Very Truly Run After

Praise for *Vikings at Dino's*

*Dino's is the first Diner I have ever regretted not visiting.
This book is pure fun, but sneaky smart, too!*
— Elizabeth Scalia (The Anchoress)

*... dry-humored prose that had me laughing out loud
every couple of pages.*
— Paul @ Amazon

... an excellent novel that fired on all cylinders.
— Jeff Miller @ The Curt Jester

... an excellent story teller ...
— Margaret Rose Realy @ Amazon

*A lot of the joy is in letting the story sweep you along.
I was greatly impressed by Will Duquette's imagination.*
— Julie Davis @ Happy Catholic

Very Truly Run After

A Novel of Squirrels and Romance

by

William H. Duquette

Zymurgia House, 2018

ZYMURGIA
HOUSE

Glendale, California
ZymurgiaHouse.com

Printed in the United States of America

First Printing, 2018

ISBN: 978-0-9998602-0-5

Cover illustration:
Jason Bach, jasonbachcartoons.com

Cover design:
Julie Davis, General Glyphics, Dallas Texas

To Julie Davis and Lizzie Scalia,

Twin Sisters of Barnabas,

With all due apologies to Miss Heyer

He went to Nqong at ten before dinner-time, saying,

'Make me different from all other animals; make me popular and wonderfully run after by five this afternoon.'
— *Rudyard Kipling*

Chapter 1

I shrank down behind the display of crab lozenges ("As good as Mother used to make!") as another round whizzed past my ear. The wrought iron of the display rack might have given me more comfort if its frills and scroll work hadn't had so many gaps in them. I tried not to think about the button nestled under my left thumb; I was longing to mash it down, but running away would only prolong the danger. Better to end it now.

Mr. Monocle glanced sideways at the contraption in my right hand.

"Bit overpowered for the situation, don't you think?" he said, returning fire with yet another carefully aimed shot from his long pistol. There was a wisp of steam and a report that was much quieter than I would have expected. "This is small arms work, what? But perhaps you know your business best."

"It's all I've got," I said.

He was looking down his pistol's iron sights when I said it, preparing for his next shot, but so help me he lowered the gun and studied me with his un-monocled eye.

"All you've got?" he said in a tone of faint consternation. He continued to study me until the next bullet from the fellow down the aisle knocked the natty bowler off his head. Unless it was a derby; I've never been clear on the difference.

"Oh, blast," he said. "Brand new, that was." Turning back to the matter at hand he fired a quick shot—"Hah, that will teach him to show his head!"—and then applied himself once more to looking down the sights.

He was a sight himself. He was wearing a form-fitting coat of blue broadcloth, equally form-fitting cream trousers, and high black boots. Around his neck was a cravat sort-of-thing that had the artless folds that (I am assured) only come with untold hours of practice. There was a long knife tucked in a sheath on the outside of one of his boots, and a holster of plain black leather at his waist. The holster was empty, of course.

"I, uh, I left my pistol at the gunsmith's counter," I said, trying not to flinch as another shot from down the aisle burst a package of Maundelson's Finest Patented Engineer's Biscuits on the shelf over my head, showering us with crumbs. I hadn't seen a gunsmith's counter, but somehow I felt sure that there would be one if I looked for it. "It's been pulling to the right, and I didn't expect to need it while I was shopping. I grabbed this when the trouble started."

I poked the contraption around the base of the display, pointed it generally down the aisle and pulled the trigger. The bright red quarrel leaped away and skittered down the polished tile toward the stack of tin cans where our attacker was crouched. It glanced off of the left-most can in the bottom row and slid to a halt a foot or two further on without having any other effect. Not bad shooting under the circumstances, I suppose, but useless. I cursed myself for believing what it had said on the package.

Mr. Monocle *tsk*'ed gently, never taking his monocle from the sights. "Eternal vigilance—oh, I do believe I winged him— eternal vigilance is the price of freedom, my boy. You should have brought a spare pistol. You'll know better next time."

I'd already gathered that not carrying an arsenal about my person was unusual (and, given current events, possibly fatal); I now realized that it was also socially incorrect. I'd brought the wrong weapon to a gunfight, and in doing so I was letting down my fellow Man-with-a-Monocle, as you might say.

"I'm not going to argue with that," I was saying, when a boom louder than any of the preceding gunshots shook the floor. I peeked through the wrought iron, and there was a cloud of smoke billowing from where the quarrel had slid to a halt. Cans were scattered everywhere, many of them oozing a brownish liquid. I wasn't close enough to read the labels, so I have no idea what was in them; maguffins in aspic, possibly, or perhaps some stewed whatnots.

"Ah," said Mr. M. "Well, that's done it. Congratulations. I shouldn't have thought it possible to do the thing so cleanly, given your equipment." Rising to his feet, he holstered his pistol and shot his cuffs in one smooth motion. He looked down at me. "But do find a proper weapon," he said as he brushed a few remaining crumbs from the shoulders of his coat. "Good day to you." And then, with every sign of aplomb, he collected his shopping cart and trundled off. He gave no sign of hurrying away, or of trying to avoid further involvement with an unpleasant situation; the affair was simply at an end, and it was time to get on with his business.

I watched him go; and when there were no further shots I peeked carefully around the display again. The smoke was clearing, and I saw a pair of legs in black trousers sticking out from behind the remains of the cans. I moved quickly.

Of course, everything I said about leaving my pistol at the gunsmith's was purest hooey. I hadn't brought a pistol with me. I don't carry a pistol, first because in Corey's End I don't need one, and second because I hadn't planned on going anywhere where I *would* need one. I never plan on going anywhere where I'd need one, because when you're small for your age you don't go looking for trouble. I've been small for my age since just after my tenth birthday, and not looking for trouble has become an engrained habit.

And on top of that I actually hadn't planned to go anywhere at all until morning, because I'd been in bed. But when you're small for your age, you don't always get what you want.

Bernie was on a weekend trip with her mother, and I'd gotten to bed late after an evening out with Joe McGillicuddy and Brother Bear. I hadn't been asleep long when I awoke to the sound of Buster barking his head off downstairs. The clock read 2:31 AM.

I didn't hesitate. No one has a key to the house but Bernie and I; and Bernie wasn't due back until the following afternoon. I slipped out of bed, and into the pair of trousers that (Bernie being away) I'd left in the chair by the bed. It's more convenient that way. I stepped into a pair of sandals, and then grabbed my backpack from the floor beside the bedside stand and slid my arms through the straps.

It was 2:32, and Buster was still barking. I grabbed my finder from its place on the bedside stand; the marks on the stubby cylinder shone blue briefly, and then subsided. Its case was already attached to my belt from the day before, but I kept it in hand, my left thumb on that big round button. Things would be trickier if Bernie were home, but with her gone Plan A-Prime was almost certainly the best response.

The barking increased in volume, and then there was a sharp *yip*. Poor Buster! It was 2:33. I knelt down in the darkness by the side of the bed to wait, doing my best to think thoughts of safe havens.

Muffled footsteps come softly down the hall, and the door to the bedroom swung open. The black-clad gentleman that opened it certainly wasn't Bernie, and he had a gun in his hand. My stomach clenched, and I pressed the button. There was a timeless moment of avoided mayhem, and then I was—

Chapter 2

—kneeling in the aisle in the middle of Walmart.

At least, it looked like Walmart, or some similar cornucopia of predictable goods at affordable prices. I mean, except for the cast iron shelving and the floor of gleaming black and white marble tiles. When you're a Traveler, you learn not to sweat the little details. It was brightly lit, especially after the darkness of my bedroom, and I winced.

As soon as I could see I stood up, trying to look natural and hoping no one had noticed my sudden and unnatural arrival. I pretended to study the items on the shelf in front of me while scanning the aisle to my right and left out of the corners of my eyes. There were only a few shoppers in view. There was something odd about them, but none seemed to be looking in my direction.

So, that was Plan A-Prime successfully executed. I took a deep breath, resting one hand on a shelf. Plan A-Prime might be all I needed. If the intruder were just a run-of-the-mill burglar then I had nothing to worry about; he couldn't follow me, and when I returned to Corey's End I'd call the police from Dino's and not go home to clean up the mess until Maynard or one of his cohorts had given me the all-clear.

But I didn't relax too much. Corey's End has a low crime rate, and burglars are scarce. If the intruder were a Traveler, as seemed more likely, then I'd no doubt he'd be toddling along after me—having found me once, he could find me again. But I didn't think he'd seen me in the bedroom, and it would take him some time to verify that I'd flown the coop. Plan A-Prime had bought me a little time, then, but I couldn't keep running indefinitely, and Plan B was useless under the circumstances. That left Plan C, which is never my first choice. At least I had a little time to find a better place to wait for him.

I took a quick look around, just to get my bearings. The name emblazoned high on one wall in big red letters was not "Walmart" but "Mordred & Sons," or at least that's how it looked to me. How it looked to the locals was anybody's guess. Bernie could have told me, but Bernie wasn't here.

I seemed to be in the toy section. There were the usual brightly colored boxes and toy animals and other gizmos, and I was about to move on when something caught my eye.

It was a crossbow, of all things, attractively displayed on the diagonal in a square package. It was painted in primary colors like a toddler's plaything, with a blue stock and a yellow bow iron and cocking lever. A spray of five bright red quarrels filled the foreground. But it wasn't a toy; it looked to be a real working crossbow. I slid my finder into its case on my belt, and picked up the package.

"Armstrong's Best Beginner Crossbow with Genuine Explosive Quarrels!" it read. "Range up to 50 feet! Guaranteed Radius of Effect, 3 Feet! Ages 5 to 7." The back of the package showed a black and white engraving of a couple of cheerful youngsters in knee breeches waving crossbows in the air and examining the smoking wreckage of some small no-longer-identifiable structure that had once been five feet or so across.

I hoped whatever kid got this wasn't too disappointed when the reality didn't live up to the advertising copy. I put the crossbow back on the shelf, and considered my next move.

I had real shoes and a nicer looking shirt in my backpack, along with one or two other useful items I'd prefer to have secreted about my person rather than out of reach, but I couldn't change in the aisle. Perhaps there was a public restroom somewhere in the store. Also, I was going to need to eat soon.

As I walked down the aisle toward what seemed to be the front of the establishment I studied the other shoppers. I could well understand why they'd looked odd at first glance—they all seemed to be escapees from some PBS miniseries based on a classic English novel, as sponsored by the NRA. Every one of the men was neatly and elegantly dressed, and each was packing more heat than a summer day in Las Vegas. The women were less obviously armed, but they were mostly wearing long flowing ankle-length dresses with puffy sleeves, and you can hide a lot in sleeves like those. Some of them were wearing lacy caps with pearl-framed goggles pulled up on their foreheads. I only saw a few children, all of them boys, but each was wearing knee breeches like the boys on the crossbow package, and each had a holster on his right hip. I hoped the holsters contained toy pistols, but I decided to make it a point not to find out. I began to have second thoughts about that crossbow.

I drew glances from the shoppers I passed, but no stares. It's not that they weren't interested, mind you; but staring seemed not to be the done thing, and perhaps if they ignored me I'd go away. I began to feel horribly under-dressed.

I didn't realize the extent of the personal armament phenomenon until I approached the entrance. There was an array of thirty or so narrow wooden nooks mounted on the wall to one side of the door. Each nook was perhaps four feet high, and a few inches wide and deep. From my angle I couldn't see what was in them, but as I drew nearer a young lady in a pretty blue dress entered the store and stepped immediately into a curtained alcove next to the nooks. She stepped out again a few moments later holding what back home I'd have call a sawed-off shotgun, and stowed it carefully in a nook by itself. I suppose she'd had it strapped to one leg.

These people were armed to the teeth. It seemed likely that they had reason to be, and I began to feel under-equipped as well as under-dressed.

I bit my lip. If young ladies took shotguns to go shopping,

what were the odds the little boys were carrying real pistols like their daddies? And was I in as much danger from the local residents as I was from the Man in Black?

There was a door labeled "Gentlemen" not far from the entrance, but instead of going there I retraced my way to the toy section. I picked up the box containing the crossbow, and then, after a quick look to make sure I was unobserved, I ripped it open and removed the crossbow and its quarrels. They were surprisingly heavy. I loaded one carefully into the crossbow— spanning it with the cocking lever took most of my strength— and slid two more into my right pocket, that being all that would fit. The other two I put in my backpack.

Time was passing. If the Man in Black was coming at all, he'd be here soon; I needed to get to cover. Leaving the tattered box on the otherwise immaculate floor, I headed back toward the entrance and the men's room.

The first shot came as I swerved around the display of crab lozenges. Mr. Monocle, who'd been passing by, joined me moments after I dove for cover. The exchange of shots played out as I've described, and the moment I saw that the Man in Black was down I was on my feet.

The cans turned out to contain Barron's Baked Beans, of all mundane things, and the Man in Black was sprawled behind them in no very good condition. An evil looking automatic lay on the floor by him, looking woefully anachronistic and out of place, but I ignored it. I was looking for—and yes, there it was.

Around the Man in Black's left wrist was a strap, like you might use on a small camera, and at the end of the strap was a small oblong object. I bent down to investigate, laying the crossbow to one side and feeling uneasily like a video game hero looting the bodies of dead enemies.

It was made of some stretchy synthetic material and might have been a camera case, but it wasn't. There was a zipper, and a flap on one side that opened to reveal a thumb-sized button.

Bingo!

I was trying to slide the strap free, and trying not to look too closely at what it was attached to, when my time ran out.

"You, lad, come away from there!"

I looked behind me. A tall man with a pencil mustache and a badge was hurrying down the aisle towards me. The local security had arrived. Abandoning finesse, I ripped the zipper-case free.

"None of that, lad. Shame on you!"

I shoved it in a pocket, and grabbed the crossbow. A heavy hand landed on my shoulder just as my heavy thumb landed on the button of my finder. There was a timeless moment of nervous tension, and I was—

Chapter 3

—alone in the desert.

Mind you, I'd have preferred to take the time to rifle my assailant's pockets more thoroughly. I don't run into other Travelers very often, or ever if I can help it, and he might have had something useful. As it was I didn't even know for sure whether he was alive or dead, and I was sorry about that.

Mind you, he wouldn't be coming after me again either way. I had his finder, and that meant that he was stuck where he was, baked beans and all. And of course he'd been trying to kill me, so my sympathy for him was limited. But still I wanted to know. I'd never killed anyone before, and it's the sort of thing you want to be sure about.

But the security guard had gotten there first, and I already knew just how a conversation with him would go. He had that polite British bobbie's voice, like Arthur Treacher in Mary Poppins.

Guard: What's all this, then, my lad?

Michael: He was shooting at me.

Guard: I'd gathered that. And then you shot a grenade at him, did you?

Michael: Well, yes.

Guard: You couldn't have found a pistol? That's quite a lot of baked beans gone to the bad, you know.

Michael: I left it with the gunsmith.

Guard: Let's go retrieve it, shall we? And then I think we should have a word with the manager. Oh, and if you'd be so good as to hand me the late gentleman's property....

And then he'd want to know whether I could pay for the damage, which I couldn't, not having any of the local money; and then he'd find the shreds of the crossbow box and want me to pay for that, which I couldn't; and then he'd want me to tell him who I was, which would only confuse him, and....

Well, it was easier just to sidestep the whole thing.

I dropped the crossbow in the dusty red sand. Bernie tells me it's stealing to take things from other worlds without paying for them, but we've never figured out how you manage to avoid it. I mean, without stealing enough local money to begin with.

My stomach gave a lurch, and then a pang, and then a sudden cry for mercy, and then I was knocked to my knees by two simultaneous waves: a wave of great and exceeding hunger, and a wave of nausea at the thought that I might have killed someone.

The hunger was no great surprise. Traveling with the finder takes it out of you, and if you don't put it back in pretty darn quick there's hell to pay. Being small for my age just makes it worse.

I slid my finder into its belt case; then I pulled off my backpack and dumped it in the sandy red dust in front of me. I'd have hated to think what that dust was doing to the knees of my chinos if I'd had any energy to spare on such foolish things. Instead I ripped open the zipper and pulled out an energy bar. I'd had the foresight to cut a notch in one end of the wrapper, and I had it open and down my gullet almost before you could say, "Cleanup on Aisle Five." The hunger abated slightly (vanquished by my body's need for food, the nausea had already crept off with its tail between its legs) and so I climbed to my feet and staggered up the wooden steps and into the battered tent cabin.

Three energy bars and a bottle of water later (these drawn from the cache in the tent, not from my bag), I rolled onto the cot and was out.

* * *

I woke up awhile later and made some beef stroganoff over the camp stove. I could have had some canned pork-and-beans, but somehow that didn't appeal.

The tent cabin was a rather spartan place when I first acquired it. There was a cot; there was water; there was a box of rather odd dehydrated meals; and that was it. I'd eaten more than one of those meals dry, and I'd had enough of that, thank you very much. Since then I'd added a propane tank, a camp stove, and a kettle for heating water, along with a couple of those bimetallic cups for backpackers that won't burn your lips if you put hot liquid in them. And a better grade of camp food. And some paper towels. And a small box of paperbacks. And a table and camp chairs. And a picture of Bernie. And....

You get the idea. I never want to have to spend a long time there ever again, but if I do I want to be comfortable.

I think of the tent cabin as my Unhappy Place. It's where I go when I need to Travel somewhere safe in a hurry, especially if I'm likely to need to crash when I get there. The location is hot, dusty, unpleasant, and nowhere you'd ever want to go on vacation. I don't know much about the world it's on, but the cabin itself is in deep desert, and I've only once seen any sign of the locals (for which I am devoutly grateful). The tent itself is literally beneath their notice.

It's no place I'd want to go with another Traveler on my tail, of course. There's no cover, for one thing; and then, the fox never leads the hounds back to its den. Hence, Mordred & Sons, not that I'd known that that's where I'd end up.

And now the Man in Black was grounded for the duration, and maybe forever, and I was still breathing. It was time to go home.

I finished the stroganoff, and cleaned up the mess. I retrieved the crossbow from where I'd dropped it outside the tent, and left it and the four remaining quarrels on the table—back home in Corey's End, that kind of thing gets you talked about in all the wrong places.

Then I thought about Bernie for a while, and when I had her firmly in mind I opened the flap on my finder's belt case and pushed the button. There was a sweaty moment of timeless dust, and then the world turned inside out and I was—

—standing in the family room of our house. Bernie was waiting, of course, sitting in her comfortable chair with a magazine in her lap; and she dropped it on the floor as I staggered over and climbed into the chair with her. She held me in silence for a long moment, and then—

"Did you get him?" she said, and at the same moment—

"How's Buster?" I said, and at the same moment—

My stomach rumbled alarmingly.

"Food," she said.

"Please," I said.

"Can you make it to the kitchen?" she said.

"I'll give it a try," I said, and because I'd just had breakfast I was able to do that thing, but I was grateful to slide into the breakfast nook and sit down. Moments later she put a peanut butter sandwich in front of me. It was cold—she'd had it ready in the refrigerator—but I wolfed it down anyway, and drank a glass of milk that had magically appeared, and finished up with an extra large hot fudge sundae. It all tasted better than rehydrated beef stroganoff. That's one upside to Traveling: when I come back, I can eat as much fattening food as I like.

"So, how's Buster?" I asked, somewhere during the glass of milk.

"He has a cracked rib and a concussion, but he's going to be fine. The vet is keeping him over night. Did you get him?"

By "him," I knew, she didn't mean Buster.

"I think so," I said. "At least, I laid him up for a while. Did he break in?"

"It doesn't look like it. The front and back doors were locked, and none of the windows are broken."

I nodded. It was what I'd expected; after all, I hadn't entered by the front door, either.

"Any damage?"

"Only to poor Buster."

Bernie and I had made an agreement before we got married that I would always let her know before I Traveled anywhere, unless Plan A-Prime was called for. I'd held to that. It was no great hardship: the only Traveling I'd done in the first months of our marriage was to get my Unhappy Place properly stocked. You know. Just in case. My father, now, he'd Traveled much more frequently than I ever planned to. Come to think of it, he Traveled so much that I'm not sure that he and his front door were actually acquainted.

But finders are rare. You can't Travel without one, and the only way to get another one—as a spare, or to give to a son, say —is to take it from another Traveler. And Bernie and I both knew that that meant that one day a Traveler would come knocking.

She married me anyway, and I try not to give her any reason to regret it.

But anyway, that's why I've got emergency supplies in my backpack. It's not quite a bug-out bag—it's my regular backpack that I carry around with me—but you never know when Plan A-Prime will be needed. That's also why we have Buster. He's not going to stop an intruder, but, as he'd valiantly shown, he'll raise enough of a fuss to wake me.

"Poor Buster is maybe the only reason I'm still alive," I said. "We need to be very nice to poor Buster."

"Yes," she said, "we do. Are we going to see him again?"

Again, she wasn't asking about Buster.

Reaching into my left front pocket, I pulled out the oblong case and tossed it on the kitchen table.

"I don't think so," I said. "I got his finder."

And then she was hugging me, and I held her while she cried.

It was after that that Bernie made me the hot fudge sundae, and I filled her in while I ate it.

"Let me get this straight," she said. "You tried to go

somewhere safe, and it took you to a steampunk regency Walmart?"

"Yeah, I guess. What do you mean by 'regency'?"

"Heh. Never mind. I'd like to meet Mr. Monocle, that's all."

"Why?" I said, stung. "I got myself out of trouble without his help."

"What's that got to do with it?"

I wasn't sure what to say to that, so instead I took my empty ice cream dish to the sink and rinsed it out.

"This is going to happen again, isn't it," she said over the sound of the water.

"You know it is."

"Then we've got to figure out a better way to handle it."

"Yes," I said. "We do."

Chapter 4

The next day I had my usual Monday morning breakfast with the Gang, that being Joe McGillicuddy, Brother Bear, and Guy Valens. Sometimes there are one or two others: Maynard the Recruiting Poster, or Bernie's grandfather Dino, but usually it's the four of us.

It's all Bernie's fault, really; after my mother died I developed a tendency to sit around and brood, and let me just say, I'm a championship brooder, I am. You'd have to be a Rhode Island Red to brood more devotedly than I can.

She put up with it for a couple of days, and then one morning Brother Bear—his real name is Alex Schafer, but I call him Brother Bear because he's tall, wide, and hairy—one morning Brother Bear came tromping up my stairs, galumphed into my apartment, picked me up out of my desk chair with one hairy paw, tucked me under his arm, and took me to breakfast. With the Gang.

By the third day, I actually got to ride in the passenger seat of his Hummer, instead of in the cargo compartment. Brother Bear says he doesn't like driving with people who grunt at him when he tries to pass the time of day.

Bernie put them up to it, of course. Did I mention that we weren't even engaged yet?

After I'd mostly gotten over myself we cut it back to once a week; but by then it had become a habit, and I'd no more have missed breakfast with the Gang than I'd have missed my weekly bacon-cheeseburger at Dino's. (I used to have lunch at Dino's Burgers & More several times a week, but Bernie's trying to get me to expand my horizons.)

I was especially eager to talk to them this particular morning. I don't talk much about Traveling with anybody but Bernie, but the Gang is different. With them behind me I'd face any Mongol horde you'd care to name; and anyway, they all knew about it already.

We've tried a number of breakfast places, but we always seem to come back to the Pancake Hut, AKA the Local House of Pancakes. It's where I'd first met them all—well, except for Joe, who taught me English in high school. Brother B was already wedged into our usual booth when I got there, sipping from a mug of coffee, and Joe and Guy came in a few minutes later, talking about a '64 Corvette they were restoring.

I waited until we all had pancakes in front of us, except for Guy, who always orders a waffle, before I told them about my weekend.

"Let me get this straight," said Joe. He dribbled raspberry syrup on his pancakes. "You tried to go somewhere safe, and that thing took you to a steampunk regency Walmart?"

"That's exactly what Bernie said," I said.

"Heh," said Joe. "Told you she was a keeper."

Guy looked at me, a question in his eyes, and mouthed the word "regency." English isn't Guy's first language, and the finder allows me to talk to anybody no matter what language they speak, so when I'm around he relies on me to explain words he's not familiar with. I shrugged my shoulders and grimaced. I mean, I know what the word means, but that wasn't helping.

Brother Bear chewed a couple of slices of bacon with a considering look on his face.

"So," he said, "is this going to happen again?"

"Yes and no," I said. "The Man in Black won't be bothering me again, not unless he has a spare finder. And isn't dead."

"Dead is good," said Guy. "I've never come to any harm from

a dead barbarian."

Guy is from ancient Rome, or as close as makes no difference; you have to make allowances. I'm told he has a lovely accent, and that his speech is quite picturesque and colorful, but you can't prove it by me; the same faculty that lets me understand his Latin makes him sound more or less like everyone else to my ears. Pity.

"But yeah," I went on, "I expect there will be others."

"Got to do something about that," said Brother Bear, engulfing a pancake.

"You've got that right," I said. "Poor Buster got his leg broken for him. It's bad enough to have people coming after me, but if Bernie had been home things might have gone south in ways I really don't want to think about."

"Guy has a point, though," said Joe, gesturing at me with his fork. "I'm inclined to think you should take—what did you call the fellow who helped you out?"

"Mr. Monocle," I said.

"That's right. I'm inclined to think you should take Mr. Monocle's advice."

"What advice was that?"

"To get a proper weapon."

"'S'right," said Brother Bear around another expanse of pancake. "You got lucky with that crossbow."

I shook my head, because I'd been thinking about that. "No, that was the finder. I wanted someplace safe, and I had no weapon, and my finder put me right in front of it."

"Yeah, yeah, all hail the *deus ex machina*," said Joe. "What Alex meant was, you got lucky *using* it."

"Oh." Well, he had me there. But I was a little afraid of what Joe's idea of a proper weapon might be. Did I mention that before he was a school teacher, Joe was a Marine? "So, uh, what would you suggest?"

"Light," said Brother Bear, who had moved on to his fried eggs.

"Easy to carry," Joe agreed. "You don't know when one of your Traveling friends might show up, so you need to be able to carry it with you."

"A Colt .45," said Guy. Guy used to be a centurion in a Roman legion, and after the fracas in which we'd first met he'd insisted that Brother Bear teach him to shoot. I think he'd fallen in love with the Colt at first sight.

Brother B snorted. "Knock him flat on his ass," he said.

Well, it would.

"Enough with the Colt, Guy," said Joe. "Besides, I think Michael would prefer something less reliably fatal."

"All I really need to do is to disable whoever it is for a little while," I said. "If I can get their finder from them, they can't follow me."

Guy shook his head. "Dead is better," he said.

"Sorry, Guy," said Joe. "We take your point, but Michael would rather not leave a trail of bodies behind him."

Guy waved a hand dismissively.

"He doesn't need to leave them lying around Corey's End. Once they're dead he can just find a nice quiet place somewhere else."

"I don't really want to leave them lying anywhere," I said. "I just want them out of my face. And anyway, I need something I can carry without getting myself in trouble."

"No open carry in Corey's End," said Brother B. "Colt's too big for him to conceal."

Joe cocked his head at Guy, as if to say, "You see?"

Guy rolled his eyes. "You have a better idea, Joe?"

He nodded. "You know, I think I do. I need to talk to some people; I'll swing by your house tomorrow morning, Michael." He put down his fork, and picked up his mug of coffee.

"Now," he said. "Let's talk tactics."

Joe came by the next day with a small package, the contents of which he explained in detail to Bernie and me; and for the next week the two of us had to spend an hour a day down at the police station learning how to use it properly before Chief

Roderick would let me carry it around town. I didn't mind that, much; it gave me an excuse to have lunch with Bernie and Maynard at Hannity's Hamburger Hut, across the street from the station. It's not Dino's, but they do a good burger at Hannity's, and the fries aren't bad either.

And after that Joe and I had another discussion about tactics, and got them pretty well nailed down. I knew what to do, I knew how to do it, and in practice I *could* do it.

When the next attack came, we would be ready.

Chapter 5

The next attack came a couple of months later, while I was riding my bicycle to philosophy class.

Why philosophy class? That's a long story.

To begin with, my name is Michael Henderson. I'm in my late twenties, but I look rather younger—rather a *lot* younger—than that. I got married not too long ago. And I'm a Traveler.

That means that, properly equipped, I can Travel to other worlds, to alternate realities. The proper equipment is this thing I call a "finder"...but just having a finder doesn't make you a Traveler. You already have to be a Traveler to use a finder. And to be a Traveler, you have to be the son of a Traveler. Or, maybe, a daughter, but I gather that's rare: my father had never heard of a female Traveler. At least, that's what he told my mother.

How does all of this work? I really have no idea. My father was the Traveler in the family, but I don't remember him at all; he vanished under suspicious circumstances when I was a baby. When I do think of him, it isn't fondly. There are...reasons. I don't mean to say that he ran out on us, because I'm not at all certain of that. To hear my mother tell it, he left to protect us at great risk to his own life and would have returned to us if he could have. She waited for him until the day she died, but me, I have my doubts.

Travelers are seldom gregarious, at least with other Travelers, and they don't advertise. And that means that what little I do know about Traveling I learned from my mother, who learned it from my father; and as she's been dead for over a year I can't ask her any more questions. That leaves learning by trial and error, and as I'm informed that the relevant errors are likely to be fatal I'm not too eager to experiment.

But on the other hand my finder has saved my life more than once, and it's clear to me that the better I understand it the better off I'll be. And sometimes what seems like the long way round is the shortest way home.

My mother met my father, so she said, in a class on Aristotelian philosophy. His pet hobbyhorse was figuring out how finders and Traveling worked, and he was studying philosophy trying to find a metaphysical system that matched what he'd already learned. It was a fruitful line of inquiry, according to my mother; my father told her that Aristotle's theories made better sense of the whole thing than anything else he'd looked at.

Had I mentioned that my father wasn't from here? Travelers usually aren't.

I'd give quite a lot for his research notes, but if he left any Bernie and I didn't find them when we went through my mother's things. I expect my mother hid them when I was little so that I wouldn't read them and get ideas; as it was, she put off telling me about my father as long as she possibly could. I don't think she would have destroyed them, though, not something of his. But wherever they were, I had no immediate access to them.

So...given a choice between studying philosophy on the one hand, and learning the nuances of Traveling by making jumps to places I knew nothing about and perhaps finding myself twenty fathoms under water, or in vacuum, or in someplace even less healthy (they do exist!) on the other, well, I signed up for classes at the local college. I don't know if it's helping or not, but I've stuck with it—and at least in that crowd I appear relatively normal, even if I am on the small side.

I was coasting down an alley behind the college library when my next assailant appeared about twenty feet in front of me. I was irritated and fascinated at the same time; I'd never actually seen a Traveler arrive before. One moment, empty space; the next, there he was, with only a faint blue halo around him to show that he hadn't arrived in the usual way.

The halo faded in moments, and after that he wasn't anything out of the ordinary to look at. He'd chosen his outfit well, I thought; dark trousers and a red shirt. I hoped that was an omen. He had a small, deadly looking handgun in his right fist that I was hoping to get a better look at.

I stopped my bike behind him, and since he was facing mostly away from me I blew him a raspberry. His head whipped around, revealing green eyes and a nose the size of Wisconsin, and when I was sure I had his attention I pressed the button. There was an astonished moment of extreme anticipation, and I was—

—just where I wanted to be.

A finder is pretty good at finding things for you, provided that you're specific and not too picky about the little details. I think of it as being kind of like a database search. You present it with your criteria, and out of all of the infinite number of worlds it comes up with a list of places that meet your requirements.

And then instead of giving you a nice list of search results, it just picks one of them for you and—hey, presto!—there you are. Pity you didn't specify you wanted a breathable atmosphere....

But thanks to Joe, I knew pretty well what I wanted; and I got it.

I was at the base of a sheer granite cliff that stretched up forty or fifty feet above my head, and continued for a considerable distance to either side. That was so he couldn't appear behind me. In front of me there was a gentle slope of tall grass stretching down to a river a mile or so away; and in the distance the skyline of a good-sized city. The sun was about halfway down the sky to my right, and the towers in the distance were edged with light. The sky was blue, the air was warm, there was no one around, and when Red Shirt showed up he'd almost certainly be in my direct field-of-view.

I got off of my bike, which I'd brought with me—well,

seriously, it's my bike. It's how I get places, I wasn't going to abandon it behind the library—and laid it on the grass. Then I removed the weapon Joe had gotten me from my backpack and gave it a quick once over; and then, to no one's surprise, it was show time.

Red Shirt appeared in a blue-outlined crouch not quite in front of me. He might have been trying to arrive in a stealthy way; I don't know. Or maybe he was just trying to be a smaller target, so that he'd have a better chance of shooting me before I shot him. That might have worked if he'd been facing me when he arrived, because he still had his gun in hand; but as it happened he was facing pretty much straight off to my left. He was about fifteen feet away, so I ran forward a couple of steps, aimed, and pulled the trigger just as he turned his head in my direction. The taser's electrodes hit him on his left bicep, going right through the red shirt, and it was all over but the twitching. It wasn't a pretty sight, but it sure beat being shot at.

Dropping the taser, I retrieved the roll of duct tape I'd put in my backpack for just such occasions as this, and in a few moments I had his ankles and wrists taped together pretty well. I reeled in the electrodes and put a new cartridge in the taser, and then I rifled his pockets. He had a box full of extra rounds for his pistol and a wallet containing some brightly colored bills that were apparently various denominations of "queebles," and that was it. I put the bills back and dropped the wallet at his feet. He wasn't wearing any jewelry, and the holster on his belt didn't have any hidden compartments.

That left the pistol.

Maynard had insisted on adding a course in gun safety to my taser training, so although the pistol didn't look quite like anything I'd seen before I was able to identify it as some kind of semi-automatic. You'd think that a handgun from some other world wouldn't fit into our categories very well, but I guess in some cases form really does follow function. The markings on it read Ramcaster Special 0.4π. At least, that's the shape they made in my head. The box of ammo was stamped 0.4π as well, so I guess that was the caliber of the ammunition. Where Red Shirt came from, or where his gun came from, anyway, I guess they measured caliber in terms of circumference rather than diameter.

By the time Red Shirt was able to form complete sentences again I had completed my investigations and was standing well out of reach but in his field of view.

I assume he was able to form complete sentences, because he'd stopped moaning and his eyes were tracking again, but in fact he just lay there and stared at his gun, which I was pointing at his head, and didn't say a word.

"We both know why we're here," I said. "You came looking for a finder, right?"

His eyes jumped from the gun to my face and back, and he gave a cautious little nod.

"Do you have anything to say for yourself?" I said, after letting him stare for a while longer.

He shook his head very slightly.

"I could shoot you," I said, "and you'd deserve it, but I'm inclined to be merciful." I lowered the gun.

His nose twitched eloquently, and I could see that his hands were starting to work at the duct tape behind his back. I considered chiding him about that, but unless he were a lot stronger than he looked it was going to take him more time than he had to get his hands free.

"Now, I could leave you here," I said, and his nose twitched again and his eyes got wide, and his hands started working more frantically, "or I could drop you somewhere on my way home." His hands slowed down again, but his eyes got wider. "Someplace like, maybe, the Old City?" And then he just kind of deflated.

"Yeah, I've been there," I said. "It's an interesting place."

"I'll, uh, I think I'll just stay here, shall I?" he said.

"Probably a wise plan," I said, and really it was. You've no idea. "There's a city some distance south of here. I haven't been there, but I'm sure it's quite nice. You probably won't starve before you reach it."

"May I, um, would you be willing to…"

"Leave you your gun?"

"Yes, yes, that's it."

Hope was shining in his eyes, but I was feeling mean. So I said, "Sure, why not," and then sent it sailing into the tall grass as far away as I could manage.

And then I climbed on my bike, pushed the button on my finder, and went home.

I was sorry not to be able to see his face when he found it and discovered that I'd not only taken the ammo, along with one or two small but significant parts (just in case they sold 0.4π caliber ammo thereabouts); I'd also removed the finder from its custom-machined hiding place on one side of the grip.

"Here you go," I said, handing Red Shirt's finder to Bernie. "Spoils of war." It was a cute little thing about the size and shape of a quarter, made of the usual dark metal. It had a knurled button on one side and the usual glowing blue marks on the other, and I was pretty sure I needed to find some convenient place to secrete it around my person where I could get at it if my usual finder were taken from me.

I'd arrived in the kitchen instead of the family room this time. I thought that was a real time saver, especially since it was just about dinner time and Bernie was making spaghetti, but she disagreed—she hadn't realized I'd been gone, and my sudden arrival in the kitchen with a bicycle nearly caused a culinary incident. Nearly, but not quite. The pot of spaghetti sauce was saved, and I had just enough time to wheel the bike into the hallway before the hunger hit me.

I told her about it between mouthfuls.

"The taser worked a treat," I said. "Slap, bang, boom, it was all over in moments."

"Yeah, and if he'd been facing towards you?"

"I've been trying not to think about that." It was as much for distraction as anything else that I pulled Red Shirt's finder out of my shirt pocket and handed it to her. The marks flared as I pulled it out, and faded when she took it from me. Then I got some more spaghetti. I really prefer spaghetti the second day, when the sauce has soaked into the pasta, but I wasn't complaining.

Bernie was frowning at the finder. "How many is that now?" she asked. "Four?"

"Attacks? Two. What, you think I've been attacked more often and haven't told you?" I raised an eyebrow.

"Not attacks, Michael, finders."

"Oh. Yeah, I've got four now. There's the one you and I found together, and that one that my dad left for me, and the one that I got at the steampunk Walmart, and this one."

"*Regency* steampunk Walmart," she corrected me, and I rolled my eyes.

"And you're keeping them where?" she said.

"With me, of course. I can't leave them lying around. I keep the first one on my belt, and the others in my backpack." I yawned. "I don't know where I'm going to keep the new one, but I'll think of something."

"Hmmmm," she said. "Now, could you please get your bike out of the house before you fall asleep?"

I did the first of those things, and then I did the second.

Chapter 6

The next attacker showed up when Bernie and I were on our way to her mom's house for Sunday dinner. It's a habit we'd gotten into soon after we got married—going to her mom's for Sunday dinner, not getting attacked on the way.

Well, actually, it's a habit we'd been gotten into at our wedding reception. As we were heading out of the reception hall, Bernie's mom told us, "Now, I won't see you for dinner tomorrow, because you'll be on your honeymoon, but I'll expect you *next* Sunday. Have a good time!" Bernie's mom has a way of arranging things like that. Some guys might resent that kind of thing, but it's what got me through my mother's funeral, and I'm grateful.

But that's beside the point.

When Bernie and I got married I sold the house I'd shared with my mother and we got a larger place a few miles away. Among other things, that meant that we could walk to her mom's for dinner, and we were doing that when a fellow leaped out from the bushes in front of 2743 Mercator Street and tackled me. He knocked me down, and we both of us rolled over the curb and into the street. I'm not sure whether he was planning a simple snatch-and-grab of my finder, or a more complicated snatch-and-grab of *me*, or whether he just wanted to throttle me before moving on to other activities, but in the event it mostly involved him crushing me to the pavement while we both tried to get my finder out of its belt case.

Then, of course, Bernie shot him in the face with pepper spray.

I love Bernie. She has *savoir-faire*.

I got a whiff of it too, naturally, but not like he did. Bernie pulled him off of me, pulled me to my feet, sat me down on the curb, and shot him in the face again for good measure.

"Thank you," I said as soon as I was able. It took a while, what with the wheezing and the shakes.

"No problem," said Bernie. She handed me an acorn-shaped object of dark gray metal. It was about two inches long, with a button where the acorn cap would be. The letter-like marks that spiraled around the sides writhed and flashed blue in the usual way when I took it from her.

"It was in a little pouch tied around his waist," she said.

I slipped it into my pocket, and we contemplated my latest assailant.

He was short, only a foot taller than me, and he was wearing a karate suit in dark brown with black piping. His head was shaved, or maybe just naturally bald, and his head and hands (and all the rest of him, for all I know) were tattooed all over with images in the most appalling taste. He was curled up in a fetal position, moaning and wiping at his eyes to no great effect.

"I'll meet you at your mom's," I said. "This shouldn't take long."

"I'll tell her not to hold dinner," she said.

I knelt down, took the Illustrated Man by the front of his brown suit, and pressed the button. There was a whimpering moment of non-Euclidean geometry, and we were—

—somewhere that looked quite nice.

It was some kind of garden, with camellia plants and ferns and ponds and little streams and mossy stones, and here and there small Japanese-looking huts joined by boardwalks. (Someday I really need to take an architecture appreciation class, so that I have the vocabulary for all the things I see.) There was the scent of cherry blossoms. There were ooohs and aaahs from a number of pretty girls in kimonos. There were stern looks from a number of samurai-looking gentlemen.

If this seems like an unusual place for me to have brought the Illustrated Man, well, you're right. But on reflection it seemed to me that he'd only been after my finder, not my life, and frankly I found that refreshing. And he'd left Bernie alone.

I felt almost a little grateful to him, despite my bruises. So since I was going to be stranding him somewhere where he didn't know anybody and didn't speak the language, I asked my finder to find us a place where he could be reasonably happy.

Three of the samurai-looking gentlemen were striding in our direction, hands on their sword hilts and top-knots bobbing comically with each step. I gave them a cheery wave, and said, "Take good care of him!" And then I mooned them for good measure before I pushed the button and rejoined Bernie at her mom's.

We had lasagna, which was just about perfect under the circumstances. It's filling, high in calories, and takes enough eating that I didn't have to say much. Which was good, because about all I had to say was, "This can't go on."

After dinner we walked home, holding hands. I won't usually hold hands with Bernie in public; she's so much taller, and I hate looking like a little kid walking to school with his mom. Tonight, though, I wanted the contact.

"You mooned them?"

"I don't think they liked me anyway. And I figured, the more they disliked me, the less likely they'd be to take it out on the Illustrated Man."

"The enemy of my enemy is my friend?"

"Something like that."

"He didn't seem like he really knew what he was doing. I mean, none of your attackers seem to be all that good at it, you know?"

I thought about that. "For a Traveler, I suppose attacking

someone is kind of an unnatural act. Although, Red Shirt had his finder embedded in the hand grip of a gun. Shows a bad attitude, in my view."

I suppose we seem remarkably blasé about my being attacked so often, but that's only from the outside. And what are you going to do? I didn't like it, Bernie didn't like it, but either you cope or you melt into a puddle—and puddles aren't so good at self-defense. Bravado is easier, even if neither of you believes it.

"Have you noticed," said Bernie, "that the time between attacks is getting shorter? The first was a couple of years after we met. The next was a couple of months after the first one. This time it's only been a few days."

"Yeah. It's one damned thing after another, isn't it. I wonder why? I sure hope it doesn't become a daily experience."

"I've been thinking about that," she said.

"Do tell." I squeezed her hand. She squeezed back.

"Why are they looking for you? Dumb question, I know, but bear with me."

"To get my finder, of course."

"Right. But your father lived with your mother for some time, and he had a finder, and as far as you know he was never attacked at home."

I frowned. "I don't know that, actually. I don't even know how much time he actually spent at home. But Mom never mentioned it if he was."

"And then, you didn't have any trouble the whole time you were growing up, until the thing with the Vikings."

"I beg your pardon," I said. "I had a whole lot of trouble."

"With Travelers, I mean."

"That's true."

We crossed the street, and entered a little park that occupies part of a block not far from our house. It was a beautiful night, and somehow I didn't want to go back to the house quite yet. I nodded over toward a bench with a nice view of the sky.

"Want to sit down?"

"Are you going to fall asleep on me?"

I thought about it.

"I don't think so," I said. "Your mom's lasagna is really good. I wonder what she puts in it."

"If she won't tell me, she won't tell you," said Bernie. "And she won't tell me."

"Maybe she should go into business selling lasagna to Travelers. I'd buy lots."

I could hear Bernie smile.

"So, no trouble with Travelers until the Vikings showed up," I said.

"No trouble for over two decades. And *they* weren't looking for your finder."

"That's true," I said, resting my head on her shoulder. I don't mind doing that when it's just the two of us. It seems kind of backward to me, but it's a matter of simple geometry—Bernie can't rest her head on my shoulder without getting a crick in her neck.

"And then, a couple of years later, the Man in Black shows up."

"Yeah."

"So what changed?"

"That's a good question. My dad's finder was here all the time, but no one came looking for it."

"Do you remember when we found Red Mustache's finder, how you spent hours playing with it, trying to get it to do something?"

"Oh, yeah. It took forever, and then *bam!* Blue everywhere."

"How long did it take you to activate your father's?"

"What? No time at all, I guess. I just touched it."

"And the one you got from the Man in Black?"

"Same thing."

"So for over two decades you had a finder in the house, and there was no trouble. Then in a matter of a few days you had *two* active finders. And then three. And then four."

"And now five," I said. The pattern was blindingly obvious now that I came to look at it. I muttered a few rude words.

"You can say that again," said Bernie.

You remember I described using a finder as something like a database search? How the finder finds a bunch of worlds, and picks one arbitrarily? Apparently the choice wasn't as arbitrary as I'd thought.

"If every Traveler has a single finder, then a finder search will pick one of them randomly."

"But if one Traveler has a bunch of finders, then that result bubbles to the top," said Bernie.

It was more complicated than that, I was pretty sure, but....

"What are we going to do?" I said.

Bernie didn't make the obvious suggestion, which was to drop all of them in the Pacific. In the Marianas Trench, say.

"Let's go home," she said, and we did that thing.

Chapter 7

I was at home for the next one. Bernie was at work, and I was sitting at my desk working on an essay on Aristotle's *De Anima* for philosophy class. Buster was snoring on the couch under the window. He usually likes to sleep right behind my chair, so that I bump him when I try to slide the chair back. I don't know why he likes to lie there; it certainly isn't something that *I* would do. But today he was on the couch.

So I was wrestling with the Philosopher, and Buster was chasing rabbits or something, legs flailing in his sleep, when the air in the room changed. I don't know quite how, whether there was a sound, or maybe I got a slight reflection of blue on the screen of my laptop. But Buster barked and leaped to his feet, and I spun around, and there was yet another damned attacker. I began to think I should order them in bulk, and save on postage.

This one was in black.

I don't know what it is with other Travelers and their costumes. Seems to me, if you're going to be Traveling to another world you don't want to stand out when you get there. Perhaps that's my father's influence talking; he did his level best to slide through the world unnoticed even at home in Corey's End. But of the four I'd seen in the last year, only one was dressed to fit in. The first was in black of the burglar variety, with one of those black knit wool beanies; the third had those atrocious tattoos; and this one was in a kind of black ninja outfit with a wicked looking knife in his fist and a surprised look on his face. I think he expected me to be taller.

It's possible, of course, that he was trying to dress for his notion of the occasion.

My backpack was across the room, and like an idiot I'd left the taser in the backpack. I had my finder on my belt, but no other supplies. I'd execute Plan A-Prime if I had to, but I needed that backpack first. The basic Plan A was out; he was between me and the door, and I'd never make it through the window. Plan B was out; there was nowhere to hide except under the desk, like that was going to work. So...an immediate Plan C, then, followed by Plan A-Prime if possible, and a basic Plan A if not.

And just like that I launched myself at him. Cool assessment first; shakes and meltdowns *afterwards*.

I've noticed that people like me who are built to a more compact scale have a real advantage over people of height when it comes to hand-to-hand fighting: we're low to the ground, and not where we're expected to be. He was coming for me with weight forward on his toes when I cannoned into his shins. People of size have such a high center of gravity that when his lower legs stopped his upper half kept going. He tumbled over my back, and I think he hit his head on my desk chair when Buster jumped on him.

I kept going, too, across the room to my backpack. I grabbed a strap and hit the button. There was an adrenalin-fueled moment of fear and trembling, and I was—

—crouching next to a hedge, in a park. I knelt there for a bit, until my heart rate was back to something approaching normal, then stood up and looked around.

I was standing on a broad gravel walk next to a low hedge. On the other side of the hedge was an expanse of grass around an ornamental fountain—the kind with a central figure spouting water in the middle of a shallow pool, the whole encompassed by a stone rim broad enough to sit on. The central figure was standing on a tall plinth of baroque design, in the middle of something like a large birdbath, with spouts on the side from which water poured into the lower pool. He was a heroically built gentleman wearing a top hat and long coat, and he was holding the breach of a double-barreled shotgun in his right hand, with the butt resting on the ground by his booted foot. His expression was stern and solemn, and yea verily he looked off into the future with the intensity of a prophet.

On the other side of the walk another expanse of turf sloped down to an irregularly shaped pond, perhaps fifty yards across and a hundred yards or so in length. The water was that opaque green you get in places like that.

Men dressed in tight-fitting coats with fancy cravats walked on the grass, next to women in flowing dresses with puffy sleeves. The gravel walk made a long circuit around the pond, and other walks led off from it deeper into the park. In the distance I could see folks on horseback promenading (if that's the word I'm looking for) on another path that led around the outer perimeter. Beyond that were buildings of various sorts. And all of the folks near me were scrupulously avoiding looking at me, and each of the men had a holster on his hip and some kind of long-arm strapped to his back.

It all looked distressingly familiar, and all the more distressing as I'd meant to return to the place where I'd taken care of Red Shirt. It wouldn't have been exactly the same world, of course, but it would have been close enough for me to cope with the Black Ninja in reasonable safety. Instead I had ended up in another steampunk sort of world. "*Regency* steampunk," I imagined Bernie whispering in my ear.

Well, I might be underdressed again but at least I had my taser with me. There was a gap in the hedge a few yards away, so I went through it and over to the fountain, carrying the backpack by one of the straps. I sat down on the rim and retrieved the taser from my backpack, and then I put the backpack on so that I wouldn't accidentally leave it behind. Then I stood up and prepared to wait. There was nowhere in sight that was any better than where I was standing; I had the fountain at my back, for all the good that did, and everywhere else was even more open. I could always use my finder again, but that would just make the hunger come more quickly. I couldn't afford that right now.

"So, lad, is your long-arm at the gunsmith's as well?"

I did a double-take. Mr. Monocle, the man himself, was walking towards me over the grass. I wasn't in another steampunk—oh, very well—another *regency* steampunk sort of world, I was in the same one. How could that be? I had no anchors here. I began to wonder if my finder was messing with me.

"It's presumptuous of me to speak to you, of course," he said as he came up to my side, "but after the minor bit of unpleasantness some while ago I suppose I can claim acquaintance. And it's clear that you need guidance, lad. I'm glad to see you have a small arm with you this time, though I don't recognize the model, but to be out in Remchester Park without a long-arm!" He shook his head. "And in those clothes. Have you no father, lad?"

It felt very odd to be addressed by someone in another world who wasn't trying to kill me. Perhaps that's why I answered as I did.

"I never knew my father, Mister—"

"Monocle, lad." He drew a square of pasteboard from the pocket of his waistcoat and handed it to me. It read, "Tristram J. Monocle, Esq."

Humph. That was the finder doing its translation thing again. I'd never know what he was really called. I'd dubbed him Mr. Monocle when I first met him, and now he'd be Mr. Monocle forever.

"And in fact, Squire Monocle—Squire? Is that right?"

His mustache gave an odd tilt. "A courtesy title, only. 'Mister' is the normal usage."

"Mr. Monocle, then. You should know, I'm much older than I look."

He raised an eyebrow, and waited. Clearly he was ready for

me to elaborate, but he wouldn't be so ill-bred as to interrogate an acquaintance.

I had no such qualms. "How old would you say I am, Mr. Monocle?"

He looked surprised. "I'd say you were a lad of perhaps ten years. Possibly eleven if you were small for your age."

"Oh, I'm small for my age, Mr. Monocle. Would you care to hazard a guess?"

His mustache slanted to one side, and there was an ironic gleam in his unmonocled eye. "I would hate to take the risk of offending."

"I'm tw—" I began, but I was interrupted by a loud cry from behind me.

"Ware gulls!" cried the voice. "Ware gulls! Everyone turn to!"

"And here you are, with no long-arm," said Mr. Monocle. "You need a keeper, lad." He scanned the skies in all directions. "And there they are!" And he pointed out over the pond.

With calm, practiced motions he unslung the rifle from over his shoulder and worked the action, verifying that it was loaded. All over the park, men and women were doing the same, though most of the women appeared to have been carrying their weapons under their skirts, just as the young lady at Mordred's had done. There were no alcoves with privacy curtains in the park, but that didn't slow any of them down.

The voice came again, louder this time: "Ware gulls! Look to the south! Ware gulls! Look to the south!"

And we all did that thing. I followed Mr. Monocle's gaze, and saw in the distance a flock of birds soaring in our direction. Apparently seagulls were not well liked in this world. I was wondering how the locals felt about pigeons, and thinking that the statue in the fountain was surprisingly unstained, when I realized that the gulls were still getting bigger. Or, to put it another way, they were much further off than I'd realized. As they got closer and I could relate them to the things around me I saw that each one was about the size of a pony. They still looked mostly like the seagulls I knew, but there were differences. I've never seen a seagull with talons, for example.

"What on earth are those?" I said. I didn't squeak, but it was a close thing.

"Why, gulls, of course," said Mr. Monocle. "They come for the snapping trout that swim in the Turpentine down there, but they've been known to carry children off before now. Not the worst thing that could have come along today, but quite the nuisance."

And then the shooting started. I didn't participate; a civilian-model taser has a range of about fifteen feet, and none of the gulls got that close. Most, in fact, tumbled into the pond—the Turpentine, as Mr. Monocle had called it—and the rest fell on the bank, close to the water. There was a churning and a bubbling and the white-fledged carcasses slowly began to sink below the water line. Apparently the snapping trout had as much of a taste for gull as the gulls had for snapping trout. I saw a carcass with just one wingtip in the water dragged bodily off of the bank.

"That's that," said Mr. Monocle, lowering his rifle. The others around us were doing the same, and down near the pond a team of men was beginning to drag the outlying gulls closer to the water.

There was a blue flash in the corner of my eye, and I turned to see the Black Ninja on my flank. He had a black eye and a bloody nose, and he'd ditched the knife in favor of a pistol. There was a loud report, and a blow to my shoulder. As I went down, spun to one side by the blow, I saw rifles and shotguns coming back up. I heard a massive roar as I hit the ground, and through the pain I remember thinking that I wasn't going to be having any more trouble with the Black Ninja.

Chapter 8

I'd like to be able to say that everything faded to black and I knew no more, because that sounds a lot more comfortable and also easier to describe than what really happened.

I remember Mr. Monocle kneeling by my side and pulling his cravat from around his neck. I guess he must have used it to stop the bleeding, because I'm still here. He looked funny without it, but he seemed to know what he was doing. After a while he was replaced by a severe-looking woman in a grey cap with bronze goggles on it who insisted on leaning on my shoulder with all of her weight, even though I repeatedly asked her not too. I wondered what the goggles were for. I tried to ask her, but she just kept leaning. Then there was the sound of horses, and a voice said, "Lift him up, gently! There we go." I came down on something soft, and then Mr. Monocle was beside me again and we went rolling away.

Buildings passed by for a while, bumping and jolting in a way that must have been really uncomfortable for the people who lived in them. At one point Mr. Monocle said, "Hold on, lad, we'll soon have you set to rights!" And then I was being lifted down, and carried, and I heard Mr. Monocle say, "Summon Dr. Hampstead." The pain was intense by that time—you know how real pain takes all of your attention? I was put down on a bed, and I wondered vaguely where my backpack was. Then there was poking and prodding, and a taste of something that must have been brandy, and then something that tasted much worse, and then I drifted off leaving the pain on the bed behind me.

Eventually the pain drew me back, and I found I was lying in a soft bed in a dimly lit room.

"Ahhh, you're awake. I'll tell the master."

I looked to my right, where the owner of the voice was rising from a chair beside the bed. He was a thin fellow with a receding hairline, and he was dressed more simply than anyone else I'd seen in this world. He had a deep, slow, country sort of voice.

After he left the room I made one attempt to sit up, and then thought better of it: my left arm seemed to have no strength, and trying to move made the pain redouble. The rest of me didn't feel much better. I wasn't going anywhere, so I lay there and did my best to take stock.

I was lying in bed wearing some kind of long nightshirt, with my left arm in a sling. There was a window to one side, with drapes drawn shut and a sliver of light peeking through, and a wardrobe in the corner. There was a washstand with a bowl and pitcher, and a small fireplace with some sort of metal contraption in it. There was a light sconce by the door that provided what little light there was. There was dark wainscoting below figured wallpaper that looked like it might be bright and cheerful in better light. There was a glass of water on a small table next to the bed, but although I discovered I was quite thirsty I couldn't bring myself to try to pick it up.

I saw no sign of my clothes or my backpack.

I was relieved, in a way. If I'd still had my belt on, I'd have been torn between going straight home and trying to recover my backpack first. If I'd had my belt and my backpack handy, I'd have been torn between going straight home and just lying there. Since I didn't feel like I was in any shape to recover anything it was nice not to have the option. Anyway, I really didn't think Mr. Monocle was going to steal from me. It wasn't done.

After ten minutes or so, Receding Hair—um, that is, the fellow who'd been sitting with me—came back with a bowl of something. Mr. Monocle came in a few moments later. I had a little speech in mind—I thought Mr. Monocle really ought to know about my attackers—but I didn't get to use it. Steam was rising from the bowl, and in moments a smell that was probably plain enough in normal times had my full and complete attention. My stomach roared to life, and I made an involuntary move to sit up. It didn't work, of course, but I produced an impressive gasp when I tried it.

"Just a minute, lad," said Mr. Monocle. He set a mug down on the little table by the bed, and then he and his...servant? Valet? Whoever he was, the two of them helped me to sit up a bit. Mr. Monocle lifted me with a hand between and below my shoulder blades, supporting my left arm with the other so that it didn't dangle and pull at my wound, and his helper filled in behind me with pillows. Then Mr. Monocle sat down at the foot of the bed, and his helper moved the chair so that he could sit close by with the bowl.

"Now, lad, rest easy and let Thompson give you a bit to eat."

Thompson! A real name! Thompson gave me a drink of water, and then commenced to feed me some kind of hot cereal that was savory rather than sweet. I felt like a goldfish, opening and closing my mouth at intervals, or possibly a baby bird, straining forward to get each spoonful as quickly as possible. It's the sort of reflection that really gets my goat, because I hate feeling like a child...but truly, in that moment I was incapable of feeding myself.

The bowl was empty all too soon, and although my arms and legs were feeling a fraction less heavy and immobile, my stomach still felt as empty as a cavern.

"More, please," I managed to croak.

"Yes, yes, lad, certainly," said Mr. Monocle. "But first, drink this."

I nodded my head, which ached, as Thompson put down the bowl and retrieved the mug from the little table. Could it be coffee? Tea? Something with caffeine? I leaned forward eagerly as Thompson held it to my lips and took a big swallow before I'd quite tasted it.

I nearly choked at the bitter flavor, but it was too late; the first swallow was done, followed by several more as Thompson expertly poured the rest down my throat.

I was already beginning to feel a slippery detachment when Mr. Monocle said, "There you are, lad. You'll rest easier, now." And then to Thompson, "We'll give him a few minutes, and then see to that dressing." He sounded matter-of-fact rather than worried, which I suppose would have been comforting if I were still in the vicinity. As it was, the pokings and proddings and wrappings of bandages seemed to be happening to someone else.

And after that, I really didn't know any more for some period of time.

The next thing that I remember is hearing some loud noises, but they weren't very interesting. I think there was some shouting, and maybe a loud bang, and perhaps a crash or two; but I was still drifting, and the pain was still remote and unimportant, and it was dark, and the bed was warm and cozy, and if I was still hungry, well, that was remote and unimportant too. And anyway there was no one in the room to talk to, even if I could have gathered the gumption to say anything. I think I went back to sleep, but it's so hard to tell.

Quite some time later, I think, I woke with a start.

The pain was quite thoroughly present.

The hunger was quite thoroughly present, too, and it had brought a fair amount of thirst along with it.

"Ah, you are back with us."

Mr. Monocle was sitting in the chair by the bed. He had an open book in his hands, a bandage on his arm, and another one on his forehead. He was bare-headed, of course, and the monocle was dangling from a string on his chest instead of screwed into his eye, which made him look younger. Or no, I realized, it was the monocle—and his general air of competence

—that had made him seem older. In fact he was not that much older than I was, four or five years at most.

The bandages seemed to remind me of something, and suddenly I remembered the loud noises that had seemed so uninteresting. Not only was Mr. Monocle taking care of me, he was taking care of my business, too. He was a full-service sort of Samaritan, Mr. Monocle.

Now I felt hungry *and* guilty.

"We need to talk," I croaked.

"In due time," he said, and then, while holding a glass of water for me, "In...due...time." He left the room, returning momentarily with Thompson, another bowl of something, and another mug of something else. In the meantime I tried to figure out what to say.

I let them sit me up and feed me first, of course. I'm small for my age, but I'm not stupid.

"We need to talk," I said when I was done eating, just as Mr. Monocle was reaching for the Mug of Oblivion.

"In due time, my boy. You've a good stretch of recovery ahead of you yet."

The "my boy" exasperated me. Here I was, trying to let him know what he was in for, and he was patronizing me.

"I'm not a boy, I just look like one," I said. I'm sure my tone was even and mature.

Mr. Monocle glanced at Thompson, and Thompson shrugged back at him. I managed to raise my right hand and bat at the mug. (I missed, if you want to know.)

"And I don't want that yet. I need a clear head." I'm sure I didn't whine even a little bit.

"Indeed," said Mr. Monocle. "Thompson, could you lend a hand?"

"Yes, sir," said Thompson, and started to move in from the other side.

In desperation, I blurted out my hole card. "The man who broke in! What was he carrying?"

Mr. Monocle raised an eyebrow, still looming over me. "That's nothing for you to worry about, lad."

"But it is, you have to listen. Dark gray metal, with a button! And some odd writing. I don't know what shape, but he'd have had it handy."

Then I started coughing, which was no fun at all, and when I was done I got to drink some more water. Except that it wasn't water, but more foul-tasting stuff from the mug. It took both of them, and when they were done Thompson sat down by the bed and Mr. Monocle left with the bowl and the mug, pausing to turn down the light somehow on his way out.

As I faded out, body aching from the exertion, I thought, well, I'd tried.

Chapter 9

I didn't see Mr. Monocle for some time after that. The next time I woke up, I was fed by Thompson and another fellow, similarly dressed but much younger, whom Thompson addressed as "Bodger." I stoutly tried not to call him anything at all, even in my head, in hopes that his real name was something nicer than "Bodger" and that I might learn it one day. They got me fed and cleaned up, and then Dr. Hampstead came in. He was fat and he was jolly and he was patronizing and I loathed him on sight.

"Well, my boy! And how are we doing, hmm?" He sat down in the chair beside the bed and continued to make ludicrous and condescending noises while checking my pulse, my heartbeat, my tongue, and, eventually, my wound. I'll spare you, except for the bottom line: "Well, that seems to be healing quite nicely, hmmm, yes. Be patient for just a few more moments, and I'll have it all wrapped up again, my little man."

I refrained from giving him what for, but I have to say I found it encouraging that I had the energy to want to. I also felt thinner than I'd been just a few days before, which given the low diet I'd been on shouldn't have surprised me. This was the first time I hadn't been able to eat my fill after Traveling, and I was glad I was only recovering from the one jump.

"How bad is it?"

"How bad is it? Nice clean wound, no bones broken—a lucky break there, ha ha—you'll be up and about in a day or so. But you must always wear your sling, for the next fortnight at the least and possibly longer. After that it will be just a matter of exercise until you regain full use."

He bustled off not a moment too soon, and then Thompson came back with some water and the Once and Future Mug, and another object he laid beside them on the table. This time I was able to take the cup of water from his hand and drink it by myself, and when he brought the mug over I took it in the same way.

And then, laughing hysterically, I threw it in his face, leaped from the bed, and dashed for the door…collapsing halfway there, having run out of energy and also having cut my foot on the remains of the mug.

Well, no, I didn't do that thing. As annoying as it was that no one was listening to me, Mr. Monocle and his servants were taking good care of me. I was feeling better every day.

And so I just said, "Thank you, Thompson."

He looked surprised, but said, "Not to worry, lad," in that slow, country way of his.

"Will Mr. Monocle be returning soon?"

I must have sounded better, because I actually got an answer.

"The master is attending to some business, lad. I expect you'll see him this evening, or tomorrow morning as it might be."

"Thank you, Thompson," I said again, and drained the Mug in one long gulp. You taste less of it that way. Shortly after that I drifted off, wondering how many times Bernie was going to kill me when I finally made it home, and whether it would be more painful than getting shot. I don't know what Dr. Hampstead put in his medication, but it didn't lend itself to clear thinking.

Had I mentioned that Thompson had a new bandage around his forearm that I hadn't seen previously? He also had a number of new bruises, and was walking like a guy who'd rather not. And his helper, whom I was steadfastly not thinking of as "Bodger," had a black eye, though it didn't seem to slow him down any. Apparently another enemy had come to play, and Thompson and company had dealt with him in Mr. Monocle's absence.

And the thing about servants is that they are always listening, whether you think they are or not. The other object Thompson had placed on the table when he entered the room was a spindle of dark metal with a button near one end.

"It seems I owe you an apology, lad…or perhaps a good thrashing, I'm not sure which."

It was the next day, I think, when I awoke and found Mr. Monocle sitting in his usual spot, book in hand, monocle dangling on its string. The drapes had been drawn back for a change, and the room was bright and cheerful. Mr. Monocle, for his part, seemed rather more rueful than cheerful.

"You found it, did you?" I said.

He raised an eyebrow, and placed a second finder on the table, next to the one Thompson had left there. This one was a small cube with marks on five sides and a button on the sixth.

I nodded. "And the fellow who shot me in the park? He had one, too, I'm guessing."

He raised the other eyebrow, making two raised eyebrows in all, as he pulled a black glove out of his pocket and handed it to me. There was a flattish disc sewn into the wristband of the glove, with a neatly hemmed opening revealing a silvery button surrounded by dark gray. I handed it back to him, careful not to touch the finder itself.

"But," I continued, "the fellow who was shooting at us at Mordred's didn't have one."

I think Mr. Monocle would have liked to have raised yet another eyebrow, but he couldn't afford the ante. Instead he lowered both of them (preparing, I suppose, for next time), and pulled a fourth finder out of the side pocket of his coat. This one was a flattish hexagon. He held it up in the air, and looked at me quizzically.

"But he couldn't have," I exclaimed. "I took it with me when I left. Did he have two of them?"

Mr. Monocle emitted a sound that might have been a chuckle on a good day. "So that is what you were doing. I heard something about that. No, in fact he didn't. This one was delivered here in person a few hours ago."

Uh-huh. "I'm sorry about that," I said.

"Are you?"

"Yes. Also, I'm grateful. I never meant to involve you in my problems."

This time the chuckle was more cheerful.

"No, lad, let us by all means give credit where credit is due. I involved myself in your problems when I brought you here. I simply didn't expect them to be so…numerous. Or so frequent."

"You were expecting trouble?"

"Are you forgetting, lad? Twice we have met, and twice someone has tried to shoot you. And the second time, witnesses are agreed, the scoundrel appeared out of thin air and tried to shoot you in the back. Very bad *ton*, I must say, for which he paid dearly. Dueling in a public place like Mordred's is hardly good *ton*, but at least that gentleman waited until you were facing him."

"The…gentleman…at Mordred's…did he live?" I didn't need to ask about the scoundrel in the park. I wasn't sure what *ton* was, but it was clear that bad *ton* was a thing I wanted to avoid.

"Briefly, though I am told he never regained consciousness. The point is moot, however, as he'd have been hanged by now."

I must have looked questioning.

"He had initiated an exchange of shots in a public location to no good end; of course he would have been hanged." Mr. Monocle studied me. "At least, I presume he had no good end in view."

"If you mean, was he trying to put an end to an evil villain who devours puppies and small children and uses the wrong fork at dinner, no, he didn't."

"That is rather what I thought," he said.

"What led you to that conclusion?"

"I think an evil villain would be better equipped."

"I can't argue that." I mused for a moment. "What about the ones who have shown up since I got here?"

"Two are in custody awaiting trial. Unfortunately, Thompson and Bodger were unable to subdue the middle one without killing him."

"What will happen to the other two?"

"I have no doubt that they will be hanged in due course."

"Bad *ton?*"

"It is hardly a question of good or bad *ton*. A man's home is his keep, and even more so under the Commonwealth than under the Kings. Invading a dwelling with intent to violence is a quick road to what the lower orders call 'the nubbing cheat.' Though these two are foreigners, so my friends at the Bailey tell me; they don't seem to speak even the lowest forms of English."

English! I'd been assuming that we were able to communicate by virtue of my finder...but it occurred to that I had no idea where my things were, or how close at hand my finder needed to be in order to do its translation gimmick. Was it possible that we really were speaking English?

"Now," said Mr. Monocle, "it pains me to question a guest... but I am afraid I really must know what is going on."

A fair question. "In due time," I said, thinking quickly.

Mr. Monocle pursed his lips and made as if to speak, but I held up a hand.

"First," I said, "I need to write a letter to my wife."

Mr. Monocle sat back in his chair. "Your...wife?"

"I told you I was older than I look."

He blinked several times.

"And how old would that be, pray?" he said after some moments of silence.

"Twenty-eight."

"Oh, dear." He straightened up, bowed slightly in his chair, and said, "I humbly beg your pardon, la—" and then stopped in confusion.

"Henderson," I said. "Michael Henderson."

He nodded.

"I humbly beg your pardon, Mr. Henderson. I intended no disrespect, and apologize for any offense I might have caused. If you require satisfaction, I will of course provide you with the direction of my seconds."

"Seconds?"

"Certainly, should you wish to demand satisfaction on the field of honor."

I stared at him.

"Are you asking me whether I want to fight a duel with you?"

He nodded his head stiffly.

"Well, of all the—" I broke off. I could see he was in earnest, and it would be foolish to make light of what I'm sure he considered to be his finer feelings. At the same time, I was surprised to discover that his treatment of me, which at one time I'd have hated as "condescending" and "patronizing," in fact distressed me not all.

"Mr. Monocle," I said, in the most serious tones I could manage, "May I speak plainly?"

"Certainly," he said, with the air of a proud man expecting the worst.

"I'm small for my age, and that's caused no end of confusion in my life. I used to resent that. But you meant no disrespect, and you've done me nothing but good since we first met. You came to my defense when I was attacked. You brought me to your home and got me medical attention when I was shot. Since then, you've been fighting off my enemies at great personal risk. And now you're worried that you might have wounded my tender sensibilities? It seems to me that I ought to be begging your pardon, not the other way around."

His eyes relaxed, and his mustache gave a little twitch.

"The risk hasn't been so great as all that, in point of fact. Your enemies, as you call them, are singularly inept."

"Hah. Singularly is right."

"Very well, then, Mr. Henderson." His mustache twitched again. "Though I admit, I long to know what kind of absurd contraption you would choose for us to fight with."

"Please," I said, "call me Michael. Where I come from, friends don't stand on ceremony with each other." I thought about Joe

McGillicuddy and the Gang, and wished that Mr. Monocle could join us for breakfast. It might take him a little while to get used to them, but I thought he and Guy Valens would see eye-to-eye on a number of topics. "I've made some very good friends in the last few years, men who have stood by me. I'd like to count you as one of them."

"Very well, then, Michael," he said, and I could tell he was much moved. "Thompson will be here shortly with breakfast, and I shall bring you pen and paper."

He rose, and paused when he reached the door. Turning to me, he said, "My name is Tristram, Michael."

Chapter 10

Thompson came in a short while later with a real meal on a tray, the kind of tray with legs so that I could sit and eat in bed. My left arm was still useless, and moving caused dull pains in my left shoulder, but I managed to scoot myself up into a sitting position without help.

"Thank you, Thompson," I said.

"It's good to see you sit up by yourself, lad," he said.

"It's good to do it," I said. I thought about correcting him as to my age, but it didn't rankle the way he said it...and of course, Thompson is much older than me. Apparently Thompson felt the same way, because "lad" I was and "lad" I've remained.

He left, and I dug in. There were fried eggs, and bacon, and slices of toast in a little metal rack, and butter, and marmalade, and a glass of orange juice and a small pot of tea, and I have to say that I enjoyed it all thoroughly. Although, I really don't understand the little metal rack. It's like they want their toast to get cold.

Mr. Monocle—Tristram, that is—came in with pen and paper as I was finishing the tea. Caffeine is a wonderful thing, and I'd been thinking. After Thompson carried away the breakfast things, leaving me the tray as a writing desk, I said, "Tristram, may I ask a favor?"

"Certainly."

"Would you write a few lines for my wife as well? She worries, and if I simply tell her I'm doing okay she might think I'm making light of my injuries. I'm sure Dr. Hampstead has spoken more freely with you than with me."

"Certainly," he repeated, and left me alone to write my letter.

I had some trouble with the pen. It wasn't any kind of ballpoint, not that I'd expected one, but it didn't look like a normal fountain pen, either. It was fairly big around, and the tip looked like something the evil villain would use on James Bond.

I couldn't get it to produce any kind of mark on the paper until I noticed a small stud on the barrel. I gave the stud an experimental flick. It slid perhaps a millimeter, and then the pen started to hum—or maybe 'hiss' would be a better word. The tip got a little blurry, and very small puffs of steam started issuing from the opposite end.

I spent a sheet of paper just playing with it. It left a nice, crisp black line that didn't smudge or streak or blot, no matter how fast I wrote or how I held it. Nice.

I kept the letter short, because what I had in mind was kind of an experiment. Or, really, two experiments. The second was to see whether Bernie could read Tristram's writing. I had an idea that she could, but no way to be sure on my own.

The first was more questionable.

My finder is capable of finding worlds that meet particular criteria and taking me to them. In this case the criteria was "the world containing my wife Bernie"; and in that phrase the word "wife" is key. Bernie's my anchor in that world: there are maybe an infinite number of worlds containing Bernie's close counterparts, but I'm married to only one of them. (And let me tell you, finding the wrong one is distressing, as I have reason to know.)

But I didn't actually want to go home yet. I was still convalescing; and with all due apologies to Mr. Monocle I was safer in his home than I'd be in my own. On top of that, it was a mystery to me how I'd arrived in his world twice in a row. I had no anchors here, and I wasn't at all sure that if I left I'd be able to find my way back. I owed him an explanation, and it would be poor repayment for his kindness to vanish without giving him one.

At the same time, I needed to let Bernie know that I was okay. So...the finder allowed me to Travel to other worlds; and when I Traveled I could take other things with me. Was it possible that I could *send* things while remaining where I was? I was pretty sure that it couldn't hurt to try: I'd verified some while back that pressing the finder's button had no effect if I had no wish to go anywhere.

It turned out to be three experiments, actually, because as soon as I was done writing the letter I climbed out of bed. It wasn't too bad, so long as I kept my left arm in its sling. (Yes, I tried removing it, and no I didn't try that again.)

My things were in the wardrobe, as I'd expected. It was a big one, big enough on the outside to suit those who are old school in their taste for inter-dimensional travel, but it wasn't filled with coats. Inside the left door I found my trousers and shirt hanging neatly in splendid isolation, with my backpack on the floor; inside the right I found drawers and shelves. My belt, complete with finder case, was coiled up on one of the shelves next to my keys and my wallet. I took the belt and the backpack with me when I went back to my pillows. Nothing had been touched.

Mr. Monocle returned some while later; I imagine he wanted to give me plenty of time to write my letter. He had one of his own, sealed with a button of red wax, and a small device that turned out to be a sealing wax dispenser.

"I see that you have found your things," he said. "Good. Now, I can frank that for you, if you like."

"Frank it?"

"So that your wife needn't pay the postage."

"Oh, I see. Thank you, but that shouldn't be necessary." Have you ever noticed how you start to talk like the people around you? I suppose it's useful.

He raised an eyebrow, and waited.

I grabbed my belt, and pulled my finder out of its case. I held it up.

"Indeed," he said, matter-of-factly, but I think his mustache twitched a little.

"This is something new I'm trying," I said. "May I have your letter?"

He handed it to me and sat down in the chair, folding his hands across his chest.

I folded my letter, tucked his inside, and wrote "Bernie" in big letters on the outside. I held the combined letters in my left hand. I held the finder in my right. I thought of Bernie receiving the letters, of them appearing on the floor next to her while I stayed right where I was.

When I thought I had it all clear, I pushed the button.

The letters vanished, and the red button of wax from Mr. Monocle's letter fell in my lap.

"Was that supposed to happen?"

"Could be worse, I guess. I could have sent the paper and left the ink behind. That would have been messy."

Mr. Monocle nodded.

"Now," he said, "I believe you have a story to tell me. We can stay here, or if you are feeling up to it we can adjourn to the library."

"The library, by all means," I said.

"I will send Thompson to help you dress."

Twenty minutes later found me slippered, wrapped in a burgundy dressing gown, and ensconced in a wingback chair by the fire, with a cup of tea at my elbow and a taser in my lap. I hadn't intended to bring the taser, but Thompson wouldn't let me leave my room without it.

"Now then, lad, it's not all vermin as walks on four legs. The Master tells me you've got a sidearm, so you'd best be bringing it with you," he said as I was heading for the door. "Especially these days, it seems."

I made him unzip my backpack for me, which delighted him—he'd not seen a zipper before and thought it a capital invention—

and rummaged through and pulled out the taser. I showed him how to check whether it was loaded, which it was, and then I tucked it in the pocket of my dressing gown, next to my finder.

Then I slung the backpack over my right shoulder by one strap.

"You won't be needing that, lad," said Thompson. "It's only along the corridor and down the stairs."

"It isn't safe to leave it alone," I said. "It's what the vermin are looking for."

"Is it now, lad? Have you told the master?"

"I'm about to."

Thompson nodded. "As you say, lad."

I started to leave and then considered that there were four more finders on the table by my bed. I was about to try to transfer them into my backpack when I considered that perhaps they weren't mine. Or, at least, I'd shed blood for the one in the glove, but not for the other three. And then, I didn't want to risk activating any of them.

"Thompson?"

"Yes, lad?"

"Would you gather those up and bring them down to the library as well? Your master will want to keep an eye on them."

He nodded, and in lieu of a bag or other container tucked the three loose finders into the glove in which the fourth finder was sewn.

Mr. Monocle greeted me as I entered the library, ushered me to my seat, and saw me sitting comfortably before settling into the chair opposite mine. Thompson deposited the backpack next to my chair, placed the bulging glove on the table at Mr. Monocle's elbow, and then took himself off.

I pulled the taser out of my pocket and placed it in my lap. "Thompson insisted."

"Quite right," he said. "I intended that he should. Now, Michael, you were intending to explain the shocking parade of incompetence my home has witnessed over the last few days." His mustache twitched on the words, "shocking parade of incompetence."

"It's a long story," I said, as Thompson returned with a tea tray. It was late morning, not tea time, but I wasn't about to complain.

"Not to worry," said Mr. Monocle. "I have no further duties today, and if we are interrupted we shall know what to do."

Fair enough, I thought.

So I told him.

Chapter 11

"You'll have figured out," I began, "that I'm not from here."

"Indeed. Though just where you might be from has been a particular puzzle to me. From your command of English, odd though it is, I at first assumed you were from one of the Colonies." Mr. Monocle shifted in his chair. "No offense meant, but colonials are not highly thought of, and one might believe almost anything of them."

"Almost anything?"

"I have never heard of any that had the power of vanishing in a twinkling of an eye, as I have learned that you were seen to do." He paused to reflect. "At least, not in a place such as Mordred & Sons. I'm told they can be quite stealthy in the forest."

"This is true. Although your guess about the Colonies isn't as far off as you think. I'll get to that."

I pulled my finder out of the pocket of the dressing gown and held it up in the air for a moment.

"It's all about these," I said.

"We do seem to have acquired a sizable collection of them."

"You have no idea. I've got four more in my backpack."

Mr. Monocle's brows shot up. "Four more," he said. "Do you mean to tell me that you dealt with four of these miscreants on your own? Well done."

"Three," I said. "The fourth was a special case. And also I had help."

"Indeed. I should like to hear further details."

"In due time," I said. Turnabout, after all, is fair play. "First," I continued, "I want to explain what these things are."

He nodded agreeably, crossed his legs, and had a sip of tea. "I am seated comfortably."

I took a deep breath, and held up the finder again.

"My father called this a finder. He was a Traveler, which means he could use finders to Travel from one world to another."

Mr. Monocle tilted his head. "A Traveler—Do you mean, a gypsy?"

"No, not in the sense you mean." I thought for a moment. "Although, maybe something like. I'll have to think about that."

"And then, you say he could travel from one world to another…I presume you don't mean from the Commonwealth to the Continent."

"No…but I'm not sure how I'm going to explain just what I do mean. Hold on a sec." I thought as fast I could. "Tell you what, may I ask you some questions?"

"The Socratic method, eh? Very well."

"From what you've said, we're in a place called the Commonwealth—is that right?"

"Yes, certainly."

"And what is the Commonwealth?"

"The government of our land. To give it its full name, it is the Civil Commonwealth of Britain and the Isles."

"Can you tell me more? Assume I don't know anything about this, because I don't."

"Let me see. The Commonwealth is presided over by the First Lord, Lord Remchester, who rules in the name of the Assembly and People of Britain."

"So, no Parliament then?"

"Oh, no. Parliament," he began in a voice that suggested that he was quoting, "was an outmoded form of government entirely beholden to the noble classes, and was swept away during the glorious revolution that ushered in our current era of freedom and prosperity." There was a tone in his voice that I thought I recognized.

"Oh, really? And when was this?"

"In the first year of the New Order, of course."

"And the current year is?"

"15 N.O."

"Uh-huh. And what year is it really? I mean, what year would it be had the glorious revolution not occurred?"

Mr. Monocle leaned forward. "That, friend Michael, is a perilous question," he said. "You are in no danger from me or from Thompson, but I would not advise you to ask such questions more widely. Not that the other servants would betray you on purpose, but they are woefully open-mouthed."

I nodded, and he leaned back into his chair.

"1802," he said.

"So, there are no noble families any more?"

"Not as such, no." His mustache tilted down at one corner.

"What about the king?"

"After George of late unlamented memory, we decided that we had had a sufficiency of them."

"That would be George III?"

He nodded. "Just so."

"And the Colonies—they lie across the western ocean?"

"Yes, on the continent of New Albion."

I nodded. "Okay, that gives me enough to get started." I sipped at my tea, just to have some time to collect my thoughts.

"I come from a place," I said, "that is very similar to this world of yours. But in my world, Parliament still governs Britain. There is a Queen; her name is Elizabeth II, and if I remember correctly, she is the umpty-times great granddaughter of your George III." I shook my head. "Our George. Our equivalent of your George."

"My word. I seem to have fallen into *A Midsummer Night's Dream*, and the fairies have captured my wits. I say, my head looks the same as always, does it?" He shook his head. "This all seems excessively unlikely."

I shrugged. "You saw the guy in the park appear 'in a twinkling of an eye,' as you put it."

"So I did." He frowned. "And you are from this Britain where Elizabeth reigns?"

"Nope. My home town is in what you'd call New Albion."

"The Colonies? Well, that would explain a few things."

"In my world, the Colonies rebelled in 1776...and won."

"You interest me strangely. Two worlds, so similar and yet so different."

"Different is right." I pointed at the light sconces by the door and at the lamp hanging in the middle of the ceiling. "In my world, the kind of lights you have in your home weren't developed for another hundred years—well, assuming that these work the way ours do. Your world seems to be about two centuries behind mine, in terms of chronology, but the technology you have here is much better than any of my ancestors would have had. Well, and we don't have any gulls the size of yours. Or snapping trout, either."

"Technology?" He frowned again. "The word appears to be from the Greek, but I'm not familiar with it. The study of craft, would it be?"

"Close enough. What we mean by it is different kinds of machinery and other devices. Your lights, for example, or your guns."

"Ah. Yes, I see. We would say *armamentaria*. And your... finder...is a kind of *technology* that allows you to travel between your world and this one, is that it?"

"Yeah, I guess."

"So, then, this steady stream of ruffians is from your world? I shouldn't wonder that you'd come here to escape them, if that be the case."

"Actually, I'd be surprised if any of them came from my world —or any two of them from the same world. There's an infinite number of worlds, you see. Or as close as makes no difference."

"An infinite number—That will take some getting used to, Michael."

He sipped his tea, which had gone cold. He made a face, and rose to ring the bell for Thompson.

"Yes, sir?"

"Take this away, Thompson, and Michael's as well, and bring us brandy and soda."

"At this hour, sir?" From the tone of Thompson's voice, I thought he was shocked.

"It is medicinal."

"As you say, sir."

Mr. Monocle returned to his seat, pursing his lips under the mustache. I stayed quiet, and let him ponder. Well, it was a lot to take in.

Thompson returned with two glasses of brandy and soda, and handed one to each of us. I put mine on the table where my tea had been. Mr. Monocle sipped at his pensively. At last he spoke.

"Why," he said, cocking his head at me, "do you call it a finder?"

"Because it finds worlds. Worlds with particular things in them."

He cocked his head. "Indeed. Am I to conclude, then, that they are coming here because this world has a particular thing in it? A particular thing named 'Michael'?"

"Not precisely," I said. "I mean, it does, because here I am. But they aren't looking for me, not me specifically." I held up the finder. "They're looking for this. Well, this and its friends in my backpack. And on the table, there."

Mr. Monocle considered, brandy glass in hand.

"These 'finders' are valuable, I take it? Hard to come by?"

"Literally priceless. The only way to get one is to take it from someone who has one."

He looked at me over the rim of his glass. "Let me see if I understand the position. You began with two of these items—and, I confess, I shall want to hear how you came by them."

I nodded.

"And then, beginning last May, you have received a stream of visitors from other worlds, each intent on taking them from you?"

"That's right."

"A stream of increasing frequency."

"That's about the size of it, yes."

"Why?"

"Bernie has a theory about that. When I direct the finder to take me to a world with particular characteristics, there are usually many worlds that fit the bill. The finder picks one somehow, and there I go. We used to think the choice was arbitrary, like the throw of the dice, but in this case, well...." I shrugged. "There was a famous bank robber in our world. When he was caught, someone asked him why he robbed banks."

"And what did he say?"

"He said, 'Because that's where the money is.'"

"In other words, two finders are more attractive than one?"

"So it seems. And I gather that having two is most uncommon. The usual number is one." I quirked my lips. "Well, actually, the usual number is zero."

Mr. Monocle finished his brandy and soda and stared into the fire.

"I am filled with so many questions," he said, still looking into the fire, "that I am unsure where to begin."

The fire crackled, and I was beginning to consider drinking some of my own brandy and soda when Thompson re-entered the room and addressed his master.

"You have a visitor, sir. That Miss Stavely."

"Blast. I am not at home, Thompson." He looked ruffled. So did his mustache.

"I've told her so, sir, but she don't take no for an answer."

"I suppose I must see her. Michael, I am afraid it might be best if—"

"—I were to make myself scarce? Gladly." I didn't know who Miss Stavely was, but I didn't want to meet any callers in my pajamas. I started to pull myself out of the chair, but it was too late. Miss Stavely was upon us.

She was a slight figure in a grayish-blue dress and an erect, superior attitude that made her seem larger than she was. The dress had the usual puffy sleeves, and though she'd forgone the goggles she had some kind of device strapped to her left forearm, just visible under her sleeve. It seemed to be about six inches long, from the shape it made under the fabric, though I couldn't tell what it was.

She was accompanied by a smaller woman in black who seemed to want to slide into the woodwork and be forgotten. Once they were fully in the room, Thompson slipped out behind them and shut the door.

Mr. Monocle rose to his feet. I decided that discretion was the better part of valor, and sat quietly back, hoping not to be noticed.

"Miss Stavely," he said, inclining his head. "To what do I owe the, ah, extreme pleasure of your visit?"

"Mr. Monocle," she began, then seemed to noticed me for the first time. I suddenly had no doubt that she'd spotted me the moment she entered the room. She looked at me—her eyes were a steely gray—and then looked pointedly at him, and waited.

He looked from her to me in some little confusion, and then rallied.

"Miss Stavely," he said, "may I introduce to you Master Henderson. My cousin, you know, from the Colonies." And then, to me, "Michael, this is Miss Melissa Stavely." And then to Miss Stavely, "Please excuse Master Henderson for not rising; he is recovering from being shot in the park a few days ago."

"Miss Stavely," I said. I did my best to incline my head as Mr. Monocle had done.

"Master Henderson," she said. "I have heard of that affair." From her tone, it was clear she thought it disreputable. "I trust your injuries are not too serious?"

"The doctor says I will be just fine in a fortnight or two," I said. I had the sense of tip-toeing through a minefield.

"I am glad to hear it," she said, in tones of icy politeness. Having done the necessary, she turned her steely gaze back on Mr. Monocle.

"A relation on your father's side, I presume?"

"Quite."

I could see her file that tidbit away for later; then she went on.

"I had hoped to speak to you in private. It concerns a matter of some importance."

"As you see, I am occupied this morning."

"My father is most insistent. He has already spoken with Lord Remchester."

"Very well," he said. He turned to me and said, "Begging your pardon?"

I nodded. I wanted to grimace in commiseration, but I didn't dare.

Mr. Monocle led Miss Stavely to the door of the library, opened it for her, and followed her out. Her attendant toddled on behind, shutting the door behind them, and leaving me with much food for thought.

Item: Mr. Monocle had struck me as unflappable, but even he wasn't proof against Miss Stavely.

Item: I was now meant to be Mr. Monocle's cousin from the Colonies; and his *minor* cousin at that, if I'd understand the local lingo correctly. Bother.

Item: Lord Remchester was the current leader of the Commonwealth.

Item: Lord Remchester had opinions about Mr. Monocle's marriage prospects.

Item: Mr. Monocle was better connected than I'd realized.

Item: Judging from the tones in which he'd spoken about it, Mr. Monocle had reservations about the Commonwealth.

Conclusion: the local political situation was fraught, and if I were going to stay here much longer I'd need to find out more about it.

I glanced at the waiting glass of brandy and soda, and then got myself to my feet and found the bell pull. Thompson was there in moments.

"Yes, lad?"

"Thompson, could I have some fresh tea, please?" I indicated the glass of brandy. "I feel the need of something, but if I drink that, well…," and I waved a hand at myself, indicating my small size.

"She takes people that way, lad, that she does." He glanced toward the door, then shook his head. "I'll have it for you as soon as maybe."

Chapter 12

I took a look around the library while I waited. It was well named, as shelves lined three of the walls. Two tall windows in deep embrasures peeked through the shelves on the wall opposite the door. The two wingback chairs I've mentioned were on either side of the fireplace on the fourth wall; opposite them was a large desk where I imagined that Mr. Monocle conducted his personal business. Having exhausted the furniture, I got up, careful not to jostle my arm, and amused myself by browsing the shelves.

The books were a mixture of matched sets and individual volumes, all bound handsomely in leather. I was unsurprised to find both Plato and Shakespeare, as Mr. Monocle had alluded to both of them, though I was surprised by some of the titles: *Love's Labor's Lost* was followed by *Love's Labor's Won*, for example, and there was also a play called *Scipio Africanus*. I didn't see anything by Aristotle, though I might have missed him. There were books on history, both natural and otherwise, and a range of novels, none of which I recognized. (I'm not a lit. major. So sue me.)

Among what seemed to be the newer acquisitions were two that looked like they might have some bearing on current politics: *The Steam Revolution*, by Jno. Roehampton, and *The Founding of the Civil Commonwealth of Britain and the Isles* by one Tm. Monocle, Esq. I brought them back to my chair—or, rather, Thompson did, having providentially arrived with my tea—and then settled in for a good browse.

I turned first to *The Steam Revolution*, which turned out to have nothing to do with political events and everything to do with technology, being, as its subtitle assured me, an "encyclopedic and universal guide to the modern armamentaria of industry and domestic life." There were sections on aetheric power generation and transmission by means of steam piping, and on steam motivators and other vehicles, with bonus details on the excavation of the "mighty steam tunnels of London," along with a visual guide to small steam-powered appliances "to ease the heart of any housewife." Apparently photography hadn't yet been discovered, as the visuals consisted solely of black-and-white engravings.

It was while reading through this section that I discovered the reason for the goggles—apparently some of these "labour-easing appurtenances" had a nasty tendency to spit boiling water and other noxious substances at inopportune times, and "the wise mistress of the house will never neglect to protect her eyesight." I was left to wonder why men weren't similarly advised; or perhaps the man of the house simply had nothing to do with "Johnson's Patented Steam-Etheric Auto-Seamstress" and its homely companions, the "Aetheric Oven" and "Hansen's Steam-Powered Egg Flagellator."

I marked my place with a finger, and turned to the opening pages. The publication date was 14 N.O., which meant that steam-aetherics were the very latest thing; and if wide-spread adoption of aetheric power was more recent than Tristram's house then the lighting must have been retrofitted. I looked around at the ceiling lamp and the wall sconces. A little pipe ran along the ceiling from the lamp to the crown molding. It was pencil thin and painted the same color as the ceiling. Similar pipes ran up the walls from the sconces. And there, on the wall by the door, was a little box with five little knobs on it. Five little pipes ran up the wall from it; one slightly larger one ran down to the baseboard.

One ceiling lamp, four sconces, one steam supply. And five little valves to turn the lights on and off. Simple.

The thought of pencils prompted me to look up writing implements, and I found a drawing of the very pen I'd used to write my letter to Bernie. It used no ink; apparently one loaded it with a thick stick of graphite, or something very like it, which was used as both fuel for the pen's minuscule steam engine, and as pigment for marking the paper. It was, in fact, a steam-powered pencil.

I'm a technically minded kind of guy, but I have to say that the "glorious" and "marvelous" descriptions of the "advanced science" that underlay the "near miraculous armamentaria of steam" left me completely befuddled. How could you build a steam engine that small? How did you turn steam into lighting? What were "aetherics"? Was the "steam" the book spoke of the same thing I meant by the word? I'd taken it for granted that the laws of nature were constant across the infinite set of worlds the finder gave me access to; now I began to wonder. It was an unsettling thought.

It's said that the physical constants of the universe we live in are fine-tuned for the existence of life (or, possibly, life is fine-tuned for the physical constants we have). My body was intended to work within a particular physical context, a particular set of natural laws. What would happen if I Traveled to a world with laws that were subtly different? Would I be able to live there for long? Would the air and food nourish me, or would my body go slowly wrong? From my perusal of *The Revolution of Steam* this appeared to be no academic question.

Or perhaps the finder fixed things up as part of the transition from one world to another? That would take energy, which would explain why Traveling made me so hungry. But this was all speculation. There was so much I didn't know.

Eventually I laid Roehampton's tome aside, amusing though it was, and took up *The Founding of the Civil Commonwealth*, by the suggestively named "Tm. Monocle, Esq." I wanted to know more about the differences between this world and my own, of course, but my first goal was to discover whether the author was in fact my good friend Tristram. I had not far to seek, as he might say, for the book began with one of those long-winded tributes to the patron in whose honor the volume was published. The author signed himself "Tristram J. Monocle, Esq., London, in the 7th year since the founding of the New Order," and the patron was Lord Remchester himself.

The tribute praised Lord Remchester both generally and personally. Generally, for his leadership of the nation during the "heady days of the revolution in which the monarchy and Parliament were overthrown," Parliament that was "an outmoded form of government entirely beholden to the noble classes," and which was "swept away during the Glorious Revolution that ushered in our current era of freedom and prosperity." Personally, for taking the young Monocle under his protection and guiding him "through the vicissitudes and complexities of the New Order after the successful and profitable conclusion of our noble rebellion."

I was fascinated. So Mr. Monocle was in some sense Lord Remchester's protege, and author of what appeared to be the official history of the Glorious Revolution. Judging by the tone of the dedication it was a history that hewed closely—perhaps even slavishly—to the party line; and yet Tristram himself seemed to take a rather sardonic view of the whole thing.

I heard the door open, and drained my teacup so that Thompson could refill it.

"I see that you have uncovered my youthful sins."

It was Mr. Monocle, not Thompson. I jumped, which I immediately regretted. He looked harried, if a bit less ruffled, and his handlebar mustache had that slight tilt to it that I was coming to recognize as a sign of rueful resignation. He didn't sit down, but just rested one hand on the back of his chair.

"I've only read the dedication," I said, "but I have to admit it's intriguing." I glanced at the door, which he'd closed behind him. "Is she, uh, is she…"

"Miss Stavely is gone from our midst, yes."

"Did it go well? You don't seem too happy about it."

"In due time," he said, taking the monocle from his eye and polishing it with a cloth he removed from his vest pocket. His mustache twitched. "Luncheon has been laid on in the small saloon, if you would care to join me."

"I do apologize for casting you as my minor cousin," Mr. Monocle said as he led the way to the small saloon, which was directly across the hall from the library. "It was the best I could think of in the moment to explain why I had taken you under my wing, as it were."

"It's okay," I said. "I really didn't want to explain myself to Miss Stavely, and it's probably easier to just let people assume I'm the age I look."

"Hmmm, yes, that was my thought as well. Although I am concerned that Lord Remchester—but let us leave that aside."

The small saloon proved to be what I'd call a dining room; and luncheon proved to be a light meal of cold roast beef, thinly sliced, with roasted potatoes and some kind of green vegetable I didn't recognize. (During my bachelor years vegetables were a thing that happened to other people, and after almost a year of marriage my acquaintance with them is still mostly hypothetical.)

I ate everything, including the Mystery Greens, and as we ate Mr. Monocle told me his story.

"No doubt you've been wondering about that book; and also about Miss Stavely. And I am sure you have been wondering why I chose to take you into my home instead of leaving you to the good offices of the City of London. It so happens that these three subjects bear on one another, and since I have every intention of plumbing the depths of your life story it seems only fair to be beforehand with mine. I only ask that you keep the, er, more *personal* details to yourself.

"My mother was the daughter of the Earl of—well, it doesn't matter, you wouldn't know the name anyway. It suffices that she was the daughter of what was referred to as a 'noble line.'

During her coming-out season she met my father, who I am told was a personable young fellow though he belonged to no family anyone had ever heard of, and had no fortune that anyone ever saw. He was charming, she was smitten." He waved his hand in the air, as if to say, you know how these things go. "My grandfather forbade the match, of course, but they married anyway, I am not sure how or where, and my grandfather cast her out. Or perhaps they didn't marry, but just ran off. Thompson might know, but he won't talk about it.

"I was born the following year; and the year after that my mother died in childbirth along with one who would have been my sister." Tristram—it seems appropriate to call him Tristram, since he was baring his soul to me—paused for a few moments. Outside the window the sun shone brightly on a kind of garden in the middle of the square. I studied the statue in the center of the garden, and waited for him to continue. "My father seems never to have recovered from this. I gather that he sent a single letter to my grandfather, and then disappeared. I have no idea what became of him."

Up until this point, Tristram had mostly been looking at his plate, but now he looked me in the eye. "And that is why I brought you home. I asked you if you had no father, and indeed you hadn't. It is a state I am all too familiar with.

"It was inexcusably familiar of me to ask such a question, and I beg your pardon; but there it is."

"Granted," I said. "Thank you."

He nodded. "My grandfather," he continued, "had no wish to see me or speak with me; but he sent Thompson to look after things for me, and paid for my support and education." He paused. "I want this clearly understood," he said, his voice deepening. "After what had passed between my grandfather and my parents, he felt I had no claim on him, no claim whatsoever; and yet I sit before you an educated gentleman, and it is due solely to his support. I won't call it generosity, for I am sure it was no such thing; and yet, I am grateful."

"A proud, stiff-necked man, but your own," I said.

"Quite." He took a deep breath, let it out. "And so I grew to manhood, studying with tutors primarily, learning my Greek and Latin and my history, with Thompson teaching me to ride and shoot. I did not go out into society, but I was made to learn everything a gentleman ought to know. Thompson was a stern task master when he had to be, and I gather he had had detailed instructions from my grandfather."

I nodded.

Tristram's plate was empty by this time, so he looked out at the square for a moment.

"And then three things happened almost simultaneously," he said. "First, Lord Remchester raised the flag of revolution against the nobility; and second, my cousin Richard was killed in one of the early battles, defending my grandfather's estate against the rebels. As he was my grandfather's only other grandson, that made me the heir to the earldom—though I didn't learn that for quite some time. And third, it seems that the revolution and the loss of his heir was too much for my grandfather, for he died only a few days after Richard."

"Did he die of the shock? Or was he murdered by the rebels?"

I regretted the question the moment after I asked it; all I can say is that I was caught up in the story, and I have a suspicious mind.

Tristram shrugged. "I don't know. For the sake of my own peace of mind, I like to think that it was the shock; and indeed my grandfather was advanced in years, and of a choleric temperament."

I nodded. "And that made you the earl."

"Legally, yes; but in the chaos and confusion of those times the normal legalities did not apply. Travel was difficult, and communications irregular, and as I say, I had no notion of it until quite some time afterward.

"And then somehow I came to Lord Remchester's notice—I imagine he went through my grandfather's records—and when the dust settled.... When the dust settled, I am afraid I was exactly what Lord Remchester was looking for."

"Let me guess," I said. "You were a member of the higher nobility by blood and by law, but not actually by upbringing; and Lord Remchester had every reason to think you would have hard feelings toward your grandfather, and every reason to sympathize with his cause."

"Precisely," said Tristram. "You are astute, I find.

"Well, and so I was living in the country in those days, in a cottage provided for me by my grandfather, and the progress of the revolution was but a distant rumor. We knew that it was happening, and that the rebels were in the ascendant, but our small corner of England was untouched…until the day when Lord Remchester himself rode up to my door. He had heard good things of me, he said, that I was a studious young man, he said. His New Model Army was in the vicinity, passing through, as they say, and his secretary had been killed by a stray bullet early in the previous week. Would I care for the position?

"He gave me no opportunity to think it over, or to discuss it with anyone; he was moving on in the morning, and if I cared to accept I needed to come immediately. But indeed, I had no need to discuss it with anyone, for I already knew what Thompson would say; he'd said it to me more than once.

"'This rebellion is a bad business, lad, especially for one with kin such as you've got,' he'd said to me. 'Best you keep your head down and give the rebels no reason to remove it.' Now I had the leader of the rebels himself asking me to take service with him.

"What was a young man to do, a young man most interested in preserving his own skin? I didn't think of grandfather's fortune or title, for I still didn't know that I was his heir. It seemed that I couldn't keep my head down; at best, I could try to make it too valuable a head to separate from its shoulders." His mustache acquired that rueful tilt. "And indeed, Lord Remchester was most charming. I became not only his secretary, but his aide, his protege. He took me everywhere with him, and presented me to every one. It was only later that I found out what everyone else knew, what he was saying of me when I wasn't in the vicinity."

"You were his poster boy," I said. "The one he could point to, to show that he wasn't slaughtering the families of the nobility willy-nilly."

"But only when they forced him to it by their continued resistance," he said, nodding. "Precisely. I am not familiar with the term 'poster boy,' but no matter. I was the sign of his forbearance and his beneficence, and a sterling example of the treatment reasonable individuals might expect."

"And it was such a pity how few of noble family chose to be reasonable?" I asked.

"Quite so." He rose from his seat, and went to stand by one of the windows, continuing to look out. "After a number of months Lord Remchester admitted to me, as he had known all along, that had the revolution been unsuccessful I would now be the Earl of Uxbridge. As a reward for good behavior I was granted the bulk of my grandfather's money (though none of his land), always provided that I showed my willingness to renounce his title and family. By, say, continuing to support the New Order, and by changing my name."

"Aha!" I said. "So 'Monocle'—"

"—is an assumed name, yes. I was in the habit of wearing one even then, and it had become something of a nickname among Remchester's cronies."

"Why not just keep your father's name?"

"His lordship felt it was better for me to have a new name, as a sign of the new era. It was all part of the game, you know. I was far from the only remote scion of the old nobility to resort to it."

I nodded. "I gather that writing the history of the Revolution was one of your first tasks. Once it was over, I mean."

"Quite. I was both wary and somewhat dazzled in those days, and completely in Remchester's control. I am no longer dazzled, and I have recently moved out of Remchester's circle as far as I dare." He glanced at the door. "If not quite so far as I would like."

"Hmmm. I've not read the book yet; can you tell me what the revolution was about?"

"In a word, envy. Jealousy. In those days, English society was dominated by what was called the *haut ton*, the Thousand Families. The heads of the families controlled the House of Lords, and their scions, of noble blood if not yet of title, controlled the so-called House of Commons. Such power leads to wealth and disregard for others, and those lead to jealousy and anger."

"On the part of the common man? The working classes?"

"Not so common as all that, friend Michael. We leave that to the French. No, the revolution was a revolt against the Thousand Families by the more prosperous gentry and merchant families, those who could clearly see the power and state of the Thousand but could never rise to it."

"Got it. Back home, we call that a glass ceiling."

"Hah! An apt term, indeed. Yes, Lord Remchester's goal was to smash the glass ceiling, as you call it, not so much to destroy the *haut ton* as to replace it."

"You used that word before—good *ton* and bad *ton*."

"Yes; it means the proper manners of the *haut ton*, or, as it called now, simply the *ton*. Having supplanted the ancient nobility, their successors choose to ape their manners." He grimaced. "Not that I am in a position to criticize, aping as I do the manners of those my grandfather would have termed the 'lower orders.'"

There was an uncomfortable silence.

"So where does Miss Stavely come into this?" I asked, because, you know, I'm nosy.

"Oh, yes. The Stavely." Tristram turned to face me, and leaned against the window sill. "Odd, isn't it, how much easier it is to speak of the faults of others rather than one's own?" His mustache twitched, and settled on a more even keel.

"The Stavelys," he said, "are long time allies of Lord Remchester. Lord Stavely—"

I held up a hand. "Wait a minute. The revolution was against the nobility. How do you still have lords running around?"

"Oh, we still have titles, of a sort. Anyone with a seat in the Assembly is entitled to be addressed as 'Lord,' and those who have been of special assistance to the Commonwealth are dignified with the title of 'Esquire'—though no one is meant to use it as a term of address. In theory neither of these titles is hereditary, but we shall see."

"So Lord Stavely is a member of the Assembly."

"Just so. He is also an inveterate gamester, and as he has no skill in gaming his 'dibs are no longer in tune,' as they say. He is in danger of being completely rolled up."

"I'll take a stab at that," I said. "Lord Stavely wants you to marry his daughter so that you will be obliged to save him from financial embarrassment."

"In a nutshell, yes. He can be quite charming, of course—in his own way, and when he chooses."

"When he wants something."

"Quite."

"And you don't want to give it to him. Well, who would? It was all I could do not to run away and hide."

"I have known her these fifteen years, and I have often wished to do so. Can't, of course. Bad *ton*."

"Well, what if you were to marry someone else? Present Lord Stavely with a done deal?"

"A brilliant notion, if only I had begun on it some years ago. But alas, I am too closely associated with Lord Remchester."

"I don't get it. I'd have thought that that would be a good thing, socially."

"Oh, I have had any number of young ladies casting themselves in my way—or, rather, in the way of Lord Remchester's wealthy young protege, on the orders of their ambitious mamas. The Stavely is only the most persistent."

I thought about Bernie for a moment. "I can see how that would be off-putting. And I suppose the young ladies of, um, sounder character…"

"…wish to have nothing to do with a traitor to his own class—not that they approve of the class to which they assign me. Were I the ambitious sort all would be well, but I prefer a more comfortable life."

"Miss Stavely doesn't seem likely to give you a comfortable life."

"No more does she, and thus far I have been successful in putting her off. But there are complications."

"I heard her mention Lord Remchester." I yawned. It had been a busy morning, after having spent several days in bed, and my stomach was full, and I'd had a glass of wine, and my shoulder ached.

"Precisely. But I see you are tired, Michael." And he helped me up to bed, taser, backpack, finders, and all.

Chapter 13

I napped away most of the afternoon, but when Thompson looked in on me I'd been up for maybe an hour, writing a letter to Bernie.

"Dinner will be laid on in the small saloon in twenty minutes, lad, if you're wishful of coming down for it."

"I am. Give me a moment, please."

I signed and folded the letter, pictured it arriving next to Bernie, and pressed the button on my finder. Then I hurried downstairs. There was something that had been bothering me as I dozed, and I wanted to talk to Tristram about it.

"Tristram," I said after the meal had been served, "I'm sure you're now aware that I could have returned to my home any time in the last day or so. Have you wondered why I haven't?"

His mustache twitched; it seemed to be a sign of amusement.

"Not at all. I understand it perfectly well: you have been winged and you are not yet up to snuff. And you believe yourself to be safer here than you would be in your own home." He carved me slices from the breast of some kind of fowl and put them on my plate. "And you are quite right to think so. I will not hear of you leaving until your shoulder is sound once again... and even then I would prefer you to stop here where you are safe until you have a plan for terminating this on-going comedy of errors."

"Thank you," I said, and you can believe that I meant it.

"That's a big part of it, though I hate subjecting you to it. But there's another part."

"Oh?"

"Yeah. You asked me the reason for the on-going comedy of errors, and I haven't finished explaining. It seemed rude to go off before I did that, especially since I'm not one-hundred percent sure I could find my way back here."

"Hmmm, yes. Uncomfortable feeling, that, knowing that as I speak there are thousands or millions of me doing the same thing."

"There aren't, actually."

"There aren't? But you said—"

"There's only one me, so you're the only you that's met me. None of the others of you can possibly be having this conversation."

His brows raised, then he nodded.

"Just so," he said.

"But I don't know if that's enough to find you again. It might be; I did something similar once, but it involved having most of a town that knew me. Even then, I think my father would have said it wasn't possible." I grimaced. "That's something else you need to know. I don't really understand how any of this works. All I know is what my mother told me about what my father told her decades ago, and what I've learned by direct experience. I don't know how much she forgot, or what he over-simplified or left out or flat out lied about. I never had the chance to speak to him myself. In fact, I've only ever spoken to one other Traveler, and him I didn't trust any further than I could sling Lord Remchester. We aren't especially gregarious."

"I can see why that would be so, if having several finders in one place causes the kind of high frolics you have been experiencing."

That was a new thought. I hadn't put those things together before, but they came together with an almost audible click. And that meant—

"That bastard!" I said. I wanted to hit somebody.

"I beg your pardon." There was a cold tone in Tristram's voice I hadn't heard before, and I realized that I'd offended him, but I wasn't sure how.

He must have seen my puzzlement, because he elaborated in the same frigid voice.

"That term is not used in this house."

Oh. Yeah. He wasn't absolutely sure his parents had married, and that probably mattered a lot here.

"I'm sorry, Tristram," I said. "I guess people have accused you of that?"

He nodded stiffly.

"I humbly beg your pardon. But it would never have occurred to me to aim that term at you, even if it were legally accurate," I said. "Where I come from it usually means something different." I scowled. "Anyway, I was referring to my jackass of a father."

Now he looked puzzled, and I think a little distressed at my lack of filial piety—and maybe at the tone of my voice.

"Let me explain," I said.

He nodded, frowning.

"My father, as I've said, was a Traveler. I don't know what his home world was like, but he came to mine in pursuit of Greek philosophy. Don't ask; we'll get to that later, maybe. He met my mother, they married, they had me."

"It seems a familiar tale."

"Doesn't it just. My father was trying to figure out everything he could about how finders work. Apparently he did lots of Traveling in those days, and he could always come home because he and my mother were married; that made her his *anchor*."

"Anchor?"

"There's only one of my father, and he had only one wife. He said that the marriage relationship was *ontologically significant*, which is a hifalutin' way of saying that it changes who you are. My mother might have had a myriad of doubles in other worlds, but only one was married to my father. He had a special relationship with her. That mean that he could always find her again, without error." I grimaced. "I found the wrong Bernie once, before we got married. She didn't know me. It was awkward."

Twitch, twitch, went the mustache. "I can see that it would be."

"Well, so, when I was a baby my father went off on a trip, looking for another finder—just like these jokers you've been dealing with. He came back, gave my mother his old finder to give to me when I was older, and then left again. He said that he was being followed, and that he'd try to lead his pursuers away. He said he'd come back when it was safe. He never did, the—" I stifled whatever word was trying to climb out of my mouth. "My mother waited for him until the day she died. And that's why I'm so angry. If you're right about why Travelers aren't gregarious, then it means that my father was telling my mother the truth. He really was leaving for our protection, and the safe time to come back was never."

"But surely—"

"And Dear Old Dad would have known he'd have to do that when he went off to get a second finder. It can't be because the person he'd taken the finder from was going to follow him; after all, how could he?"

"Ah," he said, much struck. "Oh. Oh, dear."

"He couldn't have waited until I was older, no. He had to do it when I was a baby, and then abandon us." I was furious. I'd been suspicious of my father's actions since my mother had told me about them, but my suspicions hadn't had any kind of logic behind them, just a bad feeling. Until now.

"Oh, I say. Bad *ton*. Very bad *ton*. The ill-bred rotter!" He blushed a little. "Begging your pardon, Michael. One ought not speak poorly of another man's father. At least, not in his presence."

I waved a hand in pardon, and took a few deep breaths. In and out. In and out. I don't usually curse when I get angry— nothing looks sillier and than an angry ten-year-old filling the air with four-letter-words. But I was sorely tempted.

Tristram waited for me.

"I am going," I said carefully, "to change the subject."

Tristram nodded.

"Just so."

"You wanted to know how I came by all of the finders I brought with me."

"Quite."

I paused to consider how best to start. From the beginning, I decided.

"You've heard about my father's, though I didn't know about it until later. This one, the one I usually use, Bernie and I found together." I pulled it out of my dressing gown pocket and waved it at Tristram, then dropped it back in my pocket again. "The Traveler I took it from was already dead when I found him, and as he'd unleashed a boatload of rapacious Vikings on my home town we didn't mourn him particularly. We didn't know what it was, but we guessed it was what he had used to bring the Vikings to come and play. I only found out how to make it work by accident, and that's an interesting story all by itself." I shuddered, thinking about it. That had been a long day.

"Well, so Bernie and I had some adventures, and then finally we made it back to my mother's home, because parent-and-child is also an ontologically significant relationship. We appeared in the middle of her living room, and got sand all over the carpet; and that's when she told me about my father and gave me *his* finder. She'd been putting it off. I think she'd have preferred to put it off indefinitely."

Now it was my turn to get up and stand by the window and look out, except that now it was dark outside and Thompson had drawn the curtains, so I stayed in my chair and stared at my plate.

"I used his finder for a while after that; but it's much larger than this one, and harder to carry around inconspicuously, so I switched back to the one I'd found for myself."

"Do you think he killed someone to get his replacement finder?"

I nodded. "I don't know, but it seems likely. That's another reason I switched. Red—the guy who had this one— wasn't killed for it."

Tristram looked me a question.

"He made the wrong person angry. Justifiably so, I might add."

Tristram murmured a noise of approval. "And the other three were all attackers?"

"Yeah," I said, and told him those stories. He especially liked the one about Bernie, the pepper spray, and the Illustrated Man.

"Sounds like a very proper kind of young woman. Resourceful. I think I should like to meet her one day. Though I may say I do not understand your world's attitude towards arms. Pepper spray seems a slender reed upon which to lean."

"It works better than you might think, though it's only good at close range."

By this time Thompson had removed the plates and serving dishes and replaced them with what Tristram called "a sweet." It was a messy-looking mixture of jelly and whipped cream and short cake, and since it wasn't really my kind of thing and anyway my stomach felt kind of sour I just trifled with it. Tristram seemed to like it well enough, though. At length he pointed a fork at me.

"The number and frequency of the attacks depends on the number of finders you have in hand."

"So I assume."

"And it seems that you don't like to *Travel*, as you call it."

"I don't. I'm a homebody, me."

"So why not get rid of them? Leave them somewhere far from your home, and walk away?"

"I've asked myself that," I said. "The problem is, I don't think it would be wise."

"How so?"

"It's more or less what my mother tried. You'll notice that we were never directly attacked while I was growing up. Bernie thinks that it's because my father's finder wasn't active. But it also seems likely that that the guy who brought the Vikings down on us was drawn to my world because I was there. So——"

"A moment. What do mean by saying it wasn't active?"

"You might almost say, awake. When a Traveler picks up a finder to use it, it activates it, wakes it up. You've seen how the writing on this one glows when I pick it up."

Tristram nodded. "It would be difficult not to."

"It didn't, at first. It took me hours of playing with it to get it to wake up the first time. But it was the first finder I used. After that, it seems that just touching one is enough to activate it."

"I have noticed that you haven't touched any of the ones that have been, er, *delivered* since you came here."

"That's right. I don't know how long it takes a finder to deactivate itself, but I'm afraid that if I activate any more it will be Grand Central Station in here. We wouldn't be able to eat dinner without needing to use this." And I pulled my taser out of the pocket of my robe and held it up.

There was a blue glow, and Tristram looked at something over my shoulder. "And no more can we, it seems. *Thompson!*"

Chapter 14

I turned and looked where he was looking. Blue suit, blue eyes, a light brown Fu Manchu mustache; and a big axe, which was already in motion. The axe was a surprise; I hadn't seen one of those since the Vikings had shown up outside Dino's place. I potted him with the taser, he twitched, and the axe shattered the arm of my Windsor chair, missing my own arm by a fraction of a millimeter. He fell to the floor, still twitching, just as Thompson and Bodger came in at a run.

They removed the axe and the pieces of my chair, which would never be the same; they removed various other pointy and dangerous objects from around the Blue Man's person, including his finder; and, at Tristram's signal they removed the Blue Man himself from the room.

The finder was larger than most I'd seen. It looked rather like a pencil: perhaps five inches long, half-an-inch in diameter, hexagonal in cross section, with a sharp point on one hand and a button on the other. The button was even a kind of pinkish color.

"I am surprised," said Tristram, who hadn't stirred from his seat. "That device of yours is more effective than I imagined."

"It's good up to about fifteen feet," I said. "At point blank range, yeah, it works pretty well."

"How does it work? I have never seen a weapon like it."

"When you pull the trigger it shoots out a pair of electrodes. They administer an electric shock that stops the target in his tracks for a while without injuring him."

"Electric shock?"

"Aetheric power, I guess, or something like that."

I laid it on the table, and pulled a fresh cartridge out of my dressing gown pocket. "Could you, um…"

"Reload? Certainly."

He looked the taser over carefully before popping the old cartridge out and popping the new one in. He held up the old one.

"And what is this, precisely?"

"It's just a compressed air cartridge. Think of it as stored steam power—the force of the air makes the electrodes shoot out. At least, I think that's all it does. It might generate the electric charge as well, I really don't know."

"May I keep it?"

"Sure. It's not every interesting, though."

"Nevertheless."

"Enjoy. So, what will happen to the Blue Man?"

"I rather expect that our visitor in blue is already being escorted to the Bailey—the Runners have been keeping an eye on this house after the last few days. Quite a savings of time, that, as I needn't send Bodger running for assistance. He will be ensconced in the Bailey within the hour. Why, would you like to speak to him? I could arrange that for tomorrow or the next day. Justice is swift in the Commonwealth, but not that swift."

I thought about that. "Yes, I think I do. Not that I'll be able to trust anything he's likely to tell me," I said.

"I suppose someone who would attempt theft at axe-point is not likely to be scrupulously honest."

"No! Well, yes, I agree. But what I mean is, how much would he really know? The scientific mind set is alive and well here in your world, and my father was attempting to learn everything he could about finders; but how common is it really? I'm guessing that most Travelers are in my boat: they know what they were told, and what they've experienced themselves, and how reliable any of it is, is anyone's guess. It isn't like there are schools to go to."

"How do you know?"

I laughed ruefully, not having a mustache to tilt. "I don't. But given your conjecture about why Travelers of a feather don't flock together...."

"That is so."

"So as I was saying before we were so rudely interrupted—" and again, Tristram's mustache twitched—"we had no troubles and no attacks so long as my father's finder wasn't active. Except that we did. The previous owner of this finder showed up and caused no end of trouble. He wasn't looking for a finder; we think he showed up in my home town because I was a Traveler, even though I'd never Traveled. He didn't know I was there, and mind you he wasn't looking for me. I had to use his finder to make the trouble go away, and if I hadn't had access to one I don't like to think what would have happened.

"Now, Bernie and I expect to have children, and it's likely that some or all of them will be Travelers."

"And you don't want them to be unarmed. Quite so."

"Exactly right." He got it; I'd thought he would. "And then, these are priceless. Yes, I took them from other Travelers; but I didn't go looking for Travelers to steal from and possibly kill."

"Spoils of a defensive war, in other words."

"Yeah, exactly. And then, of course, if *I* have them then no one is using them to invade someone else's home. It seems wrong just to let them go."

"What if you were to...I don't know...make them inactive, somehow?"

"We have a saying: it's a neat trick if you can do it. But I've no idea how." I reflected for a moment. "Or, at least, I've no idea how to do it without killing the owner. That should do it pretty quick—but it seems a little hard on Bernie."

"Perhaps it would be best if I retained this one, then." He indicated the pencil-shaped finder on the dining room table.

"And those," I said, waving at the finder-filled glove Thompson had left on the sideboard for me. "I'd really rather not touch them, but someone should keep an eye on them."

"I have a strongbox," he said, diffidently.

"How well hidden is it?"

"Quite well, I should say."

I thought about it. There was nothing to stop a Traveler from Traveling in, locating the strongbox, and Traveling out again, taking the strongbox along for the ride…but in order to do that they'd have to find it first. Easier said than done. "That should work for now. It's not a long term solution." But, I thought, it might have short-term advantages. "Would you mind if I added my others as well? I want to keep this one handy, but I'd as soon not have to carry the rest around the house with me."

Tristram looked surprised. "You're very trusting," he said.

"And you're a man of honor," I said. "I've been young and foolish—I'm probably on my way to old and foolish—but at least I've learned to trust my friends."

"Quite," he said, and sent Thompson for a bag in which to put the finders.

Chapter 15

Once Thompson had seen me to bed I took my finder, thought of Bernie, and pushed the button. There was a quiet moment of intense longing, the world turned right-side-out, and I was in the family room of my home. There was a plate of sandwiches on the coffee table (neatly sectioned, so that I could eat them one-handed), and a glass of milk, and Bernie on the couch with Buster lying next to her.

Now, I know what you're thinking. You're thinking that I abandoned Mr. Monocle, that I'd decided that I could live quite happily with a single finder, that I was going to let Thompson and Bodger take their lumps, and that I'm a cold-hearted scoundrel who left without saying goodbye.

Well, maybe, but not really. I wanted to see Bernie, and I'd left my father's old finder in Tristram's strongbox. I was pretty sure I'd be able to find it again; finders are true singulars, and I was pretty familiar with it.

I kicked Buster off of the couch and greeted Bernie as thoroughly as I could before the hunger kicked in and I had to greet the sandwiches instead. This was not especially thoroughly given the condition of my shoulder and Bernie's reaction to the regency steampunk nightwear I had on, which was loud and raucous and took a bit of quelling on my part, but I tried.

"Oh, it's good to see you," she said when she was once again able. "But you're a sight for sore eyes."

I rolled mine, which made her laugh again.

"I see you got my letters," I said.

"I did, which is why I didn't worry."

"You didn't worry?" I was taken aback, and maybe a little hurt. I'd been picturing her walking the floor at nights, worrying about whether I was alive or dead. I mean, I didn't want her to be miserable, but still.

"No, of course not. Not after you got shot in the shoulder."

I stopped eating long enough to give her a good look. "I got shot...and so you didn't worry."

"It's because you were shot in the *shoulder*."

"Would you mind explaining what my shoulder has to do with it?"

She shrugged and grinned at the same time. "Regency steampunk is still regency."

"And what's this 'regency' stuff? You've got me using the word, and I don't even know what it means."

She just grinned, and waggled her eyebrows at me.

"So, no problems here?" I asked. "No midnight visitors or Sunday Travelers?" I'd been worried about that.

"No, nothing. I guess I'm not much of a draw all by myself."

"No accounting for taste, I guess," I said, lightly, but I was relieved. It made sense, though—with my finders gone there was no reason for a Traveler to come calling, and maybe no way for J. Random Traveler to pinpoint our home to begin with.

But Bernie was speaking.

"I've packed a suitcase for you to take back with you when you go."

"You don't mind my going back?"

"Of course not. I'm sure Mr. Monocle needs your support."

"He's quite capable, you know."

"Is he married?"

"No. What does that have to do with anything?"

"Given he's capable, quite a lot. I expect there's some designing woman trying to force him into marrying her because she wants his money and position. She's undoubtedly the latest in a stream of them. But he's not going to marry a woman like that." She paused, and pursed her lips. "Does he have a fortune?"

"A small one, I think."

"Then I bet his family wants him to marry some dragon he's known for an age but has no desire to marry, probably in order to restore *her* family's fortune."

"Aha! You're wrong. He doesn't have any family."

"Really?" Bernie looked shocked...and maybe a little worried.

"Well...he's got a patron of sorts."

"Aha! And what about the rest of it?"

I ate the last bite of the second sandwich (ham on rye, if you care), chewed it carefully, swallowed.

"How do you know all of this?" I said. "I didn't have time to write down the half of it."

Bernie relaxed at my tacit confirmation, and then looked smug. "Regency steampunk is still regency," she said again.

I considered forcing her to tell me what regency meant, but having uttered her gnomic utterance she hopped off of the couch and went to the kitchen. She came back after a few minutes—during which I scratched behind Buster's ears and under his chin, and completely failed to figure out what she meant—carrying a suitcase in one hand and a hot-fudge sundae in other. She put the sundae in front of me and the suitcase on the floor, and then handed me a spoon.

"So what did you pack for me?"

"Things," she said evasively. "Some fresh clothes. Food for when you get there, and a bottle of water. My camera, so you can take pictures of Mr. Monocle and company. Send it back when the battery's gone. Oh, and a present for Mr. Monocle."

And, I thought, possibly one or two other things she was choosing not to mention. Uh-huh.

After that we talked for a while. I told her about Thompson and Bodger and Miss Melissa Stavely, and she looked smug some more, and about Lord Remchester and the Commonwealth, and about Tristram's background.

"How old is he?"

"Early to mid-thirties, I think."

"That's really quite suggestive," she said.

"Yeah, isn't it though."

"And you're using *that* finder?"

"Yup."

"Finder bias?"

"Let's just say I'm keeping my eyes open. That's another reason I want to go back. Besides which I like Tristram, and if you're right I want to be on the spot."

Then I told her my theory about why my father had never come back, and she got a fierce look on her face that I'm glad wasn't aimed at me.

"Well," she said, and I almost looked to make sure she wasn't burning a hole in the far wall. "That explains why we haven't been able to find his notes."

"Ahhhh. Yeah, that would be it." If he hadn't intended to come back, he'd have taken them with him.

"That—," she began, and it only got more colorful from there. She pulled out a lot of the words I never use (she's full-size, she can do that without looking silly) and a lot of others it wouldn't have occurred to me use, and I just sat back and listened.

After that we went on to talk about other things. And then, just before I left, Bernie said, "It's certainly quieter around here with you gone. I haven't had to pull out my pepper spray in a couple of days." And then, "Would you like me to tell the Gang you might want their help?"

"There's a thought. Not just at the moment, I think, but maybe. I'll let you know."

"Good." She hugged me, quickly. "Try not to get crumbs on the bed."

Neither of us talked about the fact that I was really going in order to keep Bernie safe while I healed up, but we both knew it. Marriage is like that.

I thought about my father's finder, blast him, and pressed the button. I swirled into angry red, and then I was—

***

—in the dark.

It took a moment for my eyes to adjust enough to realize that I was in Tristram's library. I headed for the door, and nearly tripped over the suitcase.

Oh, yeah.

My left arm was still in its sling, so I picked it up with my right, and groaned. I didn't know what Bernie had loaded the suitcase up with, but it seemed to weigh almost as much as I did. There was no way I'd manage to lug it up to my room.

There came an ominous **–click-click–**, and then a man's voice: "Stand easy, whoever you are. And shame on you for breaking into an honest man's house." I didn't recognize the voice.

"Is that you, Bodger? It's me, Michael."

"Master Michael, sir! What are you doing down here in the dark?"

"Accepting a delivery. Would you carry this up to my room for me?"

"In the dark, sir?"

"I couldn't find the valve for the lights."

"Oh, I see, sir." Bodger went out and came back with a candle —apparently aetheric flashlights hadn't been invented yet—and picked up the suitcase without seeming to make any effort at all. Show off. We trundled upstairs to my room, where he put the suitcase on the floor, gave me another puzzled glance, and left. I dove into the suitcase, hoping for more sandwiches.

What I got was energy bars. I ate a few, and drank some water from the pitcher on the washstand, and climbed into bed. The rest of the stuff in the suitcase would have to wait until morning.

I was up in good time for breakfast in spite of being up half the night; a few energy bars will only take you so far when you're Traveling. I found Tristram in what Thompson called the breakfast room, where I gladly put Bernie's package, wrapped in blue and red birthday paper, on the table. I'd needed

Thompson's help to pick it up, and it was a bit heavy.

Tristram eyed it but said nothing, gesturing at the sideboard. There I found plates and chafing dishes filled with good things, and by holding a plate carefully in my left hand (with my arm still in the sling) I contrived to fill it with eggs and bacon and what I thought were quite possibly scones. I even managed to convey it to the table without spilling anything.

"You are feeling more the thing this morning, I see," said Tristram. A restful person, Tristram; he'd have helped if I'd asked, or if I had clearly been incapable, but he wasn't inclined to coddle me. Which suited me; I'm rarely inclined to be coddled. Well, except when I get *really* hungry.

"Bodger tells me you have been Traveling. He didn't put it that way, of course. I presume all is well at home?"

"Yes, it is. Bernie asked me to thank you for your note, and she had me bring this back for you." I indicated the package.

"Really? You must thank her for me."

"I will." I ate some bacon. "You can open it any time you like. I know it says 'Happy Birthday' on it, but you don't need to wait until then."

"Very well." He pulled the package across the table, a little surprised by its weight. "What could it be? Some arcane device? A quantity of sand?"

"I really have no idea. She wouldn't tell me."

Tristram examined the outside of the package from all directions; then, taking a folding knife from his pocket he cut the tape where the package was sealed, being careful to damage neither the paper nor the contents. Then he removed the paper in one piece, rather than ripping and tearing in proper Christmas fashion, and folded it and placed it to one side.

The object thus revealed was a boxed set of books I remembered having seen on our shelves, though I'd never read it. Tristram read the title slowly: "*A History of the English Speaking Peoples*, by Winston Churchill, in four volumes." He looked at me with wild surmise. "Is this a history of England in your world?"

"I guess it is. I'd mentioned to Bernie in a letter that this was something like our England, and that you were an historian. I guess she thought you'd enjoy comparing our history with yours."

"What a delightful surprise. I must write her another letter."

"She'd like that."

He was clearly eager to dig in, but instead sat down and finished his meal. I suppose reading at the breakfast table was bad *ton*.

At length he finished. "I must go out and attend to some business today, Michael. Thompson will be here; ring for him if you need anything. And feel free to read anything you find in my library...though I hope you'll pass over my history of the revolution. I shall return for dinner."

I nodded, as I buttered a scone. I think it was a scone, though it certainly wouldn't be a scone for much longer.

"Oh, and might I borrow your weapon?" he said.

"What, my taser?" It was in the pocket of my dressing gown, of course; and after the Blue Man incident I found I was reluctant not to have it by me.

He interpreted my question correctly, and going to the sideboard drew a small handgun from a drawer. "This will be harder on the wainscoting should you need to use it, but it should give you no trouble." He showed me how it worked and how to load it and how to prevent it from going off in my pocket. It was some kind of revolver, but the outside was encrusted with brass piping, and the mechanism was unlike anything Maynard had shown me at the shooting range. Still, it had a grip and a trigger and a barrel, and I thought I could manage to point it in the right direction. "Front toward enemy," as they say.

"Another miracle of steam?" I asked.

"Of course."

"Uh-huh. Well, all right." I handed him my taser, and put the steam revolver in its place in my pocket.

He paused by the door. He looked uncomfortable. "Michael... I thought you weren't sure you could find this place again."

"You've got my father's finder."

"Well, I can see you'd want it back, but—"

I waved my hand dismissively. "No, no, not that. It's just that Finders are true singulars, like Travelers. Any true singular is easy to find once you're acquainted with it."

"Ah. So there was not much risk involved."

"Not once I'd left it with you, no."

He looked happier. "Is that why——"

"It's one reason. Another is that I was tired of lugging it and the others around the house with me."

"Ah," he repeated, mustache twitching merrily, and then he was gone.

Chapter 16

After breakfast I went back to my bedroom and continued exploring the contents of my suitcase.

Bernie had included some of my clothes, of course, which made me happy; not that I owned anything that wouldn't look outlandish on the streets of Tristram's London, but I was tired of wearing regency steampunk pajamas all day long. There was the promised camera (a small digital point-and-shoot) and a sack of energy bars, and several bottles of water. There was even a bottle of Tylenol, which I made immediate use of. (I'd been avoiding the local painkillers, as I really did want my wits about me.) There was even a picture of Bernie in a little frame, which I put on the table by the bed.

And there were several books, of a sort that normally I'd never, ever, read—but I found the word "regency" on the cover, so I had to assume that Bernie had put them in on purpose and meant for me to take the time to read them. I put them in my backpack, and then I got dressed: chinos and a short-sleeved button-up shirt. I used to wear blue jeans and T-shirts pretty much exclusively, but Bernie put her foot down: just because I look like a ten-year-old, she'd said, that was no reason to dress like one. I mostly agree with her—I feel a lot less conspicuous when we're out together if I'm dressed like a grown-up—but I still prefer to wear T-shirts around the house. It was much easier not having to pull the shirt on over my head, though, even if I did have to button it up one-handed. Then I put my left arm back in its sling. It all took me a while, but it was nice to be able to do it.

I didn't put on my shoes, but instead put on the carpet slippers Tristram had loaned me. There are limits.

As I put them on, it struck me for the first time: Tristram wasn't a family man. Unless he'd been carting his boyhood clothes around with him he must have bought the slippers and dressing gown and so forth just for me. I'd have to ask him about that.

Then I put the dressing gown back on, slipped Tristram's steam pistol into the pocket, grabbed my backpack, and went to sit in the library because I'd had it up to here with sitting in bed. I snagged my usual chair, and looked through the books Bernie had provided for me. They all seemed much of a muchness, but one had a sticky note on it saying, "Start here," so I put the others away and settled in to read.

It was a romance novel—that had been clear from the cover illustration, which featured a couple in old-fashioned dress—so I admit that I was fairly determined not to like it. But the gentleman, if he *was* a gentleman, was wearing a cravat rather like Tristram's, and if there were neither guns nor goggles, the rest of their apparel had a familiar air to it. Perhaps there was something in this "regency" thing after all.

I was plowing through the first chapter by main force when I surprised myself by chuckling out loud. By the third chapter I was hooked. I was on my second cup of tea, neither coffee nor cola being available, when Thompson came in.

"The tailor's here, lad. Shall I show him in? Or he can take your measurements in your bedroom, if you prefer."

"Tailor? What tailor?"

"I collect the master sent him. I can see as how your clothes might be all proper and correct by your lights, lad, but the master is wishful of taking you out into London with him, and for that they will not do at all, at all, however fine they are by Colonial standards. So I'll bring him in, shall I?"

Judging that I'd no hope of winning a battle with Thompson over London vs. "Colonial" standards—and besides that, being eager to get out of the house—I put my book aside and got measured. I was curious to see what sort of steam or aetherically powered device the tailor might use to take my measurements, but was I disappointed. Whatever fascinating armamentaria he might have back in his shop, for the current task he used a simple cloth measuring tape and wrote the measurements down in a tiny notebook using one of the ubiquitous steam pencils.

He was a small man, in a white shirt and a little gray vest with pins stuck in it, and a little gray mustache, and when I saw him out he put on a little gray bowler that he'd left on the hat rack. He didn't say much: "Arm up, please, Master Henderson. Stand straighter, please, Master Henderson. Hold still, please, Master Henderson. Arm down, please, Master Henderson. Step out of the slippers, please, Master Henderson. There, all done, Master Henderson." He made a few more notes in the little book. Then he turned to Thompson. "Please tell your master that I'll bring the first suit for fitting tomorrow morning."

The first suit? How big a wardrobe was Tristram having made for me?

Then off he went; Thompson brought me some fresh tea, and I went back to my book.

It was set in more or less the time and place in which I found myself: England, a little after 1800. Steam armamentaria, giant gulls, and Lord Remchester were notably lacking, but the flavor of the language and dress were similar. (I don't know whether everyone was packing heat or not; the author didn't say.) There was a wealthy old guy named Sylvester who was dying, and his great nephew, who seemed a sensible kind of guy, and his heir, who seemed a bit of a skunk, and his real heir, a young guy who'd had to flee to the continent because he'd been accused of murder. There was also Sylvester's ward, a young lady with a French accent and truly nutty ideas. Oh, and there were smugglers and innkeepers and Bow Street Runners (whatever they were), and like that.

Tristram had used the word "Runners." I'd have to ask him.

I was quite a ways in when I figured out why Bernie had marked this one, "Start here." The young guy who'd been accused of murder was spending his time adventuring with smugglers, and had recklessly come to his home county on a smuggling run; and then he had to help the nutty young lady run away from home in the middle of the night because she didn't want to marry the young guy's sensible cousin (who didn't want to marry her anyway) and while he was doing that they came across some of the local authorities and the reckless young guy was shot.

In the shoulder, natch.

He and the young lady holed up in a local inn (though, quite properly, in separate rooms); the innkeeper had known him since he was a boy, and was one of the smugglers' chief customers in the area besides.

I've since done some research; the usual outcome of being shot in the shoulder is shattered bones and all kinds of trouble, but in his case it was just a flesh wound and he'd be fit as a fiddle if he'd only rest and not go outside and catch the attention of the authorities. Uh-huh.

There was a lot more to it; the young guy's sensible cousin figured largely, as did a judge and his unmarried but whimsical sister who were staying in the inn due to the high quality of its cellar, which in turn was due to the innkeeper's relationship with the smugglers; and there was some foofaraw about a ring, and of course they had to keep the young guy from being arrested while trying to figure out who killed the guy the young guy was supposed to have killed.

It was all pretty goofy, but the dialog was fun. Of course, being the kind of book it was, a lot of it was devoted to feelings and details of how people were getting along, and who was going to end up marrying whom (which was pretty obvious from early on in the book, in my view), but it was a pleasant enough ride.

I was only interrupted once more during the course of the day, but that was by Miss Stavely. I heard Thompson expostulating with someone in the hall—I think that's the word I'm looking for —and then the door opened and Miss Stavely came in like a super-tanker coming to its mooring. I don't mean to imply that she was stout, far from it; just that there was a kind of smooth inevitability about her entrance, and the sense that she was likely to crush anyone who got in her way, effortlessly and without having taken the least notice of their presence.

Having entered she stopped; and without any haste or moving anything but her head she examined all parts of the room. At last her gaze rested on me, still sitting in my chair.

"Master Henderson," she said. Today she was dressed in ice blue, which went well with her tone of voice.

Oh. I was still sitting. I popped to my feet.

"Miss Stavely," I said, bowing my head. "Tris—Mr. Monocle is not here. May I be of any service?"

I tell you, you can't be too careful what you read.

"It is unlikely in the extreme," she said. "Is that what they are wearing in the Colonies these days?" I might have imagined the note of distaste in her voice—after all, when you're already at absolute zero there's only so much farther you can go.

"Yes," I said. "Yes, it is."

"Indeed. No doubt you are but recently arrived on our shores. How is that you had reason to make such a lengthy journey?"

"My parents, miss. There was an illness in my town, and my mother died, and—"

She raised a finger, and I stopped.

"And how did you come?"

By this time I'd figured out that she was pumping me for information, possibly on her own account—I think I puzzled her mightily—and possibly for sale to her father or Lord Remchester. Well, said I to myself: if I'm to be ten years old, let me be ten years old. I gave her *The Revolution of Steam* with both barrels.

"On a steam leviathan, miss!" I let myself get a little excited. "It was all the crack, miss! I made friends with the hands, and got to explore the leviathan's power room. Did you ever see a leviathan's power room, miss?"

"Never." Nor would she ever, given a choice, I thought. "What vessel was it?"

But I was in full flow. "There are aetheric transmission pipes running from the captain's bridge to a box in the power room. It's up on the wall over the steam generators. He just spins some valves on the bridge, and flags on the box show the power room mates what they need to do! It's the completest thing, and so much faster than sending a messenger like they used to. That's what the mates told me. And—

She raised a finger again. "Indeed. I see that Mr. Monocle is not here. Good day."

"Oh, but miss! I haven't told you about the stateroom appurtenances, yet!"

But she turned and launched herself into the open waters of the hallway. I let her go, and when she was gone I returned to my book. I heard Thompson's voice from downstairs; the front door opened and closed; and a short while later Thompson returned with more tea, some things that might have been scones but were probably cakes since there was no butter, and a wide country grin. I gave him a thumbs up and a grin of my own, and then made the cakes disappear.

Tristram returned late in the evening, and found me in the library.

"Good evening, Michael. Have you had a pleasant day?"

"Surprisingly, yes."

"Here, you will be wanting this." He handed me my taser, and took the steam pistol in exchange. I was glad to have it back, as I'd been having worried thoughts about the wainscoting.

Dinner was quieter than usual; Tristram seemed preoccupied. Not ruffled, mind you; *he* hadn't had to entertain Miss Stavely. I told him about it in between bites, to many twitchings of his mustache.

"Hidden depths you have, Michael," he said, eyes twinkling, "hidden depths. I do wish she had not seen you in your own clothes, as it might encourage the curiosity of those whose curiosity is…intrusive. Still, well done in a tight spot. I am glad I need not tell you not to confide in the Stavely."

I shrugged. "I'd as soon confide in Lord Remchester, and I imagine the effect would be similar. Anyway, I figure if I need to pretend to be ten years old I might as well enjoy myself. Heaven knows I didn't enjoy it much the first time. Oh, that reminds me."

"Yes?"

"Thank you for the clothing I've been wearing; and for the clothing I guess you've ordered for me."

"Ah! The tailor was here."

I nodded. "I got measured up one side and down the other, please Master Henderson, and backways and frontways, please, Master Henderson, and he will bring the 'first suit' for fitting tomorrow morning, please, Master Henderson."

"I suppose you are not used to such deference from tailors and the like?"

"I've never gone to a tailor in my life. When I need clothes I go to a clothing store. At least, I used to. These days I usually order them on-line, and they get delivered to my house."

"It was ostentatious of me to go to a bespoke tailor, I fear; it's the done and patriotic thing these days to purchase clothing made in the great steam manufacturies of the north of England. But I could not think how to get you to a clothing mart without attracting undue attention."

I nodded. "I get that. But I have to ask, how dire is it going to be?"

"Dire? Whatever do you mean?"

"Will there be knee breeches? With straps and buckles and like that?"

"I confess, I had rather anticipated there would be. But you may console yourself: dressing as a young lad you shall not have to learn to tie a neckcloth."

I contemplated the elegant folds of Tristram's own snowy-white neckcloth, accented by the monocle dangling on its string. I hadn't thought of that.

"Ah. Knee breeches. Lovely. Just the thing."

"Just so." He grinned at me.

He was quiet for the rest of the meal; and afterwards I went gladly off to write a letter to Bernie, and then to bed.

Chapter 17

"There is, in fact, a gunsmith's counter at Mordred & Sons," said Tristram, "but no one with any sense shops there. Steam manufactury is all the crack, but one's arms are a matter of life and death. Fortunately for you, I know a man."

We were riding briskly through the streets of London in Tristram's town curricle, a light carriage with two seats and wheels taller than I am, with thin pneumatic tires and a surprisingly comfortable suspension system. I suppose you might call it a "horseless carriage," as there were no horses in evidence, or a "steamer," because it was steam-powered; but I use the word carriage exactly, because the engine wasn't part of the carriage itself. Instead, the engine, or "motivator," as Tristram called it, it was a separate thing with its own drive wheels. It was harnessed into the curricle's traces rather as a pair of horses would have been, but there the resemblance ended. It was in fact roughly oblong in shape, and festooned here and there with pipes and levers and valves.

The motivator had a metal seat mounted toward the rear, and could be controlled directly by what Tristram called a "postilion"; at present, however, Tristram was driving it using a pair of reins and a number of levers and dials mounted on the dash of the curricle and connected to the motivator by means of aetheric control lines. I couldn't tell from looking at it how it worked—my knowledge of steam engines comes mostly from seeing steam locomotives in old movies—but I didn't see any sign of a boiler or firebox, and I wondered again whether "steam" was really the correct word.

We passed many similar vehicles. The carriages were of all sizes and shapes, and like Tristram's appeared to have been originally built to be drawn by horses. The motivators were similarly varied but seemed to fall into three or four basic designs. (Tristram's, I later discovered, was a Royce-Lesney Patented Steam Auto-Motivator, and it was painted a light brown with cream pin-striping and brass fixtures.)

"Tristram, I'm kind of vague on what happened just after I was shot, but I'm nearly certain there were horses. Or did I imagine it? I'm not seeing any horses on the streets."

"Oh, one would never bring a motivator into Remchester Park. The *ton* go there to promenade and be seen, you know, and motivators are far too noisy. Also, they spit from time to time, which offends the ladies." He shrugged, as if to say, "What would you?" "And of course, it is a sign of distinction to stable horses in London these days. Riding is more common in the park than driving a team, however, so you are fortunate that there was a horse-drawn carriage to hand. Which reminds me, there is a call of ceremony we must make, now that you are up and about."

I was wearing my new school boy's clothes: a flat cap, made of a grayish tweed; a frilly white shirt, buttoned up to the neck; and a gray waistcoat and coat over knee breeches that were blessedly lacking any sign of straps or buckles around the knees. And my sling of course, so that left arm of the coat hung loose. For the moment I wore my own shoes, though we'd need to do something about that. Oh, and goggles; men, I discovered, wore them too, but only when driving. Tristram, ever prepared, had had a pair ready for me.

The tailor had bristled when I exclaimed at how comfortable my new outfit was, and I had had to hasten to reassure him.

"It's just that back home—in the Colonies, you know—I'd always heard how uncomfortable English clothes were. I'm glad to see I was mistaken."

I could see he was only a little mollified by my explanation, but he unbent enough to say, "And so they were, once, Master Henderson, though I am sure I never minded it. Such outfits I used to make, Master Henderson! But things have changed. The young need to be able to move freely, so they tell me, Master Henderson." I could see that *he* didn't approve of the change, but I surely did.

I had no holster, so my taser made an uncomfortable lump in the pocket of my coat.

"Tristram," I'd said after the tailor left, still pining for lost velvet and buckles, "should I have a holster if I'm to look like the boys I saw at Mordred's?"

"Indeed you should, but your weapon is of an unusual shape. We shall attend to that at once, now that you are properly dressed."

And so I found myself riding through London, seeing clearly at last the streets and houses that I'd seen in a jumble when I was carried to Tristram's home. Lamp posts lined the streets, the steam lights at their tops turned off in the morning sun. The buildings were a mixture of what I thought of as old-fashioned brick and wooden structures, all cheek-by-jowl, alongside newer brick structures with large windows. The lower floors were often given over to shops and other businesses; and many of the shops had colorful signs of stained glass with internal lighting. It was all much cleaner than the historic London I carried around in my head, and again I wondered whether Commonwealth-style steam plants would work in Corey's End and what relationship aetheric power had to the electrical power I was used to.

Tristram stopped the curricle in front of a neat two-story brick building. The sign hanging over the door featured crossed revolvers on a red background, and proclaimed it be *Adolphus Arms, Gunsmith to the Assembly by Commonwealth Warrant.* Hanging just below that on a pair of chains, a smaller metal sign said "Est. 1 NO."

Inside it was brightly lit; a wooden counter stretched the width of the shop from left to right, and behind the counter stood a fat man in plain clothes and an apron with hints of oil stains on it. Behind him were racks of various kinds of pistols and long arms, shelves containing small boxes all neatly stacked, and a door leading further into the shop. The general air was one of tidiness and precision, with deadliness just under the surface.

It kind of reminded me of Tristram.

"Now then, Mr. Monocle," said the fat man. "And this young lad 'll be your cousin what you told me about." And he nodded at me in greeting.

"Indeed he is, Mr. Adolphus."

"Then I have your things ready for you, lad," he said. "I have them right here." So saying, he reached under the counter and pulled out a holster on a belt. The leather had been dyed gray, and was a pretty good match for my waistcoat. He also placed a small parcel on the counter. "May I see your weapon, lad?"

I handed him my taser.

"Thank you, lad." He inserted it into the holster and tested the fit. "That'll do," he said. "You won't find it falling out on its own, and it'll come to your hand when you want it." He laid the taser on the counter, and held out the belt and holster to me. "Now then, you'll want to be trying this on." I took it, then stood there helplessly. It's nearly impossible to fasten a belt with one arm in a sling.

"Oh, but you'll be needing help, won't you." He lifted a section of the counter and stepped out, then frowned—not in irritation, but in thought. "I have it rigged for a cross-draw, but I think you'll be wanting a right-handed draw for the nonce, eh, lad? You won't be wanting to jostle your injured arm."

"Yes, I think so."

"Very good!" He rearranged the holster on the belt, knelt down with surprising ease for a man his size, and buckled it around my waist. Rising, he said, "There. Give it a try, lad."

I drew the taser and returned it to the holster a couple of times. Mr. Adolphus was quite right: it was a snug fit, and I could draw it quickly if I needed to. I also noticed that my coat was cut so as not to get in the way.

"Thank you, Mr. Adolphus," I said. "This is great, just what I needed."

He beamed all over his round face.

"And the, er, *other* accessory, Mr. Adolphus?" said Tristram.

"Now that was bit of work, Mr. Monocle, and I'm sure I could do a better job given more time. Still, it should serve." He opened the small parcel and handed me an oddly familiar metal object—oddly, because I'd never seen anything quite like it, and yet the shape reminded me of something. There was what looked to be a small valve on one end, and a small unscrewable cap on the other.

"What is this?"

"An aetheric steam cartridge for your taser, Michael," said Tristram. "It should be good for a great many shots without reloading, and it is powered by the same carbon rods as a steam pencil. You'll note that there is a pouch for additional rods on the face of the holster."

"A great many—I like that, Mr. Monocle," said Mr. Adolphus. "As little power as it takes, that cartridge should be good for several hundred rounds before it needs to be refueled. There are five more rods in the pouch, lad, but when you might need them I am sure I don't know."

I might never need to reload again, I thought. "Thank you, Mr. Adolphus. This will be a great help."

Mr. Adolphus continued to beam. "Let me load it for you, lad." I handed him the cartridge, and then the taser. He popped out the old cartridge, which I pocketed, and then tried to insert the steam cartridge. "Not quite," he said. "A few moments with a file and I'll have it set to rights, lad, see if I don't." And he popped through the door into the back of the shop.

"Your idea?" I asked Tristram.

He raised an eyebrow. "I, a gentleman, engaging in artifactory? I am shocked that you would suggest such a thing." Then his mustache twitched. Uh-huh.

"Oh," I said, making a mental note to tell him about flash lights. "Forgive me."

"Of course."

Mr. Adolphus popped back out again, and handed me the taser. "There, lad. The cartridge fits snugly, as it should, but pops out and in again as easy as kiss my hand." He paused, considering me. "Would you care to step into my workshop for a test firing?"

I didn't need Tristram's look of warning to know to step carefully—it was clear that this was an offer not often made. I dialed my boyish enthusiasm up to about +3. (Miss Stavely had gotten the full +10.)

"Oooooh, could I, Mr. Adolphus? I'd like that very much."

"Well, then," he said, "Step on back. You too, Mr. Monocle, should you care to."

"I should indeed," said Tristram. "A rare treat."

Adolphus' workshop was as neat and tidy as his storefront, and every bit as well lit, though more worn: this was clearly a place where serious work was done. Through another door at the back was a one-lane firing range that ran the width of the building, perhaps twenty feet. There was a bench at the firing line, and downrange there were stands for targets. The walls were padded with mattress-like pads, I guess to prevent ricochets and maybe also to muffle the sound of gunshots.

"Here we are," said Mr. Adolphus. "No good for long arms, of course, but adequate for pistols." He stepped forward to set up a target on a stand. "Fifteen feet I believe you said, Mr. Monocle?"

"Just so."

He adjusted the stand, then hurried back behind the firing line.

"Give it a try, lad."

I took up my stance at the bench, remembering Maynard's instructions. I decided to go for precision rather than speed, so I drew the taser slowly, held it in both hands, and fired.

Wham! The electrodes hit the target hard enough to knock the stand askew. "That was…unexpected," I said. I reeled them in and prepared it to fire again. This time I went for speed. I still hit the target, though farther from the center, and the stand was knocked further askew.

"I can see you've been properly brought up, lad."

"But it seems a little overpowered, Mr. Adolphus," I said.

"The better to knock your man down," he replied. He looked slightly ruffled, and I remembered to dial it back up to +3.

"It's the aetherics that do the trick, Mr. Adolphus, not the force of the blow. And the normal cartridges aren't that strong, sir. What if it snaps the wires?"

He considered. "A good point, lad," he said, as I reeled in the electrodes again. "Let me adjust it."

I handed him the taser, and he bustled into the main part of the workshop.

Tristram said nothing, but gave me a nod. I smiled back. I'd been a freelance software developer for years. Mr. Adolphus was a craftsman rather than a customer, but it didn't do to offend either one.

Well, unless you wanted to; but I liked Mr. Adolphus. He didn't bow and scrape.

I went downrange and repositioned the target on its stand, and was back behind the bench when Adolphus returned. He glanced downrange at the target, and nodded.

"Try it now, lad," he said, handing me the taser.

I took up my stance, aimed, and fired. The target jumped just a little as the electrodes made impact. I reeled them in and slipped the taser into my new holster. Then I repeated the process. Then I turned and beamed at Mr. Adolphus, being sure to write joy all over my face.

"That's aces, Mr. Adolphus."

He beamed back.

"I think that will be all for today, Mr. Adolphus," said Tristram. "Do let me know about that other matter, won't you?"

"Never you worry, Mr. Monocle. I'll send round the very moment as I have an article for you to look at."

Adolphus then escorted us back into the front room.

"Be sure to bring it back if you have any trouble, lad," he said.

"I will, Mr. Adolphus. Thank you, I have enjoyed myself very much."

"Come back any time, lad. I shall be glad to see you."

"A good day to you, Mr. Adolphus!" said Tristram.

"And to you, Mr. Monocle, a very fine day indeed!"

Tristram helped me back into the curricle and I settled into my seat.

"Not to pry," I said, "but I gather Mr. Adolphus is going to try building himself a taser."

Tristram's mustache twitched, as I'd known it would.

"So much easier on the wainscoting," he said.

"It's a pity that gentlemen don't engage in artifactory," I said. "I've no doubt one could realize a tidy profit from such a thing."

"Yes, isn't it," he said in a voice rich with satisfaction, as he pulled the curricle into traffic.

Chapter 18

Fifteen minutes of driving found us in a rather more upscale neighborhood. The shops had been replaced by large, elegant houses—larger and more elegant than Tristram's, at any rate—grouped around large, elegant squares. The lamp posts were fancier, and there was much less traffic. The few carriages I saw were richly appointed, and there were even a few riders on horseback. Tristram nodded at a few of these, and they nodded back.

We stopped in front of a smaller house painted an eye-catching shade of yellow with gray accents, and mounted the steps to the front door (yellow, magnificently paneled, gleaming brass fixtures). Tristram touched a button by the door, and a few moments later it was opened by a fellow who reminded me of Bodger, only with nicer clothes and a sour look. He was carrying a silver tray.

"Yes, sir?"

Tristram took a small card from his pocket and placed it on the tray. "Is Miss Clarenton at home?"

"Allow me to inquire, sir."

He closed the door, which struck me as rude but Tristram seemed undistressed. Instead he turned to me and said, "When we are presented it will be appropriate for you to bow. As best you can with your arm in the sling—this is the lady who prevented you from bleeding to death while I sought help."

"As deeply as I can manage, then."

"No more than halfway, mind. Any deeper would be seen as mockery. Bad *ton*, especially in this instance." He said nothing more, but I got the sense that he really wanted me to make a good impression...that this was no ordinary social call.

"Got it."

The footman—I guessed he must be a footman, because he didn't seem nearly magnificent enough to be a butler—returned in just a few moments.

"Follow me, please." And so saying he led us through an entry way and up a flight of stairs into another hall, and then into a drawing room at the front of the house. Tristram took off his hat as we entered the house, and I was quick to do the same.

Miss Clarenton was seated on a grand kind of sofa near the windows, where the light was good. There was a basket beside her that looked to contain sewing materials. Or embroidery, or knitting, or something like that. Bernie would probably know.

An older woman in black was sitting nearby but I had no doubt the first was Miss Clarenton, because I recognized her immediately—I'd seen her face over and over again while I was delirious. She was the severe looking woman who had leaned so hard on my shoulder after I was shot. She was younger than I had remembered, perhaps just a little younger than Tristram.

"Mr. Monocle," she said. She didn't seem too pleased to see him. Then she looked at me, and I thought she looked a shade more welcoming.

"Miss Clarenton," he said, sounding unusually stiff. "May I present to you my young cousin, Michael Henderson?"

I knew a cue when I heard one. I decided on a +3 for boyish solemnity.

I bowed, using my right arm to keep my left from dangling, and made it to about 45 degrees, which would have to do. Then I stepped forward.

"I remember you, ma'am." I said. "Thank you for not listening to me when I asked you to stop leaning on my shoulder. I hope I didn't ruin your gown."

That actually got me a small smile.

"You are quite welcome, Master Henderson. A gown is of little important next to a life, I believe. May I present to you my aunt, Mrs. Illridge?"

I turned and bowed, though not so deeply, to the older women, who smiled at me.

"Won't you be seated?" said Miss Clarenton.

"For a moment, only," said Tristram, and did so. I sat down beside him, rather on the edge of my seat. Tristram turned to Mrs. Illridge.

"My condolences on the loss of your husband, Mrs. Illridge. I regret that I haven't been able to offer them until now. He was always very good to me."

"Very prettily said, Tristram," the older woman replied, smiling broadly at him, "though that was always your way. I am sure he thought the world of you as well."

Miss Clarenton was looking severe again. Pointedly ignoring Tristram, she addressed me.

"I am glad to see you looking so well, Master Henderson. How are you finding England?"

"What a question to ask the boy, Louisa!" said Mrs. Illridge. "I daresay he hasn't seen much beyond his sickroom."

"That's true, ma'am," I said. "I had just arrived when I, well…"

Mrs. Illridge leaned forward.

"Have you discovered anything about the man who shot him, Tristram? Such a strange looking man, Louisa tells me." Then, to me, "Was he from the Colonies as well, Master Henderson?"

I could tell she was dying to hear all manner of lurid details about life in the distant Colonies. I was rather at a loss, not knowing anything much about them, and was chiding myself for not having looked up something about them in Tristram's library when I saved by Tristram and Miss Clarenton.

"Alas, we've no idea where he was from—" Tristram began, and—

"Now, Aunt Maria, I'm sure Master Henderson—" Miss

Clarenton began—

And they looked at each other for a moment. Tristram's mustache made as if to twitch and stopped in that rueful slant, and I'm pretty sure that the corner of Miss Clarenton's mouth began to go up before she made all severe again.

"I beg your pardon, Miss Clarenton," said Tristram, and the moment ended as quickly as it began.

After that we spoke of generalities: the beauty of London; the kindness of Mr. Monocle; the sad loss of my mother; the magnificence of the modern steam leviathan; and after about half-an-hour we rose and took our leave.

"I am so glad you were well enough to come today, Master Henderson," said Mrs. Illridge. Miss Clarenton shot her a warning glance, but she went on, "for tomorrow we are returning to our home in the country and should have missed you."

"I'm glad too, ma'am," I said; and then Sour Not-Bodger escorted us to the door.

"Thank you, Michael," said Tristram as we drove away. "That is the first time Miss Clarenton has been 'at home' to me in many, many years."

Tristram was quiet for some time after that, giving his full attention to the task of negotiating the increasingly busy streets, and I left him alone with his thoughts.

Regency steampunk London had embraced the motivated carriage, but had not yet learned to cherish such corollary items as traffic signals, lane striping, or cross walks, and the going was sometimes a wee bit fraught. In addition to the various private conveyances I saw any number of motivated wagons, including a massive barrel hauler having an altercation with what I can only call a London proto-bus. It was bright red, with the usual two decks, and pulled by a heavy motivator; and it was so long that it had a second postilion at the back to steer the hind end around corners. Fortunately we were able to turn onto another street before we were fully ensnarled.

After a time, he said, "Michael, do you still wish to speak with the gentleman in blue? We are near the Bailey."

"Yes, I do," I said.

Our visit to the Bailey was a bust.

It started well. I could tell they knew and respected Tristram there, for the man at the desk hopped to his feet when we entered and greeted him warmly; and we were ushered down to the cells with every sign of respect and courtesy.

The Blue Man was sitting on a cot in a tiny cell by himself, staring at the floor. He didn't look up as we approached, or show any sign that he had noticed us.

"'E never says a word," said the jailer who was escorting us. "We 'ad to put 'im in a cell by 'imself. The other prisoners wouldn't leave 'im alone."

"Let me try," I said.

The jailer looked at me funny, but Tristram held up a hand to forestall any commentary.

I stepped a little closer to the bars—though not too close. "Good morning," I said. "Why did you shoot me?"

There was no response.

"You're being foolish, you know. If you'll answer some questions for me, I might be able to help you."

The Blue Man raised his head and looked at me—and then, quite deliberately, spat on the floor. Then he lowered his head again.

I tried several more times, but got no further response. "What will happen to him?" I asked Tristram.

"He entered a home and attempted violence on one of the residents. In most cases, such an individual would have been carried out feet first. In the case of our friend here, he'll receive a fair trial and then he'll be hanged."

"That's what I thought."

I had the power to save him from that end. All I had to do was prepare my mind and push the button. But he'd tried to kill me, and come frighteningly close to succeeding. By comparison, the

Illustrated Man had only knocked me down.

"We're done here," I said at last.

"Quite," said Tristram.

Chapter 19

We were around the corner from Tristram's house when he pulled back on the reins, slowing the curricle to a standstill. Crossing through Maudlin Square a hundred feet or so ahead of us was a fancy-looking red-and-gold carriage hitched to a fancy-looking red-and-gold motivator. Both were considerably larger than Tristram's. There were two postilions on the motivator, two footmen standing on a kind of step at the back of the carriage, a purely superfluous coachman in a top hat seated at the front, and an ornate "R" on the door.

"That's Lord Remchester's carriage," said Tristram. "I fear he intends to pay me a visit."

"And that would be a bad thing?"

"He will want me to offer for Miss Stavely. Our dealings with each other are such that I should find it difficult to refuse him to his face if pressed—and accepting his plan would be fatal." He took out his monocle and polished it with a cloth he drew from his pocket. It was clear that there was more going on than the prospect of a life hitched to the Stavely, but I wasn't sure what.

"Also, I fear he may have become curious about you." He reinserted the monocle and looked down at me. "It is rarely a good thing for the small to come to the notice of the powerful. They might become tools to his hand." Slant. "Still, I suppose I must see him."

I took a good look to the right as we entered the square.

"Yup," I said. "He's stopped in front of your house. I think I saw the front door close."

Tristram said nothing, but drove on around the square and brought the motivator to a stop behind Remchester's carriage. Thompson met us at the door.

"His Lordship's waiting in the drawing room, sir." His tone was even, but his eyes urged caution.

"Indeed," said Tristram. "I surmised as much. Thank you, Thompson."

We found His Lordship's footmen standing one on either side of the door to the drawing room, and the man himself enthroned in the best chair at the far end. He'd clearly had the chair moved so as to dominate the room; I could see the marks on the rug where it had formerly sat. A cup and saucer stood on a little table at his elbow.

He rose as we entered. I'm afraid that fifteen years had left little of the heroic figure in the long coat depicted by the statue in Remchester Park. The present Lord Remchester had a red face under mutton chop whiskers, and he was wearing a gray bowler and striped trousers. A gold watch chain adorned his ample vest, and all in all he seemed more like a wealthy merchant out for a drive than the ruler of a country. He looked at us expectantly.

"Good morning, your Lordship," said Tristram.

"A very good morning to you, Tristram," said His Lordship. "Your man assured me that you would be home for luncheon, so I took the liberty of waiting for you."

"It was no liberty, sir; you are quite welcome."

Remchester inclined his head, then turned it in my direction.

"And you must be Tristram's young cousin from the Colonies."

"Yes, sir," I said. I bowed as I had for Miss Clarenton, and did my best to continue looking wide-eyed. It wasn't hard.

"I am glad to see you looking so well after that unfortunate incident in my park, lad." He smiled avuncularly, and I began to see how he might have dazed the young Tristram back in the day.

"Thank you, sir," I said. "Cousin Tristram is taking good care of me."

"Of course he is. He is just the man for taking care." He smiled again, then snapped his fingers. "But I am forgetting my manners. Do sit down and be comfortable, both of you."

He resumed his seat, and he beamed at us as we found ours.

"To what do we owe the pleasure, sir?" asked Tristram.

"Why, I miss you, young Tristram. After so many years of working together, I find that my day is quite empty without that mustache of yours around the place. Surely that's enough?"

"Yes, sir, I am sure it is. And yet, I have never known you to do anything merely for the pleasure of it. I presume you have come on Miss Stavely's behalf?"

Remchester laughed. "Straight to business? Well, you're quite right, young Tristram. You have found me out."

"It would be strange if I had not, after so many years." He took out his monocle and let it dangle. "Well, sir, I am listening."

"It's you I'm thinking of, young Tristram. A handsome buck like you needs to marry someone. Why not Stavely's daughter? It will give you a stronger position in the New Order, and it will allow her to live as she is accustomed. And perhaps you might pick up Stavely's seat in the Assembly in the fullness of time."

There was a moment of silence, during which Remchester regarded Tristram soberly. "And I don't mind saying," he said, "that I'd take it as a personal favor." I don't think I imagined the extra emphasis on the word "personal."

"Yes," said Tristram, "I quite see that. I shall think on it, your Lordship."

"Very well, but not too long, young Tristram. Time's a-wasting."

I noticed that neither of them mentioned Lord Stavely's finances, at least not directly; or the possibility of Stavely's sons following in their father's political footsteps. The message was clear enough: satisfy me, Remchester was saying, and I'll see you in the Assembly. Fail to satisfy me, and there will be repercussions. Carrot, meet stick.

His Lordship rose to his feet, and so perforce did we.

He paused in the doorway of the drawing room. "I'll be

waiting for the happy news, young Tristram," he said.

"As you say, sir," replied Tristram.

His footmen restored His Lordship's chair to its original location, and then followed him down the stairs.

I went to the window, and watched as the First Lord's carriage rumbled away over the cobblestones.

"And there he goes," I said.

"And so ought we, I think," said Tristram. "Come."

Tristram proceeded out of the drawing room and up the stairs to his bedchamber; and leading me to what I took to be a closet door, he unlocked it to reveal a small windowless room with a table and two chairs.

There was another door on the far side of the room; and by it, mounted on the wall, a round brass plate with a button in the middle. Tristram pressed the button, then gestured for me to take a seat.

"Thompson will be here as soon as may be," he said in hushed tones. "That button triggers a signal that only he will notice. In the meantime we may converse quietly."

"What are you planning?"

"I believe that I have just received word from my man of business that there are matters to which I must attend in the country."

I was puzzled. "I thought Lord Remchester had taken all of your grandfather's property."

"Nothing so grand as that, alas; but I still possess the cottage in which I grew to manhood. When my grandfather provided for my support after my mother's death, he transferred a minor family property to my name, along with a bit of surrounding land, and that property I retain."

The bedroom door's latch clicked quietly; moments later Thompson entered the little room, closing the door behind him.

"I've seen Lord Remchester off, sir," he said.

"And well do I know it," said Tristram. "However, I find that I've received urgent word from Grayrigg, and must go into the country post-haste."

Thompson nodded knowingly.

"Please prepare bags for me and for Michael. You know my needs." Tristram looked at me.

"Have the remainder of my new clothes arrived yet?" I asked.

"Yes, lad, not an hour a-gone."

"Then I'll need whatever clothing you think I should take with me. Also, please put all of the non-clothing items from my suitcase into my backpack, and include that as well."

Thompson nodded again, then looked at Tristram.

"Bring the bags here; and then bring the traveling phaeton around to the back door. Should anyone come and ask, you can say where we have gone; but you needn't volunteer the information."

"As you say, sir."

Tristram nodded approval. "Also, I would like you to stay here; there may be unwelcome guests popping in, and you and Bodger will need to deal with them. I do not wish to leave the house unguarded."

I could see that Thompson didn't quite like that, but he said nothing.

Tristram saw it, too.

"Yes, Thompson, but Michael can't tiger with that arm of his, and I wouldn't ask anyone to tiger all of the way to Grayrigg, even if he could."

"Yes, sir."

"In the meantime, you know how to reach me. I'll send for you if I have need."

"Yes, sir."

Thompson left, closing the door behind him.

"So," I said, "why the cloak-and-dagger stuff?"

"Cloak and dagger?"

"Sorry; it's a figure of speech where I come from. Why the secrecy? Why shouldn't we just leave openly?"

Tristram began to speak, then stopped. His mustache assumed that rueful tilt as he thought, and then twitched.

"Habit, I suppose," he said, giving me a frank look. "I have sometimes had reason to be discreet about my comings and goings. I'm done with that, now, but my precautions have become second nature." He cast that to the side with a wave of his hand. "Also, I suppose there is a smattering of what we used to call *noblesse oblige*," he said. "It wouldn't do to openly flout Lord Remchester, and I prefer not to put my people in a position where they must cover for me. It is better for them; and of course, what they don't know they can't tell."

"What about Thompson, then?"

"Oh, Thompson has been my man for over three decades. He would no more share my business than fly. More than that, no one would expect him to, not even Lord Remchester."

"Bad *ton?*"

"Just so."

"But won't your other servants notice that he's packing for you?"

"It is not likely. I don't encourage curiosity, and the only live-in staff are Thompson and Bodger. Cook and the housemaid live elsewhere." He shrugged. "This way, not even Bodger will know that we have left London until some time has passed."

Thompson returned shortly after that, carrying two leather satchels and my backpack. At least, I think they were satchels; they might have been portmanteaus. (I have the same trouble with luggage that I do with architecture.)

Tristram opened the door on the far side of the room, revealing a dimly lit flight of stairs leading down. Then he reached for one of the satchels.

"Not to worry, sir. I have it in hand," said Thompson; and so saying he went nimbly down the steps with a bag each hand and one under his arm. We followed rather more slowly; the stairs were steeply pitched, and I was glad of the hand rail.

There was a narrow passage at the bottom, floored with brick; it ran for about forty feet to a plain wooden door with a small hatch at eye-level.

Well, at eye-level for a person of size, anyway.

Thompson put down the bags and opened the hatch briefly; then he nipped out the door, closing it behind him.

"It opens on the lane behind my home," said Tristram in low tones. "We should be well away without anyone knowing that we left directly upon Lord Remchester's departure."

Then we waited in the passage while Thompson fetched Tristram's phaeton, more suitable for an extended journey than his curricle; and in twenty minutes we were on our way out of London.

Chapter 20

I'd left the Big Bag O' Finders in Tristram's strongbox, the circumstances of our departure having prevented either of us from retrieving them, and as we drove away from the vicinity of Maudlin Square I found myself consumed with curiosity. It was pretty clear that the steady stream of Traveling chums we'd been entertaining were ending up in Tristram's house because there were so many finders present. But what were they looking for?

I mean, yeah, sure, I know what they ultimately had in mind. They were looking for a guy with a finder that they could abscond with. But what was their search target? What did they ask their finder to find? Were they seeking any arbitrary man with a finder, and finding me because the search algorithm was weighted that way? Or were they seeking an easily acquired finder, and finding me because I happened to be in the vicinity of a bunch of finders? If it was the former, Thompson and Bodger would have a busy time of it, and Tristram and I would have a peaceful journey. If it was the latter, then acquisitive Travelers would be another of the hazards of the road.

I admit, I was hoping for the former: a peaceful journey. Yes, I actually thought that was possible.

All told, the trip from London to Grayrigg took us about a week, driving easy stages each day. In the old days it would have taken up to ten days if you changed horses every fifteen miles, and rather longer if you were driving your own horses and had to let them rest between stages—and longer still if the weather was bad. So quoth Tristram. It wasn't that the steam motivator pulled the phaeton that much faster than horses would have, because it didn't. But it didn't need to rest, and it couldn't be spoiled by overwork. And then, one of Remchester's early acts as First Lord was a program for improving the major roads to each of the English counties.

"That sounds worthwhile," I said.

"Oh, it has been. Trade has improved remarkably," he said, gesturing at a passing freight wagon. "The best roads are between London and the steam manufacturies of the North." He glanced at me, unmonocled-eye twinkling. "And, of course, it is ever so much easier to move the Army about the countryside."

Had we been responding to a real crisis we could have reached Grayrigg in three or four days, but as Tristram's only pressing motive in going to Grayrigg was the desire to be out of reach of Lord Remchester and the Stavely while he considered his options, we took our time, turning aside to look at this and that, and lingering over our meals.

"Riding hour after hour grows tiresome even in the best phaeton," said Tristram. "One of Remchester's cronies is working on a scheme to build something he calls land-leviathans, something like motivators but much larger, and running on a dedicated roadway with metal rails. They will carry passengers, though of course the primary purpose is freight hauling. If he succeeds I foresee the day when one can travel anywhere in the Commonwealth in reasonable comfort. In the meantime we have the choice between the main roads, which are well-paved and choked with freight wagons, and the side roads which are neither."

Our first stop once we got out of London was at a Mordred & Sons—in Reading, if I recall correctly, though it might have been closer to Oxford—to buy some items for the journey. Notably, this included a pair of shoes that wouldn't get me talked about. They were bootish and seemed to have an excessive quantity of laces, but they fit well enough, and I was pleased to discover that even with my sore shoulder I could lace them up and tie them by myself. (Up until then I'd been wearing a pair of loafers I'd nabbed from my closet on my brief trip home.) The store itself wasn't quite as big and fancy as the one in London, but the floors still gleamed and the patrons were still armed to the teeth.

There were more young people about than I'd seen at the Mordred & Sons in London, and I noticed a number of younger ladies in somewhat more revealing styles—by which I mean, their forearms were shockingly exposed. Like Miss Stavely, most of these had a metal device strapped along the backs of their left forearms. Many of them were highly ornamented, but they all had one feature that had been hidden by Miss Stavely's sleeve: a little round hatch at the wrist end, about three-quarters of an inch around. I later found out that they were steam-powered bolt throwers, something like a crossbow without the bow.

I did not investigate the children's weapons aisle, though I was sorely tempted. Tristram certainly wouldn't have willing to buy me anything we found there, though.

We were approaching the cashiers when Tristram was hailed by another shopper.

"I say, Monocle! A word with you!"

The speaker was of a distinct type—dressed more or less as Tristram was, but with the dial turned up to eleven. He wore boots with tassels, like Tristram, but his boots were as shiny as patent leather where Tristram's were a plain, serviceable black. He wore the same kind of cream-colored trousers and brown coat, but his appeared to be spray-painted on. His shirt collar rose to absurd points on either side of his face, and his extravagantly folded neck cloth pushed his chin so far up that he could only look down his nose at us. He wore no hat, but instead had his hair brushed straight forward all around his face. The butt of his pistol sparkled with silver inlay, as did its holster, as did the stock and barrel of the shotgun he had slung over his shoulder. I wondered if he ever fired them.

He had various little trinkets dangling from his waistcoat and holster, and after a moment I realized with surprise that many of them were moving and giving off little puffs of steam. The largest was a sort of mechanical flower attached to his lapel; as I watched, the petals opened and closed in a hypnotizing pattern, alternately revealing and concealing a center of spinning gears. The others were similarly baroque, though smaller.

"Good morning, Stavely," said Tristram. "Michael, this is Miss Stavely's brother Cedric. Stavely, this is my cousin, Master Henderson."

"Pleased," he said, and I nodded.

"You seem to be at high water, Stavely," said Tristram. "A good day at Newmarket?"

Stavely laughed, "Got it in one, Monocle. I had a prime tip for *No Such Luck* in the fifth, and compounded with *Eagle's Eye* in the seventh. Good thing for you that I did."

"A good thing for me? How so? I don't recall having any of your vowels."

"No more you do. Got some advice for you, regarding my sister."

"Oh?" Tristram's tone was not encouraging.

"Yes. *Run away*. That's all. Just *run away*." A thought seemed to strike him. "Unless you really want to marry her, I mean. Can't see why you would. Can't see why anyone would. Not a friendly girl, my sister. Well, I mean to say. And then there's my old dad. He's pretty well rolled up, he is."

"Is he?"

"Positively at point non-plus, and itching to be bailed out by what's left of old Uxbridge's estate. Can't let your new family fall into scandal, what? And then there's my brother Beverley, who's no better and probably worse. I'm all right myself, today, but tomorrow? When this lot is gone I'd gladly waste your blunt with the rest of them. Expensive family, the Stavelys. Always were."

He glanced at me; I was still studying the various devices that were suspended from his waistcoat. Most were simply whirring congeries of gears, like an open pocket watch; others were small sculptures. One was a tiny octopus with tentacles that writhed endlessly.

"I see that you're admiring my whatnots, Master Henderson. And well you should, for they are the talk of London!"

"I've never seen anything like them," I said. That turned out to be the right thing to say, for he beamed at me.

"I should hope not," he said. "But one or two of them are languishing, I'm afraid, so I've come to get some oil to put them right." He showed me a small can with an applicator tip. "Waterston's Whatnot Oil," he said. "It's the very thing to keep them running smoothly. I don't know how I would live without it."

"I am surprised to see you buying it here, though," said Tristram. "I would have thought that McMullin's would be better *ton*."

"What price fashion, eh, Monocle?" said Stavely. "And indeed, most of these came from McMullin's own hand. But the prices are so much better here, you know, and I am afraid that Mr. McMullin has expectations of me. If I *were* to visit him today I am afraid I should be forced to leave most of my winnings with him. All that lovely lolly gone, and nothing to show for it! No, no, Mordred and Sons is here to stay, and one most move with the times!"

He laid a hand on Tristram's arm and leaned in. "I like you, Monocle; always have. You don't want to get mixed up with my family. Bleed you to death. Done it to one fortune. Felt I needed to tell you." He seemed to consider. "Surprise to me, don't you know. Didn't think I had a better nature. Maybe there's hope for me yet."

"Thank you for your advice, Stavely."

"Thank Newmarket. I'd have said something different otherwise. Good day!" And he strolled languidly off.

"There goes a veritable rose of the *ton*, Michael," said Tristram, watching him go. "He is right, of course. They *are* an expensive family, and I have no desire to frank them. My grandfather would turn over in his unmarked grave."

"What are you going to do?"

"I am not sure yet."

We stayed at a coaching inn that night, had a leisurely breakfast, and were on the road again.

I have to say I enjoyed it all immensely. I'd never done any real traveling (with a small T) as a kid, so it was all new to me; and Tristram's England was a beautiful place, if frightfully unpaved by my standards. I was trying to maintain a +3 boyish enthusiasm whenever other people were around, and I found it to be no great effort.

Not that it was all lolling about on the phaeton's comfortable bench seat, watching the scenery go by. We did a lot of that, but we always had to keep one eye open for the local vermin—of which there were many different sorts, to the point that I began to wonder how anyone lived in the countryside at all. We were attacked by gulls several times, in twos and threes, when the road went through more open country. Tristram kept a shotgun in a kind of holster mounted on the side of the phaeton, and two rounds of buckshot seemed more than adequate to make most gulls lose their appetites. What we'd have done if the gulls had come in the numbers I'd seen in Remchester Park, I really don't know. We only killed one of them, and lacking a convenient pond of snapping trout to feed it to we pulled it out of the road and let it lay.

"Are we just going to leave it here to rot?"

"What would you? We won't be eating it, and there is no other reason to take it with us. Nor any room."

"*Do* people eat them?"

"I suppose they might, if they were quite hungry indeed. But in the present case, I think we can safely leave it to the spider-moles," said Tristram. "It won't be a nuisance for long."

"Spider-moles?" I hopped back into the phaeton, and nearly resolved then and there not to get out of it again until we were in a town with properly paved roads and sidewalks.

"Oh, yes. Lovely creatures, not at all dangerous so long as you don't trip and fall."

"And if you do?"

"You do carry a knife, don't you?"

I did; but as it was a small pocket knife I mostly used for trimming my nails and opening packages I was not comforted.

After the gull attack I remembered Bernie's camera. I hadn't had occasion to show it to Tristram yet, and he watched curiously as snapped I pictures of the gull, the phaeton, the motivator, and Tristram himself.

"And what is this object, may I ask?"

"It's a digital camera."

"Ah. I see. All is now clear." Twitch, twitch. "And what, pray, does a digital camera do?"

"It takes pictures." That got his attention. I waved him over, and showed him the pictures I'd taken. He stared at the screen on the back of the camera, utterly amazed, both eyebrows up and mustache unusually still.

"I had no idea that this was possible. How does it work?"

So I showed him how to work it, well enough for snapshots, anyway, and he snapped a picture of me standing next to the dead gull.

But that hadn't been what he was asking. He didn't want to know how to work it; or, rather, he did; but he mostly wanted to know how it took pictures, and what one could do with them, and how he could build one of his own, and of course gentlemen don't engage in artifactory but...

I had to disappoint him; your average digital camera depends on technology and manufacturing processes and materials that Tristram's England simply wasn't going to be able to develop in the near term. But I got to explain computers and software and digital image processing and integrated circuits and data storage, all of which I know something about, and the economics of manufacturing complex electronic gizmos, about which I waved my hands, and also about optics and analog photographic processes, about which I waved my hands even more. When I wrote to Bernie that night, I asked her to find some detailed books on early cameras and photographic processes for me.

The first interruption of major significance occurred late on the second day, while Tristram was teaching me the rudiments of driving a motivated carriage. We were on a side road that passed through a stretch of woodland—Tristram called it woodland, but to me it looked like the Forest Primeval—when I noticed shapes moving between the trees on either side of the road. I couldn't quite make out what they were: just that they were long and low and gray, moving through the shadows and pacing our vehicle.

Tristram caught me looking.

"Ah! So you've noticed the squirrels."

"Squirrels? But they're enormous!"

"Oh, are they smaller where you come from? These are perfectly normal squirrels, I assure you."

"Much smaller. Are they dangerous?"

"Why do you assume that all of the living creatures we run into are dangerous?" Twitch.

"Because so far, they all have been? And I'm including the Stavely in that assessment."

"Hah! I will not dispute you on that score. But the squirrels are perfectly harmless so long as we stay on the road. Under the trees might be another matter; they are fiercely territorial, you see, and this is a particularly fine stand of chestnuts."

Lovely.

So we motivated around a bend in the road, squirrels watching us suspiciously from the shadows on the left and the right, and almost hit an answer to one of my questions. At least, the guy in the middle of the road with the leveled rifle wasn't a local, not in that red spandex suit; and judging from the look on his face when we first came into view and the warning shot he fired over our heads, he meant us no kind of good.

You slow down a motivator by hauling back on the reins, and I'd done that instinctively so as not to hit him; but Tristram seized the reins and moved a small lever on the dash and suddenly we were going very much faster, faster than I'd known a motivator *could* go. The phaeton shook and fishtailed as it gained speed.

The Man in Red had just shouted what I heard as, "Stand and

deliver!" when he realized that we weren't slowing down. His eyes widened, and dropping the rifle he dove to one side.

I kept my eyes on him as we went by. I'm still not sure whether the body of the phaeton clipped him, or whether he stepped on a loose stone, but either way he stumbled into the shadows under the chestnut trees—and was immediately lost to sight under a swarm of gray bodies with big poofy tails. It would have been comical if it weren't so grisly.

Tristram stopped the motivator as soon as he could, a tricky business at that speed, but it was too late: in two shakes of a squirrel's tail the spandex suit had been reduced to shreds, along with its owner. The squirrels themselves, now looking rather two-toned, lined the edge of the road between us and the body, as if daring us to make something of it. They were bigger than any house cat I'd ever seen, and quite literally red in tooth and claw.

Tristram moved the lever back to its original position. "The highwayman routine is effective with horses," he said, "but motivators are less inclined to shy."

But my attention was on the wildlife.

"These are meat-eating squirrels? Only I thought squirrels were herbivores."

"No, no, they aren't carnivorous, not usually; they are just extremely thorough."

"Oh." I stared at the squirrels. One of them was out in front of the others. He had bright, beady yellow eyes and a belligerent look on his fuzzy little face, and I could tell he was just itching for us to make a false move. "Perhaps I should, ah, think *twice* before making any sudden move to recover the unfortunate gentleman's finder, then?"

"I expect that would be wise, at least until the squirrels have moved on."

"Are they likely to?"

"I would tend to doubt it."

"Chestnuts?"

"Just so."

I tried to think, but Mr. Squirrel was making pugnacious little motions with his paws, and slavering. It was distracting.

"Can we drive them off somehow?"

"Not easily. My shotgun would do for some of them; and then the rest would be upon us. They hunt in a pack, as you have seen. There are ways and means, but we would need a much larger group of men."

"So we're out of luck."

"I should say so, yes. I will report the tragedy at the next village, of course, but it won't help the poor fellow. In any case, he will be gone before anyone could return to look for him."

"Spider-moles?"

"Indeed."

I considered trying to mark the spot, just in case we should come back another day when the squirrels were on hiatus, but I'd have had to get out of the phaeton. Mr. Squirrel's eye was on me, and under his hungry gaze I soon decided that the local scenery was quite sufficiently marked as it was, and that I needn't make my own contribution to the decor. I leaned back in the seat instead. Tristram took that for acceptance of defeat, which it was, and got the motivator into gear with a flick of the reins.

"I wonder what other creatures your country is going to surprise me with," I said, looking back. "I wouldn't be surprised to see a lion jumping out at me."

"Unlikely, I'm afraid. The unicorns saw to that a hundred or more years ago," said Tristram, drily. He might have been joking. But then, he might not have been. I can't say, because my eyes were on Mr. Squirrel, rather than on his mustache.

So, to any Traveler who might be reading these words: if you're in need of a finder, you might be able to find an unused one in a spider-mole burrow by the side of the road in a forest in Warwickshire. Just look for the burrow lined with shreds of red spandex. But don't trip, or it will be a case of finders, weepers. I'm just saying.

Mr. Squirrel scampered redly into the middle of the road behind us. I took his picture, beady eyes and all; and then he watched us until we were out of sight.

Chapter 21

That settled that. I didn't know what Thompson and Bodger were dealing with back in London, but at least some of the eager throng of Travelers were still going to be heading in my direction. So much for abandoning the finders somewhere; if I hadn't activated so many of them it might have been a possibility, however unwelcome, but as it was I'd have to find some other solution. It didn't give me a happy feeling in my stomach.

As I mentioned earlier, we'd spent the first night on the road in what Tristram called a "coaching inn." It was called the Oaks—at least, the sign said the Oaks, though I heard people calling it the George—and it was a typical example of the species, being U-shaped: three wings with a large courtyard in the middle and a gate on the fourth side. I guess the courtyard had contained stables once upon a time, but no more; now it was just a nice, wide open space with plenty of room for guests to park their motivators and carriages. The inn itself was clean and reasonably comfortable, if rather busy and noisy, and the service was excellent—Tristram barely had to look up and cock an eyebrow for a footman to leap into action. If the service was also a bit impersonal and maybe even a little standoffish I didn't see anything odd in that; I just put it down to the constant flow of guests in and out of the place. After all, we were just two among many.

The second night was similar. The inn was smaller, but

otherwise nearly identical, and the standoffishness of the staff was if anything more marked—where we were concerned, at least. Other guests seemed to be treated more warmly. But Tristram took no notice, and so neither did I. When you're small for your age it's often a good thing not to attract too much attention.

The third night we stayed at an honest-to-goodness hotel called the Eagle. It was in Wooster, the largest town I'd seen since we'd gotten properly out of London. Tristram was known there; the moment we stepped in the door a short man in suspenders with a neat apron wrapped around his middle bustled up to us, drying his hands on a towel tucked into the apron strap. Well, I call him "short"; he was taller than I am, but not so foolishly gigantic as most people of size I run into.

"Now then, Mr. Monocle," he said, looking up at Tristram. He didn't sound unfriendly, precisely, but he seemed wary, and there was a bit of an edge to his voice.

"Now then, Mr. Charleston," said Tristram. "I will be needing two rooms, for myself and my young cousin here, and if you have one I would like a private parlor for dinner."

"I might and I might not, Mr. Monocle," said Mr. Charleston. He tucked his thumbs behind his suspenders. "Would it be his lordship's business you're after, Mr. Monocle?"

"No, I—"

"For I'd not want to inconvenience his lordship in any way, you may be sure, but—"

"I am simply going—"

"—you remember your last visit for his lordship, Mr. Monocle, and—"

"—to my country place—"

"—we still haven't gotten the stains out of the rugs, and—"

Tristram held up his hand, quellingly.

"—and, well, you see how it is, Mr. Monocle. I'm a business man, I am, and it's difficult enough to keep body and soul—" he said, then ground to a halt.

"Mr. Charleston," said Tristram, "allow me to relieve your

fears. I am not here on his lordship's business. My cousin and I are simply traveling up to my place in the Westmorlands. I assure you, I anticipate no undue wear and tear to your furnishings."

"That's good to hear, Mr. Monocle, but handsome is as handsome does. You gave me a chit on his lordship's treasury to cover the damage, and neither hide nor hair of any payment have I seen."

That took Tristram aback; then his mustache slanted.

"None at all?"

"Not a hairy farthing."

"Oh, dear. I find I must beg your pardon, Mr. Charleston. And I shall have to see what can be done about that when I return to London. In the meantime, I promise you that I shall personally make up any damage that comes about due to our presence."

"No chits, now, Mr. Monocle!"

"Good English pounds, I assure you, Mr. Charleston."

And at that Mr. Charleston relaxed.

"Very well, then, Mr. Monocle. You've always been a gentleman, and I don't care who hears me say it. A private parlor, you were wanting? And I'll have the boy carry your cases up to your rooms." And shouting for the boy he escorted us into a well-lit parlor. It was a pleasant room, paper above and wainscoting below, with a good fire and a variety of pictures and other objects on the walls, including some funny looking brass things mounted on leather straps. A rug nearly filled the floor, and there were comfortable chairs by the fire, as in Tristram's library, and a table set for four. I found myself surreptitiously eyeing the rug, looking for stains.

"Don't bother," said Tristram once Mr. Charleston had left us. "Charleston has certainly mended whatever damage there was long since, whatever he may say, and this room was spared in any event."

"Will you be looking into getting his chit paid out, then?"

"Certainly. I find it distressing that it wasn't paid long since. Distressing, but not, alas, surprising. Lord Stavely is not the only profligate member of the Assembly."

"So what happened?"

Tristram's mustached tilted again as he considered, then relaxed.

"I think we won't talk about that just now, Michael. It belongs to a part of my life I have left behind. Perhaps later, when we reach Grayrigg."

Just what *had* Tristram done for Lord Remchester? He'd said he was Lord Remchester's secretary, but I thought it went deeper than that. Secretaries weren't usually the cause of bloodstained carpets.

But then, I thought, this was the Commonwealth; maybe they were.

We had a good dinner; and after dinner I wrote a letter to Bernie, and then read for a while. I'd have liked to go home for a visit instead, but the only anchor I could be absolutely sure of was the Big Bag O' Finders. That would put me back in London, which was a fine place, to be sure, but there wasn't much point in my hanging around this world if I weren't hanging around Tristram.

Mind you, I was safer here than I would have been at home. It occurred to me, not for the first time, that Tristram and his countrymen were a lot like the local wildlife: perfectly harmless unless you threatened them or trespassed on their territory, and then, *wham!* Sudden death. In Tristram's presence, the reflection was surprisingly comforting.

And on that note I took myself off to bed.

It was raining hard the following morning, so we stayed over at the Eagle rather than drive in the cold and wet. Tristram's phaeton has a folding canvas top that's quite good at fending off the noonday sun or light rain, but it doesn't handle really bad weather all that well. We spent the morning sitting before the fire drinking tea and talking—technology, mostly; Tristram was fascinated by the idea of computers, and wanted to know more and more about them. I mentally added books on Boolean logic and digital circuit design to my list. In between conversations

Tristram wrote in a small black notebook and I read another of Bernie's novels. It was about—

But there's no need to outline any more plots. The point is that by the end of my time with Tristram I understood why Bernie had told me, "Regency steampunk is still regency." People didn't often get shot in these books, but when they did it was in the shoulder, and it only inconvenienced them for as long as the plot demanded it. When the men got shot, I should say, because so far as I saw the ladies never got shot—more's the pity, in some cases. Instead they caught interesting fevers, with sprained ankles for variety, so as to give the male lead the opportunity to be devoted and miserable and show his interest by various acts of service.

Speaking of service, we were treated very well at the Eagle, and I could tell that Tristram was both known and liked by the staff; but all of the folks who waited on us had a kind of sideways look in their eyes, as if they were just waiting for mayhem to leap out of the woodwork and wanted to be ready to meet it. Tristram was clearly regarded as being Dangerous to Know. It would have been funny if I hadn't been unpleasantly dangerous to know myself.

But nothing disturbed our peace that morning, and when the rain stopped that afternoon we went for a bit of a walk around the town. The sky was still cloudy and the pavements were still wet, but my new boots made short work of the puddles; and everything had that fresh, clean smell I associate with the countryside. I have never figured out how Tristram's "steam power" works, but it clearly doesn't involve burning anything.

I enjoyed myself, but as we walked I was starting to get that itching between my shoulder blades that tells me that I'm being watched. I could have been imagining it, of course, but I didn't think so; after so many years of dodging bullies who weren't even a little bit small for their ages, my spider sense is pretty finely honed. I did my best to study the people around us without being too obvious about it. I dialed my boyish gawkiness up to +10, looking here and there and everywhere at every new building; I turned and walked backwards so I could explain to Tristram how exciting everything was; I gaped at shop windows, hoping for reflections.

But Wooster was sadly under-equipped with shop windows, at least by the standards of Corey's End—or even of Tristram's London. There were a few newer buildings, of the "modern" brick style I'd seen in London, and one or two of these had large windows; and the aetherically-lit street lights and stained glass shop signs were everywhere. But most of the buildings were older, and the bulk of the shop windows I saw were small with multiple panes. And it being a gray day, all of the shop windows I saw were brightly lit from within. They looked quite cheery; but the gray light filtering down from the cloudy sky couldn't compete, and so there were no reflections worth speaking of even on the few large windows.

My efforts were both fatiguing and fruitless, and I was grateful when we turned away from the center of town and toward the river. The River Severn, that is. At least, that's what we call it, as I later discovered; I never heard it named by anyone in Wooster.

The Wooster skyline—I know I'm not spelling it right, but never mind—is dominated by a gothic cathedral that stands hard by the Severn. It was massively impressive, cross-shaped with an enormous square tower rising from where the arms of the cross come together, and much lighter in color than I expected. We turned towards it when we reached the river bank. There were no docks along that stretch, just a foot path, and then a wall, and then the cathedral grounds. There was no one around, perhaps because of the damp. My shoulder blades relaxed, and I dropped the ten-year-old act.

"You do put your heart and soul into that," said Tristram, "but perhaps it isn't necessary at this stage of our journey. Perhaps you could dial it back by five points or so?"

"I was trying to watch the people around us without obviously watching the people around us."

"By looking at everything while leaping about like a bumptious frog with the ague?" His mustache twitched. No, I wasn't looking at him; sometimes it comes out in his voice.

"Just so," I said. Turnabout and that.

"Ah. Well, I certainly didn't suspect you of anything more than a puerile delight in hoodwinking the locals, so your actions were effective to at least that extent," he said cheerfully; then his voice took on a serious tone. "You think we are being watched?"

"Not just at this precise moment, no, but yeah, I think we're being watched. When you're small for your age, you learn to notice things like that."

Tristram accepted that with a nod.

"Given the stories you have told me, I am sure you do. Well. It is certainly possible. Cedric Stavely saw us in Reading, and what Cedric knows everyone knows."

We turned up some stairs and through an archway into the churchyard, which was filled with long grass and headstones.

"Who do you think it is?"

"I couldn't say. It will surprise you to learn this, but after my time in His Lordship's service I am not universally loved. And then, it is possible that His Lordship himself is having me watched."

"Um. That's not good. Aren't we supposed to have urgent business in Grayrigg? Yet here we are, lollygagging in Wooster."

"I would ask you to define 'lollygagging,'" said Tristram, "but on reflection I find the meaning to be peculiarly obvious. I would much rather lollygag here in Wooster than in Grayrigg. So little scope for it there, you know." His voice was cheerful once again, but there was an odd note in the midst of it. He spoke of Grayrigg with affection, and yet…there was something there that he wished to avoid.

"Seriously, though, Tristram. What's Remchester going to do when he learns that you're dawdling like this?"

"Lord Remchester surely knows we are gone by now; and I doubt he has illusions about why I vanished so precipitously. He intended to force my hand, and so he has. The main question is, what will he do about it? He won't be pleased with me, but he won't be nearly as angry as he would have been if I had defied him openly. Very concerned with his honor and reputation, our

Lord Remchester. And besides, it provides him with an excuse for Lord Stavely."

Tristram threw out his chest, and swaggered. "Young Monocle is merely assuring himself of the state of his affairs prior to signing the wedding articles. He'll be back in town and come bang up to scratch in a few weeks. Count on it, Stavely!" He resumed his normal posture. "No, so long as it doesn't become generally known why we truly left London I believe it shall be well enough."

"You don't sound too worried about it."

"Worrying ought not be confused with careful preparation."

"Oh. So are you preparing? Carefully?"

"I shall make it my primary goal. In the meantime, you might continue to keep an eye out, if you can manage to do so without attracting attention. But only at +5, Michael. +10 is too fatiguing to contemplate."

We came around the corner to the front of the cathedral, which had lovely tall windows of stained glass and a surprisingly lack of statuary. I was disappointed; I'd been wondering as I walked whether even the saints went armed in Tristram's world, and if so what with?

"And what does his Lordship say about that," I asked Tristram, gesturing at the cathedral.

"In public, of course, he is all for it. The Glorious Revolution wasn't meant to up-end the status quo, you know. It was simply meant to replace one aristocracy with another."

"And in private?"

"It is hardly the sort of place he would feel comfortable."

Wooster was built on a small scale, and on leaving the cathedral grounds we soon found ourselves back in the heart of the town. Traffic was heavier than when we'd started our walk, though still much lighter than in London, and people seemed to be dressed much the same. I even saw a whatnot or two, though I saw no one dressed quite like Cedric Stavely. Apparently "roses of the *ton*" didn't bloom in Wooster.

We'd had no other end in stepping out of the inn but to stretch our legs, but a particular shop caught my eye. It was one of the older buildings, which is to say it looked like a house but with a small illuminated cubby behind a window near the front door. Through the bright glass panes I saw a small selection of books.

"Tristram, would that happen to be a bookseller?"

"Indeed. Are you in need of more reading matter? Judging from your frequent guffaws this morning, I would have thought you well provided for."

"I need something on the Colonies. I know something of their history in my world, but nothing about what they are like here and now—and it's going to come up. I'd have given the game away to Miss Stavely if I hadn't looked at your book on the Steam Revolution."

"Ah. Yes, we should remedy that."

So we went in; and it wasn't the kind of a bookshop I'm used to where you browse the stacks and find something that interests you, and then something else, and then something else, and then eventually you take a stack of books to the checkout counter. Rather, it was the kind of bookshop where the books are all behind the counter and you have to talk to the proprietor about what he has in stock, and he says he doesn't have what you're looking for, there not being much call for histories about the Colonies, and then you ask about novels and mention an author's name, and he allows that he has heard of such but he doesn't think he has any, and you press him to go look, and he demurs, so you insist, and eventually he comes back with a volume that he almost seems not to want to sell you because he's not sure you can be trusted not to dog-ear the pages, but you insist some more until with a long-suffering and suspicious air he wraps it in brown paper and ties the parcel with twine, which parcel you then have to ransom by leaving a bag of money behind the statue of Lord Remchester at midnight. Don't talk to the police, or the books will die!

It's precisely the sort of bookshop that when you go back to look for it again, you find it exactly where you left it. Alas.

I let Tristram get on with it. Me, I just set my boyish sulkiness and boredom to +5, and kept my mouth shut.

As I was carrying the parcel back to the Eagle that spot between my shoulder blades began itching again. I kept a subdued eye out, but didn't spot anyone.

Chapter 22

We did have a visitor at breakfast the following morning. I tased him, he fell down, Tristram relieved him of his finder, and the footmen carried him off to the local jail. Or, I suppose, *gaol*. I didn't even need to get out the duct tape. No muss, no fuss, no heartache, and no extra charges on our bill.

Truth to tell, I got lucky. I had just gotten up from the table and was heading for the door when he appeared right in front of me. I'd been practicing my quick-draw, and, well, down he went. Mr. Charleston was touchingly gratified, and so was Tristram.

"I begin to see why you're so interested in my taser," I said as we waited for the phaeton to be brought round. My pulse rate was back to normal by then.

"I am a private citizen, now," said Tristram, being careful not to grin. "I have to be careful of my expenses."

"And it's so difficult to get good wainscoting these days," I said. "Quite."

My feelings of being watched had gone away after we'd returned to the Eagle, but they returned full force as we drove out of Wooster on the road toward Lancaster—I know how to spell Lancaster—and then slowly subsided as we got away from the main road and its heavy traffic, and out into the countryside. Tristram didn't give a reason for leaving the main road, any more than he had earlier in our journey, but I figured it was as much to avoid spying eyes as it was to avoid the traffic. Then I began to wonder whether he'd had spying eyes in mind from the get-go.

The day passed peacefully. I practiced driving, and enjoyed the scenery; and if my shoulder blades got just a little itchy as we drove through the larger towns I tried not to worry about it. We stayed at a coaching inn that night (the Elms & Haddocks, if you're interested), where we had no visitors, expected or otherwise, and attracted no overt attention that I could see—and you can bet I was paying attention.

On the afternoon of the sixth day life got more interesting, and also much yellower.

It all began pleasantly enough. We got a late start, and lunched at an inn called the Bartholomew that sat by itself along the main road. Tristram had been looking forward to the Bartholomew for several days; he told me that the beer was famous, but being undercover as a ten-year-old I didn't get to find out. Barley water, however, is vile.

A few miles north of the Bartholomew Tristram turned out of the traffic onto a side road, and handing me the reins settled back to enjoy the ride. We were passing through farming country—at least, there were fields with green things in them. The road was bordered by thick hedges, for which I was grateful because every so often I saw cows in the fields beyond them. Perfectly ordinary cows, I hasten to say. At least, I hoped they were perfectly ordinary cows. I didn't stop to check, because they might be standing in prime fields of clover and I didn't want to them to think I had designs on their territory. I approved of the hedges, as I'd approve of anything that separated me unequivocally from the local livestock.

"Tristram?" I said, after an hour or so.

"Yes, Michael?" His voice had an odd note to it, and when I glanced over I noticed that his eyes were closed and his monocle was hanging loose, lost in the folds of his neckcloth. Apparently my driving was improving.

"Is there anything I should know about these cows?"

"Nothing that I can think of. I am sure they are perfectly ordinary cows."

"I wouldn't want to offend them."

"It wouldn't matter if you did."

"So they're harmless, then?"

"Well…I don't suppose I would want one dance the quadrille on my ribcage. But the chances seem remote. Placid creatures, cows. For the most part." Tristram sniffed, then opened his eyes and sat up in his seat. "Although," he said after stretching a bit, "that bull over there might cut up rough if you were to take too many liberties. You, ah…you do have bulls, where you come from?"

"No, no bulls. None whatsoever. Just cows. *Small* cows. Massive herds of minuscule bovine spinsters, covering the land from one horizon to the other."

I glanced over to see Tristram's reaction to my flight of fancy, but he was looking intently down the road.

"That is odd," he said. The road ran straight for quite a long ways ahead of us, just there, which I can tell you was not the usual way, and in the distance I saw a small figure walking by the side of the road in the shade of the hedge.

That wasn't so odd in and of itself; we'd seen many pedestrians already that day. But almost all of those were out in the fields, wantonly ignoring the bovine threat. They all had the look of locals going about their daily business: farmers walking from field to field, local gentry out for a stroll, and like that. There were funny stair-step things Tristram called stiles they used for crossing over the hedges between the fields, so they could go pretty much anywhere they wanted in the vicinity without ever walking on the road. I couldn't blame them; the road had no margin and was just wide enough for two carriages to pass if their occupants held their breaths.

Also, all of the pedestrians were wearing appropriate clothing for rambling through fields and country paths. The figure walking ahead of us, by contrast, was wearing a bright yellow dress. I'm no expert in fashion at home, let alone in the

159

Commonwealth, but it looked to me like something one would wear for a dinner party, rather than for walking in the sun on a country road. She was wearing a hat, or perhaps a bonnet, of the same material. Well, I say, "walking." It was more a kind of limping. Or perhaps lurching. I thought maybe she'd lost the heel to one of her shoes.

"That young lady appears to be in some distress," said Tristram. "I fear I shall have to consign you to the tiger's perch— I hope your shoulder is up to it."

I don't know how Tristram identified her as a *young* lady; she was a long ways off, and because she was walking away from us her hat hid her face and hair completely. But distressed she certainly was. She was carrying a couple of cylindrical objects that she kept transferring from hand to hand—from my reading of Bernie's novels, I thought they might be band-boxes. She looked quite pitiful, hobbling along like that.

"She'll be running away from home," I said, without thinking.

"Will she? Whatever for?"

I hadn't meant it as a serious comment; whatever Bernie might say, I didn't really think that Tristram's world was governed by the constraints of mid-20th-century regency romances. But Tristram sounded so surprised that I decided to go with it anyway.

"Could be any of several things," I said. "She might be a poor relation who is tired of being mistreated by her aunt who's jealous of her because she's prettier than any of her cousins. Though it's possible that she's the only granddaughter of a stodgy old general who won't let her marry the man she loves, so she's running off to punish him, and maybe to find her beloved. Either way, I expect she's planning to find work as a governess until some man comes along to sweep her off her feet."

Tristram was quite struck by this. "An impressive flight of whimsy, Michael. Why a governess, pray?"

"A girl's got to eat. I gather that it's the only honorable occupation open to an unmarried young lady of good breeding.

It won't work for her, though. Well, unless she's ugly, but I wouldn't bet on that."

"And why won't it work? I've no children of my own, but it seems to me that many of the families of my acquaintance do have governesses."

"She's a beautiful young lady of good family; the eldest son is guaranteed to take an unwarranted interest in her, and if he doesn't the man of the house will, the scoundrel. That's what the lady of the house will think. Either way, she won't want the little trollop around. So, no position as governess. Besides, she probably doesn't know how to draw or speak French or teach geography, her education having been neglected by her wicked aunt."

"Trollop's a hard word to use for someone you've only seen from a distance, Michael."

"Tell the lady of the house that. It's her word, not mine."

"Very well; she won't succeed as a governess." Twitch, twitch. "Why do you assume she's running away?"

"Look at her limp. If *I'd* twisted my ankle while out on a walk, I'd be trying to hitch a ride from the first carriage to come along. She ought to be waving at us and carrying on. Instead, she's ignoring us, and I'm sure she can hear us coming. Seems to me she's afraid of being caught!"

"Perhaps she is simply a modest girl who has been warned against accepting rides from strange men. And while I don't want to point the finger, Michael, you are indeed—"

"And besides," I broke in, "if she were just out walking she wouldn't be carrying those band-box things, and if she were on a normal journey of any distance she wouldn't be on foot."

"Quite so," Tristram conceded. "Whether or not, we still need to stop and offer our assistance."

"Sure. But you'll regret it."

"How so?"

"You're thinking we'll be able to drop her off somewhere close and then continue on our way. But these things never end well. Or, rather, I suppose they always end well, sort of, but the interval in between is likely to be unpleasant and filled with inconveniences."

"How—or, rather, *why*, do you think you know all this?"

"Narrative causality," I said, darkly. "That's what Bernie would call it."

We'd nearly reached her by this time. She hobbled gamely on, looking down at the ground in front of her.

Tristram shook his head. "Not only young, but foolish as well. She's unarmed."

"How can you tell?"

"The lines of her garments. Stop the phaeton, please, Michael."

So I pulled to a stop a few yards past her.

"Leave me alone," she said, still hobbling.

Tristram had been correct; she *was* a young lady. I could tell from her voice, which was loud, tired, frustrated, and surly. I couldn't tell what she looked like; the hat turned out to be a kind of sun bonnet, and since she was keeping her head down I couldn't see her face.

"My dear girl, I can hardly do that," said Tristram. "Here you are, miles from anywhere, on foot, unarmed and with a twisted ankle. It isn't safe. We will give you a ride to the nearest village."

"Leave me alone, I said. I'm not going to the nearest village," she said. Hobble. Hobble.

"Not like that, you certainly aren't. You will be benighted out here if you go on as you are."

"Go away."

"I am afraid I cannot do that. It would be murder, or worse."

"You have evil designs! My aunt told me about men like you."

"Oh, come. My name, dear girl, is Tristram Monocle, Esq., and you have my word that I will deliver you wherever you need to go, utterly unharmed."

I cringed. Now we were for it.

"And if that isn't sufficient," Tristram continued, "you will be well chaperoned by my young cousin Michael."

I was tempted to try to dial up my boyish obnoxiousness to +7 or so in the hopes of discouraging her, but I wasn't sure how, and besides, you know, I'm not actually ten years old any more.

She took one more limping step, then turned around and looked from under the brim of her bonnet at Tristram, and then at me, and then the fight seemed to go out of her. She stopped where she was, and kind of slumped in place.

"Very well," she said.

To my surprise, I discovered that I'd been right as well: she was strikingly good looking, at least if you like brunettes. (Me, I like Bernie, who's currently blonde. If she ever lets her hair go back to its normal color, I'll like brunette. Note the singular.) She looked to be about sixteen or so.

Tristram indicated that we should get out of the phaeton so I climbed down. He hopped out rather more easily, and took her band-boxes from her—"I shall just put these in with ours, shall I?"—and stowed them in the motivator's luggage compartment. Then he handed her into the phaeton, where she settled herself down in *my* seat.

"I am sorry, Michael, but there is nothing else for it. Fortunately we are only an hour or so from Lancaster, where we shall put up for the night." He gestured at the rear of the phaeton. "Unless you would rather ride postilion. But if you ride here you will be able to participate in the conversation and, ah, *verify* your conjectures." Twitch.

That's when I realized the import of Tristram's earlier comment about the "tiger's perch." Said perch turned out to be a narrow shelf sticking out from the back of the phaeton, upon which I was expected to stand while holding onto the back of the phaeton's single bench seat. (A "tiger," I later discovered, was a boy brought along to open gates, pay tolls, run errands, and also feed the horses, when there had been horses.)

"Bide a moment," said Tristram. "I shall need to raise the top."

I studied the perch while he did that thing. It was deeper than it had looked at first, and had a rubber surface, so it wasn't slippery; and while there wasn't a seat, as such, there was a metal rail sticking up behind that I could lean my backside against. It would have been hard to stand there with the top down, as it folded back right into the place where my head would be if I stood upright; I'd have had to crouch, or perhaps sit on the perch with my legs dangling.

Once Tristram had the top out of the way, though, I climbed up and found that I was able to stand easy, at least while the phaeton was at rest. The question was, would I be able to hold on properly, so as to keep from falling off? I'd been using my left arm more and more over the last several days, because you really need two hands to manage the reins; but driving a motivator doesn't take a great deal of strength. Just to make sure I grabbed onto the seat back with both hands and slung myself about a bit. There were a few twinges, but I found that my shoulder had healed enough to withstand the exigencies of the present moment. How convenient! I made a mental note to point that out to Bernie.

The top didn't have a rear window in it, as such; instead, when fully raised there was simply a semi-circular gap between the seat back and the bottom seam of the black canvas; and I found that I was just the right height to have a clear view through this gap. An hour or so sounded like a long time to stand like that, but at least I had the rail to lean against.

"I guess this will work," I said to Tristram.

"Let me know if you have any trouble; we can always stop and move you to the postilion seat."

Honestly, I think there was room for me to slip into the phaeton next to the young lady; but then she would have been pressed up against Tristram, and I suppose that wouldn't have been proper.

Chapter 23

Tristram started us down the road with a deft flick of the reins, and then turned to the young lady in yellow.

"And might I have the honor of your name, miss?"

"My name is Gwen—," she started, easily enough, and then, "But I shan't tell you the rest. You'll only insist that I go back, and I won't!"

So she *was* running away. I mentally awarded myself a point.

"As you wish. And where is it that you shan't go back to?"

"It is—," she began, and then turned and glared at him. "Oh, you are horrid! I shan't tell you that, either."

"Very well," said Tristram again, not looking at her. "And where is it that you are heading to, without so much as a pea shooter? You are lucky that it has been an unusually quiet day."

"I do too have a pea shooter! At least, I have this!" And she slipped what I'd probably call a derringer out of her sleeve and waved it in the air, more or less in Tristram's direction.

I'd have pitched a fit in his position—I nearly pitched a fit myself, with a handgun being waved about under my nose like that— but Tristram merely gathered the reins in his left hand and relieved her of it with his right, with no muss, no fuss, and no bloody accidents. He slid the gun into his pocket, then took up the reins again. He clucked his tongue.

"Has no one taught you the proper handling of firearms, my dear girl?"

"I'm not your dear girl!"

"So it is; you are not my dear girl. And where are you going, Miss—"

"B—there, you are doing it again. It is most unkind of you. Please, stop it!"

"But I can't call you Gwen; it wouldn't be proper."

"You may call me 'Miss Gwen,'" she said, with the air of one conferring a favor.

"Very well, Miss Gwen. And where are you going, Miss Gwen?"

She pondered that for a moment. I'm not sure whether she was deciding where to go, or where to *say* she was going. And I have to say that despite my qualms I was enjoying myself hugely; this was the most entertaining show I'd gotten to watch since coming to stay with Tristram.

"Edinburgh," she said at last. "I have a cousin in Edinburgh who will take me in. At least, I haven't seen her since I was young, but I am sure she will remember me. And if she doesn't, I shall find work as a governess."

"Why," Tristram asked, "a governess?"

"Oh, because I must do something while I'm waiting for—" And then she broke off and glared at him, though I could hardly see that it was his fault.

Tristram glanced back at me, mustache twitching, and I gave myself another point. But I was impressed. Tristram had responded to her every sally in the same mild tone, and acquiesced to everything she said, and yet he was pursuing his inquiries like a bulldog. I began to wonder if I ought to start playing the bad cop.

"Edinburgh is quite a long way," said Tristram. "How were you planning on getting there?"

"On the public stage. But there wasn't one in the village. They told me it doesn't run from there anymore."

"I begin to wonder whether we should simply take you back to the village and see if anyone knows you."

"H—I mean to say, my aunt's home is quite remote from the

village, and I was never allowed to go there. So you see, no one there would know me. And besides, I'd gotten a ride from a carter."

"A carter?"

"Oh, yes. And not in that village, either!"

Tristram homed in on the point that puzzled me.

"And yet, if you had a ride from a carter, then how is it we found you on foot?"

"He was so rude! He laid hands on me!" She shook her head. "I am not at all sure what he wanted, but after I shot him he made me get down."

"You…shot him?"

"Yes, with my little gun. It's in your pocket."

"I am aware. Where did you shoot him?"

"On his cart, of course."

"Of course. I meant, where did the bullet hit him?"

"Oh! I see. In his boot."

"You shot him in the foot?" I exclaimed.

"No, little boy, in the boot. They were quite large boots, too, with hobnails, and I don't think he had ever cleaned them, for they were quite muddy. The bullet left quite a streak down one side of his left boot." She nodded. "And so then he made me get down."

"But why the boot, by all that's holy?" asked Tristram, clearly in great distress. "You don't shoot attackers in the boot! What were you hoping to achieve?"

"Oh! But I was aiming for his head, you know."

"Well, that's something at least. And yet, Miss Gwen, you hit his boot? Someone must surely see to your marksmanship."

"But it was a natural mistake, with the cart stopping so suddenly and all. He grabbed me, you know, and I struggled, and the reins got tangled, and then the motivator was suddenly going ever so much faster, you know how they do, and the wicked man wasn't steering properly, and just as I got my little gun into my hand, the cart hit something—I think it was a milestone—and stopped, all on a sudden, and the carter went flying through the air and into the motivator, and so I hit his boot."

"Ah. All is now pellucidly clear, Miss Gwen. Thank you. What happened then?"

"Why, he got up after a moment, and he gave me such a look as I hope never to see again, and used such words that I'm quite sure I've never heard before, and he made me get down, and then he drove away, leaving me there. May I have my little gun back, please?"

"I think I would prefer to hold on to it, Miss Gwen. You have my word that I shan't, ah, *lay hands* on you."

"Oh, but there's an enormous bird flying toward us, and I should like to scare it off."

And so there was, no more than twenty yards away and coming fast. It wasn't a gull; I didn't know what it was, but it was at least as big as any of the gulls I'd seen and had a bright red crest and a wickedly pointed beak. (Tristram later told me it was a woodpecker. I can neither confirm nor deny, but I *will* say that all of the farmhouses I saw in that vicinity were made of stone.) The wretched thing must have been in sight the whole time we were listening to her tale.

Tristram rose to the occasion, as always. He dropped the reins, extracted the shotgun from its holder, aimed, and fired, all in one smooth motion. The bird jerked in the air and then came down to an unpowered landing in an ungainly feathered lump. It hit the ground beak first, just to one side of the phaeton, and stuck there, quivering. Tristram reloaded the shotgun and replaced it in its holder; and then, dismounting from the phaeton, he drew a knife from his boot and removed the bird's crest with a deft swipe. He stowed the disheveled plumage in the motivator's luggage compartment.

"Quite the bounty on these," he remarked to me in passing.

"And you're a private citizen now," I responded.

"Just so, Michael."

I stifled a snicker.

"Thank you, Miss Gwen," he said as he returned to his seat, "for your ever so timely warning."

"Oh, you are quite welcome," she said, as we rolled off. "And indeed you are, for you said, 'Thank you,' which is a thing I never heard from my aunt."

"Yes, your aunt. I'm afraid I really must take you to your aunt's home. It begins with an 'H,' I believe you said?"

Her head whipped around.

"Oh, you mustn't, you mustn't. My aunt would beat me!"

Aunt-ish mistreatment. That made three points. Maybe there was more to Bernie's conjecture than I'd thought.

Tristram, however, was much taken aback.

"She beats you? Really?"

"Oh, yes. Not every day, you know, or even every week. But often, quite often. I couldn't bear it anymore, I couldn't, and so I left."

"And how long ago was that, Miss Gwen?"

"Why, it was—but I shan't tell you, I tell you!"

"As you say, Miss Gwen."

I couldn't condone actual beatings, but beyond that I was beginning to think Gwen's aunt had a point. The young woman was a menace.

"You are being quite inconsiderate, you know," she said. "Interfering with my plans this way. Truly, if I had taken that wicked man's cart I wouldn't be in this fix. I wish I had."

"Why didn't you?" I asked.

"My aunt has always told me that stealing is wrong, and tho' I hate to think she might be right in *anything*, I've heard the same from so many others that I fear that it may be so."

"And do you know how to drive a motivator, Miss Gwen?" said Tristram.

"No, that was the other reason."

We came to a bridge just then, a tricky bit of driving, so the conversation lapsed for a minute or two. I turned my head to look at the river as we passed over, and wondered what savage beasts lurked under its placid surface, and whether they had a taste for girls in yellow.

Tristram tried a new tack when we were safely on the other

side.

"Your aunt seems to have beaten you quite often. Whatever for?"

"Why, I don't know. It is a mystery to me."

"She must have had some reason."

"Oh, she is simply a wicked, wicked woman." She cocked her head to one side. "Which makes it all the more of puzzle that she should be right about stealing, when you come to think of it."

"Was she, ah——," and Tristram cleared his throat, "was she punishing you for stealing, perhaps? I ask only for information."

"Oh, no, no, of course not. I would never steal."

"Of course not. That is quite a lovely dress you are wearing, Miss Gwen."

"Oh, do you like it? It was my cousin's, you know."

"I thought it might be. Does she know you have it?"

"I dare say she might by now."

"And yet, I thought you said you would never steal?"

"Why, but I needed it! I couldn't find a position as a governess wearing the hand-me-downs my aunt gave me. So dingy and ragged! No, no, no, I needed something that shows that I am a young lady of good family!" She looked down at the hem. "It is a pity it has gotten so spotted with mud."

"But of course you have a change in one of your band-boxes."

"Why, no. One couldn't fit a dress like this in a band-box, not without crushing it horridly." She shook her head. "I tried, you know, and it simply didn't answer. I was compelled to leave the blue dress behind."

"Then what do you have in your band-boxes?"

"Hats, of course. The finest ladies have different hats for different times of day."

Tristram was beginning to show signs of distress again.

"You ran away from home with nothing more than a stolen dress and two hats?"

"And my little gun! You mustn't forget my little gun. It's in your pocket."

Tristram took a deep breath, and another; and then another.

Then he changed the subject.

"Supposing that your cousin will not take you in, and you cannot find work as a governess? What then?"

"Why, I shall certainly find work as a governess, and take care of the little children; and the heir of the family shall certainly fall in love with me, and wish to marry me, and all will be well! That is the most likely outcome, should my cousin fail me."

Four points. But Miss Gwen wasn't through.

"But if not, why, I believe I shall go to France and be a maid."

"I suppose being a maid is a practical step down from being a governess," Tristram said in grudging tones, "but why to France?"

"Oh, because I have always heard of French maids, so they must have a great many of them there. I ought to be able to slip in unnoticed. Though, I don't know quite where France is. Perhaps you could point me in the right direction?"

"Do you speak French?"

"Why, no. Do they speak French there? Everyone I know speaks English. My cousin's governess tried to teach her French, and I always wondered why."

"Yes, they speak French there. And have you considered that should you become a maid in France, you would not be a French maid, but an English maid?"

"Why, I suppose that that is true."

"And I may assure you, there is no great market for English maids in France. You would do far better, Miss Gwen, simply to direct me to your home. I am sure that they are distressed at your manner of leaving."

And that was a mistake. Our girl in yellow got up, eyes flashing, and shouted in Tristram's face.

"And I say I will not!" And then she dove for Tristram's pocket.

Chapter 24

"Well, Michael," said Tristram rather later that evening, "thus far your predictions have been met in every particular, and I confess I stand in awe of your gift of prophecy. Have you, in your wisdom, any advice for such a poor afflicted soul as myself?" He closed the door of the wardrobe, and turned and glared at me over the width of the bed. His tone was acerbic, but I didn't take it personally; it had been a difficult few hours, and this was our first chance to speak privately since we'd acquired Gwen that afternoon.

"You've got the tiger by the ears," I said. "It's too late to get down from his back."

"What would I want with a tiger's ears? Most tigers of my acquaintance are uncommonly grubby."

"Not the little boy who rides on the back of the phaeton. You do know what a tiger is, don't you? They have them in India."

"They may have whatever they like in India, for all of me. Indeed, I have a young lady I might easily part with, should they be so inclined. What, pray tell, is a tiger when it is in India?"

"It's a big cat, kind of like a lion, but fiercer. Orange with black stripes. No mane. They grow up to eight feet long."

"And why would I have one by the ears?"

"It's from a saying: it's often easy to start riding the tiger. The trick is getting off without being eaten."

Tristram nodded.

"Ah. Yes, you are quite right. Unhelpful, but quite right."

Gwen's attempt to retrieve her "little gun" had failed, of course—I wasn't sure, but I guessed that Tristram had hidden it somewhere in the motivator's inner recesses while stowing the woodpecker's crest—so she'd gone into the sulks.

Some people, when they get the sulks, go off and sit by themselves and eat Cheerios and don't bother anyone. Brooding, they call it, and it is a good and decent and public-spirited thing, offending no one. Our Gwen altogether lacked this kind of public spirit, and in her lack of public-spirited broodiness betrayed her ownership of a considerable store of invective. I don't believe she used any of the words she'd learned from the carter that morning, as she was clearly a very proper girl in her way, but she managed to run on for quite a time. Perhaps she'd learned how from her aunt. Along with a great many words that were unfamiliar to *me*, including some I think she made up on the spot, I counted eight *horrids*, six *wickeds*, four *ungentlemanlies* (those stung, I could tell), two *cads* (ditto), three *thiefs*, and a *despicable*, all buried in a morass of "Oh!"'s and "Why!"'s and similar interjections.

She didn't say it all at once, of course. She distributed her scathing missiles a few at a time, with seething pauses, like lava bombs ejected from a fulminating volcano. (I'm sorry if that's a bit purple. I can do purple; I can't do yellow.) She'd ended by demanding that Tristram put her on the stage to Edinburgh the moment we reached Lancaster.

Tristram bore it all with long-suffering patience, merely pointing out that the stage wouldn't be leaving until the following morning, and that as she had no money for food or passage she'd have to stick with us at least until then.

So on arriving in Lancaster at an advanced hour we'd gone to a coaching inn called the First Lord (another former "George," unless I missed my guess), where Tristram had procured two rooms: one for me and him, and one across the hall for his "young cousin Gwen." We had a chilly dinner in a private parlor —socially chilly, I mean, both the parlor and the food being heated appropriately—and then repaired to our respective rooms. In my guise as chaperone I saw Miss Gwen to her door and waited until I'd heard her key turn in the lock. From the way she was limping I thought we wouldn't have much to worry about until morning.

"Seriously now, Michael, have you anything to suggest? I am at a stand." He began counting off alternatives on his fingers. "One, I cannot in good conscience put the hen-witted goose on a stage to Edinburgh by herself. Someone would be in jail for murder before she got halfway."

"Only if you give her her gun back."

"I couldn't let her go without it, now could I?" He shook his head. Me, I sat down on the bed to unlace my boots.

"Two," he went on, "I cannot return her to her home, for she won't tell me where it is. I have tried every trick in my arsenal, all to no avail."

I nodded. "This is true." I put my boots outside the door for the boot boy, as Tristram had shown me, and pulled a nightshirt out of my bag.

"Three, I cannot take her to my home in Grayrigg without fatally compromising her. It is bad enough to be staying with her in a coaching inn; I can only thank Divine Providence that I had you along today."

"I suppose you could take her to her cousin in Edinburgh yourself, assuming you can get her to tell you her name." I folded my clothes neatly, and put them on the seat of a chair. Tristram was still standing in front of the window, fully dressed.

He shook his head. "Edinburgh is days away. I hardly think you'd want to ride perch or postilion for the whole journey, and I could not leave you behind."

I did have a suggestion, actually, but I really didn't want to make it. Narrative causality to the side, I didn't see it ending well. But needs must, when the devil-in-yellow rides.

"The usual thing, in cases like these," I said, "is to take the Young Person to stay with a lady of one's acquaintance. Someone beyond reproach, you know, who will look after her while you go seeking the Young Person's relations."

Tristram had that harried look again.

"Yes, certainly, but *who?* I have told you my story. I have no mother, no sister, no aunts (wicked or otherwise), and no female cousins."

"I do believe Miss Clarenton lives near Grayrigg," I said, diffidently. This was the bit I'd been dreading.

"Miss Clarenton! But I could never—" He broke off, consternation writ large on his face as he stared into the distance.

He wasn't going to find another answer—regency steampunk will out—but I didn't want to rub his nose in it, so I changed the subject.

"There's more, though," I said.

"What more could there possibly be?"

"As soon as we reached Lancaster I started feeling like we were being watched again."

His look of consternation now included grace notes of horror and surmise, and I could tell he'd forgotten all about Lord Remchester for a little while. Now it all came home. He'd been seen parading through a major town with a beautiful brunette, all the while he was supposed to making up his mind to marry the Stavely.

"Blast," he said weakly.

They'd made up a pallet for me on the floor, the bed not being big enough for two. I sat down on it, reclining with my back to the wall, and pulled the book about the Colonies out of my backpack. I'd gotten a few pages in when Tristram seemed to come to some kind of conclusion.

"Michael," he said, "I must step outside for a moment. I must think."

"Enjoy," I said. "Should I try to keep an eye on Miss Gwen? What should I do if she tries to climb out the window?"

"Rejoice," he said, and then he was gone.

The door closed firmly behind him. I looked at it for a few moments; then, sighing, I got up and opened it so I could keep an eye on Gwen's door across the corridor while I read. Then I settled back down in my nest to do some studying.

The book, which was called *The Pathfounder*, was a lurid tale of a mysterious figure in buckskins who scouted out new lands in the Colonies in elder days. There were a few mentions of place names I nearly recognized—Plimouth and New Hamsterdam come to mind—but most of it took place out in the wild lands, where the eponymous Pathfounder was beset on all sides by wild men and wilder beasts. I've never read James Fenimore Cooper, but suspected this was something similar. Although, I'm nearly certain that Natty Bumppo didn't have to deal with kamikaze passenger pigeons, stampeding ground sloths (they stampede slowly but inexorably, like the mighty glaciers of the North), or carnivorous lichen. And I'm pretty sure the Indians of what I thought of as New England hadn't worn turbans or smoked hookahs. In point of fact, and with all due consideration, I have to say that I suspect the author, one Cowper Madisen, of having Made Stuff Up. The trouble was, I had no idea which parts he'd Made Up, and which parts were genuinely different from my world. Given what I'd seen already, carnivorous lichen were all too plausible.

So the book was almost completely unhelpful as a source of sober information; but on the other hand I was still engrossed in it when Tristram returned a couple of hours later. (The Pathfounder was on the verge of suffering the Death of a Thousand Shortcuts.) I heard soft footsteps in the corridor, oddly doubled; then he entered, slowly and inexorably, like the mighty glaciers of the North, pushing before him a reluctant gentleman in a bowler hat and a nondescript gray suit.

Well, I say pushing; and I say reluctant; but as Tristram had one arm across the man's windpipe and his steam pistol in the small of the man's back, there was a certain spirit of eagerness to the man's general air of reluctance. I'd never seen him before, though he looked vaguely familiar.

Tristram gently swung the door shut behind him with one foot.

"I found this gentleman observing the inn, Michael," he said softly. "Now, if you would be so kind?"

The man started a bit at Tristram's voice. I saw his eyes roll in a futile attempt to look behind himself, and then he seemed to relax a little. I stared at him.

"Michael?"

"I beg your pardon?"

"His weapons, Michael."

"Oh!" Scrambling up from my pallet, and wishing I was wearing more than a nightshirt, I relieved him of the steam pistol in his holster and put it in a drawer. Then I went back for his rifle, but there I had a problem: Tristram's arm was blocking the strap.

"At your convenience, Michael," said Tristram drily.

Eventually I figured out how to detach the strap from the rifle butt (I couldn't easily reach the barrel) and slid the whole thing out from between Tristram and our guest. I stood it in the corner, behind the bed.

"And now his boot knife." The man grimaced.

"How do you know he's carrying a boot knife?"

"Of course he is carrying a boot knife, Michael. I only hope he hasn't one in his sleeve."

And indeed, there was a knife in a proper sheathe on the side of his right boot, which I should have expected, as Tristram's boots were similar. I put it in the drawer with the pistol. Then, figuring I should go the extra mile, I patted down his arms.

"I don't feel anything in his sleeves," I said.

"Very good," said Tristram, and in one smooth motion he'd holstered his pistol and spun the reluctant gentleman around so that he could see his face. His eyes widened. "Harry Lackland!"

"Mr. Monocle," said the man, with a side glance at me.

"I expected it was one of your kindred," said Tristram in unusually hard tones. "To what do I owe the pleasure? Do you bring me word from His Lordship?"

"No, sir, not as such, no. But we've been watching you, you know, just like always, and well...."

"Just like always," said Tristram. "So you have been making a habit of this?"

"Ever since you left His Lordship's service, sir." To my surprise, the man sounded positively sheepish.

Aha. So this was one of our followers. And yes, I *had* seen him before, in Wooster, though not in this outfit. He simply hadn't registered before. A useful skill, that; I wondered if he'd teach me.

Tristram was frowning.

"I don't suppose I can persuade you to forget you saw us, Lackland?"

"Terribly sorry, sir. You was always good to work for, sir, and I hate having to watch you like this. And usually you never do anything out of the way for me to report on, which makes it much easier on me sir, for I know you won't come to no harm on my account. But this *is* out of the way, sir."

"She's my cousin, Lackland. The sister of young Michael, here."

"So I've heard you say, sir. But the lad left London with you, and the young lady didn't pop up until some time today. And you've been nowhere near a port, sir." He shook his head. "I'd as soon keep it under my bowler, sir, you know I would, but there's His Lordship to think about. He sent word to watch you extra close, and if I don't send a report, well, you know how it is, sir."

Tristram took a deep breath, then frowned. "Indeed I do, Lackland," he said in softer tones. "You've got the tiger by the ears, and now you have to hold on for dear life."

"Just so, sir. I guess."

Tristram fingered his mustache, which was tilting as far as I'd ever seen it go. "Very well," he said at last. "I suppose I must let you go."

"If you please, sir."

"Michael?"

I collected Lackland's belongings and returned them to him one at a time. He distributed them about his person, then touched the brim of his hat. "I'll see myself out, sir."

"That tears it," said Tristram when Lackland had gone. "If

Lord Remchester decides that I'm mocking his authority in public, I'm for it." He took another deep breath. "You're right, Michael: Miss Clarenton it must be. Tomorrow we make for Stockwood."

Chapter 25

"Miss Clarenton is not at home." The servant's words were forbidding, but the tone was apologetic. "I'm very sorry, sir, but her orders were most explicit."

"I'm sure they were, Augustus," said Tristram. "And I expect she renewed them when she returned from London with Mrs. Illridge."

"Just so, sir."

The servant was an older man, with a soft voice just starting to quaver. Normally I'd have called him a butler, but he wasn't dressed like one—as if I would know—and then, I wasn't sure that Stockwood ran to butlers at the moment. It was a fine-looking establishment from a distance, certainly; not one of the great houses of England, perhaps, but a good-sized manor house with several wings and lots of chimneys. Up close, though, I could see the signs of maintenance deferred: the paint was beginning to peel, and trees and bushes were beginning to encroach on the lawns and nearer grounds. The grass was long on the lane leading back to the stables.

It made me wonder. Miss Clarenton seemed to be spending very little on the upkeep of Stockwood, and yet her London residence seemed well taken care of: tasteful and modern, by Commonwealth standards, if not truly "bang up to the nines." Perhaps the family was now poor, and kept up a residence in London for appearance sake? But Louisa Clarenton hadn't struck me as a lady who'd give two figs for appearances. Perhaps the London residence had been rented for the season, at the expense of the country estate?

I put the thought aside.

We'd had a somewhat mercurial morning. Gwen had been cheerful at the breakfast table, prattling on and on about her cousin in Edinburgh while saying nothing of any substance whatsoever, and encouraging us—or, rather, commanding us—to hurry up so she wouldn't miss the stage. The flow of babble continued unabated as we waited for the inn's servants to bring our luggage down and stow it in the motivator.

"How far is it to Stockwood?" I'd asked Tristram during a quiet moment after breakfast, while Gwen was otherwise occupied.

"About three hours. It sits just outside of Grayrigg, perhaps five miles further on from my home."

"Uh-huh. I think I'll ride postilion today, Tristram."

"Blast. But I suppose it *would* look odd for Miss Gwen to do so."

Riding on the motivator wasn't as much of a gain as I'd hoped. While I got to sit down without my legs dangling, the postilion seat was made of uncushioned metal and the ride was bumpier than the phaeton's. And it turned out that Gwen's voice was of a carrying nature, so I wasn't as insulated from her conversation as I'd hoped.

She remained cheerful right up until the moment she realized that we were on the outskirts of Lancaster and heading off into the countryside. I didn't bother straining my neck to watch; I just looked straight on ahead, like a good postilion, and pretended that I was listening to a radio show.

"Where are you taking me? Why aren't we going to the stage stop?"

"Miss Gwen, you have no money for the trip, and no luggage to speak of, and it is many days' journey to Edinburgh. I cannot put you on the stage."

"You wicked liar! You told me you would put me on the stage

this morning!"

"On the contrary. I merely noted that the stage did not leave Lancaster until this morning. I am not responsible for what you chose to believe."

"Oh! Oh! Why, you—" and she was off again. Tristram waited patiently until she ground to a halt. I didn't bother counting her terms of abuse, but as I recall the words "dishonest" and "treacherous" figured prominently and repeatedly.

"Miss Gwen," Tristram said when she'd been quiet for several minutes. "It has become clear to me that I must go seek your cousin in Edinburgh." Tilt. (I'm presuming the tilt.) "And I will thank you later on today for whatever information you have of her. But I cannot take you with me, and so I must take you to stay with a friend of mine."

I heard a gasp.

"A friend of yours! Oh, you wicked man, if you think I am going to stay with some friend of yours you are mistaken! I am not that kind of girl!"

"Neither is she," replied Tristram in the driest of tones.

"Oh!" And then, in a more moderate tone, "Your friend is a lady, then."

"Yes. Miss Louisa Clarenton of Stockwood. She will take very good care of you."

"Oh." A pause. "But I do not wish to be left behind. You must take me with you to Edinburgh."

"It cannot be helped. But I shall leave Michael to keep you company."

"Why, you will?"

"Hey! You're going to leave me with her?" I turned around in the seat as far as I could. "Seriously?"

"Yes, Michael." He glanced quickly at Gwen, and mouthed the word "Later."

I grimaced and turned back around. Just where I wanted to be: stuck with the miserific vision in yellow, and without Tristram's protection. I'd need to grow eyes on the back of my head.

The ride had been fairly quiet after that. Gwen had ceased to fulminate, I suppose because she figured she was mostly getting her way, and Tristram and I could hardly carry on a conversation. So we jogged on in outward and deceptive peace until we entered the village of Grayrigg.

It wasn't a large place. The road passed a few houses and then transformed into a small, old-fashioned, but attractive high street. There was an inn called the First Lord's Head, which struck me as an equivocal sort of name, and a number of shops of the multi-paned window variety. The buildings were mostly timber-framed with white plaster; I saw none of the more modern brick buildings or store-fronts that I'd seen in the larger towns.

Signs of the Steam Revolution were few. The vehicles I saw were all motivated, certainly, and there were aetheric street lights mounted on brackets on the upper stories of some of the shops and other buildings, but the shop signs were all of painted wood; illuminated stained-glass signage was wholly lacking.

Though narrow, the high street was neatly cobbled. It made for a boneshaking ride, at least for the postilion, but despite that I decided I liked the look of Grayrigg. It was neat and well kept up, and down the lanes to the left I caught occasional glimpses of a lake all set about with evergreens. The sun glinted on the deep blue water.

There were people about, and I soon realized that fashions were also slow to come to Grayrigg: the women wore plain, simple dresses with long sleeves, and not even the youngest ladies had those bolt throwers on their arms. What did they have, then? I studied them, remembering Tristram's comment about the "lines of their garments," and soon noticed a tell-tale sag in each left sleeve, and a linear bulge along each right leg that made their skirts swish asymmetrically as they walked. So, a pistol in the sleeve, and a sawed-off shotgun or carbine for more serious threats. Their dresses were cut to hide it, or least to make it less obvious, but it was there if you looked.

The men, of course, were openly and plainly armed to the

teeth, though I saw fewer steam weapons than in London. Gunpowder was evidently still a thing in the countryside.

One or two of the men nodded at Tristram as we passed by, unsmiling, while others turned their heads away; and one of these was a burly man in a white apron who was sweeping the pavement in front of the First Lord's Head. From my increasingly wide experience of inns in the Commonwealth I presumed he was the innkeeper. Tristram stopped the phaeton when we reached him.

"Mr. Wiggins," he said.

"Mr. Monocle," said the innkeeper. He looked up for just a moment, then resumed sweeping. He looked to be about Tristram's age. His expression was sour, which was odd; even the least cheerful of the innkeepers I'd met in the Commonwealth strove to at least *look* cheerful when speaking to a potential customer. Of course, Tristram had his own house in Grayrigg, so perhaps he wasn't a potential customer.

"Here on His Lordship's business, are you?" he asked, looking down at his work. And then he spat into the street, and I realized that the name of the inn wasn't equivocal at all.

"On the contrary, Mr. Wiggins," said Tristram in a soft voice. "I have left His Lordship's employ."

At that, Wiggins looked up from his sweeping. "Have you, now?" He sounded surprised, though his sour expression was unchanged.

"Yes. I wouldn't want it noised about, but he never pleased me as an employer." I looked around at that; there seemed to be no one else in earshot, and I sighed in relief.

Wiggins leaned on his broom and cocked a thick black eyebrow at Tristram, looking at him square on for the first time. He didn't seem convinced, but he was listening.

"Truly? Then, why—"

Tristram shook his head. "Once you've mounted a wasp, Bert, it's difficult to dismount without getting stung. But it's all right now."

"Aye, and the old man's a wasp all right," said Wiggins, with a jerk of his head at the inn's sign, "though it surprises me to hear *you* say it." His eyes flicked over to Gwen, narrowing, and then passed over me lightly; I guess I was just the postilion, and beneath notice. I'd half-expected Gwen to raise a ruckus, but instead of accusing us of abducting her she just looked sulky.

Tristram followed his gaze. "And these are my young cousins, Bert, Gwen and Michael."

Wiggin's eyes narrowed again. "Cousins? I never knew you to have cousins."

"It came as a surprise to me as well. My father seems to have had a brother in the Colonies that no one had ever told me of."

Wiggins nodded skeptically. "Aye, that'd be it then."

"Well, Bert, I mustn't stand here blocking the high street, and I can't stop; I have a call to make."

"Stockwood, then?" He grunted, shaking his head. "She won't see you."

Tristram said nothing, but the pain in his eyes was eloquent even without the tilt in his mustache.

Wiggins nodded back, shrugging. Clearly they both understood the situation, and there was nothing more to be said. Tristram flicked the reins, and we moved on.

I was confused. Tristram was concerned about mocking Lord Remchester's authority in public; and now he'd called him a wasp in the high street. What was he doing? And whatever he was selling, I wasn't sure Bert Wiggins was buying it.

He called my name as we were leaving the village proper.

"Michael!"

I turned and looked, raising my eyebrows in question. He jerked his head to the right (his right, not mine).

"My home."

It was a cottage, I guess you'd call it: timber frame on a stone foundation, like the other buildings, two stories but small for all that, with an outbuilding that I guessed was a stable. It was set back from the road. There was a path of white flagstones leading to the front door, and a gravel lane leading back to the stable. The yard on either side of the path was planted with flowers.

"I expected something larger," I called back.

Tristram shook his head. "My grandfather's generosity didn't extend to large establishments. But it suits me."

But we passed the cottage on by. Twenty minutes later we arrived at Stockwood, with the result I described above. We'd left Gwen sitting in the phaeton. I doubt she'd have stayed there under normal circumstances, but I think her ankle was still tender.

"I don't suppose—" said Tristram, but Augustus shook his head.

"She was most definite, sir."

I dialed my boyish charm up to +6. At least, I meant to, though I'm not actually sure I possess any boyish charm. It seems to work pretty well on Bernie, but I think she might be an outlier on the being-charmed-by-Michael scale.

"Um, Mr. Augustus?"

He looked down at me.

"Just 'Augustus,' lad."

"Augustus, would you please ask her if she'd see me? Master Michael Henderson. She saved my life in London."

"Saved your life!" Augustus looked to Tristram, as if for confirmation.

Tristram nodded. "She did. He was shot in the shoulder by a bandit, right in the middle of Remchester Park. Miss Clarenton was passing by, and she was good enough to stanch the bleeding while I went for help."

Augustus seemed quietly pleased. "Aye, she's a rare one, sir. She never said, as you can well believe." He nodded. "Well, lad," he said to me, "I promise nothing. But she might well be at home to you. I will inquire."

Then he looked at Tristram, pursed his lips, and sighed.

"It's not proper to leave you standing at the door, sir, but truly I mayn't let you in. I beg your pardon."

"Do not be troubled, Augustus. The situation is hardly of your making."

Augustus nodded, and grimacing in apology closed the door in our faces.

Tristram looked down at me.

"Thank you, Michael. I see that I must trust to your wisdom and address."

"Turnabout is fair play," I said. "I'll do my best to work things out."

Chapter 26

"Good morning, Master Henderson," said Miss Louisa Clarenton.

"Good morning, Miss Clarenton," I said, standing just within the door of the library.

After Augustus had left on his mission there followed a not-very-brief interlude, during which Tristram mostly stood looking at the grounds, his face rigidly controlled. I could tell he didn't want to talk about it, but I did seize a moment to ask about Bert Wiggins.

"Tristram?"

"Yes?" He didn't look at me.

"Your conversation with Mr. Wiggins in the high street—how was that not publicly mocking Lord Remchester's authority?"

"It was, I suppose. But nobody in Grayrigg would give Lord Remchester a brass farthing if they had a choice about it, Michael. And Bert Wiggins is, or rather, *was*, an old friend—we grew up together. He was much hurt when I went away with Remchester, and blames both of us for it. And then, he's the innkeeper. We'll have a much easier time here with him on our side." He continued to stare into the distance. "And just perhaps, I might have put him into the way of being able to forgive one of us."

I left that to the side. "But won't he tell everyone what you said? I've not been here long, but I know what innkeepers are."

"I am relying on it. He will quietly pass the word that I'm no longer working with Remchester, and he will broadcast my, ah, *familial* relationship with Miss Gwen to the skies."

"I'm not sure he believed you."

"No doubt you are correct, but the fact that I said it is too juicy to keep to himself."

"Uh-huh. Well, you know best."

"Thank you, Michael," he said, glancing sidelong at me. "But what assures you of that?"

And then we just waited by the door, tilting ruefully, until Augustus returned and announced that Miss Clarenton would see me in the library.

"I'm sorry, sir, but she won't see you or the young lady. Though you may wait in the drawing room, if you please, rather than at the front door."

"Thank you, Augustus," said Tristram. "I know where the drawing room is, of course. I will escort my cousin there while you take Michael in to Miss Clarenton."

"Very good, sir."

And they did that, and I followed Augustus to the library. I was interested to note that the air of decay extended indoors: everything looked tidy, and, indeed, well-loved, but there were signs of encroaching shabbiness here and there: faded wallpaper and drapes and worn spots and the like.

Miss Clarenton was seated at a desk in the library, studying a ledger; she rose and greeted me warmly when I entered, taking my hand and leading me to one of a pair of threadbare chairs in the corner.

"I am glad to see you looking so well," she said. "You seem quite recovered."

"Thank you, miss. It's good to be feeling so well."

"Now, how may I be of service to you?"

I was surprised to discover that she truly seemed pleased to see me; but she didn't seem happy. I didn't know if it was something about Tristram, or something about the family finances, but I could tell that there was something on her mind.

Now came the difficult moment. If I simply made a plea for her to see Tristram, I was sure it would fall on deaf ears. I needed to catch her attention somehow, and lead her to where I wanted her. This isn't my usual kind of thing, and I hoped I was up to it. I pushed my boyish earnestness to +3.

"Well, it's about the young lady, miss."

"Yes, Augustus had mentioned that there was a young lady traveling with you." Miss Clarenton's expression darkened. I could see she didn't want to talk about Tristram, but in the end she couldn't help saying, "I trust they shall be very happy together."

"Oh, they aren't married, miss."

"What? Not married!" She seemed utterly shocked, and I shivered. I'd thought I'd understood Tristram's predicament from Bernie's books; now I began to understand it in my bones. This was no joking matter. But I tried to speak matter-of-factly.

"Of course not, miss. In fact, we aren't sure who she is."

Miss Clarenton looked flummoxed. I'm not sure I'd ever seen flummoxed before, not the pure article, but there it was, large as life.

"But she—but it's—isn't it Melissa Stavely? As was?"

"Miss Stavely?" That wasn't a name I'd expected to hear from Miss Clarenton's lips, and I had no need to add extra surprise to my voice. "Oh, no, miss. No, no, no. Tristram would never marry that old steam leviathan. Tristram's got too much sense."

Augustus chose that moment to enter with a tray of tea and cakes, which allowed Miss Clarenton to collect herself. She poured out the tea, and I took a couple of cakes with every sign of boyish enthusiasm.

"You oughtn't to speak of your elders in that way, Master Henderson," she said as she poured. Her tones were severe, but I could tell her heart wasn't in it.

"Oh, but she is, miss. I mean, have you met her?"

"I have."

"Well, then," I said, nodding decisively. "So you know what she is." I took another cake; they were quite good. "These cakes are delicious."

Miss Clarenton looked like she wanted to agree—about Miss Stavely, not about the cakes—but changed the subject. I suppose it comes of being well-bred.

"You were speaking of the young lady," she said.

"Yes, Miss Gwen her name is. At least, that's what she says. We don't know her family name or where she comes from. We picked her up on the way to Lancaster. Well, we had to."

"And why was that?" Miss Clarenton's tones remained severe, and I began to feel like I was being interrogated. But I could tell she was becoming intrigued.

"Well, we were driving through farmland, with nothing but hedges and cows on both sides, when there she was, hobbling along the side of the road with a twisted ankle. And she was unarmed! Completely unarmed, except for a little bitty toy of a pistol that wouldn't hurt a mouse. She's lucky she wasn't skewered, miss, as we came upon a woodpecker just a few minutes later. Cousin Tristram potted him with his shotgun."

"Unarmed?" Miss Clarenton was as shocked as Tristram had been. "I can see that Tris—that *you* behaved very properly in taking her up. But why bring her here? Surely you should have returned her to her home."

"That's the difficulty, miss. She's a girl of good family, that's plain, but she won't tell us which one. She says she's running away."

"Running away? From what?"

"From her wicked aunt, so she says, miss. Her aunt beats her, she says." I shrugged, as if there was no accounting for the ways of aunts. "Well, we couldn't leave her on the road, nor in Lancaster, for she's got no more sense than God gave a goose, nor any money, nor any change of clothing."

"Beats her!" Miss Clarenton sounded appalled.

"So she says, miss. So she aims to go to a cousin of hers in Edinburgh."

"Beats her. Well." Miss Clarenton shook her head. "And so, Edinburgh. The sooner she gets there, the better."

"Yes, miss. Tristram agrees. But Tristram and I can't take her there. It was bad enough that we had to stay at an inn in Lancaster last night."

Miss Clarenton's face darkened again.

"Tris—*your cousin* stayed at an inn with this girl?"

"It's all right, miss. She got her own room, and he bunked in with me. He put it about that she's his cousin, my sister. He said the same to Mr. Wiggins in the village, just now."

"And he dares to bring her here?" I've seen storm clouds that looked less ominous. But I shook my head.

"Oh, not him, miss. Me. I had to argue him into it, and it took a bit of doing." I said, and her brows rose in surprise. It was like flabbergasted emotions week, watching her react to each new enormity.

"Well, she needs to stay with *someone* while Tristram goes looking for her cousin, doesn't she? And I said, Miss Clarenton lives near here. She's a rare good 'un, I can tell. Well, look at how she took care of my shoulder, with me calling her names and all. She wouldn't leave Miss Gwen hanging, even if Miss Gwen *is* a bird-witted watering pot. That's what I told him."

Miss Clarenton stared at me in confusion, and I left her to it. I sipped my tea, and had another cake. I might have swung my legs a bit, but if so I'll never admit to it.

"To be perfectly clear, Master Henderson," she said after a while, in a faint voice, "you have brought a foolish young lady of unknown family to stay with me, while you and your cousin go on a wild goose chase to Edinburgh."

"Just Tristram, miss, I'm afraid. He wants me to stay here to keep an eye on Miss Gwen. And it's more of a chase on behalf of a wild goose, I think, miss, than to catch one. But you'll see."

She continued to stare at me for another long moment. I could almost see the wheels turning in her head. Eventually, I guess, she came up with the same answer Tristram and I had. As a gentleman, Tristram couldn't abandon Gwen; and he truly had nowhere else to take her.

"I suppose I shall," she said, and her mouth tilted to one side.

She had no mustache, but otherwise the expression seemed awfully familiar.

I followed Miss Clarenton into the drawing room, which proved to be a long room much festooned with couches and occasional chairs. Tea was set out on a small table, and Tristram and Gwen each had a teacup and a crumb-filled plate at their elbows. At least, Gwen's plate was crumb-filled (and in the process of becoming more so), while Tristram's crumbs were still disguised as a pristine teacake.

Tristram looked up as we entered, his face giving nothing away —but then, I gathered he'd had lots of practice at that in the usual course of business.

Miss Clarenton inclined her head in his direction, and said, "Mr. Monocle."

He replied, "Miss Clarenton, I—," and she held up her hand and looked at me.

"Miss Clarenton," I said, "this is Miss Gwen. I'm sorry, I don't know her last name. Miss Gwen, this is Miss Clarenton."

Then I matter-of-factly got myself a plate and added a couple of cakes to it, partly because my ten-year-old persona demanded it, but mostly because it enabled me to wait and see where Miss Clarenton sat down. She chose a chair next to Miss Gwen; and so I went and sat across the room where I could watch Tristram and Miss Clarenton at the same time.

"Miss Gwen," said Miss Clarenton.

"Oh, Miss Clarenton," Gwen said, "thank you so much for these lovely cakes! I could eat a dozen of them!"

It was a pretty speech, except possibly for the last clause, but it was almost the only pretty thing about Gwen at the moment. Her fancy yellow dress was spotted and bedraggled, there were dark circles under her eyes, and now that she'd taken her bonnet off I could see that her hair needed some expert assistance. She'd started her journey looking her best, but she seemed less than expert at maintaining it. The forlorn-waif-of-good-family look served Gwen well, though, because I could see Miss Clarenton's doubts evaporating the moment she laid eyes on her.

"You poor dear! You have had a time, haven't you."

"Why, yes, Miss Clarenton!" Gwen nodded, eyes wide. "I'm so very tired, and my ankle hurts so much, and, Mr. Monocle won't return my little gun to me. It was in his pocket, but he put it somewhere else when I wasn't looking. It was very rude of him."

"Miss Clarenton, I—" began Tristram with a note of ill-use, but Miss Clarenton held up her hand and looked at me.

"It's true enough, miss," I said, "but she was waving it about like a flibbertigibbet. Irresponsible, I call it, and I was glad when Tristram took it away. Besides, it's the tiniest little thing, hardly worth carrying."

Gwen frowned me her deepest frown, so I made a face back at her. Verisimilitude in all things!

"That will do, Master Henderson," said Miss Clarenton.

"I'm sorry, miss," I said, and picked up a cake. Miss Clarenton turned back to Gwen. Her expression was still sympathetic, but her tones were business-like.

"Now, Miss Gwen, if I am to take responsibility for you I must know more about you and why you are here. Would you please explain to me how Master Henderson came to find you all alone on a country road?"

"Oh, I'm sure I don't know how he came to find me, miss, except that he happened to be passing by. I suppose he could have been looking for me, though I can't think why he would have wanted to do so."

"No, no, Miss Gwen. I mean, how did you happen to be there?"

"Why, I'd run away of course," said Miss Gwen, nodding. She had resumed her most wide-eyed and sincere expression, and she had little sprays of hair sticking out in odd directions. If the governess gig didn't work out, she could always try to find work as an anime star. "It was because of my aunt. I went to live with her when my father died, and she beat me, and so I had to run away."

"And where does your aunt live?"

"Oh, she lives in—" and then she frowned her deepest frown at Miss Clarenton. "Oh! How horrid! Why, you're no better than he is."

I could see that she disliked the comparison, but Miss Clarenton continued straight on.

"And where do you hope to go?"

"I have a cousin in Edinburgh. She will take me in, I think. At least, I only met her once, when I was quite young, but she was so tall and pretty and kind. I am sure she will remember me. Her name is Eliza."

That was a new bit of information. I filed it away, and from Tristram's expression he was doing the same.

"Do you know her family name?"

"Why, no! I've only ever called her Cousin Eliza. Her mother was my mother's sister."

"And your aunt who beats you is your father's sister?"

"Yes, that's right!" Gwen smiled brightly.

"Do you know her direction in Edinburgh?"

"Direction?"

"She means, do you know where she lives," I said.

Gwen looked at me, all wide-eyed again.

"Why, yes. In Edinburgh! I've told you that ever so many times. I think your memory must be very bad."

Miss Clarenton glanced at me, and then at Tristram; I thought I detected a gleam of reluctant sympathy, and maybe even a hint of rueful humor. I know I saw that rueful tilt of her upper lip. I glanced at Tristram; sure enough, he had the same tilt. I wished I dared pull out my camera. When I looked back at Miss Clarenton, she was frowning a little.

"Well, Miss Gwen," said Miss Clarenton, "if you are to stay with me you must agree to behave yourself, and to do as I say."

"Oh, but Miss Clarenton, I don't want to stay here. I want to go to Edinburgh."

"And so you will, in due time. Your cousin must be found first."

"Why, I am sure you are all making it much too difficult. We shall simply go to Edinburgh and ask."

"Miss Gwen," said Tristram, "how many people do you imagine to live in Edinburgh?"

"Why," she said, "I am sure that it is at least as big as Grayrigg."

"It is considerably bigger, Miss Gwen. I—"

Miss Clarenton held up her hand.

"I'm sorry, Miss Gwen," she said, "but you will have to stay with me for a time."

"Oh, very well. But I think it is too silly."

Pot, meet kettle, I thought.

"Miss Gwen has certain pressing needs—" began Tristram, but stopped before the hand was properly up. Then he sighed, and both he and Miss Clarenton looked at me.

"I guess she hasn't anything to wear but what she has on," I said. I glanced at Tristram, who gave me a pleading look. "Oh, and Tristram says she needs to be taught how to use a gun properly." He nodded his thanks. "And she has a twisted ankle, which should be looked at."

"I shall—" said Tristram, and up came the hand.

"I shall attend to these things, Master Henderson," said Miss Clarenton.

"Thank you, miss," I said.

"And you shall be staying here as well, Master Henderson?"

"I think I should like to talk about that with Tristram," I said.

"Michael," said Tristram, and waited. But apparently he was allowed to talk to me, because the hand, it stayed down. "I have one or two things to attend to at my cottage before I set off for Edinburgh. Should you like to see it while Miss Gwen gets settled in? I can bring you back when I leave Grayrigg."

I looked at Miss Clarenton, and she nodded her agreement.

"Yes, please," I said.

Miss Clarenton politely escorted us to the door, but no more words were passed.

Chapter 27

"Well done, Michael," said Tristram. The motivator was chugging down the road, drawing us behind it, and the lake was shining gloriously in the sun to our right. I'm not sure which lake it was; they have quite a few of them around about there, and I never did get the names straight. (I tried to look it up on-line when I got home to Corey's End, but the geography is a little different—there is a Grayrigg in my England, but it is nowhere near a lake.) In the meantime, I was rejoicing in not having to talk like a ten-year-old.

"She really *doesn't* want to talk with you, does she. What's her problem?" I tried tilting my lip ruefully; it's harder than it looks. "If you don't mind me asking, that is."

Tristram showed me by example how the trick was done.

"It's easily told. She despises me for throwing in with Lord Remchester." He fell silent for a moment. "Have you read the rest of my book about the Revolution?"

"No. You suggested that I not."

"Perhaps I was misguided. I wouldn't advise you to trust it too far, but it would have provided at least the skeleton of the sequence of events. Let me see.... Well, as I've told you the Revolution was a revolt against the Thousand Families by those who wanted to take their place."

"I remember."

"Of course. In theory, the Revolution was a broad-based

movement arising equally from the old gentry in the countryside and the new merchant and industrial leaders in the cities. In practice, it arose only from the more ambitious and pushing members of either group, those who were dissatisfied with their current places in society."

"Let me guess: there were many more of those in the cities."

"Quite correct. Most of the men involved in the Steam Revolution were sons of the artisan class. They became wealthy due to their inventions, and powerful due to their wealth, but socially they were accepted by neither the Thousand Families nor by the majority of the gentry. For such men it was intolerable." He paused. "Lord Remchester is one of these, you understand." Twitch.

I nodded. I hadn't thought about it, but I'd kind of tacitly assumed it, if you know what I mean. "And Miss Clarenton's family is an old one?"

"Her mother's family, properly speaking. The Illridges are not of the nobility, but they have been the lords of the manor in Grayrigg since shortly after the Conquest, and have always been highly respected in this vicinity. A family having less in common with the New Men of the cities would be hard to imagine."

"I met Mrs. Illridge in London; I guess she's Lord Illridge's widow?"

"'Squire' is the correct term, rather than 'Lord,' not that anyone's been permitted to call him that since the Revolution. Yes, she's Squire Illridge's widow."

"How does she come to be living with Miss Clarenton?"

"It's quite the other way around. Miss Clarenton's parents died in a coaching accident when we were both small, and she came to live here, with her aunt and uncle." Tristram turned and looked sharply at me. "Who were both uncommonly kind to her —and to me as well, though I was an outsider—and who never beat her at all."

I nodded. I'd only spent half-an-hour in Mrs. Illridge's presence, but I quite liked her; and the thought of her beating anyone made my mind boggle.

"Of course, she *is* the heir. And then," Tristram continued, "when Squire Illridge passed away some years ago, Louisa—that is, Miss Clarenton—perforce took over the management of the Squire's estate, what remains of it. Her aunt is quite unsuited to the task."

"That sounds like a difficult job," I said.

"Miss Clarenton is equal to it. She has always been the heir, and as she is unmarried she always knew the task would fall to her. Squire Illridge instructed her well."

"Stockwood's not looking too good, though. I guess she's short of money."

"Yes, well. That's the other reason she won't speak to me." He shook his head, mouth tight. "Squire Illridge didn't oppose Lord Remchester, not forcibly, but he didn't support him either. There were many such scattered about the counties of England, and Lord Remchester made examples of a number of them by stripping them of the bulk of their real property and selling it to his cronies. The Illridges once held a good deal of land around and about Grayrigg; now, Stockwood is all that is left." He looked at me, to see if I was following; at my blank look, he continued, "He took the productive land, and left them the estate without any means of supporting it."

"I see. And, uh, who bought the rest of their land?"

Double tilt. Long pause. Deep breath. Then he looked me square in the eye.

"I did," he said at last.

That sounded bad. "Do you want to talk about it?" I asked after a while.

"Not at present. I would prefer to let my actions speak for themselves."

Oooookay, then.

We continued on in silence until we reached Tristram's cottage. To my surprise, Tristram didn't stop.

"I do wish to show you the cottage, and I hope you will make it your base while I am gone," he said. "But first I wish to make you known to my man of business, Harry Bartlett." And then, "We must go see him in any event: the cottage is all in Holland covers. In the ordinary course of things I would have sent him word of my coming, and all would have been arranged ahead of time. As it is, it isn't fit to live in.

"And in addition, he must find you a manservant. You have become a good hand with that taser of yours, but I should feel more comfortable in my mind if you had proper support."

I nodded vigorously. "So would I. I'd been worrying about that."

Tristram brought the phaeton to rest before a modest house in the high street, where a placard by the door read, "H. Bartlett." We dismounted, and Tristram rang the bell.

"Mr. Monocle? My word!"

I looked up; a head was extended from one of the second floor windows.

"Mr. Bartlett," said Tristram.

The head vanished, only to reappear in short order at the front door.

"I wasn't expecting you, sir, I am sure of that," said Bartlett, ushering us through a hallway and into an office with a broad desk and several chairs. He was a middle-aged man with spectacles, soberly dressed though he appeared to have donned his coat in a hurry. "Had you sent word, sir?"

"My apologies, Bartlett, but I was obliged to come in haste; and I find I am obliged to leave in haste as well," said Tristram as we sat down. "However, I wish to make known to you my cousin, Michael Henderson, who is newly arrived from the Colonies. He will be staying in my cottage while I am gone."

Bartlett showed signs of professional distress. "My word, sir! Nothing is prepared! I shall notify Mrs. Williams at once, of course, but the cottage will not be fit to live in until tomorrow."

"That is satisfactory, Bartlett. I fancy Master Henderson will be welcome to stay at Stockwood for the night."

"Truly?" Bartlett looked surprised. "My word." He looked down at his desk for a moment, and then said, "How lies the wind in that quarter, if I may be so bold, sir?"

"Unchanged; but Master Henderson and Miss Clarenton became acquainted in London. He is on much better terms with her than I am, I am glad to say."

"Ah. Well, Mrs. Williams is available to cook and clean, as usual. Is Thompson with you?"

"No, he is not; and speaking of Thompson I wish you to find someone to wait on my cousin while I am gone."

Bartlett nodded. "What kind of person are you looking for? If you wish me to find a suitable governess or a tutor, my word, I should have to send to York, or perhaps even to London."

I was still trying to decide how to explain politely that I didn't need either a governess or a tutor without blowing my cover when Tristram did it for me.

"There is no need for that, I think. As he is newly from the Colonies he can best augment his education by being out and about and so come to know how things are done in the Commonwealth. So I wish you to find him a stout man, ready for any adventure or trouble that might arise; and he should be a trustworthy guide and a man of discretion, one in whom Michael can confide if necessary."

Bartlett looked somewhat disappointed in Tristram; apparently Tristram thought so as well, for he added, "It will not all be bread and circuses, Bartlett. Master Henderson is somewhat older than he appears, and is used to studying on his own; and I have ample reading material for him in my cottage. Never fear, I shall not scant his education."

I tried to look studious (boyish intelligence +4), and Bartlett looked happier. He nodded. "In that case, I have just the person in mind—my younger son, Frederick. He's just turned eighteen, and would gladly enter your service, sir. He's a bright lad, and reasonably steady, if I do say so myself. He knows how to keep his tongue in his head. And, of course, he gets on well with Mrs. Williams."

Tristram nodded. "He will do admirably." He paused. "Now, then. Are there any matters of business we should speak of?"

Bartlett pondered. "No, sir; your properties are all in good order, and the rents are no further in arrears than is normal at this time of year. Plus there's the accumulated surplus. And you've seen for yourself how things are at Stockwood."

"Yes. Well, in that case we must be off. I have urgent business in the north country; Michael will explain it to you at his leisure. And I must show him the cottage before I go."

"Very good, sir. I'll have Freddie and Mrs. Williams there first thing in the morning; and I'll make bold to predict that all will be set in order by noon."

"Thank you, Mr. Bartlett," I said. "I expect I'll be back to speak with you sometime in the next few days."

"Call at any time, young sir. I am at your service."

"I shall enable the steam plant myself, Bartlett," said Tristram, "but your Frederick shall manage it from here on."

"Of course, sir."

As the door was closing behind us, I heard Mr. Bartlett say, "My word! My word, indeed!"

Chapter 28

The day was still bright outside, but the interior of the cottage was dark and silent and cold. The light from the open door cast a cheery rectangle on the hardwood floor of the entry way and on the gun rack just inside the door, but made it nearly impossible to see anything else.

"A moment," said Tristram. He vanished into the interior; I heard a door open, and footsteps going downstairs. Apparently the "steam plant" was in the basement. Or perhaps it was in the cellar. There was a bit of dragging things around, I think, and the sound of a heavy door closing, and then the footsteps reascended and lo! There was light.

I glanced into the rooms on either hand; the drapes were closed (and the shutters were closed on the outside, as I'd seen as we drove up), and, yes, indeed, the furniture was swathed in white covers. But Tristram didn't give me the opportunity to look around.

"You will see it all in better light tomorrow, after Freddie and Mrs. Williams put the place to rights, and then you can explore at your leisure," said Tristram, "not that there is much to explore. Though you might find the steam plant of interest; it is down in the undercroft. But today there are one or two things I wish to show you."

In the undercroft, was it? Well, la-di-da.

Tristram led the way up a flight of stairs to a hallway that ran from one side of the cottage to the other. "There are five principle rooms on this floor. The main bedrooms are on the front of the house; mine is just here, with my study across from it, and the spare bedroom is down at the other end, across from Thompson's quarters. You'll have the spare, of course, and young Freddie will use Thompson's for the time being. Thompson won't like it, but you will want him close by. The little room between my study and Thompson's quarters is the bath."

Tristram showed me the spare bedroom, which was outfitted similarly to the room I'd had in his town house: bed, wardrobe, table, chair...but also bookcase. I'd investigate that later.

"Now, come and see my study." He led me out and down the hall to the study door, which he unlocked with a key he removed from a ring in his pocket. As the door swung open I noticed it was much heavier and thicker than the door to my bedroom.

The study looked as though it would be a pleasant room if the drapes and shutters were open. There were windows on two sides, and a desk, of course, with a chair; a long, low credenza occupied the wall that was common with the hallway, and built-in bookcases lined the wall that ran between the study and the bath. A guest chair stood in the corner, by the credenza.

"Now, attend closely," said Tristram. "First, I close and bar the door." I thought he was speaking quaintly, and then I realized that he wasn't talking about the lock he'd unlocked earlier, but about a heavy deadbolt mounted on the back of the door with iron straps. The deadbolt extended the full width of the door, and had cog-teeth on its lower edge; and as he turned a metal wheel mounted just below it the deadbolt slid at least four inches into an iron socket in the door jamb. "Now you try."

"Okay..."

The bolt was heavier than it looked, but well greased; it took a fair amount of strength to turn the wheel to slide it open and then closed again. I managed it without too much difficulty. Mind you, I was careful to let my right arm do most of the work.

"Next, come over here." He knelt down in front of the first bookcase on the left, and put a hand under the kick rail. There was a quiet thunk, and the bookcase swung out into the room like a door. I couldn't see what was behind it, because the bookcase itself blocked my view, so I walked around and stood between the desk and the window. From there I could see that the recess behind the bookcase held four shelves at the top, with a number of drawers below. All of the shelves were empty.

"This is where I kept my correspondence and other papers for my work with Lord Remchester when I was in residence here in Grayrigg," he said, standing. "There was never that much of it here, as I was so rarely in residence, but one must keep up appearances. Of course it is all gone now." He closed the swinging bookcase, which latched, and waved his hand at the hidden switch.

I knelt down where he had, and felt under the kick rail. Near the left end I felt a lever, or button; I pulled on it, and felt and heard it unlatch. Standing, I swung the bookcase out as Tristram had.

"Very good. Now, one more thing." He crossed to the window, which had a wide sill, and did something I couldn't quite see. I looked at him, puzzled, until he gestured toward the open bookcase. I turned, and watched as the hidden unit with the shelves and drawers slid slowly and silently to the right, revealing a dark opening. "There is a push-valve under the sill. A second press will close it again."

I knelt down by the window, and looked up under the sill. Sure enough, there was a pushbutton tucked into a neat recess on the underside.

"And there's a steam line running through the walls?"

"Just so."

The sill was well below eye-level, even for me, and the button was clear across the room from the bookcases. Unless you knew it was there, you'd never go looking for it.

I pressed the button, and watched the hidden shelves slide back into place.

"Got it," I said. When it was fully closed, Tristram nodded approvingly.

"Now, open it again and have a look. There is a valve for the lights on the right as you go in."

I turned and looked at his expression, which was serious, but somehow serene. Then I did as he said.

The hidden room—or, perhaps, the hidden closet—was even smaller than the hidden room in Tristram's town house, being not much more than three feet square. The doorway was on one side; the other three sides were lined with shelves, and the shelves were lined with a variety of things. There were notebooks of different sizes, including a shelf of serious looking ledgers, and rows of wooden and cardboard boxes. The right-hand set of shelves was about half-empty; the rest were snugly packed. It smelled musty, like old books, but it was surprisingly dust-free. I took a good look around, and stepped back out into the study.

"Now close it all up," said Tristram, so I crossed the room and pressed the button; and when the shelves had slid back into place I swung the first bookcase closed until it latched.

"Note well," he said. "The bookcase can be unlatched and swung open at any time; but the sliding unit behind will only open if the bolt on the study door is fully engaged."

"So even someone who finds the first hidey-hole probably won't think to look for the second," I said. "And if they do find the button they probably won't find out what it does. Nice. So what's in there that's so secret? And why show it to me?"

"What is in there, Michael, is the story of the Revolution as it truly was. I had no choice but to write Lord Remchester's history for him; but I could not bear to leave it at that. And as Remchester's secretary, certain…information…came naturally to my hand. My plan is to arrange for the contents of that room to be published after Remchester's death…though, I hope, rather before my own.

"And I show it to you because I wish you to read it. You will no doubt hear rumors and tales about me while I am gone, and I should wish you to know the truth of things. It is not always an admirable truth, I fear; but if you are to think poorly of me I should prefer it to be because of what I have done, rather than what others will say I have done." Tilt. "I should start with the notebooks, if I were you. The ledgers contain records of certain accounts, and the boxes contain various documents and corroborating material." Twitch. "Should you find them too dry, as who would not, my *official* history is available on the, ah, *open* shelves."

He sighed. "Until now, only two have known about that room: myself, and Thompson, who helped me construct it. And now you. I trust you will keep its existence a secret."

Then he had me slide the bolt back; and after I'd locked the door behind us with the key he gave me, he led me back down the stairs.

Chapter 29

"I hope you will look in on Miss Gwen once in a while," said Tristram on our way back to Stockwood. "It would be rude in the extreme to require Miss Clarenton to have her sole care."

"Yeah, it seems that way to me, too. How long do you think your errand will take?"

"At least a week, and probably longer. The roads are not so good in the North Country, and of course there is the needle to find in the haystack of Edinburgh. But I think you will find you are fully occupied."

"If...when...I have to tase somebody, what should I do with them?"

"I would apply that admirable substance you showed me... duct tape, was it?" Twitch.

I rolled my eyes. "Well, yes. And then what? Seriously, Tristram, you're as bad as Miss Gwen."

"Hah! At Stockwood, I would inform Miss Clarenton, or whichever of the servants comes most easily to hand; the individual in question will send to Grayrigg for the beadle. In Grayrigg, I'd inform young Frederick, who again will inform the beadle. I am well-known here, if somewhat equivocally; I have made you known at both Stockwood and in Grayrigg; there should be no complications."

"All right; and if there's trouble anyway? With Miss Gwen around, anything might happen."

"If necessary, you will simply have to take Bartlett into your confidence. It may take some doing, mind you; Harry Bartlett is a worthy man, but he is not as unnaturally gifted with imagination as I am. I suggest you show him your camera, if necessary."

"Hmmm. Here's to hoping there's no need; the battery is almost dead."

"Quite," said Tristram. "In the meantime, you will need a way to get about. I must take the phaeton with me, but there is a small motivator-and-cart at the cottage. I have not used it in some time, but Bartlett will have ensured that it is in working order as a matter of course."

"Good. I was worried about that. I see a few horses around here, and I really don't want to learn to ride one."

"No?"

"Who knows what one of your horses might do to an unsuspecting newbie? I don't want to get eaten."

Twitch.

"And what about Lord Remchester? Should I worry about him while you're gone?"

Tristram was silent for a moment, then spoke.

"As long as Remchester is content to watch, you should have no reason to worry. Otherwise, you shall simply have to trust in your own resourcefulness."

"I was afraid you'd say that."

They were watching for us at Stockwood, and when the phaeton stopped in front of the manor house Augustus emerged with a footman to retrieve my bags and Miss Gwen's two band boxes. (The footman retrieved the bags; Augustus supervised magisterially.)

Tristram frowned as we dismounted, then took me aside. "Michael, I would prefer not to see Miss Clarenton," he said, "but all the same, I must discover whether Miss Gwen knows anything more about her cousin. Would you be so kind as to—"

"You mean, you'd prefer not to waste any more time interrogating such an unsatisfactory subject. But yes, I'll go ask."

"Thank you, Michael." The early afternoon sun glinted on his monocle as he turned away. I felt sorry for him; he was bent on doing the right thing at great cost to himself, and Miss Clarenton still wouldn't give him the time of day.

Then I followed Augustus and the footman into the house, where I found Miss Clarenton manifestly not peering at Tristram through the curtains. She had her back to them, in fact. I pretended not to notice.

"Master Henderson," she said.

"Please call me 'Michael,' Miss Clarenton," I said. "When people call me 'master' I don't know where to look, and Cousin Tristram said I might be called Michael among friends."

"Very well, Michael." Tilt. Side-long glance at the curtains. Well, I *had* mentioned Tristram.

"Please," I said, "has Miss Gwen said anything more about her cousin in Edinburgh? Cousin Tristram needs to know."

"Why, yes, she has." Tilt, but this time with a lady-like glare towards the ceiling that I was pretty sure was aimed at Miss Gwen. "Oh! Oh!" she said in a voice quite unlike her usual, very breathless and giddy, "Cousin Eliza is a great lady, she must be, for she was dressed in the first stare of fashion when Miss Gwen saw her, and so she must live in a grand house, and surely everyone in Edinburgh will know who she is. And oh! If Mr. Monocle will only return her little gun, which he had in his pocket, she would be quite able to go to Edinburgh and help find her. Oh!" Then she sighed, deeply.

Her mustache didn't twitch, since she didn't have one, and neither did her upper lip, because that would be foolish and un-ladylike. But I bet her lip was thinking about it.

"That's our Gwen all right, miss."

"But of significant detail she said nothing to the point. She is asleep at the moment, or I would let you ask her yourself."

"Oh, well. I'll let him know. Oh, and Cousin Tristram means to return her pistol; I'll remind him. But she really does need training in how to use it safely."

"I shall see to that myself, as soon her injury permits."

I bet she would, too.

"One other thing, miss. Cousin Tristram would prefer me to stay in his cottage while he is gone; he's engaged Mr. Bartlett's son Frederick to wait on me. But the cottage won't be ready until tomorrow, so may I stay here tonight, please?"

"Certainly, Master—certainly, Michael. I shall be pleased to have you as often as you like." She seemed to mean it, too.

"Thank you, miss. Now I have to go give Tristram the bad news."

She nodded, and escorted me to the door; and then, to my surprise, escorted me out to the phaeton, stopping a few yards away from it. Naturally, I kept going.

Tristram was standing by the motivator with his back to the manor house, looking out over the countryside. Stockwood was on rising ground, so he had a fine view of the lake. At least, he had a fine view of *a* lake. Whether it was the same lake I'd seen earlier, I'm not sure.

"No luck," I said to Tristram when I reached him. "Cousin Eliza is a fine lady and dresses well. Oh, and you need to give me Gwen's little gun so Miss Clarenton can teach her how to use it properly."

"Ah," he said. "I have it in my pocket." Tilt. Twitch. "Here it is." And he handed it to me.

"Thank you," I said. I…well, I put it in my pocket. What else would I do with it?

"Good luck on your search," I said, finally, trying not to acknowledge that sinking feeling in the pit of my stomach.

"Thank you, Michael."

He was silent for a few moments, still looking out at the landscape.

"Stockwood was one of the great joys of my existence when I was young, Michael," he said at last. "It pains me to see it looking this way."

"You may rectify that whenever you choose, Mr. Monocle," said Miss Clarenton from behind us. "Is it not yours to do with as you will?" I was surprised by the bitterness in her voice.

Tristram turned. I don't think he'd realized she was there, as his mustache was more profoundly tilted than I'd ever seen before.

"If it were truly in my power to have things as I wish them," he said, "then things would be far different, Miss Clarenton. But still, they need not be as they are at present. I have perfect confidence in your management."

"If you thought you could salve your conscience by sharing your ill-gotten gains with me, you were gravely mistaken, Mr. *Monocle*." Her tone was sharp enough to slice bread, and angry enough to mangle the remains. "And why should I spend our scarce household funds on a property from which we might be evicted whenever it suits your purpose?"

Aha. She'd been holding *that* in for quite some time, or I was no judge.

Mr. Monocle looked at her for a long moment. I could see the pain in his eyes, and I think maybe she could too, because she looked away.

"It is true that I once hoped to make my home here," he said. "But your departure from Stockwood has never formed any part of my plans, Miss Clarenton."

And with that he climbed into the phaeton, flicked the reins, and drove north.

Chapter 30

I enjoy people-watching to a surprising extent for a guy who spends so much of his time alone; I started doing it as a means of self-defense back in the day, and it's become habitual. But I have to say, the Tristram and Louisa show was even more fascinating than the Tristram and Gwen show, and I was looking forward to writing my nightly letter to Bernie even more than usual.

But it was sad, too. There had been real anger in Miss Clarenton's voice, and real regret in Tristram's, and it was a little shocking.

Apparently Miss Clarenton found it shocking, too, for she was rooted to the spot for several minutes after Tristram's dramatic exit. I don't know whether her lips tilted ruefully during that period of time or not because when I looked at her and saw her expression, I was the one who had to look away. Then she ventured a quiet, "Come inside, Michael," and I walked back to the house with her.

Augustus met us at the door, having returned from watching the footman deliver my stuff to my room.

"Are you all right, miss?" he said, voice warm with concern and thin with worry.

"I'm fine, Augustus," she said, in the same quiet tone she'd used when asking me to come inside, and I immediately saw that A, she wasn't, B, he didn't believe her, but C, he wasn't sure what he could do about it. (These old family retainers have the most expressive faces!) But I didn't have time to reflect on it, because my ears were assailed by a cry from Mrs. Illridge, who was descending the stairway.

"Master Henderson! Why, I am so surprised, I do declare, I never expected to see your face out here in the country! Is young Tristram with you?"

"He's just left, ma'am," I said. I smiled at her as broadly as I could manage without it looking creepy. It was maybe a +5.

"Oh, it is too, too bad," she said. "I had a sick headache this morning and so I took to my bed, you know, it is the only thing when you're not feeling quite the thing, that is what my husband always said, though personally he preferred the hair of the dog more often than not, and justly so, but I am quite sure that if I had known he was here I would have found that I felt quite the thing in no time. Tristram, that is, not my husband. His conversation is such a pleasure to me!"

There was a stifled noise, and then an "I beg your pardon, Michael. Mrs. Illridge will look after you," and then Miss Clarenton proceeded up the stairway at speed. Mrs. Illridge watched her go with a considering look, and then turned back to me.

"My niece has a sick headache herself, I shouldn't wonder. Young Tristram always does have that effect on her, these days. Did they have words?"

"Sort of. I guess."

"Ah. Well, young man, isn't it time that you should be eating something? Lads your age are always hungry, and older lads, too, come to think of it. My husband always was. Come with me, Master Henderson, and Augustus will find us something sustaining."

"It's Michael, if you please, ma'am. Cousin Tristram said my friends might use my given name."

"Michael, then," said Mrs. Illridge, pleased. "Now, Augustus, you will find us in the drawing room. Please bring something more sustaining than those little cakes Louisa favors. After all, we have a young man to feed!"

"Certainly, ma'am," said Augustus, who looked glad to be given a task within his capabilities.

"Now, then, Michael," she said. "Do you play backgammon?"

Dinner that evening was not what I had expected. I had expected Miss Clarenton to be kind and warm, Mrs. Illridge to be gossipy and cheerful, and Miss Gwen to be grumpy and inane. Instead, Miss Clarenton was quiet and distracted, Mrs. Illridge was quiet and watchful, and Miss Gwen was quiet and, not to put too fine a point on it, miserable. I'd thought I'd known how Miss Gwen behaved when she was unhappy: with torrents of verbal abuse erupting periodically from seas of simmering resentment. She didn't go for quiet; she went for loud, persistent, and nonsensical. Yet her she was, hang-dog, looking down at her plate, looking like she wanted to be alone.

I'd have expected Miss Clarenton to be all over that. I'd experienced her good heart first hand, and also her severe attitude with foolishness; I'd expected her to insist that Gwen cheer up and enjoy her dinner, and to be full of plans for the next day. Instead she was looking off into space as she chewed her food, and she said no more than was necessary for politeness' sake.

And then Mrs. Illridge—but I should go back a bit.

I'd spent the early afternoon with Mrs. Illridge. I spent the first bit getting myself around the massive roast beef sandwich that was Mrs. Illridge's idea of "sustaining food," while she had something rather lighter, and after that she taught me to play backgammon. (For the record, the sandwich was delicious. It wasn't a cheeseburger, but it was the closest thing I'd had in weeks.) She was a good teacher, and between explaining to me about stones and points and blots and bearing off and gammons and backgammons and doubles and so forth she kept up a steady flow of local gossip.

I did manage to get a few words in; I figured I needed to warn her about Miss Gwen, since she'd been indisposed on Gwen's arrival. So I explained about Miss Gwen, and how we'd met up with her, and how we'd told people she was my sister but she wasn't really, and where Tristram had gone. She listened to it all with great interest, and then the sorry tale inspired her to new heights. I heard about several not very similar adventures that had happened to people she'd known during her girlhood, or at least to their remote relations, my gracious, and all of them ended well, well, except for *that* one, but we don't talk about *that* one, dear, no, that was an extraordinary case, not at all like your Miss Gwen's case, and didn't it all make you think? I agreed that it did, it really did.

She didn't ask me about myself, precisely—I think she thought it rude to question a guest. But she had a habit of dropping subtle queries at the end of her sentences, invitations to agree with her about something and possibly give examples of my own. At one point she mentioned a local dispute over a collision between a cow and a motivator down on the high street, "And what the cow was doing on the high street, I am sure I shall never know, Michael, but people will do the oddest things. Don't you find it's the same in the Colonies?" Or "I am so glad you had such a pleasant trip up from the City. It was quite different when I was a girl, of course, all slow cramped stages that smelled of tired horses and had to stop every fifteen miles. That was before I married my husband, you know, for he would never have sent me to London on a common stage, dear me, no, but a coaching inn was a coaching inn however you happened to arrive there. Did you have to travel on a stage like that to New Hamsterdam?"

I wasn't sure whether she was asking because she was merely curious, or to give me opportunities to participate in the conversation, or because she was trying to pump me without making me suspicious. Too late, if so. I'm *always* suspicious.

Not that I could have given her satisfactory answers in any event. I still had no real idea how things were in the Colonies, nor any real notion of how I would have gotten to New Hamsterdam had I ever gone to New Hamsterdam, so instead I enthused about the accommodations on the steam leviathan I would have boarded in New Hamsterdam had I ever boarded a steam leviathan, and all about the adventures I might have had on it and the way I might have befriended the power room mates; and when I'd exhausted that I talked up the dangers of the Western Wilderness, from carnivorous lichen to drop bears, and how we all had to be *so* careful about where we sat down and what trees we walked under. Mrs. Illridge thought it all sounded perfectly homey, and that she'd quite like to go visit someday.

After an hour or so of backgammon I commenced to yawn somewhat ostentatiously, and she had Augustus show me to my room. Once there I wrote a letter to Bernie and sent it off; and then I actually did take a nap.

I was awakened by a bonging noise; and a few minutes later Augustus came to tell me that that was the gong, which meant it was time for dinner.

"Just come as you are, lad," he said, smiling. "There's no need to dress for dinner, as Miss Louisa hasn't opened the formal dining room these past five years. I remember the old days: the family and their guests would gather in the drawing room, all wearing their best, and go into dinner together, two-by-two, the ladies on the arms of the gentlemen. Now it is just the two ladies, and they take their meals in the breakfast parlor."

So I combed my hair as quickly as I could, and then followed Augustus parlor-wards.

The breakfast parlor was on the eastern side of the house, and had broad windows to let in the morning light. I suppose that had been an essential feature of a breakfast room before the Steam Revolution and the advent of aetheric power. Tonight the curtains were drawn, and the room was brightly lit by a fixture over the table. The steam tubes were plainly visible on the wall, just as they were in Tristram's home.

I found the three ladies—I use the term charitably in Miss Gwen's case—already seated, and I apologized to Miss Clarenton as I took my seat across from Miss Gwen. Mrs. Illridge was to my right, with Miss Clarenton across from her.

"I'm sorry I'm late, miss. I was napping."

"Oh, Michael, there you are," said Miss Clarenton, seeming to notice me for the first time. "It's quite all right. Augustus, you may serve."

"Yes, ma'am."

"Good evening, Michael," said Mrs. Illridge. "You are well rested, I hope? When a boy wants a nap that is no time to stand in his way, no it isn't, for surely he needs it." I assured her I was, and she said little more. She wasn't distracted, mind you, not off in another world; I rather thought that the rest of us had her full and complete attention. But what ever she might be thinking about us all, she wasn't saying.

Miss Gwen was staring at the table, as I've said, and she didn't look up.

We began with ox-tail soup, so Augustus told me as he put the bowl in front of me. Miss Clarenton ate quietly and neatly; Mrs. Illridge ate quietly, neatly, and watchfully; and Miss Gwen stared at her bowl. The soup was good, but once I'd finished it I had nothing to do but watch Miss Gwen brooding on the other side of the table. And I have to say, this was full-on world-class the-world-can-go-to-hell-for-all-of-me brooding. I almost wanted to jump home and get some Cheerios for her. I might have, too, if I'd been sure I could get back to Stockwood in any reasonable amount of time.

Eventually Augustus returned with some fish, by which time I'd exhausted my patience.

"What's the matter, Gwen?" I asked. "You're not usually so quiet. Is your ankle bothering you?"

Miss Clarenton didn't seem to hear me, though Mrs. Illridge gave me a quick look; and Miss Gwen said, "He went without me. And he took my little gun with him." She didn't look up, but spoke directly to her untouched fish, which had replaced her untouched soup.

"What's the big deal with your little gun, anyway? It isn't much of a gun, after all."

"My father gave it to me," she said. "To keep me safe."

Oh. I might have winced a little.

"But Tristram didn't take it with him," I said. "I have it right here, in my—he gave it to me before he left."

I thought she'd go ballistic, or maybe leap across the table, but she just looked up, eyes widening.

"May I have it back now, please?"

I pulled it out of my pocket. "Ought I to give it to her, Miss Clarenton?"

Miss Clarenton seemed to wake up a little at the sound of her name, and her eyes focussed for maybe the third time since the meal began. "What was that, Michael?"

"I have Miss Gwen's little gun here. Ought I to give it to her? Only, she hasn't had any lessons, yet."

Miss Clarenton pursed her lips. "Give it to me, please, Michael. Miss Gwen, you may have it back to keep when you have learned how to manage it properly." So I stood up and handed it across the table to Miss Clarenton, butt first. She laid it on the table next to her plate…and was soon lost in thought again. Miss Gwen watched the little gun like a hawk as I passed it across, and then stared at her fish. She actually had a bite or two after that.

Then we had some beef, and then a sweet, which Mrs. Illridge and I enjoyed; and then Mrs. Illridge bid us good night after a lingering glance at her niece. A minute or two later Miss Clarenton rose silently and wandered off without a word, and there were just the two of us. Well, and Augustus who watched them go, and sighed, and then carried off the remaining dishes.

I looked at Gwen, and she looked at me; and then *she* rose and left the room, limping only slightly.

In her distraction Miss Clarenton had left the little gun on the table, and Gwen scooped it up as she went by. She didn't look at it, but just casually let an arm dangle and snatch it as she passed. I frowned, but I wasn't about to fight her for it. It was hers, anyway.

Then I found my way back up to my room and settled down to read more about the Pathfounder and the dangers of the Western Wilderness.

Chapter 31

I woke up late; or, actually, I woke up early and lay in bed thinking about Tristram and Miss Clarenton until it got late. He was sweet on her, that I knew. I'm not terribly observant about such things, but in this case I hadn't had to be; and anyway, his comment about living at Stockwood and Miss Clarenton not leaving had been about as direct a declaration of his attachment as I could well imagine, especially given that she wasn't willing to listen to him. And I'd seen signs of past friendship, from the little looks they sent each other while listening to Gwen to that odd tilt of the lip that they shared.

And yet, Tristram's declaration seemed to have taken Miss Clarenton by surprise. And more, it had distracted her for the remainder of the day. I could only conclude that she really hadn't known how he felt, and now that she did it was making her... thoughtful.

Had Tristram never told her before? That struck me as unlikely. But on the other hand, when had he had an opportunity? She hadn't been willing to receive him in many, many years; he'd only gotten in the door this time because of me. Come to think of it, that took in our morning visit in London as well. And he couldn't very well have protested undying devotion while she was preventing me from bleeding to death in Remchester park. Not at all the done thing, you know. Not good *ton*.

But before that…what had happened to damage their friendship?

It was the influence of Lord Remchester, of course, at least in part; Tristram had said so himself. And Tristram had mentioned that the ladies who chased him were after his position, and the ladies who weren't wouldn't speak with him. I didn't think I was stretching things to put his childhood friend as the chief—and maybe the only important—member of that second group. So she hadn't liked him going off with Lord Remchester. He'd been sixteen then, if I remembered correctly; too young to have made a formal offer of marriage, and—

Oh. Of course. At that time, he was nothing more than a poor relation of the Earl of Uxbridge. He'd had a gentleman's education, but not a married gentleman's income; he had no prospects; and he had no expectations of further aid. Miss Clarenton was the Squire's niece, and heir to the manor. If he loved Miss Clarenton even then, and I daresay he did, I've no doubt he kept that information to himself. In that time and place and under those circumstances he had no business asking a young lady for her heart; and knowing Tristram, he'd have taken that seriously.

And if nevertheless she was expecting him to declare his love one day, and I daresay she was, and then he went off with her uncle's enemy…would that be enough to account for her continued anger and disdain?

I didn't know. I mean, me, what do I know about romance? I'd recently read a few books that I was already trusting farther than I trusted them, if you know what I mean, and anyway they weren't meant as guide books. And Bernie, well, Bernie; some days I found it very hard to account for Bernie's continuing presence in my life. From her point of view, I mean. From my point of view…there aren't words enough.

Still, I thought there must be more to it, something I was missing. And it had to be in the past; and I rather thought it had to do with the ownership of Stockwood.

Tristram had more or less begged me to dig into his past

activities when he showed me the secret room in his cottage. I thought I'd see those activities and raise them with some investigations of my own.

In the meantime, I was a growing boy and a fine upstanding young man and in need of a sustaining breakfast, so I got dressed and went to look for one.

I found it in the breakfast parlor, all neatly laid out under covers on the sideboard: cold eggs, cold ham, cold toast, warm butter, marmalade, and some cold fishy things I thought might be kippers. I'd call that the penalty for being late, except that I suspected it was normal. I took some of everything but the kippers.

No one else was in evidence, but I'd brought my book with me, so I took my food and sat down to read about floods on the Great Western River as experienced by the noble and intrepid Pathfounder. Apparently the flood waters could extend for miles through the trees on either side of the river, and woe betide you if a storm caught you in the flood plain without a boat during the rainy season. Short of climbing a tree, there was often no way to get out of the water; and you *really* wanted to get out of the water. According to Cowper Madisen, the local children had a saying: "The guppies will get you if you don't watch out!" However, our intrepid Pathfounder managed to extricate himself from danger before he was more than slightly nibbled, and built a raft from the boughs of the tree using his belt knife and strips of the belt it had used to hang from, for he was a man of infinite resource and sagacity.

When I was done eating, I sipped at a cup of tea and considered my next move. It was mid-morning, and I wasn't expecting Tristram's cottage to be ready until noon. For that matter, I wasn't sure how I was going to get to the cottage. It was farther than I wanted to walk, especially armed with nothing more than a taser, and I didn't have a bicycle. But I tabled that after my second cup of tea. Either Freddie Bartlett would come collect me, or I'd beg a ride from Miss Clarenton; and after that

I'd just use the motivator-and-cart to go back and forth.

But all that could wait; I had a couple of hours to fill, and I wanted to know more about Tristram's childhood. But who to ask? I pondered my choices.

Sometimes the indirect approach is best. There was nowhere to put my dirty dishes, so I tucked my book under my arm, picked up my plate and teacup, and went looking for Augustus.

"Master Michael! Whatever are you doing with those dishes?"

I'd run the butler to ground in a small room on a narrow corridor behind a fabric-covered door in the main hallway. I had figured that the fabric, which was fastened to the door with a neat pattern of brass tacks, was more than likely baize; and if it was baize then, according to my recent reading, I ought to find the servants on the other side of it. It was red baize when it should have been green baize, according to my sources; assuming it was actually baize. It was a felty kind of material, and the tacks were nice and shiny.

Behind the door was the corridor, and off the corridor was the small room, and in the small room was an armchair, and in the armchair sat Augustus in his shirtsleeves, book in hand. His coat was hanging on a hook by the door. There were some pictures of horses on the wall, and a little desk with ledgers and notes and things, with an aetheric light hung over it, and a small fireplace in which a fire crackled. It was simple, but cosy.

He looked shocked to see me. I gave my brightest and friendliest ten-year-old smile and best Colonial manners.

"Hi, Mr. Augustus! It didn't seem right to just leave these on the table, and I figured you'd know where I should put them."

"Indeed, Master Michael, you *should* have left them on the table. Crosley would have collected them in due course." And so saying he climbed to his feet and insisted that I hand them to him.

"Oh, it was no trouble," I said, handing them over. "I'm glad to help!"

His face said that it was really no help at all, but I didn't let on. Instead I hopped up onto a stool that stood in one corner, and asked the question I'd really come about.

"Mister Augustus?"

"Just Augustus, lad!" he said, standing in the doorway of his little office, plate and teacup in hand. He was half turned away from me, and looked at me over his shoulder.

"OK, Augustus, then. I guess you knew my cousin Tristram when he was a little boy?"

"Know him! Of course I did. Didn't he grow up in Grayrigg, lad, from the time he was small?"

"I thought you had," I said, coloring my voice with all of the boyish enthusiasm and satisfaction that I could muster. It was +6 at least. "So please, could you tell me…."

"Yes, lad?"

"What was he like? I haven't known him for very long, you see. And I don't quite like to ask Miss Clarenton."

Augustus regarded me gravely for a moment, the enormity of my presence warring with his obvious liking for and approval of Tristram. At last Tristram won; and setting the plate and cup on his desk he resumed his seat and looked into space.

"Well, I'll tell you, lad. He was a lot like you, d'ye see. Smart as paint, he was, but he didn't seem to know it himself. We all knew he was the grandson of old Uxbridge—did he tell you about that, lad? For I don't want to go talking out of school."

"Yes, he did, and how Thompson came and brought him here after his mother died and his father…after his father went away." I stopped myself before letting my chin quiver. Ten-year-olds aren't much for pathos. Had I really been a ten-year-old, I'd have found Tristram's story delightfully gruesome.

"Just so, lad. Well, we knew he was Uxbridge's grandson from Thompson, or we wouldn't have known it at all, for young Tristram never said a word about it, once he was old enough to talk, that is. Smart he was, and cheerful, and always willing to be pleased—you see all kinds in service, lad, and a master who is willing to be pleased is a treasure to be cherished, though I say it as shouldn't.

"He had a talent for making friends, too. Many's the time I've known him to sneak through the red baize door when no one was looking and come and perch right there on that stool, right where you're sitting. Seeing you there, well, it takes me back, lad."

"How did he come to Stockwood?" I asked. "It's a long way from Grayrigg to get here."

"That was Thompson's doing, lad; or, I suppose, old Uxbridge's. The Squire (for I'll not call him anything else, not here in my own cubby) had a letter of introduction from Uxbridge. He wanted your cousin brought up as a gentleman, and truly, lad, you cannot learn to be a gentleman all by yourself."

Augustus puffed up a little. "And I'm proud to say, lad, that the Illridges have been the squires of this manor for longer than anyone can remember. Young Tristram once told me that the Illridges have been at Stockwood since the Conquest, lad, and you can't say fairer than that. So this is where young Tristram learned to shoot, and to ride, and to treat young ladies with respect." He pursed his lips at that final clause, but didn't elaborate. "There's no one could have taught him better how to be a country gentleman than the Squire, lad. And after he came into our lives, why…we found we couldn't do without him."

He looked into space for some moments after that.

"Well, we'll not be teaching you to ride, for there are no more horses at Stockwood, and I collect that Tristram has already taught you how to drive a motivator. But I expect that Miss Clarenton will want your help teaching Miss Gwen to shoot." He winced, very slightly.

"I can do that, Mr. Augustus!" I said, cheerfully, not that I really wanted to spend more time with Gwen. But I owed it to Tristram, and it would also mean spending more time with Miss Clarenton—and who knows what she might let drop.

"Now then, lad, it is time for my rounds." The interview was over.

"Thank you, Mr. Augustus," I said, sliding off of the stool. I hadn't found out what I wanted, not yet, but I'd laid a foundation.

"And you just leave your plate on the table in future, lad," he said, as I slipped boyishly out the door. But there was a smile in his voice.

Chapter 32

I still had some time left after that; and as it seemed much the most likely thing that Freddie Bartlett would come and get me, I took my book to the front garden to find a spot where I could read and wait for him.

I found a kind of bower, I guess you'd call it, not far from the front door of the manor house: a wooden bench tucked into the hedge that divided the drive from the rest of the grounds. At a guess it had been put there to be a comfortable place to wait while one's carriage was brought around, but it was perfect for my purposes. It was both comfortable and shady; it had a direct view of the road and drive; and I had a thick hedge at my back. It had been several days since the breakfast attack in Wooster, and I was worried that I was due for another—and without Tristram's backup. There in the bower, there was no way for an attacker to sneak up behind me. He'd have to come in head on, and I had my taser to hand.

Better yet, the hedge was considerably overgrown. If I sat with my legs up on the bench, I could see out without being easy to see. When you're small for your age, that's a good thing.

So I settled in with my back to one end of the bench and my face to the road, and settled down to read. The light was a little dim, but I managed.

Traveling under Tristram's protection led me into bad habits, because I became so engrossed in the book that I didn't see

Freddie coming. The Pathfounder had survived the floods and the vicious colonial guppies; he'd lost a horse to a prairie dog swarm in a feeding frenzy; and he was on the verge of being fed to a hill of fire ants (as a sacrifice to a native tribe's six-armed goddess of doom, natch) when the sound of tires crunching on the gravel announced Freddie's arrival. Typical. Company always shows up just when you get to the good part.

He drove past me on a bright yellow motivator, which he pulled to a halt in front of the manor house. He was of the tall persuasion—exactly the kind of guy I used to lie awake plotting the destruction of, in days gone by—but I was pleased to see that he drove the motivator with an air of confidence and experience. I use the words "drove the motivator" advisedly, because he was in fact riding postilion.

The motivator was pulling a rather rustic-looking two-wheeled farm cart. The cart had none of the flair or elegance of Tristram's phaeton. Despite having a bench seat at the front it was clearly intended for hauling cargo—groceries and other such household goods, say, or perhaps sometimes more bucolic materials—rather than passengers. Worse, it lacked the hookups and instruments that would let one control the motivator from its seat, so Freddie was riding postilion from necessity rather than choice.

I stood up, closing my book, and said, "Hi."

Freddie turned around at the sound of my voice, but I was still in the shade of the bower, and in the bright sun I was well nigh invisible. He climbed down from the motivator, and pulled a shotgun out of a rack by the postilion seat and slung it over his shoulder. There was no hesitation, but rather second nature; Freddie, I rather thought, would no more leave home unarmed than he would leave home unclothed.

"Master Henderson," he said once he located me, and after he trotted over he executed a half bow and came up smiling. He was neatly dressed and properly armed, and I suspected him of being one of those fellows who wakes up feeling cheerful.

"Yes, I'm Michael Henderson. You must be Freddie Bartlett."

"Yes, Master Henderson. Your cottage is ready, and so am I—to bring you home to Grayrigg, I mean. Uh, at your convenience."

I hid a smile. He was trying to do the servant thing, but he hadn't had any practice. Perhaps if I were more imposing he'd have been cowed into maintaining the proper staid and servile demeanor; as it was, his natural good spirits were bubbling over, and I realized with a start that this was an adventure for him as much as it was for me.

"But you mustn't call me 'Freddie,' you know," he said. "You must call me 'Bartlett.'"

"But isn't your name 'Freddie'?"

"Oh, yes, that's what everyone else calls me. But it will go hard with me if my father discovers I'm encouraging you to call me 'Freddie.' He would say I was taking liberties."

"But you're not encouraging me to call you 'Freddie.' I'm choosing to call you 'Freddie.'" I gave him a +3 look of boyish quizzical perplexity. "If I'm the master and you're the servant, why can't I call you whatever I like?"

"You can, of course," he said, smiling even more broadly. "I'm afraid I *am* taking shocking liberties in even presuming to instruct you. But I'm in a cleft stick, you know. On the one hand I'm supposed to maintain the proper distance; but on the other my father told me you weren't used to servants, having been raised in the Colonies, and that I should do what I could to show you how we do things in the Commonwealth."

I needed to know that.

"But 'Bartlett' sounds so stuffy," I said. "What if I call you 'Bartlett' when anyone else is around, then, and 'Freddie' the rest of the time?"

"If that's what you wish, Master Henderson. But it would be a kindness if you'd simply call me 'Bartlett,' as I'm going to have enough trouble learning to answer to it as it is. When I hear it I look around for my father." He made a show of looking around.

"Well, OK. If you say so, Bartlett."

"Thank you, Master Henderson."

"Do you have to call me that? My name is Michael."

He cocked his head. "Why, yes. I think I do."

"Oh. What about 'Master Michael,' then, instead of 'Master Henderson'?"

He considered. "Are you the eldest? Or do you have an older brother?"

I frowned. That was an interesting question, and one that had been on my mind since my chat with Augustus. "I'm not sure," I said. "I think I might have had a brother once."

"Oh! How sad for your parents." A look of commiseration passed across his face, and was gone. "But if you are now the eldest, then I must certainly address you as 'Master Henderson.' That's what the books say."

"Well, as far as I'm concerned you can call me 'Master Michael.'"

"All the same, sir," he said brightly.

"Sir! That's almost worse than 'Master Henderson.'"

"It is a hard life we lead here on this earth, Master Henderson, and we must simply make the best of it that we can."

From some people that would have been prim, sententious, and exceedingly irritating; but Freddie said it with the air of letting me in on the biggest joke in the world, and so cheerfully that I found myself laughing. I had the notion that he was quoting his father, and I found myself liking him despite his enormous height.

"Very well, Bartlett." I shook my head, and decided not to slant my lip for fear he might misunderstand. "Is that Mr. Monocle's cart? He told me he had one."

"It is, sir, freshly washed and at your service."

"Then I suppose I'd best collect my things."

"Oh, no, sir!" said Freddie. "I see Crosley waiting at the door, and he and I will make short work of it. Leave it to us, while you go and say your goodbyes."

"Oh. Is that how it works?"

"Most certainly, sir."

"All right, then, Bartlett."

He beamed at me. "There you go, Master Henderson. You're quite getting the hang of it. Shall I pack your book, sir?"

I nodded, and handed it to him, and he trotted off and vanished into the house behind Crosley.

I found Miss Clarenton in her library, working on accounts or some such. At least, she was sitting at the desk, with a ledger in front of her and a pen in her hand, but when I entered she was staring into space. She might have been thinking, but she looked tired and I thought she might have had a sleepless night.

I cleared my throat, and she started, looking around before settling her gaze on me.

"Oh, good morning, Michael," she said.

"Good morning, miss," I said. "Bartlett is here to take me back to Tristram's cottage."

She winced slightly at Tristram's name, then looked confused.

"Bartlett? But I thought young Freddie was going to fetch you."

"He is," I said. "But he says I have to call him 'Bartlett' or his father will think he's taking liberties."

She nodded. "Yes, that is right. I hadn't thought." She paused. "But I do hope we will see you again soon," she said, rising from her chair and coming over to me.

"Uh-huh. Tristram told me I needed to come over and spend time with Gwen every day."

"That would be exceedingly kind of you," she said. "And my aunt and I will expect to see some of you as well."

"Certainly, miss."

"Please," she said, "I think you must call me Miss Louisa, now that we are better acquainted."

"Thank you, Miss Louisa."

She walked me to the front step, where Freddie was stowing my bags in the cart.

"Thank you for taking care of Michael for us, Freddie," she said.

"Good morning, miss. I suppose I shan't be able to persuade

you to call me 'Bartlett'?"

She shook her head. "After all these years? No, I don't think so."

"Ah, well, miss." He went and stood by the motivator.

"Thank you for everything, Miss Louisa," I said. "I expect I'll be by tomorrow afternoon."

"We shall expect you for the noon meal."

I gave her a cheery grin, and climbed up onto the seat of the cart.

"To the cottage, Bartlett!" I cried.

"Very good, Master Henderson," said Freddie, and so saying he mounted the postilion seat and we were off.

Chapter 33

Once we got out onto the high road I was pleased to discover that he was a careful driver in the Commonwealth sense. That is to say, he kept his shotgun ready to hand; and while keeping an eye on the road he also kept one on the sky and another on the margins, checking for imminent danger. If that's too many eyes, I'm sorry; that's just life in the Commonwealth.

Freddie and I didn't talk much on the way. We couldn't, really, with him sitting about five feet in front of me. As I was more or less useless in the event of aerial attack, being armed with nothing but my taser, I left it to him and enjoyed my view of the lake.

In due time Freddie brought the motivator-and-cart to a halt in front of the cottage, hopped down (grabbing his shotgun), and trotted over to help me down. Fruitlessly, because with my shoulder back in good shape I had no trouble hopping down myself and already had feet to gravel. I grinned up at him, and he smiled despite himself.

"I'll just get the bags, then, shall I, Master Henderson?" he said, retrieving my backpack and the satchel (unless it was a portmanteau) that I'd borrowed from Tristram from the back of the cart.

"I'll need the backpack," I said, and he handed it to me. "As for the other, I guess you're going to unpack that for me, too?"

"That's what I'm for, Master Henderson. One of the things,

anyway."

"OK. Well, when you've got that done come find me, all right? I'll be somewhere about."

"Certainly, sir! Mrs. Williams is out shopping, but I can bring you some tea if you like."

"Do that," I said; and then I followed him up to the door, which he opened for me, and into my new temporary home.

I'd been dreading this moment, but gone were the shadows and the holland covers and the dust and the gloom. I poked around a bit, surveying the decor (masculine) and the furnishings (comfortable, if just slightly shabby), then headed up to Tristram's study. Begin as you mean to go on, they say; and I had a feeling that Freddie and I were going to need to have a talk. He clearly felt somewhat *in loco parentis*, and while I needed a guide I didn't need a keeper.

Tristram's official history of the Revolution was on one of the "open" shelves in his study; I was sitting at Tristram's desk looking at the table of contents when Freddie came in with my tea and my feeling was proven right.

"There you are, Master Henderson!" He paused, and looked uncomfortable. I just looked at him and waited. "But should you be in Mr. Monocle's study, sir? There's a pleasant sitting room down—"

"Yes, Bartlett, I should be; and in fact I plan to spend quite a lot of time in here."

"Oh, but—"

"Freddie."

He cleared his throat. "Um, yes sir?"

"Mr. Monocle wishes me to continue my education while I'm here in Grayrigg, and before he left he gave me the run of the books here in his study, which is the closest thing this cottage has to a library."

"Yes, sir?" He looked puzzled; there were a lot of books in the room, certainly, but even at a glance none of them looked like the sort thing a ten-year-old would find interesting, or even intelligible.

"Bartlett, did your father tell you that I'm older than I look?"

"What? No, he didn't—I mean, no, sir!"

"I thought he hadn't. Tristram told him, but I guess it didn't register. Well, Bartlett, I know I look like a ten-year-old, but I'm rather older than that."

Freddie put the tea tray down on the table.

"How much—I beg your pardon, sir, may I take the liberty of asking—"

"Old enough that I'm tired of explaining to people that I'm not actually ten years old."

"But my father—"

"I'm sorry to keep interrupting you, but it will go quicker this way. Tristram and I decided not to go into detail about it with your father. Tristram was in a hurry, and as I say I'm just tired of the whole thing. But your father assured Tristram that you were both quick and discreet, and I think we'll get on a lot better together if I can get it through your head that I'm small for my age but I'm not a small boy."

He stared at me, with that deer-in-the-headlights look I know so well; but he was both perceptive and resilient, and once he got caught up to the fact that ten-year-olds just don't talk like that a look of horror swept over his face. It was just for a moment; and then he stood up as straight as he could, looked straight ahead, and steeled himself to speak.

"I beg your pardon, sir. I have been most awfully free."

I closed my eyes for a moment, and took a deep breath. Then I shook my head.

"You know, Cousin Tristram said almost the same thing."

"He—he did, sir?"

"More or less. In fact, he offered to give me satisfaction if I thought it necessary. But really, Freddie, what were you supposed to think?

"Now, would you please sit down for a moment? Yes, I know you're not supposed to; I promise I won't tell anybody."

He sat down on the chair by the door, perching right on the very edge.

"Let me make some things clear. First, I might not be ten years old, but I *am* a stranger to this part of the world, so I'm going to need your guidance almost as much as if I were."

"All right, sir," he said, uncertainly.

"And I'm sure that there's a host of things to be done around here that you're already planning on doing for me, right? Seeing to the steam plant and suchlike."

He nodded.

"So you'll do that. And I'm going to need your skill with a shotgun when I go out driving—unless you know somewhere I can get a shotgun that won't send me flying head over heels?"

He brightened a little at the word "shotgun."

"I might be able to help you with that, sir."

"Good. You'll need to show me how to drive the motivator, too. I can drive Cousin Tristram's phaeton, but I never tried to do it from the postilion seat."

He nodded again. "Yes, sir."

"Now, I've got some work to do for Tristram; I'll probably be spending my mornings in here doing that. In the afternoons I'll be going over to Stockwood. And I'll want to spend some time getting to know Grayrigg; in fact, I'd like you to give me a tour of the high street after lunch. Um...there *will* be lunch, won't there?"

"Yes, sir, as soon as Mrs. Williams gets back."

"OK. So we'll take that tour right after lunch. In the meantime, I have a question or two."

"Yes, sir?"

"First, who are you working for?"

He frowned. "I don't know what you mean, sir."

"Well, you're a gentleman's gentleman, I think the phrase is. Isn't that right? So are you working for Tristram? Or for your father? Or for me?"

"Oh, I see. Well, I had thought I was working for Mr. Monocle, keeping an eye on his young cousin. I see now that I was mistaken. Unless—you're not just angling for me to let you run wild, are you? My father wouldn't approve of that at all."

I shook my head. "How wild can I run? I don't smoke, and as for strong drink," and here I waved at my minuscule form, "drinking to excess is really far too easy to be any fun. And besides, my wife will kill me if I pick up any new vices while I'm away."

I have to say, It was fun watching his expression run from suspicion and concern to amusement to deep shock.

"Your...wife?" He looked around wildly, as though she might pop out of the woodwork. Somebody might, actually, but it wouldn't be her.

"Yup. Her name is Bernie. She stayed home when I came for a visit to Cousin Tristram."

"How old are you, really?"

"Twenty-eight."

Freddie blinked, slowly, several times.

"But...Mr. Monocle...does he know?"

"Oh, yes. He's fully aware. You can ask him about it when he gets back; in fact, I'd like you to do that." I smiled at him. "It's a lot to take in, I know. But you can see why I get tired of explaining this to people. Back home, everybody has known me since I was supposed to look like this, and they've gotten used to me. Here, well..."

He was nodding. "I can see that, sir."

"So I want to be clear. Are you working for Mr. Monocle, or for your father, or for me?"

He straightened up. "Oh, I'm working for *you*, sir. That's how it works, in service. A gentleman's gentleman's loyalty is always to his gentleman first. That's what the books say."

"And second?"

"That would be to Mr. Monocle, sir, as head of the family."

"Then I think we'll get along fine, Freddie. I mean, Bartlett."

"Thank you, sir."

"Now, I don't want you running off and telling everyone that I'm so much older than I look."

"No, sir? I could smooth things over for you, like. Pave the way."

"If I'm here long enough for it to matter, I might take you up on that. But for now, it will be much simpler if everyone goes on thinking that I'm the age I look."

But Freddie was looking worried.

"Yes, Fred—Bartlett? What is it?"

He looked up at me. "What am I to call you, sir? I can't call you 'Master Henderson'; you're of age, it wouldn't be right."

I pursed my lips and thought quickly.

"In private you can go on calling me 'sir,' since I can't persuade you to call me 'Michael.' In Mr. Monocle's presence you can call me 'Mr. Henderson,' if you like. But in public I'm afraid you'll need to go on calling me 'Master Henderson.'"

He still looked unsure, so I resorted to threats. "You'll call me 'Master Henderson,' Bartlett, or I'm afraid I'll have to start calling *you* 'Freddie' at every public opportunity."

He stifled a chuckle. "Very well, sir. 'Master Henderson' it is."

"That's all, I guess. How do I call you if I need you?"

He stood up and indicated an embroidered strip on the wall behind his chair. "This is the bell pull, sir. Just give it a tug and I'll come. And I'll come when luncheon is ready, sir."

"Thank you, Bartlett."

That got a quick smile, and off he went. Resilient lad, Freddie. I thought we'd get on famously together.

Chapter 34

I had a lot to ponder that evening as I prepared for bed, and a longer than usual letter to write to Bernie. What I wanted more than anything was to head home and talk things over with her; but I had to stay put if I wanted to be useful to Tristram. It was annoying.

See, I get these ideas; and sometimes they make sense and sometimes they don't. When it comes to software I make my own judgments, but people, now…when it comes to people I rely on Bernie to let me know what's what. In this case I thought she'd agree with me.

But I'll get to that.

After a simple and perfectly adequate lunch of bread and cheese and cold meat that Freddie fetched from the pub because Mrs. Williams didn't have the kitchen *quite* in order yet, we sallied forth to investigate the glories and wonders of Grayrigg High Street.

It was market day in Grayrigg, and as we walked we passed quite a number of people, both pedestrians and (for lack of a better word) motorists. To my surprise, I attracted a fair amount of attention; I guess Bert Wiggins had been busy. Most of the passersby looked at me with open curiosity but continued on their way without really acknowledging my presence; and there were a fair number who turned up their noses outright. I pegged these as folks who shared Miss Clarenton's view on one Tristram

J. Monocle, though there was one older lady who seemed personally affronted that my short pants had no buckles at the knee.

The countryside, I decided, was *different*. The anonymity of London had no place among the townsfolk of Grayrigg.

A very few wanted to meet Tristram Monocle's young cousin, motorists not excluded—and they served to confirm that everyone knew that I was Tristram Monocle's young cousin.

Driving in Grayrigg is a rather sedate affair, given the narrowness of the high street; and there are no sidewalks. Motivated vehicles mostly went right down the center unless they had to pass one another; and then the pedestrians had to give them room. And of course all of the vehicles were open, and none of the drivers showed any compunction about stopping in the middle of the street to say hello or give me the cold shoulder.

So. As he'd hinted, Tristram wasn't necessarily well-regarded in Grayrigg, and that attitude was slopping over onto me. I'd have to make my own friends among the locals if I wanted to get along, and I was puzzled as to how to start. In the stories, the hero always goes down to the pub and talks to the landlord, and maybe with the folks in the public bar—or, if he's too high and mighty for the bar, perhaps the parlor. He stands a round or two, and doesn't put himself forward or give himself airs, and after a while he's accepted and all is good. But when you're small for your age, though, and (more to the point) when everyone thinks you're ten years old, that approach isn't going to work.

I was still pondering when I caught sight of that temple of craftsmanship and aetheric wonders known as Mortimer's Motivator shop. It was on a lane about three quarters of the way down the high street from the cottage, on the side opposite the lake. A former livery stable, it consisted of a barn, a workshop fronted by a row of double doors (now standing open) that looked to have once been a carriage house, and an open air forge. A red motivator was stopped half-in/half-out of one set of double doors, and the place had that look of grime and controlled chaos you find in garages everywhere.

What had caught my eye was the stained glass sign saying, "Mortimer's Motivators," the only one of its kind I'd seen in Grayrigg, and it gave me an idea. Not the one I mentioned above —this one was an unequivocally good idea, and one that I didn't need to discuss with Bernie (though I did tell her about it in my letter).

What forward-thinking ten-year-old boy doesn't love motivators? And what country gentleman forward-thinking (and eccentric) enough to get into the motivator business in a country town like Grayrigg wouldn't be pleased as punch to have an intelligent and (above all) *polite* young lad come and listen to him go on about his steam-powered obsessions? The lad could make friends; and then perhaps the young lad could listen in on the gentleman's conversations with his customers, and maybe get to know some of them, too; and maybe after a couple of weeks, he'd find he was getting somewhere. It turned out that I didn't *have* a couple of weeks, mind you. But it was still a good idea.

So that was one idea; and I had another that went with it, that I'll get to. (No, still not the one I mentioned above.)

As we walked up to the workshop a man stepped out, wiping his hands on a dirty rag. He was a thin man of mostly reasonable height, with a flat cap and grease stains. He looked to be about my age, or perhaps Tristram's—young enough to be motivator-mad, and old enough to be doing something about it.

"Now then, young Freddie," he said to my companion. "And you must be Tristram Monocle's cousin."

"Yes, sir, I am."

"And what brings you here afoot? I happen to know that your cousin owns an Ermintrude & Sons Rustic Express, and it is in perfect working order because I serviced it just last month." He looked at Freddie, raising an eyebrow to let him know what he thought of people who walked when a motivator in perfect working order was available.

"Master Henderson wanted to walk around the town and get to know people," said Freddie.

"That's right," I said. "And I particularly wanted to come

here!"

"Oh, really, lad?" said Mr. Mortimer. "And why would that be?"

"Because motivators, of course," I said, in the voice of a ten-year-old explaining the obvious to an older person who just doesn't get it. Freddie looked bemused, but Mr. Mortimer nodded vigorously, as if to show me that *he*, at least, thought that was the best reason ever. "But also," I said, "because I want to see if you can make me something."

The eyebrow, which had come down, went back up. "And what would that be, lad?"

Boyish enthusiasm +2. "Back home, we call it a bicycle. It's got two wheels, and you ride on it, and—"

"Oh, a velocipede. What would you want with one of those, lad?" He looked sincerely puzzled. "Not that I couldn't make one given time, you understand. I've got the materials, and I could fire up the forge if I had to. The front wheel would be tricky, being so large, but perhaps I could make one from a cartwheel—but that would be dangerously heavy—"

"Oh, no, no, sir." I kicked it up to +3. "I've seen that kind, and it's not what I want. We have a different kind at home. And I have an idea—"

"Do you, now?"

"Oh, yes sir!" I hadn't really engaged his attention yet, I thought; he was still indulging a customer's young cousin. Time for +4. "You make both wheels the same size, and—do you have something I could draw on?"

Both eyebrows went up, but he stepped into the workshop and returned with a slate that might have been liberated from a class room. I knew he'd have something to sketch on; a man getting into motivators at this point in their history couldn't help but have aspirations to design and build as well as service.

I took the slate and roughly drew out the frame, wheels, handlebar, and saddle of a basic single-speed bicycle, but I didn't add the pedals, sprockets, or chain.

Mortimer watched with interest. "That does look more

stable," he said. "And you might be able to get off it without breaking your neck." He rubbed his chin, then pointed at the front forks. "That bit there," he said.

"The forks, they call them."

He nodded. "Yes. Why did you draw them at that angle? With that curve at the lower end?"

That was a really good question. I shrugged.

"I don't really know, sir; that's just what they look like back home. Maybe it makes them easier to steer?"

"It might," he said. "It just might. Worth a try, anyway. Now, how do you make it go? Push with your feet?"

"Steam!" I said. "You could call it a steam velocipede."

But Mortimer was shaking his head. "No, no, lad, it can't be done. Before the motivator had gone ten feet you'd be dragging rather than riding."

"Oh, but that's the brilliant thing, sir!" +5. "You don't use a separate motivator. You build the steam power into the velocipede itself, like riding postilion!"

He stopped, mouth open. Then he started to say something, then stopped again. Then he said, "Hand me that slate, lad." He pointed at the open spot in the middle of the frame. "I suppose I could sling a steam plant just there...it would be a small one, but this device would be much smaller than a motivator, and you're not so big yourself, are you lad?"

"No, sir," I said, beaming. Beaming, because I wasn't so big! It felt odd.

"But how would I get the power to the wheels?" he went on, mostly to himself.

"Back home," I said.

He looked up from the slate. "Yes, lad?"

"Back home—in the Colonies, you know—bicycles like this have pedals. The pedals turn a metal wheel with teeth on it, and there's another one on the back wheel, and a chain that connects them." He handed me the slate, and I drew them in. "So you pedal, and it turns the back wheel. But I was thinking, why pedal when you could use steam?"

"That would work, right enough...but perhaps I might do something better." He took the slate back from me, and stared at it. "If I were to..." he mumbled, and his voice trailed off. And then, "I wonder...."

And then he wandered back into the workshop, and we heard the sounds of drawers opening and closing and bits of metal banging against each other.

Mission accomplished. I'd made him see me, rather than Tristram, and given myself an excuse to come back.

I looked up at Freddie. "You said something about a shotgun my size?"

He nodded. "Right this way, Master Henderson!"

They take shooting seriously in the Commonwealth. Tristram's cottage had a service porch at the back, and the service porch had a gun closet, and one of the objects in it was a pump-action shotgun of what seemed an absurdly small caliber. Tristram's grandfather had seen to it that he'd acquired all of the skills appropriate for a country gentleman—and given the wildlife of Tristram's country, an ability to use a shotgun certainly counted. And it made sense that he must have started to acquire that skill when he was too young to use a full-sized gun. I mean, this was a country where you could buy a child a crossbow with explosive quarrels. And here it was.

"It isn't a proper steam gun, sir," said Freddie, "not modern at all, but an old one that uses gunpowder. But you should be able to manage it well enough." He handed me the gun, and dropped a couple of boxes of tiny shotgun shells into his pocket.

There was a shooting range back behind the cottage. "The town has a common range, sir, but a proper gentleman's house always has a range of its own, my father says." The range was about thirty yards long and bordered on three sides by an earthen berm, and metal targets hung from stands at the far end. The grass was long on the three segments of the berm, but the ground in the middle had clearly been mowed in the last twenty-four hours, and the targets were painted a fresh deep black. That seemed silly to me, but I supposed it hid the rust.

"You don't usually shoot at metal targets with a shotgun, sir," said Freddie, "but we need to work on basic skills." I took that to mean, "We need to be sure you won't shoot things you'd rather not, like, you know, your valet."

"Besides," he went on, "these cartridges aren't powerful enough to bring down a clay pigeon."

"Then why bother? If it can't bring down a clay pigeon, how is it going to be a help against a gull or a woodpecker?"

"Let me show you, sir."

He opened a box of shells and showed me one of the cartridges, which was made of thick paper with a brass base. Drawing a knife from his belt he sliced it open, and poured a stream of white grains into my hand.

"Rock salt," he said. "It won't take down a gull, but it will make one think twice, and if you get it in the eyes it won't have any attention left to spare for you. You might drive it off, and you can buy yourself time to get under cover."

He showed me how to load the shotgun and had me fire a number of rounds at the targets, correcting my stance and technique after each shot. I now saw the reason for the black paint: it made it easy to see whether I'd hit the target or not.

"Did you repaint the targets this morning, Freddie?"

"Bartlett, sir. Yes, I did. My father said that everything needed to be made ready for a young gentleman."

I practiced for about an hour, and by the end my right shoulder was quite sore; but when we were done I was able to sling the shotgun over my back without feeling like a complete poser.

"You should spend some time practicing every day for the next week or two," said Freddie, quite forgetting to call me "sir." "I'll keep the closet stocked with cartridges."

And then, of course, Freddie led me back inside and showed me how to properly clean and oil the shotgun. Because, he said, "Mr. Monocle would expect you to know how to do it, sir." He would, too, I reflected as I took the gun to pieces for the third time.

After that I had a bath, and then an excellent dinner, served by Freddie; I still hadn't laid eyes on Mrs. Williams. And then I spent an hour or so with Tristram's official history before settling down to write to Bernie. My camera's battery was dead, so I sent it off home with the letter.

All through that long afternoon and evening the idea I mentioned had been niggling at me. The older residents of Grayrigg, those who had deigned to speak to me, had all uttered some variant of the sentence, "Now then, you'll be Tristram Monocle's young cousin. You couldn't very well be anyone else, for you have just the look he had at your age." And Augustus had said much the same thing, though it hadn't registered with me until later.

I hadn't noticed any such resemblance, but then I wouldn't have. Still, I found that I was quite ready to believe it.

My finder, as I have reason to know, has a bias for finding latent Travelers. It's a bias that had been amply (and somewhat horrifically) demonstrated a couple of years earlier.

That my finder had brought me back to the Commonwealth a second time—to the exact same world, not simply to another one like it—indicated that there was a latent Traveler somewhere in the vicinity, and logic dictated that it must be Tristram. Bernie and I had already discussed that on my last visit home. And then there was Tristram's story, and our respective ages, and the fact that my father had shown up in my mother's philosophy class not long after the time that Tristram's mother died and his father went missing....

Tristram wasn't really my cousin—but all in all it seemed to me that he might actually be my half-brother. I wanted to help him anyway, for his kindness to me, but if I was right it made helping him that much more urgent.

Chapter 35

I won't bore you with a recap of Tristram's *The Founding of the Civil Commonwealth of Britain and the Isles*; it went pretty much as I'd expected, given what Tristram had already told me. The noble merchants and manufacturers—noble in character, if not in so-called "birth"—the makers, I say, of the modern world—having been oppressed and crushed by the backward, dilatory, and frivolous drones of the countryside, naturally rose up on behalf of the common folk and instituted a New Order of prosperity, bliss, and consumer products for all.

I spent a good bit of the morning with it, skimming the unfamiliar names and trying to read between the lines to get a notion of the character of Lord Remchester and his cronies. It was hard-going, especially since I was training Freddie not to bother me while I was in Tristram's study, which meant I had to get my own tea.

Tristram was a gifted writer, I must say. I had feared that he was going to lay on the praises of Remchester with a trowel, but he didn't. Instead, he had told it straight, merely being carefully selective as to the motives he ascribed to Remchester and his opponents. I learned two things from this: first, that Tristram hadn't been willing to wholly sacrifice his integrity on the altar of survival, and second, that Remchester might be a cad, but he wasn't the kind of fool that surrounded himself with flatterers and toadies.

In Tristram's account, Remchester's motives were invariably pure and aimed toward the good of the country as a whole, and his achievements were both laudable and beneficial. There was a large measure of truth to that, from what I'd seen: Mordred & Sons was a sparkling and well-stocked concern; the towns I'd seen were all prosperous, their buildings bright with paint and their folk with good cheer; the main roads were wide and well-maintained. If there were sinks of Dickensian misery I'd seen no signs of them.

The former nobility and higher gentry naturally came in for a fair amount of dispassionate and clinical abuse. They were foursquare opposed to progress, to science, and to the steam revolution, and they wanted to keep the common folk of Britain in bondage to the service of the land and themselves. Slavishly wedded to their own interests and unwilling to compromise, they had had to be forcibly put down for the good of the nation.

It was all deftly done, and by the end of the book I was nearly ready to acquit Remchester of all wrong-doing and place him firmly on the side of the angels. At least, I might have if I hadn't been aware of some the details Tristram had left out of his account, and if I hadn't become acquainted with some of the gentry and common folk in question. However hidebound the landed elites might have been, I was confident that they'd been "put down" without reference to their individual views or willingness to compromise; and given the rancor I'd detected here and there in my journey from London, and most notably from Bert Wiggins at the First Lord's Head, there must be downsides to Remchester's rule that weren't obvious on the surface.

As for Remchester's motives, well...however shiny his official motives were, I'm sure he had whole stableful of ulterior ones just waiting for Tristram's shovel. I was quite looking forward to investigating the contents of Tristram's secret cupboard.

After finishing my studies for the morning I spent an hour

practicing with my little gun, which by no means fit in my pocket, and then set out for Stockwood with Freddie. He drove, while I rode in state in the humble farm cart, pulled by that noble example of the modern steam armamentaria, the Ermintrude & Sons Rustic Express, as kept in perfect running order by Mr. Mortimer of Mortimer's Motivators.

I had my little gun to hand and spent the ride scanning the skies. I was rather hoping for an attack of gulls so that I could try it out while I had Freddie and his much bigger gun to keep an eye on me, but the skies remained clear and we reached Stockwood without incident.

If the trip was uneventful, however, our arrival was less so. As we pulled up before the manor house Miss Louisa rose from the bench I'd sat on the day before and hurried to my side. I noticed with surprise that the bower had been much trimmed back.

"Michael," she said, "have you seen Gwen?" She seemed nearly frantic, which wasn't a usual sort of look for her.

"Um, no. Why, is she missing?"

"We haven't seen her all morning. Her bed has been slept in, but she never came down to breakfast. I thought nothing of that, for she has been so sullen, but just now I went to look for her and she wasn't there. Oh, I had hoped you might have seen her on the road."

So Gwen had bunked off. Typically bird-witted of her; I guessed she'd gotten tired of waiting for Tristram. Or had she? Last I'd seen her, she hadn't seemed up to walking long distances.

"What about her things?" I asked. "Did she take her things with her?"

"What had she to take? That gown of hers was quite ruined. I had set her to altering an old frock of mine, not that she was making any great progress."

"What about her band boxes? She had some fine hats in them, I guess, and I don't think she'd have left them behind."

"I don't know," she said. She led me to the house, and sent for a small housemaid I'd not met.

"Beth, were Miss Gwen's bags missing when you checked her

room this morning?"

"No, miss, the band boxes are still there. Ought I to go and check again?"

"No, that will do."

"I expect Miss Gwen is somewhere about the grounds, then," I said. "Shall I go look around for her?"

"Would you? It's dangerous for her to be out unarmed, and I see that you now have a shotgun with you."

I frowned, then shrugged. "She has her little gun, you know."

"She does?"

"You left it on the table last night."

"I did?"

I nodded.

"Oh...I was..."

She went from frantic to flustered in three easy steps.

"It's OK," I said. "I'll go take a look. And should I send Freddie to drive north along the road?"

"Yes," she said. "The very thing. But I'll have Augustus talk to Freddie. Please, go and look for Gwen! I'll send Crosley out as well, as soon as I find him."

And so saying she led me to some french windows at the back of the house and I ventured forth into the fabled grounds of Stockwood.

There was no formal garden of the sort I'd half-pictured in my mind, no mazes or faux Greek temples; I suppose that wouldn't have been in keeping with the humble nature of the Squires of Grayrigg. But there were shrubs and hedges and gravel walks and flower beds and a sundial, and if I'd actually been ten years old I've no doubt I'd have delighted in exploring all of the ins and outs. It was all overgrown and untended, but even still it would be a pleasant place to stroll with Bernie. I made a mental note to bring her someday, if all went well.

But I didn't really think I'd find Gwen out in the open or skulking among the hedges. She knew the dangers of the open skies, and her little gun was a slender reed to lean on in the face of woodpecker attack. Nor did I think she'd try to go far on foot, not with a sprained ankle. Her previous attempt in that line hadn't worked out too well for her.

No, I thought she'd try to find some kind of ride. There might no longer be horses at Stockwood, but there ought to be some kind of conveyance—Miss Clarenton of Stockwood surely didn't walk to town.

And bird-witted as she was, Gwen possessed a certain low cunning; and while I was fairly sure she hadn't gone, at least not yet, I thought she might be scoping out her options. With that thought I set off down a gravel walk in the direction of the old stable.

The stable was a long, low building with a peaked roof, topped with what I'd call a cupola except that it ran the full length of the building. The outer walls were unbroken except for a pair of double doors on the near end, but the cupola-thing had windows running the length of both sides. The stable had once been painted white with green trim, but now there was more gray than white.

One of the leaves of the double door stood open about a foot. Aha! Miss Louisa might be refusing to maintain the grounds as a matter of principle, but outright neglect was another thing. She'd keep the stables buttoned up tight so as to limit the damage from small animals and the weather. And that meant that Gwen either was or had been inside.

I had just swung the doors wide, blinking into the dimness beyond, when I heard a noise behind me. Before I could react, an arm snaked round my neck and yanked me off my feet.

It was a thick arm, and hairy, and it took me right back to eighth grade.

That was a problem. I had my taser by my side, and my right arm was still free; if I'd grabbed for the taser immediately I might well have been able to stun him long enough to get loose, assuming I didn't accidentally tase myself in the leg. Even there, the spasms might have caused him to drop me, not that that would have helped me in the long run.

Instead, the attack triggered exactly the reaction I would have had fifteen years earlier: I tried to drive my right foot between his knees.

I know what you're thinking, but it's a lot harder than you'd imagine to immobilize someone that way unless he's a lot taller than you. But if you can hook your foot behind his knee you can make him trip; and that has definite possibilities, especially if you manage to land on his solar plexus. Land hard enough, and you'll find you can run quite a long distance before he starts breathing again.

This guy was more than tall enough for the full treatment, but he was also smarter than my middle school banes had been. As my foot moved he swung me around in a circle, so my legs extended and I missed my target. It also meant that his grip tightened around my throat, which wasn't a sustainable situation —well, not for me—and also it made it impossible for me to bite him. I don't make a habit of biting people, but any port in a storm, you know? Meanwhile, he kept whirling so that I saw the manor house in the distance then the dimness of the stable, then light, and then dimness. The barrel of my little shotgun dug painfully into my shoulder blade, and my only consolation was that it couldn't have been comfortable for my attacker either.

I finally grabbed for my taser and found my attacker's hand in the way, and I had just settled in for a bout of kicking and flailing when I saw brown hair and a blue dress go by, and heard a familiar voice saying, "Oh! Oh! Oh! Stop it! Stop it!" The next rotation I saw the muzzle of Gwen's little gun pointing more or less at my face. There was a bright yellow flash and a loud noise, and my attacker stiffened and then fell backwards, taking me with him. I landed on top of him, my shotgun between us, and wasn't *that* a lovely sensation!

I squirmed free as soon as I could, and rolled over onto my hands and knees. My heart was pounding, and I took in big, gasping gulps of air.

William H. Duquette

When I had caught my breath, I looked up and found Miss Gwen sitting on a bench that stood against the wall, just inside the door. She had her face in one hand and her little gun in the other, and looked younger than her years in an overlarge blue dress. She was quietly sobbing.

"Thank you," I said, rubbing my neck where my attacker's arm had held me. I was glad I'd not tried to take her gun from her the previous night.

She rubbed the sleeve of her dress across her eyes.

"You're welcome," she managed after a few tries. Then, in a shaky voice, "Who was that? Why was he attacking you?"

"These things happen," I said.

I took another deep breath. I kind of wanted to go join Gwen on the bench and do a little sobbing myself, but my legs had gone all rubbery. Instead I looked at my attacker more carefully. The body lay on the ground beside me, stark in the light from the open door. She'd shot him more or less between the eyes; from what I could see, the bullet must have passed no more than an inch over my own head, way too close for comfort.

I'd been expecting a Traveler, but his apparel wasn't that out of place for a town like Grayrigg: a collarless beige shirt, unbuttoned at the neck with sleeves rolled up past his elbows; a pair of brown trousers; scuffed brown boots. Had Lord Remchester sent someone to kidnap me? I didn't have any other potential enemies, not that I could think of. Well, except for Miss Melissa Stavely and the bulk of the local flora and fauna, but I didn't think either of them would be trying to abduct me. Still, the clothing might be happenstance. I leaned in closer, and gave him a quick frisking.

"Oh! What are you doing?" said Gwen, as I pulled on a string I found around the fellow's neck. "Please, it's horrid, come away! Oh, come away!" There were more sobs.

The string was attached to a little pouch, and in the pouch was a small finder, just as I'd half-expected. I pulled the mouth of the pouch closed, being careful not to touch the finder, and started to pull the string over his head...and then thought better of it and cut the string with my pocket knife.

I had just tucked the pouch in my pocket when I heard a shout and the sound of running footsteps. Crosley burst into the stable moments later.

"Master Henderson! Master Henderson! Are you all right? Did she shoot— Oh. My. Who is this?"

"I don't know. He jumped me when I opened the stable door," I said. "I was trying to get free, when Gwen shot him with her little gun." I gestured at the bench, which was behind him.

"Oh, Miss Gwen!" He blushed, I suppose because he'd just accused her of shooting me. "Are you all right?"

"Oh!" said Gwen, her voice still full of tears. "I was sitting here, on this bench, and Michael opened the door, and this man grabbed him from behind and was choking him, and he couldn't get free, and I took my little gun and, and, and…."

"She did, too," I said, as she started sobbing again. "You'd best go tell Miss Louisa. I'll stay here with Miss Gwen." I sat down beside her to wait.

Chapter 36

Miss Louisa took it much more calmly than I'd expected.

She hurried into the stable, holding up her skirts with both hands, and completely failed to recoil at the sight of the dead body.

"I see," she said. Then she turned to Gwen and I, sitting on the bench. "You are both quite unharmed?"

Gwen nodded silently; she had ceased sobbing some minutes prior.

"My neck is sore and my throat hurts, but otherwise I'm fine," I said.

Miss Louisa nodded, then turned back to our late guest.

"I don't recognize him," she said. "Michael, have you seen him before? Have you any idea who he might be?"

"I've never seen him before in my life," I said—which was completely true, if not completely forthcoming. I expected that I'd have to tell Miss Louisa the truth about myself eventually, but this didn't seem like the time.

She studied him for a moment, then clicked her tongue. She turned to Crosley, who had followed her in.

"Summon the beadle; he will need to attend to this."

"Yes, miss," said Crosley, and went off at a run.

It occurred to me, not for the first time, how much in common the people of the Commonwealth had with the squirrels I'd seen in the forest—both were polite if treated politely, and both responded to invaders with extreme prejudice. The man had invaded Stockwood and attacked a guest of the manor; and as he was now dead and his erstwhile victim was unharmed there was no reason to make a fuss. She came, she saw, she sent Crosley to summon the beadle. It was all quite matter-of-fact.

She didn't ask me why I'd been attacked, or why I thought I had been attacked, which was a good thing; I'd either have had to lie and say I didn't know, or I'd have had to make the lengthy explanations I was trying to avoid. Nor did she speculate in my presence. Instead she said, "Let us return to the house. The atmosphere here is quite unwholesome."

Although it was rising lunchtime no one was particularly hungry —go figure—so Miss Louisa took us to her library and sat us down. Augustus brought tea, favoring both Gwen and I with warm smiles.

"Now, Michael," said Miss Louisa, "please tell me what happened."

"I went looking for Miss Gwen, and thought she might be exploring the stable, so I headed that way. I saw that one of the doors was standing partly open, so I went and swung both doors wide, and then that guy grabbed me. I don't know where he came from—," and boy was that the truth, "—but he grabbed me and swung me around. He was choking me and trying to take away my taser when Miss Gwen shot him."

Miss Louisa turned to Gwen.

"Miss Gwen? What did you see?"

"Oh! I was looking around the stable, you know, just for something to do. I always liked the horses at home, but there were no horses, not even a pony, nothing at all. And my ankle hurt, so I sat down by the door." She nodded.

"And then?"

"Why, the door opened, of course, and there was Michael with that man attached to him, and he didn't seem to like it all, I mean Michael didn't seem to like it, not the man, and I asked him to stop, and he didn't and so I took out my little gun—it was in my pocket—and, and, and—"

"That will do, Miss Gwen. So, neither of you saw him before he laid hands on Michael?"

"No, miss," I said.

"Oh, no, not at all, because I was sitting on the bench, which faces into the stable, you know."

Miss Louisa made a noise of agreement, then sipped tea for a few moments, eyes deep in thought. She pursed her lips, and then nodded to herself.

"Miss Gwen," she said, "I must commend you on your swift and correct response."

Gwen's eyes widened, then she beamed. "Oh! Why, thank you, miss!"

"However, if your ankle is well enough for you to walk to the stable, it is well enough for you to handle your gun properly. This afternoon I shall take you out to the range."

Gwen deflated again. "Oh, very well. If you think it necessary."

"I do," said Miss Louisa. She turned back to me.

"I had thought to have you take Miss Gwen for a drive this afternoon, Michael, but I think you have had enough excitement for one day. Also, Dr. Smith should examine you and make sure you have no hidden injuries. I shall summon him at once."

I thought it wiser not to reject the doctor's attention, but this line of thinking was going to find me spending the night at Stockwood and lose me a day of research.

"Please, Miss Louisa," I said, "Freddie can take care of that. I'd much rather return to the cottage and have Dr. Smith see me there. It would be easier for him, too."

She studied me for a long moment.

"Very well," she said. "It speaks well for you that you are concerned with the doctor's convenience, Michael. Now, I know neither of you are hungry, but you are young and need your strength. You certainly must eat before you return to Grayrigg."

The beadle came while we were eating, driving a motivator

with a long wagon behind it. He spoke with Miss Louisa for a few moments while Gwen and I remained at the table; then the wagon trundled on down to the stable, trampling down the long grass. Not long afterwards it trundled away again. He never spoke to us; he'd had the story from Miss Clarenton of Stockwood, and that's all any of the locals would ever need. A quarter of an hour later I met Freddie at the front door and we followed in the beadle's wake.

Chapter 37

I began to tackle Tristram's Closet of Secrets the first thing after breakfast the following morning. I had Freddie bring a pot of tea and a footstool to Tristram's study, and then I swung the door closed with a heavy thud. I turned the locking wheel hand over hand and watched the heavy iron bolts slide soundlessly into place, which seemed wrong. There should have been a loud ratcheting noise. Life is not a video game, though, and Tristram's attention to detail in all things extended to keeping the machinery well oiled.

After locking the door, I knelt in front of the first bookcase and pulled the lever hidden under the kick-rail. The bookcase unlatched with a satisfying click. I swung it wide, exposing the hidden shelves; then, crossing the room I pressed the hidden button and watched in satisfaction as the hidden shelves slid to the right, exposing the hidden closet.

I won't give you a blow by blow of my first look through this cornucopia o' stuff; it was long, tedious, and dull, with much opening of boxes and skimming of files, and in the end I had to close everything up and unbar the door so that I could send Freddie for a step-ladder, because I couldn't reach the topmost shelves whether I stood on the footstool *or* the side chair.

It had to be done, though. You don't start cataloging a library by opening the first book on the first shelf and reading it through; you start by sampling the entire collection, and getting an idea of what kind of books are in it and where they are located. Otherwise you get bogged down, and while you might have a marvelous time (depending on the kind of library) you never really come to grips with what you've got.

It was frustrating, really. What I wanted to do was dig right in and find the details about the ownership of Stockwood and environs, and anything else that pertained to Tristram and Miss Louisa. What can I say? For a geek, I guess I'm a bit of a romantic at heart. But I knew that Tristram wanted more from me than that. He had bigger secrets, and he wanted me to know what they were; he wanted me to have the inside story before I heard an inaccurate version it from anyone else.

So I buckled down, and got tore in, and put my nose to the grindstone, and all that jazz, and by the end of the morning I had a pretty good notion of what I was dealing with.

The higher shelves were filled with boxes of various sizes and shapes, and these proved to hold artifacts of one sort or another. The first box I opened held a hand gun, a pair of gloves, and a wallet with a singed hole going straight through it. (I might have imagined the faint scent of gunpowder.) Another held a derby hat that had seen better days. It would have been an attractive piece of headgear if it weren't for the bloodstained dent cudgeled into one side. There was a pair of stout brown boots with a distinctive pattern of hobnails on the sole. For a wonder, the boots bore no signs of violence; I wondered who had worn them and what horrible things he had done—or had done to him.

Each item had a paper tag attached to it with string, and each tag had a number written on it in a neat black script. The tag numbers were repeated on the outside of each box in the same handwriting, which I presumed was Tristram's. The numbers appeared to be consecutive from box to box.

As I looked through the boxes I began to realize that this wasn't just a Closet of Secrets; it was an evidence locker. What role had Tristram played in Lord Remchester's administration that he was able to lay his hands on this kind of thing? Surely he hadn't been some kind of government assassin, collecting trophies; I knew him better than that. But the objects whispered of violence and sudden death. Who was it who had died? Who had done the killing?

I didn't know whether the Commonwealth had discovered finger prints, but after the first box I avoided touching any of the artifacts, just in case. Yeah, that's why.

The lower shelves contained rows of lidless wooden file boxes, each containing ten or so portfolios of stiff brown paper tied shut with silk ribbons of red or black or purple or green. Each portfolio had an index number written on the upper right corner of its front cover, often accompanied by a name. Some, like "Barton Wood," appeared to be names of places; but most seemed to be names of individuals. The index numbers ran in sequence through the boxes, from top to bottom and left to right, though the names were in no particular order.

I opened a number of the files at random, just to get an idea of what was in them. File #47, labeled "Postlethwaite," will do as an example. It was sealed with a black ribbon, and contained an assortment of sheets and scraps of paper. Some appeared to be lists of bank transactions; others were copies of tradesman's receipts. Judging from his bills, Mr. Postlethwaite, whoever he was, seems to have had a healthy source of income. But most of the scraps seemed to be surveillance reports, all written in the same crabbed, unskillful hand:

Watched A——'s residence from noon until dusk. Long visit from M mid-afternoon; brief visits from R—— and C——. At dusk A went out. Followed him to his club. A—— remained in club until after midnight, then returned home.

Each was signed "*Post,*" and was dated in Tristram's tidy script. The last report was dated perhaps five years in the past. From the fading of the ink on the earliest reports, Tristram had written the dates on receipt rather than at any later time.

The other files with black or green ribbons were similar; the only significant difference was that those with green ribbons had dates running up to the current year, while those I saw with black ribbons all ended a year or more in the past.

I thought back to Harry Lackland, our visitor at the coaching inn in Lancaster. He was a spy, and he'd evidently worked for Tristram at some point. Had Tristram been Lord Remchester's spymaster? The conclusion seemed to be unavoidable.

The files with purple ribbons contained copies of letters, more tradesman's receipts, a few news items clipped from the *Times*, and other similar matter. Each piece of paper was once again dated in Tristram's hand. I didn't recognize any of the names I saw, but judging from the tenor of the news items they were all members of Lord Remchester's new aristocracy, the Lords of the Assembly. When I realized that, I had to snicker at the choice of purple as the marking color.

The red files were like the purple, but as with the black files the most recent dates were a year or more in the past.

So. Tristram had spent over a decade running spies for Lord Remchester; and all of that time he'd been keeping records on the spies, and spying on Remchester's supporters on his own time.

So far, though, I'd seen nothing that tied it all together. I turned next to the middle shelves, the ones comfortably at eye-level. Well...comfortably at eye-level for Tristram. Me, I was grateful for the step-ladder.

On one shelf I found a row of notebooks. They filled perhaps three quarters of the shelf, with green marble bookends keeping them neatly vertical, and I guessed that they must be Tristram's journals because they were of varied bindings, sizes, and states of wear. If you're buying a bunch of notebooks all at once you tend to buy all the same kind, but journals you buy one at a time, and you buy what you can find. I've got a similar shelf of mismatched notebooks at home.

I took one from the middle of the row and examined it. It was bound in green paper, and had two dates written on the cover: 9 April 07—23 October 07. There were no other markings on the outside, so I flipped it to the middle and got my first surprise: Tristram had written in code.

I flipped quickly through the journal, just to be sure, but the pattern was consistent throughout. Entry dates were recognizable, but the entries themselves were gibberish: a hodgepodge of letters, numbers, and other symbols I didn't recognize. The entries were confined to the right-hand pages; the left-hand pages were mostly blank, though some had notations opposite one or another line on the right hand side.

I was nonplussed. Tristram wanted me to read his secrets, but they were in code. Had he expected me to crack the code on my own? I leaned back on the step-ladder and glared at the row of journals. The key to understanding the boxed exhibits and files was right there in front of me, and I couldn't read any of it!

I was about to go and get a fresh pot of tea when it hit me: yes, the journals were of different sizes and shapes, but there was a pattern. Counting from the left, the odd-numbered journals showed signs of wear—scuffs, stains, tears in the binding—but the even-numbered journals all looked much newer. I slid the journal for 9 April 07 back into place, and pulled out the one just to its right.

Bingo. This journal was *also* labeled 9 April to 23 October, but it was written in plain English. The odd-numbered journals were the ones that Tristram had carried with him; and as he'd filled them up he'd made plain text copies for ease of reference. I wondered how many hours he'd spent in this very room with the door barred, painstakingly transcribing his notes page by page. Just thinking of it made my right hand ache.

I resolved to get Tristram a laptop, if I could figure out how he could keep it powered. And a printer, definitely a printer. After all he'd done for me, I could afford to keep him in toner.

It wasn't yet time to read through the journals, but I glanced at a few pages of this one. The entries were cryptic, to say the least:

Sent H55 to observe Amberson, per R1's orders. P47 reports no contact between Carstairs and Rosemont in the past week. R1 to visit Bath Thursday next.

Was "P47" our friend Mr. Postlethwaite? Indeed it was; his file was #47. Then R1 must be...I found the first file box, and pulled out file #1. It was tied with a purple ribbon, and labeled

"Remchester." So "R1" was his lordship, "P47" was Postlethwaite, and "H55" was someone I'd not yet met.

The final journal on the shelf was about half full, and the final date was about three months in the past.

On a whim I glanced at the earliest journal and got a surprise. Not in the journal itself, which was dated 2 July 04, but in what came with it. When I pulled the journal from its shelf, something else fell to floor. It turned out to be a diary, bound in leather; it must have been resting on top of the row of journals. It was written in plain English, and the dates ran from 1775 to 1781. This year was 15 N.O., or 1802 in the old reckoning, which put the revolution at about 1777. Apparently Tristram hadn't adopted "New Order" dating in his private journals until beginning his work as spymaster.

I put the diary tenderly back on the shelf; I planned to give it some *special* attention at my earliest convenience.

So. Evidence, physical and documentary; daily activity logs; but there had to be an index. Tristram had a good memory, I was sure, but even he couldn't keep all of the boxes and files straight without help, and a man so organized wouldn't have tried.

I had not far to seek. The shelf below the journals held another row of notebooks; and unlike the journals these were all of the same size, binding, and color. The leftmost notebook on the shelf seemed to be the most worn, so I pulled it out first. It was helpfully labeled "Directory," and proved to be the index I was looking for. The first twenty-six pages were labeled with the letters of the alphabet; each page contained a list of names beginning with the appropriate letter, and next to each name was a string of letters and numbers. On the page for "P" I found "Postlethwaite, D-6, F-47, A-17".

The "F-47" was clearly "File #47". I pondered for a moment, then counted over to the sixth notebook after the directory. It was labeled, "Dossier #6." The first page held a list of names in no particular order; Postlethwaite's name was about halfway through the list. I flipped through the pages until I found him.

Postlethwaite's entry was several pages long, but I'll

summarize. It seems that one Jno. Postlethwaite had been an informer to the First Lord's office, had taken money from the First Lord's enemies, had passed on false information, and had subsequently been quietly disposed of by "N23".

I climbed to the top of the step-ladder and found the box containing the item with tag #17. As I thought I'd remembered, it was the derby with the bloodstained dent in it. Alas, poor Postlethwaite.

I put the derby away.

Toward the end of that shelf I found another notebook that began with a list of place names rather than personal names. Each name had a date by it; they ran in chronological order, with the first date being in year 1 N.O., which meant that Tristram must have compiled this information after the fact. I opened to a page at random.

It said, "Alderbridge, Hampshire. Primary seat of the Earl of Alderbridge. Valued at £250,000. R1, 17 June 01." There followed a description of the bounds and nature of the property: park, woods, farm acreage, and so forth.

I looked back at the cover of the notebook; it was labeled, "Confiscations". It appeared that Lord Remchester had taken the estates of the Earl of Alderbridge. Hmmmm.

Turning to the first page I ran my finger down the list of names; it came to a halt halfway down the page. Stockwood, 5 August 01. I turned pages until I came to the full entry.

"Stockwood, Westmorland. Manor of Squires of Grayrigg, currently Geo. Illridge, Esq. Valued at £43,000. S3, 5 August 01."

I turned back to the index. "S3" turned out to be one C. Stavely.

Stavely? I didn't know what Tristram's last name had been before he changed it to "Monocle," but it surely wasn't "Stavely". Was this Lord Stavely, father to Melissa the battleship?

But if Stockwood had gone to Lord Stavely, how did Tristram get his hands on it? He'd said that he bought it, but not that he'd bought it from Stavely.

I closed the notebooks and slotted them back into their places on the shelf. It was time to look at the journals.

Chapter 38

Well, actually, it was time for shooting practice, as Freddie reminded me by banging on the door of the study. And then it was time for lunch; and then it was time to hop up onto the seat of the cart so that Freddie could drive me to Stockwood. Time: it's just one damn thing after another.

I kept my shotgun to hand and my eyes alert along the way, and smiled at the occupants of the few vehicles that passed us by on their way into Grayrigg. Several smiled broadly at me, to my surprise, and one, a little old lady in an honest-to-goodness pony cart with a shotgun nearly as big as she was, stopped us to tell me how much I looked like Tristram when he was young, and how glad she was that he'd stopped working for that wicked Mr. Remchester. Her name was Mrs. Tolliver, so she told me, and she hoped I'd come to tea some afternoon. She lived in town just off the high street, at #3 Chestnut Lane, and anyone could tell me how to find it. We disengaged with some difficulty, and proceeded onward with all speed.

Our arrival at Stockwood resembled something of a reprise of the day before, except this time the figure waiting for us in the little bower was Gwen rather than Miss Louisa. Freddie stopped the motivator as we passed, and I hopped down, slinging my shotgun over my shoulder.

"Oh! You are very late!" she said. "We were obliged to eat the noon meal without you."

"I'm sorry," I said. "I didn't know I was expected for lunch today."

"Why, you are expected for luncheon every day. That is what Miss Louisa says." She nodded vigorously, brown ringlets bouncing. "Do you like my dress?"

"It does look rather nicer than the one you were wearing yesterday."

It did, too. It was also blue, and of a similar fabric that I'm sure I could name at a glance if I'd ever made a study of such things, and it was simple and attractive and above all it fit properly. She was also wearing a trim hat of approximately the same shade, fitted with the usual goggles.

"So, you finished making it over?"

"Why, no. Mrs. Illridge finished this one." She twirled in place. "Isn't it lovely? So much more comfortable than that nasty yellow thing I ran away in. I really don't know what my cousin saw in it."

"Uh-huh. Well, so I guess you were waiting for me?"

"Yes, yes. Miss Louisa says that you are to drive me into town so that I won't be underfoot for a few hours."

"She does, does she?"

More nodding. "Oh, yes. And I quite want to go, too."

"Let me say hello to Miss Louisa and Mrs. Illridge first."

"Oh, very well," she said. She went and stood by the cart and looked expectantly at Freddie.

He looked blank for a moment, and then said, "Oh, I beg your pardon, miss," and helped her to climb up and take a seat on the cart.

She smiled down at him, and said, "Thank you, Mr.—"

"Bartlett, miss."

"Thank you, Mr. Bartlett."

"Just 'Bartlett,' miss."

"Really? Just 'Bartlett'?"

"Yes, miss."

"Oh. Thank you, Bartlett."

"You're welcome, miss."

"I'll just run in and say hello, shall I?" I said.

"I shall wait here," said Gwen.

"I'd gathered that," I said, and trotted off to the open door of the manor house, where Augustus was beaming at me.

"Good morning, Master Henderson," he said.

"Good morning, Augustus! Is Miss Louisa available?"

"Yes, Master Henderson. She and Mrs. Illridge are in the library, and she said that you must come straight in whenever you might arrive."

"I'll do that then. You needn't show me, I know the way."

"Of course you do, Master Henderson!"

I gave him a broad smile, and dashed on in.

It's really quite odd; I was having more fun being ten years old at twenty-eight years of age than I ever had when I was actually ten years old.

I knocked gently on the door of the library, then opened it and stuck my head in.

Miss Louisa was behind her desk, as I'd expected; Mrs. Illridge was sitting in an armchair nearby with sewing on her lap. They'd been discussing something; they both looked a little heated, but they broke off the moment the door opened.

"Miss Louisa?"

"There you are, Michael. Please, come in."

I walked on in, hat in my hands, and stopped in front of the desk.

"Good afternoon, Miss Louisa!" Then, turning, "Good afternoon, Mrs. Illridge. Gwen's dress looks quite nice."

Whatever they'd been arguing about, they weren't angry with me; their answering smiles were wide and clearly genuine.

"Why, thank you, Michael. A pretty frock it is, if I do say it as shouldn't. And how are you this afternoon?" asked Mrs. Illridge.

"Oh, I'm fine," I said. "I've been studying all morning. Cousin Tristram's orders."

"And so you should be," said Miss Louisa. "And so you should get some air this afternoon."

"Yes, about that," I said. "Gwen asks whether I might take her for a drive into Grayrigg." According to Gwen, Miss Louisa wanted me to take her into Grayrigg; but if she were telling me a fairy story—as she well might be, our Gwen not being too firmly attached to reality—I didn't want to get her in trouble. She got into quite enough trouble all on her own.

"If you would be so kind, yes, I wish you would," said Miss Louisa. "She's been quite underfoot all morning, and though she's willing to help she seems to have had no domestic training whatsoever."

"That's so, so it is," said Mrs. Illridge. "I am quite out of patience with her auntie; she seems to have taught the girl absolutely nothing of any consequence. It is a great pity, for though her understanding is not *very* good I think she would respond quite well to a little kindness. But there it is, you cannot get milk from a pig, as my husband was wont to say."

"Now, Auntie, we shouldn't speak ill of people we have never even met," said Miss Louisa.

"I take people as I find them, Louisa, and in this case I'm quite sure I don't wish to find them at all," returned Mrs. Illridge.

Miss Louisa pursed her lips and elected not to reply. Two points to Mrs. Illridge.

"So, yes, Michael, please do," she said, returning to the original subject. "And since you were not able to join us at noon, I hope you will join us for the evening meal?"

"I'm not sure what Mrs. Williams is planning," I said. "I'd hate to offend her." I still hadn't laid eyes on Mrs. Williams, whom I pictured as a stout, grandmotherly lady, probably one who had helped Thompson take care of the young Tristram in years gone by and now continued to do so on a more irregular basis. All I knew for sure was that Freddie went into the kitchen and brought delicious food out to the dining room, and I wanted to make sure that that continued. You know, they make jokes about English cooking...but either they are mistaken or there's something different about the Commonwealth.

"Dora Williams isn't one to pitch a fit," said Mrs. Illridge. "Just stop by the cottage when you get into town and have Freddie give her fair warning."

"If you're sure it won't cause any trouble."

"Oh, I'm quite sure that Freddie is up to it."

"I'll do that, then."

"And if you would, Michael..." began Miss Louisa.

"Yes?"

"If you would stop at Mr. Clarke's shop? Miss Gwen has no shoes that are suitable for the countryside, and I've been told that Mr. Clarke now sells a line of shoes made in a manufactury in Yorkshire. I would never ordinarily buy such things ready made, but there is no time to have Mavisham make up a pair for her."

I said I would; then, smiling at both of them, I bowed a little and dashed off without further ceremony.

I'd been figuring on spending the afternoon mooching around Stockwood, chatting with all and sundry and looking for clues about the dim distant past, and instead I was heading back into Grayrigg with Gwen in tow. I wasn't as distressed by this as you might think; I'd been wanting to stop by at Mr. Mortimer's and see how the velocipede was coming, and I was pleased to have the opportunity to get to know another shopkeeper in town. You never know who will drop just the hint you need.

On top of that Gwen made an effort to be pleasant, which was a bit of a shock. Mind you, a pleasant Gwen was still Gwen. She began her campaign of kindness as we drove back out onto the road.

"Oh! Look at the lake, Michael! Look at how the light shimmers on the water! Isn't it beautiful?"

"Yes. Yes, it is."

"Oh! Oh! And those little islands, all covered with trees. I didn't see those when Mr. Monocle drove me here. One of them has a stone tower on it. Are they new, Michael?"

"As old as the hills, I'm sure. They were there a couple of days ago."

Gwen was silent for a few moments after that, until I began to wonder whether I'd offended her. I'd tried not to use a nasty tone of voice.

"Michael?" She didn't sound offended, which was a relief. If she started fulminating, I was going to have Freddie take us back to Stockwood.

"Yes?"

"How long have you known Mr. Monocle?"

"You'd better call him 'Cousin Tristram,' you know," I said. "Otherwise the people in Grayrigg might get confused, and Tristram might get into some trouble."

"Oh, but he isn't my cousin Tristram. Miss Louisa knows he isn't my cousin Tristram. And Mrs. Illridge knows he isn't my cousin Tristram."

I saw Freddie's ears perk up. That's right, I hadn't let him in on that part of it. I foresaw another talk in my future, but at the moment I needed to focus on coaching Gwen for her debut into Grayrigg society.

"Yes, but everyone else in Grayrigg thinks that he's your cousin Tristram, and that I'm your brother."

"They do?"

"A couple of days after Tristram mentioned it to Bert Wiggins? I think so."

"Oh. But—"

"Look, just go on calling me 'Michael.' Call him 'Cousin Tristram,' and don't be surprised if people assume we're related. OK?"

"All right. But you aren't my brother. And he isn't my cousin Tristram."

"Gwen—"

"Oh, very well, but truly I do not understand it at all."

"You don't need to understand it, you just need to remember it," I said. It occurred to me that prepping Gwen was a lot like programming a computer. Computers don't understand what you tell them, either. Not even when they seem to. It's just that some *other* human being instructed them to act that way, just as I was instructing Gwen. Now, if only I could rely on her memory....

"But how long have _you_ known Cousin Tristram, Michael?"

"Very good Gwen," I said, and she dimpled at me. "Not long at all, really. I'm not from the Commonwealth, you know."

"Is that why you speak so oddly?"

"Um. Yeah, I guess so."

"Oh. I thought so, for I have always been told that people from the Colonies have many uncouth ways."

"Thank you for that, Gwen." She dimpled at me some more. "Who told you that? I thought you were given no schooling."

"Why, my aunt did. She said it often and often. 'Gwen,' she'd say,"—and here Gwen adopted a stiff and forbidding face and tone of voice—'The manner in which you behave, you might as well be from the Colonies.'"

"A real charmer, your Aunt."

"Why, no, she isn't charming at all. I have always wondered how my uncle could have come to marry her." Then she pursed her lips and frowned. "But then, I have always wondered how my aunt could have come to marry _him_."

"Sounds like they are well suited."

"Oh! You are quite right. How odd. But then, Michael, if you are from the Colonies, how did you come to be here?"

I flashed back momentarily to the gunfight at Mordred's, and shuddered a little. I thought I wouldn't start there. On the other hand, I didn't want to lie to her; Bernie frowns on that.

"My mother died," I said, choosing my words carefully. "And then, I needed to find somewhere safe to live. So I came here to live with Cousin Tristram."

"Oh, that is terribly sad," she said, eyes wide. "How ever did she die?"

"She was killed by savages," I said. Which was true enough, even if Khazretgali's men weren't the kind of savages the Pathfounder met in his excursions in the Far West.

"Oh! I am so sorry. My mother died, too, at least I believe she did, for I never knew her, and my father too, I think, which is how I came to be living with my aunt, who is so unkind to me. I do not like my aunt, which is not very odd, you know, because she is quite an unlikeable person. But what about your father?"

"What about my father?"

"Why, what happened to your father? Your mother died, but you must have a father, too. Most people do, I believe."

"Oh," I said. Well, it was infectious. I frowned a little. "He went away when I was very small. I never knew him. I have no idea where he is, or even if he's still alive."

"But why would he be dead? It can't have been that long ago, for you are not very old, you know. You might still see him again."

"It's been longer than you might think," I said. "I'm small for my age."

"Are you?"

"Yes."

"Oh. So you left the Colonies and came to live with Cousin Tristram. I am very sorry for you, for he seems to be quite as unkind as my aunt." Now she frowned. "No, not as unkind, for he has never beat me. But he seems to laugh at me behind that monocle of his, and I don't like it."

"Tristram has been extremely kind to me," I said. I passed over her accusations of laughter, which were certainly true. I was a little surprised that she'd noticed, though. "I was injured shortly after I arrived in the Commonwealth, and he took good care of me."

"Oh, you were injured? Did you fall? I fell down the stairs once, because I stepped on the hem of the dress I had borrowed from my cousin, because it was too long, and I broke my arm, and my cousin and my aunt wouldn't talk to me for weeks, all because the dress got torn, and my cousin stole my favorite bonnet and left it outside in the rain and it was ruined."

"Um, no. Actually, I got shot."

"Shot! But who shot you? Where did they shoot you?"

"In Remchester Park," I said, before I could help myself.

"Oh! Is that in London?"

"Yes."

"But who was it?"

"I don't know really. But he didn't seem to like me."

"Perhaps he was an enemy of your father?"

"Something like that," I said. That wasn't too far off the mark, given my father's reasons for leaving us. "Yes, something like that."

"Oh! Oh! So that's what you meant!"

"What?"

"In the stable! I asked why that man attacked you, and you said, 'These things happen.' Do they really happen so often as all that?"

"Often enough," I said, shifting in my seat. I didn't like how this conversation was going. "Anyway, Cousin Tristram took pity on me, and we found that we got on well. He's an orphan too."

Her eyes widened again. "He is?"

"Yup. We have a lot in common. His mother died when he was quite small—in childbirth, he said—and then his father went away. He had it harder than me; I at least knew my mother. He never did."

"Humph!" she said. "Then I dislike him all the more. If he is an orphan then he should be more understanding!"

"Hang on just a minute, there. You realized that at this moment he's in Edinburgh, on his own dime, trying to find your cousin? He could have spent his time trying to find out where your aunt lives, instead." And he'd have succeeded, I suddenly realized. He had the skills, and he had the manpower. At least, he'd have had the manpower if he returned to Remchester's service.

"On his own dime? But I thought he went in his phaeton."

"I mean, he's paying his own expenses."

"Oh." Her brow furrowed. "Well, then I shall try not to dislike him quite so much. But it will be hard! He was rude to me, and he took away my little gun."

"But he gave it back. It's in your pocket."

"No, it isn't. It is in my sleeve. Why would I keep it in my pocket, Michael?"

I had no answer to that, so perhaps it was fortunate that

Freddie pulled up in front of the cottage just a few moments later.

Chapter 39

"Bartlett," I said, "please go in and tell Mrs. Williams that we'll be dining at Stockwood tonight."

"Very good, sir," he said, and dashed—with all due decorum, as befit a Gentleman's Gentleman—into the cottage.

"How is your ankle?" I asked Gwen. "Are you up to walking into town?"

"Why, my ankle is much better, thank you. But only look!" And she indicated her feet. She was wearing light slippers, and they were a little too big for her.

"Now, now. Would your aunt approve of you showing your feet to a young lad?" I got a glare in response. "Well, OK. So maybe we'll ride at least as far as Mr. Clarke's."

"Mr. Clarke's? But who is Mr. Clarke?"

"Apparently he sells shoes. Miss Louisa said to stop and get you some."

"Oh! Miss Louisa is quite unlike my aunt."

After that Gwen and I sat quietly on the bench seat of the cart until Freddie dashed out again, in similar manner, a couple of minutes later.

"All fixed up, Master Henderson," he said, grinning.

"How far away is Mr. Clarke's shop, Bartlett? Miss Louisa wants me to find some stout shoes for Miss Gwen."

"Clarke's is at the other end of the high street, Master Henderson."

"Then drive on, Bartlett!"

"Very good, sir."

Our progress down the high street was both very like and very unlike my walk down the high street a couple of days prior. We were riding rather than walking, of course, though as I've explained before that made less difference than you'd think. And we attracted a great deal of attention, just as I had—but the quality of the attention was different.

The people who'd greeted me two days before greeted me again—"And is this your sister? How lovely you are, my dear." (Dimples.) Several of them invited us to tea, and I had to hope that Freddie was making mental notes, because I had no idea who any of these people were.

The people who'd noticed me and then ignored me all looked much friendlier. They even seemed to look at us—at Gwen, really—with a kind of approval that I was at a loss to account for, and some of them unbent far enough to say hello, and to have Freddie introduce us.

The people who'd looked at me with out-and-out disapproval now had considering looks. Well, except for the old lady who was outraged by my lack of proper buckles on my knee breeches. But even she favored Gwen with something that might have been a smile had it been on a nicer looking face.

Something had changed, but I didn't know what it was.

In due time Freddie brought us to a halt in front of a house identical to all of the others on the high street, except that it had a square display window by the door and a hanging sign that said, "Clarke's Sundries." Inside it was about as unlike Mordred & Sons as you could imagine, with far too many goods crammed into much too small a space. It was, however, well-lit, which probably hadn't been the way even a decade earlier. Little by little the Steam Revolution was coming to the English countryside.

There was a counter, its surface covered with candy jars, tobacco jars, and piles of labeled boxes a yard high; and right in the middle of the counter was an open space about eighteen inches wide, and in the middle of the open space was a glum face with glasses and a mustache that I took to be Mr. Clarke.

I threaded my way to the counter. The glum face said, "May I help you?"

"Good afternoon, sir!" I said. "My name is Michael Henderson, and this is my sister, Gwen. Miss Clarenton says we need to get Gwen some stout shoes. Can you help us?"

The face brightened up.

"Shoes? Why, yes, I can, lad. I've got just the thing. Just a moment, just a moment, let me find Mrs. Clarke, I'll be just a moment." He vanished through a door behind the counter, and I heard a muffled "Maria! Maria!" Then he reappeared through another door into the main part of the shop, ushering in front of him a woman I took to be Mrs. Clarke.

"Maria," he said, "This lad and lass are Tristram Monocle's young cousins; and they want to buy some *shoes*!" He seemed inordinately pleased, and she seemed inordinately surprised. I concluded that Miss Louisa's lack of confidence in machine-made shoes was widely shared in Grayrigg, and not least by Mr. Clarke's better half. But she took her reversal in stride.

"Well, then, young lady," she said, placing a stool in front of us, "Just you sit down and I'll take your measurements."

Gwen sat down, and extended her feet, exposing her hand-me-down slippers and a bit of ankle. Mrs. Clarke looked sternly at her husband, who popped out the door and popped back in behind the counter. She didn't comment on the slippers—at least, not audibly—but produced a T-shaped gauge with ruler marks on it. It was labeled "Alderson's Finest Shoes, Yorkshire. *Made by Steam*."

Mrs. Clarke put the gauge on the wood floor.

"Up you stand, young lady. There, with your heel just so. Yes." Then she called out some numbers to her husband, who noted them down on a slate.

"And what kind of shoes are you in need of today?" he asked.

"Stout walking shoes, Miss Clarenton said." Gwen looked at

me, and then at the slippers. "And maybe a pair of slippers for indoors?" I added.

"Slippers, yes," he noted on the slate. "And who will be paying? Miss Clarenton?"

I'd been thinking about that.

"Does my cousin Tristram have an account here?"

"Surely he does, lad."

"Then I think Cousin Tristram had better pay for them. Miss Clarenton has been too kind to us already."

"Done," he said. I had expected some kind of haggling over the price, but apparently Miss Clarenton and Mr. Monocle were presumed to be above that kind of thing. He went into the back of the shop, and came out after several minutes with a stack of boxes, which he placed in the open space in the middle of the counter. Meanwhile, Mrs. Clarke rummaged about and came up with some black socks, though I suspect she'd have called them stockings. As they were never referred to by name in my hearing I really can't say for sure. Then Mrs. Clarke collected the boxes of shoes and came and knelt down in front of Gwen, and gave me a significant look.

"I'll just go wait outside, shall I?" I said.

She gave me an approving nod, so I went outside to talk to Freddie.

"Freddie," I began.

"Bartlett, sir," he said, looking significantly around him.

"Bartlett, then. Bartlett, do you ever visit the local pub of an evening?"

He grinned. "I've been known to do that, sir."

"I'd like you to visit it this evening, after we're back from Stockwood."

He looked troubled. "But it isn't my half-day, sir."

I looked blank. "Your half-day? What's that?"

"According to the books, sir, I get a half-day off each week."

"Oh. But I've never given you a half-day."

"It's only Thursday, sir."

"And it would look odd if you went to the pub on any other

day?"

"I should say so, sir. I'm supposed to be attending you. People would wonder at it."

"I see. But I was hoping…well, what it is, is that I'm quite curious to know why everyone is so much friendlier today."

"Oh, that, sir? I can tell you that, sir. At least, I think I can."

The door of the shop opened, and Gwen emerged with Mr. Clarke in tow. He was carrying a couple of parcels wrapped in brown paper and tied with twine, which he handed to Freddie.

"Here you go, young Bartlett."

"Thank you, sir."

And then to us, "Good day, Miss Henderson, Master Henderson."

"Good day, Mr. Clarke," said Gwen. I said nothing, because I was still gobsmacked by him calling Gwen "Miss Henderson." I mean, yes, that was the story, but still it hadn't occurred to me.

Freddie helped Gwen onto the cart, and I climbed up by myself.

"On to Mortimer's Motivators, Bartlett," I said. More than anything I wanted to get Freddie alone and find out what he knew, but that would have to wait.

Mr. Mortimer popped his head out of the double doors of his workshop the moment he heard our motivator-and-cart pull into his yard.

"Aha, there you are lad! Come in, quickly, I need you!" he said, and vanished again. A thrill of excitement washed through me, and also satisfaction—my plan was working.

"He needs you?" said Gwen. "Whatever for?"

"He's making me a steam-powered bicycle," I said. "Maybe he needs me to try it out."

"He is? But why would he do that?"

"I asked him to."

"But you have such a nice motivator, with Bartlett to drive it!"

"I thought it would be fun," I said. "You might not be acquainted with that, what with your aunt and all."

"Oh, but I am! Though it is another reason why I do not like my aunt, for she never wanted me to enjoy myself. I remember when—"

But I'd gotten down.

"You can come and see if you like."

Dimples, and a brilliant smile.

"Why, may I?"

"Oh, but miss!" said Freddie. "Please, be careful of your dress. It's sure to be dirty and greasy in there."

The dimples vanished. The smile frowned. "Oh, is it?"

Mr. Mortimer stuck his head out again. "Come, lad! There's no time like the present!"

"I'm sorry, sir," I said. "I was explaining to my sister about the steam velocipede."

"Your sister?" Mr. Mortimer looked around his yard with a puzzled expression, as if he'd heard of sisters but had never expected to actually meet one in person and wondered what they might look like. Eventually his gaze settled on Gwen. "Aha! That would be you, would it?"

There were more dimples, though I don't think Mr. Mortimer noticed.

"Heard about the fracas yesterday afternoon," he said. "Well done, miss, well done. We don't need any of that kind around here. Don't need 'em anywhere, really. Better they learn to stay away." He frowned. "I suppose you can watch from the doorway if you like, but you'd better not come in. A motivator shop is no place for pretty dresses."

"Why, thank you!" said Gwen. She looked at Freddie until he summoned up the wit to hop down from the motivator and help her to the ground.

"Now, lad!" said Mr. Mortimer, and swept me into the workshop, swinging the double doors wide. Gwen stood by one of them, keeping a careful eye on the skirts of her dress.

There was an assemblage of junk in the middle of the floor. I looked past it, and around at the corners, looking for my new bicycle. I was still looking when Mr. Mortimer waved at the assemblage and said, "Climb on!"

"Climb on? But…how? It doesn't look anything like a velocipede."

And yet, when I examined it more closely, it sort of did. There were no wheels, and no steam plant, and it was made of bits of scrap metal and wood clamped to something like a sawhorse… but there was a straight bit of pipe that might be handlebars, and a wooden block that might just be a seat, and were those foot pegs?

"Of course it doesn't, lad! But I have to know how big to make it. Climb on, and let me take some measurements."

I climbed on, and sat on the seat with my hands on the pipe and my feet on the pegs. The pipe was a bit too far away, and the pegs were a little too close, and I thought the seat could be raised a bit. But Mr. Mortimer didn't ask, he just started in with the measuring tape. After that it was like being fitted for clothes all over again, except that instead of having to try things on I was having to get on and off the model while Mr. Mortimer adjusted things. I was sorry Tristram wasn't here to watch, because I think he'd have enjoyed it.

"There we are, lad," he said at last. "Now I have a better idea of the space I have to work with. Come back in a couple of days and we'll see what we can see." And he went to a workbench and began sketching in a notebook, referring to the measurements he'd recorded on his slates.

I shrugged, and climbed off of the beast.

"Thank you, sir," I said, not that I think he heard me. Then I collected Gwen, and we went on our way.

Chapter 40

"So, Freddie," I said, as he placed a cup of hot tea on the table in front of me. I held it in both hands, letting the warmth seep into my fingers.

"Bartlett, sir," he said, hurriedly. "Must keep up appearances, sir."

"Freddie, it's late."

"Indeed it is, sir. But appearances matter, whether it's late or early. That's what the books say."

"Freddie, you're being impertinent. Thank you for the tea."

"Am I, sir? How shocking. You're welcome, sir."

As he spoke he went from window to window, closing the drapes and shutting out the darkness and cold. Especially the cold, and I was heartily glad of it. We'd left Stockwood just as the sun was setting; I'd not been out by night, much, since coming to the Commonwealth, and I wasn't prepared for how chilling the lake breeze could be after dark.

It was what Freddie was supposed to be doing, but I had the sense he was bustling about for another reason altogether.

After closing the last set of drapes he returned to my side.

"Will there be anything more, sir?" he said in hopeful tones—hopeful, that is, that I was done and he could escape.

"Yes, there will be something more. I'm beginning to think you don't want to talk to me."

"Ah...yes, sir? I mean, no, sir? Ah, why would you think that, sir?"

"Freddie, do I need to make you sit down at the table and have a cup of tea?"

"Oh, no, sir—only, I am rather chilled, sir?"

"Fine, but you're not getting away that easily. Go and find yourself some tea, or whatever you'd prefer to drink to warm you up, and then come back here. Got it?"

"Yes, sir," he said, in resigned tones. "A moment, sir." He vanished through the servant's door into the kitchen.

I didn't mind him wanting to get warm. That was only reasonable; after all, I wanted to get warm too. But this was my first opportunity to speak privately with him since Gwen had emerged from Mr. Clarke's shop with her new shoes, and I still wanted to know why everyone was so much friendlier today. I thought Mr. Mortimer's comments about the intruder were part of it, but I wanted to hear Freddie's explanation. Only now he didn't want to give it.

"Ah, sir?" I looked up; Freddie had stuck his head through the doorway. "It's most improper of me to suggest this...but it's much warmer in the kitchen, and Mrs. Williams has gone for the day, so she won't mind."

I rose from the table with all speed, teacup in hand.

"Lead on, MacDuff," I cried.

Freddie held the door for me. "It's 'Lay on,' sir," he said. "'Lay on, MacDuff.'"

"But I don't want you to lay on, I want you to lead on."

"As you say, sir." So he led me down a short passage into a part of the cottage I'd not yet seen. The walls were plastered and painted in a light beige; the kitchen was equally simple and functional, with few homey touches, but it was warm, and I settled gratefully at the small table in the corner.

Freddie came and joined me a few moments later, mug in hand. I saw a green bottle on the hutch behind him.

"Aha!" I said. I handed him my teacup, which was mysteriously empty, and pointed at his mug. "Get me one like that, please."

"One like this, sir? But—"

"I'm twenty-eight? Married? Of age?"

"Right, sir."

He filled another mug from a pot on the stove, added a slug from the green bottle, and brought it to me, and by gosh and by golly it was coffee. Well, mostly coffee.

"Coffee? You've got coffee?"

"Why, yes sir." He seemed surprised. "You've always asked for tea."

"But…but…coffee!"

"I'll keep that in mind, sir."

I sipped it gratefully. I'm not sure what kind of spirits he'd added, but it did the trick, and between that and the coffee and the warmer air I began to feel a little more human.

"Now, Freddie," I began. "Earlier you said you knew why everyone was acting so much more friendly. Was it because Gwen shot that intruder?"

He nodded. "Yes, sir. At least, mostly."

"OK. But what did Mr. Mortimer mean by 'We don't need any of that kind around here'?"

He hesitated, then spoke.

"Lord Remchester's men, sir."

I frowned.

"They think he was from Lord Remchester, and that he was trying to abduct me to put pressure on Tristram?"

"In a word, sir."

That was…interesting. I knew perfectly well that my attacker wasn't working for Lord Remchester, but no one else in town was in a position to see that. And it would explain Miss Louisa's reaction as well. She wasn't simply being matter-of-fact; she'd been expecting some such move on Remchester's part—and was perfectly content with the outcome.

"Fascinating. And that makes them friendlier, why? It seems like shooting one of Lord Remchester's men would bring trouble down on Grayrigg."

"Lord Remchester isn't very popular around here, sir. And the man was trespassing. And he *did* try to abduct you.

"But really, sir, it's a sign to everyone that Mr. Monocle really *has* broken with Lord Remchester, and that's a thing everyone is pleased to see. And of course they think better of Gwen knowing she's a reliable shot."

"How do you know all this?" I asked. "You've had no time to talk to anyone since it happened."

"I've spoken with Mrs. Williams. But I don't need to talk to anyone, sir, not about this. I'm from Grayrigg."

I nodded, accepting that at face value.

Freddie asked, "Will that be all, sir?" There was a "please" in there, somewhere, but it was silent.

I shook my head. "Not likely. You used the word 'mostly' a bit ago. It's *mostly* because Gwen shot the man that they are being friendly. So…what's the rest of it?"

"Oh, well, sir…" He looked away, and there we were. This was the part Freddie didn't want to talk about.

"Yes, Freddie? You were saying?"

"I, uh, I wasn't, sir. Saying, I mean." He drank from his mug, looking anywhere but at me.

"Oh, yes, you were. Or, least, you will be."

He took a long breath. "As you wish, sir."

"I *do* wish."

He paused, took another drink. At last he said, "It's because they've seen how old Miss Gwen is, sir."

I looked at him over the rim of my mug, puzzled.

"And because they've seen you and Miss Gwen together, sir."

I continued to stare at him. What was he getting at?

Freddie began to sweat. I made "get on with it" motions with my free hand.

"And because Miss Gwen is too old to be Mr. Monocle's daughter, sir."

I blinked. Several times. Freddie looked at his mug, and then over at the wall, and then at me, and then back at his mug, and then at the table.

"They…thought…that Gwen might be Mr. Monocle's

daughter?"

"Ah, yes, sir. They did."

"And why would they think that?"

"He's, ah, he's been away for a long time, sir. He's only been back for short visits. No one's been sure what he might have been getting up to in Town."

"Such as fathering natural daughters, I presume? Because *some* people were inclined to think the worst?"

"Yes, ah, yes, sir. And then, if he broke with Lord Remchester he'd naturally want to protect his, ah, his *family*, sir."

"Well, OK, anybody would. But hang on a minute. Why would they think that she was his daughter?"

"Because she's your sister, sir."

"Because—hey, wait a minute. They think I'm Tristram's *son*?"

He nodded sadly. "Yes, sir. Or, they did. No one had ever heard of any cousins until Mr. Monocle arrived with you and Gwen. And given your age—your *apparent* age, sir—and he put you in his own cottage...and you do look *so* like him...."

"—It was a reasonable conjecture. I see." I drained my mug, and held it out to Freddie. "I think you'd best get me another."

I thought hard while Freddie got busy with pot and bottle.

"So let me see if I've got this straight," I said. "When I showed up in town as Tristram's cousin, rumor had it that I was his natural son; and his other 'cousin,' Gwen, must therefore be his daughter. But now they've seen Gwen, and they realize that she's too old to be his daughter—unless he got busy before he left Grayrigg, and it's pretty clear that he didn't. So she must really *be* a cousin, not a daughter, and since I'm her brother I must really be a cousin too."

"Yes, sir."

"Did they really think Tristram would fob off his illegitimate daughter on Miss Clarenton?"

"Some did, sir," said Freddie, miserably. "Or worse."

"Or *worse*, Freddie? How could it be worse?"

"He might have gotten into the petticoat line, sir."

That was a term I'd run into in Bernie's books.

"They thought he might have taken his mistress to Stockwood?" I was flabbergasted. I stared at him as I tried to take it in.

"Some of them had been thinking the worst of him for a *very* long time, sir."

I looked around the room some more. There was a pendulum clock on the wall; its ticking seemed very loud.

"But now," I said slowly, "now that they've seen her...they don't think that anymore."

"I wouldn't think so, sir."

"And why is that?"

"Because she looks so much like Mr. Monocle...and like you, sir."

I was gobsmacked again. "She does?"

"Pretty close, sir."

I took a hefty slug of my fortified coffee, and then another, as I worked it out.

"So she must really be my sister, so we must be Tristram's cousins, because of her age, so he must be telling the truth, and so nobody has to feel bad on Miss Clarenton's behalf. God is in His heaven, and all is right with the world. Is that what they're thinking?"

"Yes, sir. That's the size of it," said Freddie, fidgeting with his mug. He seemed more nervous than ever. "But she's not his cousin. I heard her say so. Who is she really, sir?"

"That, Freddie," I said, "is the sixty-four dollar question. If we knew that, Tristram wouldn't have had to go to Edinburgh."

Chapter 41

"So that's what I know," I said, some while later. "She's a menace when she's not being a watering pot, and I'm just glad she missed yesterday. She was surprisingly pleasant today, though."

"Missed, sir?" said Freddie, folding up my trousers. "She hit the man square on, he was dead before he hit the ground."

"Well, that's true," I said, as I pulled the night shirt over my head. "But the shot went about an inch from *my* head."

"Oh, sir, surely you don't think—"

"—that she was aiming for me? No, of course not. I've just got no confidence in her marksmanship."

Freddie shook his head. Of course, in the Commonwealth "gun control" means hitting what you aim at.

"You yourself have improved remarkably, sir. Will there be anything else, sir?"

I settled down on the edge of my bed. "No, I don't think so." I picked up *The Pathfounder* from the side table and frowned. It looked like I had only a few pages to go; and though I hadn't given Tristram's *public* shelves a thorough browsing their contents all seemed fairly heavy. "Unless…is there any light reading in the house? Or a bookstore in town? I've nearly finished my book."

"Thompson has a shelf of novels in his room, sir. Shall I pick one for you?"

"Please," I said. "Something like this, for choice." I held up the book. "*The Pathfounder*, by Cowper Madisen."

Freddie's brows went up. "The name is familiar, sir. By your leave?"

I waved him on; he returned a few moments later with a similarly bound volume and a grin.

"I was right, sir! Thompson appears to have a complete set of Madisen's works." He handed me the volume. "This one was shelved next to *The Pathfounder.*"

I took it. It appeared to have been well and frequently read; the cover was worn, and many of the pages had been dog-eared at one time or another. The spine read, "Cowper Madisen. *The Rest of the Malthusians.*" These words were repeated on the title page, which added, "Being the continuing adventures of the Pathfounder."

I nodded at Freddie. "Thanks, Freddie. This is just what I was looking for."

He smiled broadly, then frowned. "Bartlett, sir. You did say you would try."

"Oh, very well. Thanks, Bartlett."

"My pleasure, sir. Good night."

The next morning followed the established pattern. I had a delightful breakfast, courtesy of the elusive Mrs. Williams, featuring scones with honey and the best bacon I've ever had, after which I barricaded myself into the study and got to work.

Yesterday morning I was strictly business; today I was a little more self-indulgent. My discovery that Stockwood and its estates had been forfeited to one C. Stavely, index S3, had been chasing itself round and round in the back of my head all through the previous afternoon and evening, looking for something to attach to, and finding no certainty. Was this S3 actually Lord Charles Stavely, father of the ferrous Melissa? Or was it some other member of the family? I'd met Melissa's brother, *Cedric* Stavely, but surely it couldn't have been him. Or was it some unrelated dangling Stavely of some sort? Lord Charles seemed the most likely, but I didn't know.

And then, how did it pass from this Mr. C. "S3" Stavely to Tristram? I found myself formulating conjecture after conjecture, but all of them depended on who Stavely was. I built towering structures of hypotheses over and over again, but they kept blowing away in the wind.

I've often reflected that a software engineer is a guy who builds castles in the air…but to do that you need a pretty solid keel to build on. It might be floating in mid-air, but it still has to be solid. All I had here were clouds and a high wind and a driving need to understand.

This makes for unrestful nights, especially when dream logic sets in. Before I woke up I spent hours searching Stavely's house in London for the deed to Stockwood so that Tristram could give it to Mr. Mortimer in payment for my steam-cycle in lieu of foreclosing on the First Lord's Head, which somehow was Tristram's instead of Bert Wiggins'. And all through it Miss Melissa Stavely followed me ponderously from room to room and stared at me with cold gray eyes. (I really don't know how so slender a woman can give such an impression of mass.)

On top of that, all I found were countless copies of Tristram's *The Founding of the Civil Commonwealth of Britain and the Isles*, all with copious profane annotations in red ink, and endless file boxes containing a myriad of dented bowler hats. What they were doing in the drawing room, I'm sure I'll never know. I tried to look their owners up in the index, but the numbers on the paper tags kept shifting.

Despite what Bernie says, I *can* take a hint. The first thing I did after opening the Closet of Secrets was to grab the first notebook of dossiers and flip to the third entry.

It began, *Stavely, Charles. Son of S2, and heir to Stavely Textiles. Principle ally of R1 following death of S2.* I flipped to S2, which proved to be one Jack Stavely.

The dossiers made for interesting reading. Jack Stavely had made his pile as the owner of a number of steam-powered textile mills of his own design. Socially he'd come up from nowhere, his father being a poor weaver from the north of England; but he was bright and innovative, and the steam revolution had come just at the right time. He'd grown rich, and also furious at the glass ceiling that kept him from joining those he'd regarded as his intellectual inferiors. He'd been Remchester's mentor when the latter was a young man, and the two of them had planned out Remchester's strategy in detail before Jack's death.

After that, it seemed, Remchester had more or less inherited old Jack's eldest son Charles, a man rich in cunning and vitriol but lacking any sense of restraint where money or gaming were concerned. He'd been invaluable in the early days, showing particular skill at ferreting out enemies of the revolution, and also at ensuring that portions of all confiscated funds ended up in his own pockets.

The most interesting bit was the notation, *Relieved of intelligence duties, 1 July 4 N.O.* Wasn't that...I slid the first of the journals out of its place and glanced at the cover. Yes, that's when Tristram took over as Remchester's spymaster. Remchester had replaced Stavely with Tristram; I wondered why. Perhaps Stavely had gotten a little too prone to finding enemies wherever there was money to be had? By 4 N.O. the fighting had been over for a couple of years, and stability would have been the name of the game. Perhaps Stavely had no longer been quite so much of an asset.

And yet, Remchester hadn't cut ties with him. Stavely had retained his seat in the Assembly, hence his title of "Lord," and he'd remained Remchester's close political ally. Odd.

The dossier included a list of Stavely's property transactions: confiscated, received, and (mostly) sold. I was surprised to note that the "sold" column included all of Lord Charles' father's mills. Stockwood was also in the sold column, but without any further details.

I returned the notebook of dossiers to the shelf. So, Lord Charles Stavely. Gambler; wastrel; opportunist, and very much on the make; tactically cunning, ruthless, and ultimately too extreme even for Lord Remchester.

I didn't need to ask how he got his hands on Stockwood; that was clear enough. Squire Illridge probably hadn't bowed low enough to suit him; and in return Lord C had vindictively arranged to take his lands. But how had Tristram gotten his hands on them?

I wouldn't find anything in his official journals; they started in 4 N.O., and Stockwood had been confiscated in 1 N.O. I took down the little diary I'd found, and settled down in Tristram's desk chair.

I turned to the first page.

The Journal of T. MacHendry.

3 June 1772. Thompson says I must keep a journal, because my grandfather says that gentlemen must know how to express themselves...

So Tristram had grown up as Tristram MacHendry.

MacHendry. Henderson. Now *there* was a smoking gun, if you like.

Despite having looked forward to digging into it, I felt odd peeking into Tristram's diary. The dossiers and journals were "public" documents, as it were, records of Tristram's time in public service. They were written for Tristram's own use, but were also designed to preserve details of Remchester's administration for posterity. The diary was no such thing, and I was afraid I'd come across things that I had no business reading.

The current year was 15 N.O., 1802 in the old reckoning, and I was looking for a date in 1 N.O.; so I flipped pages until I found the first entry for 1777. It read:

4 January 1777. Tea at Stwd with Sq. I—. & fam. Spoke with L— after.

A few pages later, I saw this:

8 January 1777. Mkt day. Met L— on high street.

So much for expressing himself, though I suppose brevity *is* the soul of wit. I flipped to the beginning of the diary, and saw that the entries there were rather longer; but after the first few weeks Tristram was recording only the outstanding events, either because they were out of the ordinary or because they were important to him. "*L—*," for example, appeared on almost every page.

But the event I was looking for wouldn't have happened until after Remchester's arrival; and Remchester wouldn't have been campaigning in January. I riffled quickly ahead to May, and then flipped pages more slowly looking for longer entries—Remchester would have been worthy of more note than usual.

I began seeing mention of rebellion in late May, with Remchester's name first appearing a week or so later. The entries all concerned news that had reached Grayrigg; the revolution was still distant. But then,

17 June 1777. Market day. L— did not come to town; Remchester and his men are too near.

22 June 1777. B— says Remchester seen 12 mi. south. He will be here tomorrow.

I presumed that *B—* was Bert Wiggins. Then, there it was: a rare blot at the beginning of the line, and then, in a hand rather less tidy than usual,

23 June 1777. Remchester is here. He has offered me a position as his secretary. Dare I take it? What will happen to me if I do? What will happen to L— if I don't?

On the next line, in a hand closer to his usual, unruffled script: *I have decided to accept Remchester's offer. In his employ, I may be of service to L—. If I reject him, I might well be of service to no one ever again.*

24 June 1777. I am to pack and be ready to leave Grayrigg tomorrow. Is there time to see L—?

The following days were filled with discussions of his duties and details of travel, and included references to a number of men whose names I recognized from his history, Stavely prominent among them. There were no mentions of *L—*; evidently he hadn't been able to visit Grayrigg...or perhaps he thought it inadvisable.

27 June 1777. R— told me that my grandfather and cousin are dead. His doing? Mustn't question.

Over time, Remchester took Tristram further into his confidence.

12 August 1777. R— told me that 'It had come to his attention' that I

was my grandfather's heir; my cousin had predeceased him, and so in the Old Order I would now be Lord U—. The U— estates are forfeit to the Revolution. R— says the title must be retired; there will be no patents of nobility in the New Order. However, he knows that I am 'no enemy of the Revolution,' and in reward for my work I am to be allowed to keep the monetary portion of my grandfather's bequest—provided that I renounce my new name and continue to show my loyalty to the New Order. And so I must betray my benefactor. But what else am I to do? I am wholly in R—'s power.

And then, finally:

9 September 1777. Disaster. Meeting with R— and S—. S— reports that he suspects Sq. I— of working with R—'s enemies, and that his lands must be confiscated. R— wrote up writ of confiscation on the spot. I do not believe it; but S— has been gaming heavily, and is short of funds.

L— must not be made homeless.

10 September 1777. Sleepless night. Tackled S— after the noon meal. Adopted S—'s own manner, and maligned good Sq. I— most unfairly. Persuaded him of my jealousy of Sq. I— and family, and my own desire to 'do Illridge in the eye,' may God forgive me. Persuaded him to give me the writ of confiscation (and therefore Stwd and environs) in exchange for my bequest. R— will not know; he trusts S— to dispose of confiscated property honorably.

O, the depths to which I have sunk. But L will be safe, and I have sent T — to explain matters to Sq. I—. L— must not know. As for me, I am now destitute; the income from the Illridge lands must go to Stwd. Shall I ever be able to leave R—'s service?

The next mention of Stockwood was in October, when Remchester next came swinging back through Westmorland.

7 October 1777. Visited Grayrigg to take possession of Illridge lands; I must, or S— will grow suspicious. I despise him more each day, yet I must not antagonize him.

L— would not see me.

He gave everything he had for "*L—*"; and she rejected him. Of course she did. What did she see? A lad she'd grown up with and admired, throwing away everything she valued to run off with her family's enemy. I'm sure she felt she had never known him. And then, the theft of her patrimony—I'm sure she felt immeasurably betrayed.

But why hadn't he told her? Squire Illridge, it is clear, knew all; but Tristram did not permit him to explain things to Miss Louisa.

Poor, doomed, too proud Tristram. What else could she see? He'd never declared himself; they didn't have any kind of "understanding" as Bernie's novels would put it. As a gentleman and the grandson of an earl he was of suitable rank, but with his minimal fortune he wasn't an eligible match. His sense of rectitude would not have permitted him to speak of love to a woman he could not support. She didn't know his mind, and he'd had no time to speak to her before Remchester spirited him away. When he followed Remchester out of town she took the surface view for the whole of the truth, and when he returned, writ in hand, she took it as confirmation that he was everything she hated.

Really, it *was* a plot right out of one of Bernie's novels. Tristram wanted to be loved for himself, for the young man he'd been before Remchester took him away, and not for gratitude. Or no, gratitude would have been all right. But not for *necessity*. He'd arranged things with Squire Illridge that the family would continue to live in the manor house; only the surrounding agricultural lands were to have been *publicly* confiscated. But the manor and its immediate estate couldn't remain a going concern without Tristram's help, without the income from those lands. Without that, the Illridges and Miss Louisa would descend into pauperdom.

Had he offered for her, and had Miss Louisa known what he'd done and why, her sense of duty might have compelled her to accept him in marriage; and he wanted her love, not her sense of duty. And if she married him to save Stockwood while he remained in Remchester's employ, that's all he would have gotten.

And then—oh. Of course. Even had he wished, even had she been willing, he *couldn't* have married her then without giving Remchester's game away. It suited Remchester's narrative for Tristram to take the Illridge lands out of envy; it even suited

Remchester's narrative for him to punish his former friends by letting them perch precariously on the last vestige of those lands. It made a useful object lesson to other potential enemies of the state. But for Tristram to have married an enemy of the Revolution—that wouldn't have flown. Not then. Not for the way Remchester had wanted to use him.

He hadn't told Louisa because he *needed* her to be angry with him, and to be seen to be angry with him. It was just one more way that he protected her.

I wondered if the Squire and Mrs. Illridge had argued with him about that? I thought they probably had, especially as time went on. It was clear to me—and, I thought, to everyone else in Grayrigg—that Miss Louisa was still attached to the Tristram she'd once known, despite his betrayal, and indeed even to the Tristram that still was, even if it was against her better judgement. And after Tristram's declaration on his leavetaking, there could be no doubt of *his* attachment for her. And yet here we were. The forces that had been in play in the early days of the Revolution were no longer in play; and the pair of them were both too set in their ways to bend enough to make each other happy.

I closed the diary and returned it to the shelf, depressed at how things had worked out. It was time for shooting practice, and then lunch at Stockwood; and it seemed it was going to be my turn to be distracted and uncommunicative.

Chapter 42

I got away from Stockwood as early as I could that afternoon, being in no mood for company. Freddie took me home, and ensconced me in a wingback chair in the sitting room with a pot of coffee and my book. And it was there that I sat stewing when all hell broke loose.

Mind you, it broke loose slowly. The first I knew of it was when Freddie poked his head into the sitting room.

"Sir, there's a man at the back door. He's looking for Mr. Monocle. I think you should see him."

I frowned, and marked my place—not that I'd actually been reading.

"Who is it, Freddie?"

"He says his name is Lackland, sir. He says it's urgent."

Lackland—that was the name of Remchester's agent, the one Tristram had discomfited in Lancaster.

"Show him in, then," I said in what I'm afraid was a surly tone of voice. I was still in a lousy mood, and Lackland's business wasn't likely to improve it.

Freddie half-smiled sheepishly. I think it was supposed to be apologetic, but it came out sheepish. "I'm sorry, but he won't come in, sir; says he has to fly."

I pursed my lips. I supposed that was a piece with his coming to the back door: perhaps he didn't want anyone to know he'd been here.

"Very well." Taking my book, I uncurled from my chair and followed Freddie to the rear of the cottage, where Lackland stood just inside the back door.

"Cousin Tristram's not here, Mr. Lackland," I said. "He's not back from Edinburgh. Can I help you?"

"Edinburgh!" Lackland sounded shocked. "Then it's true! Which he is betraying His Lordship!"

"Betraying His Lordship?" I said. "What are you talking about? No, he's off looking for Miss Gwen's aunt in Edinburgh."

But Lackland wasn't listening; his head was bowed in furious thought.

I stared at him in puzzlement. At last he looked up, eyes blazing.

"Tell him. He must fly—France, the Colonies, anywhere. He's not safe here. His Lordship says he's an Enemy of the Revolution. And Stavely's coming. He'll be here soon! Tell him!"

A jolt went through me. Stavely! Had Remchester given Stavely back his old job, now that Tristram had resigned? But it didn't matter, really; it was Stavely that was coming, and Stavely that was in charge, and Stavely that was going to put his hands on Tristram's assets by crook if he couldn't get them by marriage. Stavely was the last person I wanted to see. Remchester might give Tristram a fair hearing; Stavely certainly wouldn't.

Lackland gave me a long look, then nodded, satisfied. "Tell him!" he said, and whirling he tore the door open and was gone.

I watched him go. And then, moments after he rounded the corner of the cottage, I heard a gun shot; and then another, and a muffled thud. Stavely wasn't coming; Stavely was here.

I couldn't execute Plan A without getting shot; I couldn't execute plan A-prime without deserting Freddie. Plan B was a no-go; Stavely's men would be all over the cottage in moments. That left Plan C: direct action against the enemy.

"Freddie, get ready to welcome Lord Stavely," I said. "*Politely.*"

"But he—that man—"

"Politely, I said!"

And then I ran for Tristram's study.

It seemed only a few seconds but may have been as much as five minutes before I heard doors slamming and heavy footsteps on the stair. I had just sat down behind Tristram's desk with my book when I heard a hand on the door latch.

I looked up as innocently as I could as two sharp-eyed men entered the room. They wore bowlers—unless they were derbies —and like Harry Lackland were dressed in plain, functional town clothing. Each carried a drawn steam-pistol, leveled and ready.

"Here, who are you? What are you doing in here?" I said in my best puzzled 10-year-old voice. But I didn't move, and I was careful to keep my hands in plain sight.

The Bowlers ignored me as they checked all corners of the room. Once they were satisfied that I was alone, Bowler #1 took up a position by the door, gun trained on me; Bowler #2 stepped into the hallway and muttered a few words I couldn't quite make out.

And then, in came a man I knew must be Lord Stavely.

He was tall and fat, or maybe fleshy is a better word, with a red face and a sneering mouth. He wore a fine blue coat and white breeches with tall riding boots, and carried an oaken stick with a brass knob. I have to say, his cravat was nothing so fine to look at as Tristram's.

He resembled his daughter, or she him; but where she was a pocket dreadnaught, deadly and cold, he gave the impression of Juggernaut, crushing his enemies to a red paste under his wheels.

A well-bred English lad of gentle family would stand in the presence of his elders come hell or high-water; so I did that thing, clutching *The Last of the Malthusians* to my chest. I looked from Stavely to Bowler #1's pistol, eyes wide, and back to Stavely, the very picture of the boy trying to be brave and not quite succeeding. When you're small for your age, it's important for your enemies to underestimate you.

"So, young 'Henderson,'" he said. "Where is Monocle?

Speak!"

"He's not here," I said. "He went north, on business." My eyes flicked over to the gun and back to Stavely. "Who are you?"

He snorted derisively. "Take him," he said. "Put him over there." He gestured to a corner by the window.

Bowler #1 continued to hold me at gunpoint while #2 moved the side chair to the corner. Then he gestured towards the chair with the barrel of his gun. Keeping my eyes on him, I went to the corner and sat down. He came and stood by me, gun to my head.

"You can't do this," I said. "This is the Commonwealth!"

Stavely snorted again. "And your cousin is an Enemy of the Commonwealth, boy, drawn and papered." Then, to Bowler #2, "Search this room. We found nothing in his town house, so his secrets must be here."

Town house. I felt a pang for Thompson. Was he all right? Was he in prison? And then, what about the Big Bag O' Finders? Not that Stavely or Remchester would know what they were, or be able to do anything with them, but it would be a nuisance if we had to retrieve them from some government office.

I sat there, visibly fuming, as Stavely's man took the room to pieces. He started with the desk. He checked each drawer, first combing through what was inside, then, after dumping the contents on the floor, checking the underside. Then he poked and prodded the desk's scrollwork and the insides of the drawer cavities.

"Nothing here, sir," he said at last. "Just stationery and domestic correspondence, and no hidden compartments."

Stavely said nothing, but came and sat himself at the desk, stick in hand. Bowler #2 moved on to the bookcases.

It was painful to watch. He took the books down one by one, riffled through them, and tossed them in the corner. "Nothing here, sir." When the shelves were empty he began studying the cases themselves. He hit on the left-hand bookcase almost immediately.

"This one, sir," he said, standing in front of it. "It shifts slightly. There'll be a latch somewhere."

"Send for tools," said Stavely. "I am concerned with the traitor's secrets, not the state of his furnishings."

"Yes, sir."

Bowler #2 left the room. Stavely turned his chair and looked at me for a long, considering moment.

"I don't suppose…no, Monocle would not be that stupid."

"He's not stupid!" I burst out.

He snorted, and nodded at #1. I winced as he rapped me on the head with the barrel of the pistol. I glared at Stavely, and he snorted again in a more satisfied tone.

"Be grateful you're of use to me, boy. I doubt very much that Monocle will want to leave his…cousin…in my hands."

#2 returned with two more Bowlers. One had a hammer, and the other a pry bar, and between the two of them they reduced the lefthand bookcase to splinters in short order.

"Ahhhh," said Stavely as the case came off of its hinges, revealing the hidden bookcase behind it. "Here we are!"

Rising from the chair, he laid his stick on the desk and went to examine the row of mismatched notebooks I'd placed on the top shelf. He smiled as he took one down, caressing it lovingly.

"Just what I need," he said to himself—we might as well have not been in the room. Then he opened it and swore horribly.

He riffled through the pages, and finding nothing that he could read he hurled the notebook to the floor. He grabbed another, opened it, and did the same. I watched in silent pleasure. Secrets Stavely expected, so secrets Stavely would find —but not secrets he could read. If Tristram had the transcriptions, I thought he could spare the originals.

It hadn't taken more than about thirty seconds to shift the coded journals from the hidden closet to the sliding shelves. It was opening and closing the deadbolt on the study door that had given me the most trouble.

Still swearing, and growing visibly more angry moment by moment, he yet took the time to check each notebook. When he was done he cried, "Rubbish! All rubbish! This is of no use to me!"

Then, taking his stick from the desk he turned to his men.

"Burn the house. Burn it well. I want nothing to survive. And bring the boy and his man."

I'm afraid I yelped. Burn the whole place down? I felt sick to my stomach.

As Stavely turned to face me I let all signs of rebellion drain from my face.

"Please, sir," I said. "May I get my things?"

I could see he wanted to have me shot and be done with me. I watched the calculations flutter across his contorted red face.

"One bag each," he said at last. "Personal items only." Then he swept out of the room.

I began to breath easier. A *little* easier. Apparently even Stavely couldn't leave a trail of dead children behind him without it coming home to roost. That must mean that he was acting as an official representative of the First Lord's government—or, at least, that he wanted to say so later on.

Bowler #2 came over to where I still sat at gunpoint. I rose from the chair at his gesture, and stood quietly as he relieved me of my belt and holster.

He looked at me, not unkindly; I wondered whether he'd been a friend of Harry Lackland. "Behave, and you'll get this back in due time," he said. "Misbehave, and I can't answer for His Nibs."

I just nodded solemnly, and let him lead me away.

Chapter 43

Bowler #2 watched carefully as Freddie packed my backpack, and made him open each of my books so that he could see there was nothing hidden inside. There wasn't, of course, though he seemed somewhat bemused by the covers of Bernie's paperbacks, which were quite unlike anything I'd seen in the Commonwealth. Then he did the same as Freddie packed a bag for himself. Then he followed us downstairs and out the front door, where he stood just behind me. His gun was drawn but he left it his side. Freddie, who had also been disarmed, stood at my left.

A fancy motivator and carriage, dusty from the road, stood on the gravel drive. Drawn up in front of it, trampling the flowers, were two ranks of soldiers in blue coats. They were equally dusty but no less menacing for all that, and they stood with their rifles at present arms, bayonets fixed.

Stavely himself stood on the flagstone path, leaning on his stick and eyeing the muttering crowd that was collecting on the high street. Bowler #1 stood at his elbow.

There were forty or fifty of the townsmen in all. Bert Wiggins was at the front, looking about ready to breathe fire; Freddie's father had his hand on Bert's arm and was speaking into his ear. The beadle stood next to him, glaring at Stavely and the troops, and next to him a simply dressed man I'd not yet met. (I later discovered that he was the vicar at St. John's.) Mr. Mortimer was further back; he nodded at me, looking worried. I didn't see any torches or pitchforks…but in the Commonwealth, who needed them? None held a drawn weapon, so far as I could see, but each had his shotgun or rifle slung over his shoulder; and I knew from experience how quickly those guns could come into play. Stavely had only eight soldiers and a few Bowlers in evidence; it wouldn't go well for him if the men of Grayrigg decided to cut loose. I began to look around for places to get out of the line of fire.

Stavely glanced over his shoulder at the sound of the front door closing, then looked back at the townsfolk. Drawing himself up to his full girth, he draw a piece of paper from within his coat and ostentatiously unfolded it. A tail of black ribbon dangled from the bottom.

The crowd went silent at the sight of the ribbon. Bert's eyes narrowed; Mr. Bartlett went white.

Holding the paper before him by its top and bottom, Stavely began to read in a stentorian voice:

> *Due to his manifold and great crimes against the Civil Commonwealth of Britain and the Isles, and in accordance with law and custom, Tristram J. Monocle, formerly esquire, is declared an Enemy of the Commonwealth, his property forfeit. Let none aid him, let no man seek to give him comfort, but let him be brought to justice with all speed.*

> *By my hand this day. Remchester, First Lord.*

Stavely lowered the writ with satisfaction, and surveyed the crowd.

"Would anyone care to inspect the document?"

Bert Wiggins lunged forward, but Mr. Bartlett pulled him back. The vicar inclined his head.

"I would," he said.

Stavely handed the writ to Bowler #1, who carried it to him.

The vicar took it in hand and read it carefully, then squinted at the seal.

"It appears to be quite in order," he said, and handed it back to #1.

"Very well, then," said Stavely. "By my authority as a Lord of the Assembly of the Commonwealth, I declare this gathering illegal. Return to your homes."

"What about the boy?" came a voice from in back. I thought it was Mr. Mortimer. "What about Freddie Bartlett?" cried another. A murmuring rose from the crowd, and Bowler #2 shifted behind me.

The vicar turned, and made a hushing motion with his hands; the crowd subsided. He surveyed the men of his flock for a long moment, then turned back to face us.

"Yes, your lordship," he said. "What about Master Henderson and young Bartlett? Are they also declared Enemies of the Commonwealth?"

I couldn't see Stavely's face, but the back of his neck got even redder. "They are material witnesses. They remain with me until the criminal is apprehended."

"You pledge on your honor as a Lord of the Commonwealth that no harm will come to them?"

That was too much for Stavely. "I pledge nothing!" he cried. "Begone, all of you. Or there will be more writs in the offing!"

There was another long moment. Bert Wiggins lowered his head, not in resignation but like a bull ready to charge, and Mr. Bartlett clenched his fists. I held my breath. The ranks of soldiers stiffened, but held their positions. Stavely leaned on his stick, massive and unmoving, and faced them down. I leaned forward, weight on my toes, ready to hit the dirt, then felt #2's hand heavy on my shoulder.

"Easy, lad," he said. "This lot won't start no trouble. Not with the Lords of the Commonwealth."

It seemed he was right. The vicar turned and nodded at the assembled men. Bert Wiggins swore, loudly; then Mr. Bartlett led him away, though not without many an angry glance back at his lordship. The rest followed him, leaving only the vicar. He looked pointedly at me and at Freddie, then back at Stavely.

"On your head be it," he said to him, quietly, and turned to go.

Freddie and I were made to stand on the gravel drive hard by the carriage while Stavely's men fired the cottage. I'm not sure what it was they used as an accelerant; I didn't see them carrying any cans of gasoline or other fuel into the house. Perhaps they were using some substance they found inside. Was the fuel for the steam generator sufficiently volatile? I still wasn't clear how the Commonwealth's steam technology worked, but it didn't seem to involve any obvious combustion, and the only fuel I'd seen were the carbon sticks used by the steam pencils. I'd seen no sign of lamp oil, gasoline, or other flammables in my time with Tristram. But several bowlers and half of the soldiers swarmed into the house and got busy with whatever it was, and kept it up for half an hour or so. I fumed silently the whole time, wishing Stavely at the devil. My stomach was growling, but I didn't dare try to get a granola bar from my backpack.

The sun was setting and the breeze was getting chill as, task complete, the soldiers returned to their post in the flower bed and the bowlers to Stavely's side.

Stavely turned to the soldiers, and waved a beefy hand at the cottage; and stepping forward, one of them fired a single round through the front window. I flinched at the report and the sound of breaking glass.

The remaining windows glowed red in the sunset as a brighter glow rose behind them.

Stavely watched with satisfaction as the fire began to roar, then spoke to one of the soldiers.

"Jennings, post four men here to ensure that no one interferes, and that the cottage burns to the ground. Then take the rest and commandeer the inn. We shall stay in Grayrigg tonight."

The fire was hot on my back as Bowler #2 loaded us into the carriage.

Chapter 44

The next day was Interrogation Day at the First Lord's Head. What fun.

I'd expected Stavely to drag Freddie and me off to some dark dungeon and hold us in durance vile until Tristram came riding up on his white motivator and got shot in the back while trying to rescue us, but apparently that wasn't what Stavely had in mind. Instead, we stayed put at the First Lord's Head. I don't know what his plans were—we were not on terms of mutual confidence—but I suppose he expected Tristram to return to Grayrigg for me. Or maybe he just wanted to irritate the townsfolk for a day or two before he moved on.

So Freddie and I got to spend the night at Bert Wiggin's expense, each of us tucked neatly into his own cold cramped little guest room, complete with lumpy bed and guard at the door. I had to agree with a comment Tristram made the day we arrived: the Head was an inn for drinking, not an inn for sleeping. Perhaps my expectations weren't so far off at that.

It wasn't much of an inn for eating, either, at least under Stavely's management, because we didn't get fed that evening. I didn't go hungry, myself; I hadn't done any significant Traveling since my visit home, so I still had plenty of water and protein bars in my backpack. It was enough, though I'd gladly have eaten more. Poor Freddie was out of luck, and as a strapping seventeen-year-old he had to be feeling it.

So it was a long cold boring night, followed by a long stuffy boring day. I mostly sat on the lumpy bed and read *The Last of the Malthusians*, in which the Pathfounder ventured into the Far North and fought Kodiack Bears and Screaming Weevils *en route* to the fabled land of Malthusia Thule.

I did have a brief session with Lord Stavely. Bowler #1 came for me late in the morning, and ushered me down the stairs and into the common room of the inn. Stavely presided at one end, comfortably by the fire, where he lolled in what I suspected to be the most comfortable arm chair in town. He sat behind a trestle table covered with a purple cloth, on which rested a journal and a mug of something steaming. The rest of the furniture had been removed, except for a single bench in the middle of the room. #1 escorted me to the bench, sat me down, and took up station behind me. He hadn't drawn his gun, but then, he didn't really have to.

Stavely was writing in the journal when I came in, and didn't look up until I was settled in place. He didn't trouble himself with good mornings, or hopes that I'd had a good night's sleep. He just gave me a jaded look.

"Boy. Where is Tristram Monocle?" He sounded tired and bored in equal measure. I'm sure he'd taken the best room in the inn, which was probably Bert Wiggin's own bedroom; but perhaps Bert Wiggin's own bed wasn't any better than those he offered for his guests. Or perhaps it simply wasn't up to Stavely's lordly standards.

It occurred to me, watching him, that he was exactly the kind of upperclass drone that Remchester had rebelled against. He wasn't any kind of self-made man, not a successful merchant or manufacturer; he'd inherited his fortune as surely as any noble lordling, and he'd added to it only by theft, whether judicial or otherwise. He hadn't produced anything but misery in his entire life, the pernicious git.

He'd have questioned a dozen people by now, and by his bored expression he didn't expect to learn anything new from me; but by the same token I didn't dare balk him.

But what to say? I couldn't hide Gwen's presence or the involvement of the ladies at Stockwood, much though I'd have liked too; it was the talk of the town. Here in Grayrigg only Freddie knew that Gwen wasn't my sister; and he was smart enough not to let that slip. I didn't know whether Stavely had gotten around to Miss Louisa or Mrs. Illridge yet, but surely they were canny enough not to speak of that either. Gwen I was less sure of, but I doubted he'd hear sense from Gwen in any case.

So yes, Gwen remained my sister, and of course Tristram was still my cousin. Stavely clearly inclined to the "bastard son" theory, but we'd told his daughter that I was Tristram's cousin, and so I'd better stick with it. But then, how to plausibly explain Tristram's trip north? If Gwen was my sister and Tristram our cousin, then there was no reason for Tristram to go hunting for Gwen's aunt. I didn't have an answer for that, and I decided that that would have to do. Sometimes it's good to be ten.

Mind you, I didn't leave Stavely hanging there on his throne while I thought all this through. I'd had ample time to ponder my story in the middle of the night, repeatedly and *ad nauseum*.

"I don't know," I said, trying to look mulish. I wanted to give the impression of not being fully aware of the enormity of the situation I found myself in, and also the impression of not liking his lordship at all, at all. The latter, at least, was quite true.

Stavely waved a hand in the air, and Bowler #1 clouted me across the head.

"Ow!" The flat of his hand was better than the barrel of his pistol, but not by much.

"Speak politely to 'is lordship," he said.

I made a face at him over my shoulder, then looked back at Stavely.

"I don't know, *sir*," I said.

"And where did he say he was going?"

"To Edinburgh, sir," I said. "On business."

"To do what?"

"I don't know. He just said, 'on business.'" I omitted the "sir," just to see whether I'd get clouted again, but apparently I was still meeting the minimum daily requirement of *politesse*.

"To meet with enemies of the Commonwealth and plot its destruction?"

"Then he'd have waited here for you, wouldn't he, *sir.*" That one did get me a clout. Also, a sneer from Stavely.

"I suggest that you not try my patience, boy," he said. "Then he's off with that strumpet, I suppose."

Clout or not, I had to answer that in character.

"She's no strumpet, you rubbish-monger! Owww!" I rubbed my ears with both hands. I'd never had my ears boxed before, and I didn't like it. I glanced up and back; Bowler #1 smiled cheerfully down at me. "Sir," I said.

"Then who *is* 'Miss Gwen'?"

"My sister." Stavely began to raise his hand, and I quickly added, "Sir." He lowered it.

"And how came the two of you to the Commonwealth?"

Uh-oh. "On a steam leviathan from the Colonies."

Stavely smiled coldly. "The Commonwealth West India Company has no such passage on its books, not for you and not for your sister." He glanced at Bowler #1, who gave me another rap on the head. But I heard no special emphasis on the word "sister," which was interesting. He might doubt our parentage and provenance, but he didn't doubt we were siblings.

"From the Colonies, sir, truly!" I said. "A little town called Corey's End."

Stavely made a note. "And where is she?" He looked at me. "If she hasn't run off with your 'cousin.'"

"Where is who? Sir?"

"Your sister."

"At Stockwood. Sir." No reaction from his lordship; as I'd surmised, he'd known that already.

"Why at Stockwood?"

"Cousin Tristram said it wasn't suitable for her to stay at the cottage with just me and Freddie."

"And where is her maid?"

"She doesn't have one. Sir. Cousin Tristram said he'd find her one when he returned."

Stavely looked at me sourly, head a little to one side.

"And yet, he took the trouble to find you a man."

"That was so we could open the cottage."

"Hmph. Where is she, boy?"

"I told you. At Stockwood!" A hint of doubt crept into my bones. "Isn't she?"

Another snort. Then Stavely looked past me to Bowler #1, and waved his hand in the air.

"Take him away."

Gwen wasn't at Stockwood? I swore violently (in my head) all the way back to my room, and didn't stop until the door slammed behind me. Or was Stavely just messing with me? No, she had to be gone—I couldn't think of any reason why Stavely would hint that she was missing if she wasn't.

And wasn't that just like her! Of course she'd choose the worst possible moment to run off again, the moment most calculated to arouse Stavely's suspicions. Probably she'd heard Miss Louisa or Mrs. Illridge say something about him, and been afraid that he would find out who she was and send her back to her wicked auntie.

I shook my head. At least she hadn't shot anyone with her little gun. Or had she? The possibilities for disaster seemed limitless. She had to be found.

And here I was, stuck in a stuffy little guest room under the eaves of the First Lord's Head.

Well, I say "stuck." I had my finder with me, tucked into the pocket of my waistcoat; in fact, I had two finders with me, because the one I'd acquired from the late gentleman in the stable was tucked into my backpack. I was free as a bird. I could go walkabout any time I chose. Trouble was, if I vanished Stavely would presume that the locals had helped me escape, and that wouldn't go well for them. And I couldn't leave and come back unnoticed. Even assuming I could get back to Grayrigg in a timely way, I'd still have to sneak back in through the ground floor of the inn, and that didn't sound like a winning proposition.

Or could I? If I left the extra finder behind, could I use it as an anchor? I pondered that for a while, and came up with a definite *maybe*. I had no special connection to it, and if I tried to find it I might as easily find the Big Bag O' Finders, or one of those that Tristram had collected on our way north. I could activate the extra finder and leave my usual one—but I might have the same problem, and anyway I *really* didn't want to activate any more finders.

No, I'd have to have a compelling reason to run off, especially since I was in no immediate danger.

I wasn't sure I could find Gwen anyway. Tristram I could find, I was pretty sure; and enough people knew me at Stockwood and in Grayrigg that I *might* be able to return to either locale using an indirect reference, e.g., "the Grayrigg where I am known." That *might* work with Gwen, too; of all the Gwens in all of the worlds she was the only one who knew me. But was I enough of a concept in her head for that to work? I had the idea that non-essentials didn't stick too well beneath those glossy curls. Anyway, the only time I'd tried that kind of indirect reference it was with my home town, where everyone knew who I was and had for many years. I didn't know if it would work with a single person.

It was too slender a reed for me to go risking reprisals against the folk of Grayrigg.

In the end I had to put thoughts of Gwen aside and go back to my book, or I'd have started tearing at the walls. I almost did anyway, because the book didn't provide all that much comfort. The Pathfounder, abandoned by his native guide, had been carried off by the Wasps of the North to their nest, and their hungry larvae were approaching. That was all thrilling enough; but I kept thinking of Tristram in the north country, and wondering whether he was all right, and what wasps *he* was having to deal with.

Bowler #2 stopped by with a tray late that afternoon. I got stew (not bad), bread (only slightly stale), and a cup of water. He stood by the door and watched as I ate it. His pistol remained in its holster.

He seemed to be playing good cop to #1's bad cop; I decided to see how far I could push that.

"Did you know Mr. Lackland?" I asked, in my smallest voice.

"We'd met." His voice was even and non-committal.

"He's dead, isn't he."

#2 cocked his head.

"You don't want to worry about the likes of him, lad. He was an Enemy of the Commonwealth. You do, and you'll find that it's almighty catching."

"But he was just trying to warn Cousin Tristram!"

"Aye, lad, he tried to give aid and comfort to a proscribed man, properly drawn and papered. You heard his lordship."

I scowled at him. "Tristram's no enemy!"

"He's no angel, lad. I could tell you stories. And I'd advise you to hold your gab. It won't do you no good. Now, let's have the tray. Ah, ah! The spoon, too, lad."

I dropped the spoon on the tray with a sulky clunk. I don't know what I'd have done with it if I'd been allowed to keep it; I was no Edmond Dantes, to carve an escape tunnel through the solid wood of my cell with a sharpened spoon.

I lay down with my face to the wall as #2 shut the door firmly behind him. It was going to be a long evening.

Late that night I came awake with a start. It was full dark, but I had a sense of air moving: there was someone in the room with me.

Friend or enemy? Stavely had guards all over the inn, so an enemy seemed by far the most likely, just another chum after my finder—Stavely's men had no need for stealth, and no one else could have gotten in without raising the alarm

The room was small; I was wrapped up tightly in my blanket, which wasn't a good tactical situation. My only advantage was that my intruder didn't know that I was awake. He might suspect, but he didn't know. I didn't want to give that up until I knew how I was going to respond, so I lay still as I ran through the possibilities.

Plan A was out, because the door was almost certainly still locked; there was nowhere to run. Plan B was out, because I was in bed: my visitor already knew precisely where I was, and I couldn't move without alerting him. Plan C, well, that was a possibility, but I was unarmed; Bowler #2 had my taser. That left either Plan A-prime, with all of the disadvantages I'd already outlined, or screaming like a banshee and hoping my guard would rescue me before I got clobbered, which I suppose came under Plan C. I hadn't undressed for bed—I wasn't going to risk being separated from my finder, safe in my waistcoat pocket—so A-prime was a possibility, but—

You know, I'm usually pretty quick at this kind of analysis; it's a skill I've honed over many years. I guess I have to plead grogginess and a sleepless night the night before.

Well, that and having gotten used to out-sourcing my security to Tristram and Freddie.

Enough with the excuses. It suffices to say that before I'd come to a conclusion I felt a hand on my shoulder. I lunged upward, and saw stars when my head collided with something hard. A familiar voice cried, "Owwww! Be still, can't you?" There was a rush in the hallway, and then—

—blue, and an unexpected moment of timeless disorientation, and then—

Chapter 45

—I was reclining on a concrete floor. It was hard and cold even after the bed in Bert Wiggin's guest room. My head was still ringing.

Gwen knelt over me; she had one hand on her nose, which was bleeding through her fingers. Her little gun was in her other hand, but she was holding it backwards, with the barrel in the palm of her hand and her thumb on the butt, where a metal cover had been twisted to one side.

As I squinted at her, the light harsh and bright after the darkness, she rose and rushed away, just like anybody with a bloody nose would do, leaving me to climb to my feet all by my lonesome. Standing was better than lying down, but my feet were still unhappy: my shoes were back in Grayrigg.

I rubbed the back of my head—there was a noticeable bump —and looked around. I found myself in a small room, maybe six feet by six feet, and completely empty. The walls were of corrugated metal. It might have been aluminum, but it had the mottled look of galvanized. There was one light in the middle of the plywood ceiling, and an open doorway in one wall. I stretched my sore muscles, and yawned a couple of times; and then, finding no reason to remain, looked into the next room.

It was a little larger, though no prettier—more lighting, but the same walls, same ceiling, same floor—and it was as crowded as the previous room was empty. Steel shelving lined the walls to my left and right, the shelves jammed with boxes and bags of all sizes and colors. A collapsible table and a couple of folding chairs occupied most of the space between them.

Beyond that was the living area, if you can call it that. One corner held a table with a camp stove and some cooking gear, and the other held two camp cots side by side. A closed door with a security eye hole was set into the far wall, right between the cots and the "kitchen"; there was another closed door on my left, from which came the sound of running water.

There were no windows.

I recognized the place at once—not that I'd been there before, you understand, but I knew what it was: a Traveler's bolthole, fancier than my Unhappy Place in the Red Desert but no different in principle.

You ever have one of those moments where suddenly everything seems different than you thought? No wonder Gwen had been so concerned about her "little gun." She was going to have some explaining to do, and that right speedily.

Speedily. Hah! She must have made at least three jumps in the last twelve hours: one from Stockwood to somewhere else, probably right here, though it could have been anywhere; one to my room at the First Lord's Head (and how she'd known that would work, I'd really like to know); and then one back here. Three jumps in half-a-day was a lot, even if she'd taken food and a few hours rest after the first one, and that was the minimum. I knew from personal experience that I wasn't going to get much sense out of her until after she'd eaten and slept.

It was like some kind of law of conservation of dimness. First she played dumb, and so excessively that I was kicking myself for not smelling a rat; and now that she'd revealed the Gwen behind the curtain she was going to be genuinely and unavoidably dopey for hours to come.

The water stopped running, but the door remained closed. Well, she'd be out in due time; and a little after that she'd be out, period. I frowned in exasperation. God only knew what was going on back in Grayrigg, but it wasn't going to be anything good for my friends there; and my only source of answers was in the bathroom tending to a bloody nose.

I admit, I felt a little bad about the bloody nose…but mostly I just felt frustrated and angry.

Well, the sooner she ate, the sooner she'd be fit to talk to. I took a few deep breaths—dust, a hint of sage—and then maneuvered around the table to where I could examine the contents of the shelves.

It was an interesting collection, a cornucopia of products for every need of the weary Traveler, from bandages and antiseptic to a variety of food stuffs. The food was all pre-packaged and non-perishable; the thing about a bolthole is that you want to go there as seldom as possible, so you won't be stocking fresh vegetables and shell eggs. I surveyed the choices. There was a big box containing miscellaneous packets of dehydrated camp food, including one labeled "Beer and Mushroom Steganoff," whatever that was.

I had the usual problem with labels, thanks to my finder: everything looked like it was in English, even if it wasn't. I had to wonder how the finder managed that.

But even accounting for that, some of the products were shockingly familiar. I saw several boxes of Maundelson's Finest Patented Engineer's Biscuits, such as I'd once had showered over me by a stray bullet; and there were boxes of Kraft Macaroni and Cheese that I might have purchased myself.

Before I got married, I mean. Bernie won't allow it in the house.

Other shelves held food to be carried while Traveling: dried fruit, nuts, jars of Callahan's Buzzard Jerky, and boxes of "Muslin Energy Bars." I checked the ingredients list on the latter —more granola, natch, with caraway seeds and fennel. Why caraway seeds? Why fennel? Who knows?

I didn't see anything from Calahosis Camping Supply; apparently Gwen didn't shop at the same stores as Red Mustache, the fellow who'd originally set up my own bolthole. But the boxes, bags and other packages appeared to come from at least three different worlds, which surprised me a little.

The other thing about a bolthole is that it needs to be findable from anywhere, which means it needs to act like a true singular. Places are almost never singulars; I was aware of only one exception to that rule, the Old City, and while I'd once used it as a bolthole I fervently never wanted to do that again. So what you have to do is find a suitable location, and *singularize* it: change it in ways that could never have happened without your intervention so as to make it unique. The easiest thing to do is to pick a safe and suitable locale in a world you have no other reason to go to, and stock it with products from a different world. That was what the late, unlamented Red Mustache had done to create my Unhappy Place; I'd carried on in the same way.

But products from multiple worlds seemed like overkill. Why go to the effort?

And then, the presence of the Engineer's Biscuits and the Mac'n'Cheese was dismaying: that meant that Gwen had been watching both Tristram and me for some time, and had been to both of our worlds often enough to go shopping.

Two cots...perhaps it wasn't Gwen alone, perhaps she was working with someone else. But who? I filed that thought for later.

I assumed all the food was to Gwen's taste, but I was hungry myself, and I was tired of granola bars even when they didn't have caraway and fennel. Opting for the devil I knew, I took down a couple of boxes of Kraft and carried them over to the "kitchen". There wasn't much in the way of cooking gear: just the stove itself, connected to a tank of propane or something like it on the floor; one pot and one pan hanging from hooks on the wall; and a kettle already on the stove. I wasted a few moments looking for matches before I realized the stove was the fancy kind with a built in igniter.

There was no sink in the main room, but there were jugs of distilled water on one of the lower shelves and a half-full one by the stove. I took down the pot, filled it from the open jug, and put it on the stove to boil.

The Mac'n'Cheese was going to take a little while, and Gwen

was going to be out and ravenous any moment, so I opened a box of Engineer's Biscuits and put it on the table.

I tried one. It wasn't bad, actually: kind of like an animal cracker, though what it had to do with engineers is anybody's guess. I put a double-handful on a paper plate, and then I went and knocked on the washroom door.

"Food's up," I said. Then I went back to the stove and began to open the packages of Mac'n'Cheese. After a few moments I heard the door to the washroom open; when I turned to look Gwen was sitting at the table, eating Engineer's Biscuits with a furious intensity I recognized all too well. She had a black eye, a real shiner, but it didn't look like I'd broken her nose.

By that time the water was boiling. I dumped in the macaroni and the cheese powder and gave it a stir with a plastic spoon. Gwen was still going to town on the biscuits, but she managed to choke out the word "water" around a spray of crumbs. I grabbed a paper cup and filled it with distilled water; she drank it greedily. I got her another, and had a couple more biscuits, and then dinner was ready.

She ate a plateful of macaroni and cheese, and then a second, and had several more cups of water; and then without a word went and lay down on one of the cots and started to snore.

I watched her sleep as I finished off the remainder of my own modest serving. Now I knew how Bernie had felt when I zonked out after an excursion: bored and frustrated, not to put to fine a word on it. I ate a few more biscuits; then looked around for something to do.

I didn't see any books, which was a serious oversight; inconsiderate, I call it. But it occurred to me that I hadn't seen the entire place yet.

The washroom was tiny, containing only a wide sink, a mirror, and a toilet. There was a roll of paper towels, a bottle of Kirkland dish soap, and a box of tissues stamped with the Mordred & Sons logo. I wondered where the water came from, and whether it was safe to drink; the jugs of distilled water argued that it might not be.

The remaining door was locked with a deadbolt; I slid it back and opened the door, revealing darkness and an expanse of nothing-to-see-here under a sky blazing with stars. A folding chair sat on a concrete deck outside the door, just visible in the pool of light coming through from the main room. There was no breeze, and no sound but Gwen's snores. The air was cool and dry.

So much for that. I closed and bolted the door.

I was at a loss. I couldn't return to the First Lord's Head. That cat was out of the bag; the Head would be humming like the nest of the Wasps of the North by now. I hoped Stavely wouldn't do anything too awful.

It occurred to me that I had time to go home and see Bernie if I wanted to. I shouldn't have any difficulty finding Gwen afterwards; as a Traveler she *was* a true singular, and she wasn't going anywhere for a while. And then, her bolthole was findable for all the reasons I mentioned above.

That was a comforting thought. Whatever Gwen had in mind, she wouldn't have brought me here if she meant to harm me. Not that I was really worried about that; if she'd wanted my finder she could have dropped me in the stable and gotten two for the price of one.

I was so tempted by the thought of seeing Bernie that I took my finder from its pocket—but then I put it back again. I had questions for Gwen...and if I went and came back then *I'd* be the one who needed to eat and sleep while *she* waited. Turnabout was fair play, but who knew what would be happening in Grayrigg while I slept? I couldn't risk it.

I couldn't even write Bernie a letter, as I had nothing to write with or on. Damn Gwen anyway. Couldn't she at least have grabbed my backpack before she spirited me away? And what had she thought she was doing, anyway?

I shook my head and lay down on the other cot. Bloody idiot, I thought, meaning Gwen.

Chapter 46

I don't know what time it was when I gave up and got up. There was no clock in the place, and it was still dark outside. Gwen was still snoring. The floor was still cold and hard under my stockinged feet. My shoes were still back at the First Lord's Head.

Damn that girl anyway! If she simply had to rescue me, she should have taken a little more care and brought my things too. Instead she bungled it. Lord Stavely was probably writing out writs of proscription for Bert Wiggins and company right now, or calling up troops to level Grayrigg to the ground, and here I was with no shoes and no way to put things right.

There was a jar of what looked to be instant coffee—*Jakarta Joe Gets You Started on the Instant!* said the label—so I put the kettle on and made myself some. I didn't have anything to put it in but a paper cup, which I had to hold *very* carefully because it was so hot.

Books. Writing materials. A clock. Proper mugs. My list of defects was growing by the minute.

I put the coffee on the table and sat down. Then I got up and retrieved the blanket from my cot. Then I sat down again, swaddling my feet up in the blanket to keep them warm. Then I started to brood.

The box of Engineer's Biscuits was still on the table. They weren't Cheerios, but they'd have to do.

Books. Writing materials. A clock. Proper mugs. Spare shoes.

My things. Cheerios. *Damn* it.

By the time Gwen woke up I had myself in a properly foul mood.

She sat up, rubbed her eyes, yawned. Wrapping herself in her blanket like a robe, she unlocked and opened the front door, letting in the early morning light; then she toddled into the washroom. After an unconscionably long few minutes she came out and sat down across from me.

"Is that coffee?" she asked, still groggy. She sounded nothing like the bubble-headed Gwen I knew, which by this time surprised me not at all.

"The jury is still out," I said.

"Oh." She took a biscuit and nibbled on it. "Thank you for making dinner. I wouldn't have expected that from a boy your age."

"I'm small for my age," I said. I got up, leaving my blanket on the floor, and made a cup of perhaps-coffee for Gwen. I put it in front of her and sat down again, sliding my feet back into their slots in the pile of blanket. She took the cup, blew on the surface of the coffee.

"Now," I said, with what I considered to be commendable patience, "would you be so kind as to explain to me just *what the hell you thought you were DOING?*"

I hadn't meant to shout. I really hadn't. But small volumes make for high pressure, and I'd been accumulating steam for hours.

Gwen jumped. She'd just raised the cup to her lips, and she spilled a little, and I think she might have burned her mouth. She was completely awake after that, I can tell you.

"Why, sir," she said, in her most cutting Miss Gwen voice, "I was rescuing you." She simpered sweetly. "You might at least be grateful." She took a careful sip, and grimaced.

"Grateful?" The enormity of that statement filled me with rage. No books, no mugs, no clock, no shoes, no answers, and Stavely no doubt rampaging around Grayrigg like the wrath of God, and she expected me to be grateful? "*Grateful?* Do you have any idea what you've done?"

"I've kept Stavely from harming you!"

I glared at her. How could she not see it?

"He wasn't going to touch me, you bloody idiot! I was perfectly safe!"

"You know nothing about it, little boy!"

"Little boy! I like that, 'big sister.' You're practically gray with age."

She sniffed, and looked down her nose at me. "I'm older than I look."

"Uh-huh. I bet. What are you, sixteen and a *half?*"

She looked down at her coffee, and took several deep breaths.

"Rather older than that," she said in a tight voice.

"How much older?"

"You wouldn't believe me."

"I wouldn't believe anything you—" I began...and then stopped.

Of course. Freddie had *said* that we looked like family, had all but rubbed my nose in it, and I'd taken it for coincidence. *And* she was a Traveler. "I'm small for my age," I'd said. "I'm older than I look," she'd said. Had that *bastard* done it again?

He could have. He most surely could have. He'd left Mom and me and run off to who knows where; he'd have had plenty of time to find another young lady and start another family.

And then when the child had come, he'd gotten up to his old tricks. Had he run out on them, too?

It could be. Gwen might truly *be* my sister.

I'd already been angry. Now I was angry *and* curious *and* truly and memorably outraged. I'm afraid I started shouting.

"How much older?"

"Oh, what does it matter?"

"Tell me!"

She put her coffee down, then looked at me with tired eyes.

"Twenty-eight, if you must know."

I stared at her.

"You can't be."

The Miss Gwen voice came out again. "Don't be fooled by my youthful figure, sir. I assure you, I am quite twenty-eight years of age."

"But *I'm* twenty-eight," I said. "How can you be twenty-eight if I'm twenty-eight? You have to be younger than that."

She stared back at me, puzzled. "What are you saying?"

I stood up, kicked aside the blankets.

"Come in here."

I led her to the washroom. The mirror was small and at the wrong height, so I took it down from the wall, and held it so that we could both see our faces. Freddie was right. Gwen's hair was much longer than mine, but it was the same shade; and even with Gwen's black eye our faces were recognizably the same shape and cast.

"Your father did something so that you stopped growing at sixteen," I said. "Didn't he." It wasn't a question.

"Yes," she said. "Yes, he did. He said it would make people underestimate me."

"And it's a royal pain. Isn't it."

"Yes. It is."

"And everyone in Grayrigg who's seen us together is sure you're my sister, because of the family resemblance."

"They are?"

I nodded. "They are."

I looked up at her, then back at her face in the mirror, and said a rude word.

After a long moment Gwen repeated it.

"I'm sorry about the black eye, by the way. Next time you need to wake me up like that, you might want to prod me with a stick."

"A ten-foot pole, by choice."

"Nah, that'd put you out in the hallway. Attract all the wrong kinds of attention."

"You did that anyway."

"Hey!" I glared at her. "I wasn't the one who shouted."

"No, but I wouldn't have if you hadn't—"

"Look, I said I was sorry."

"Hmph."

We were sitting out on the deck in front of the bolthole. I didn't need to bring another folding chair from inside; I guess they came in sets of four, because there was a second chair already out here that I hadn't noticed in the darkness.

The scenery wasn't all that much prettier than it was in full darkness: just a rocky slope leading down to a sweep of tall grass going out to the horizon. But the sky was blue and the sun was warm and we each had a cup of Jakarta Joe's advanced coffee substitute; and the subject at hand was just too damned big to keep indoors, crapping all over the place. It needed room to run.

Not that we were finding it easy to get down to it.

I sipped my coffee. "Mugs," I said. "A clock. Spare footwear."

"Huh?"

"Mugs. These are no good for coffee. And my shoes are still in Grayrigg."

"Oh. This is true. I'll get right on it." She got up and vanished inside, which I thought was maybe a little too enterprising; but instead of making a quick trip elsewhere and delaying matters even further, she came back a few moments later with a pair of wool socks.

"Camping gear. Bottom left, opposite the food. They'll be too big, but at least your feet will be warm."

"Oh." I put my coffee on the deck and pulled on the socks. "Nice. Thank you." It was a little weird, talking with Competent Gwen when I was used to Bird-Witted Gwen, but maybe I could get used to it.

"So," she said.

"So," I said.

We looked out at the morning. Pain; abandonment; growing up small; fathers; I didn't know how to get started.

"Is your name really Gwen?"

"Yes. Gwen Hendryx. Is yours really Michael Henderson?"

"Yup."

"Hendryx. Henderson."

"Yup."

She started to speak, and I held up my hand, trying to gather my thoughts.

"My father left us when I was very small," I said. "I don't remember him—he Traveled away, and left us. Mom said it was to protect us, but I've never been sure of that. Anyway, when you said you were older than you look, I got to thinking."

"You thought that maybe he'd left you and married my mother. That's why you were shocked when I said I was twenty-eight."

"Yeah. But the timing doesn't work."

"My mother died when I was very small. That's what my father has always told me." She looked out across the grass. "Could we...do you think they...could we...maybe...be twins?"

"And after we were born, they split up? I don't know. Maybe." I shook my head. "I guess it might have been safest."

"What do you mean?"

"That guy in the stable? He's the latest in a long sequence." I filled her in as quickly as I could. "We figure it started because I had two active finders, and that Dear Old Dad left because two Travelers in a world are asking for trouble."

"We? You mean you and your mother?"

I swallowed. "No, I meant me and Bernie, my wife. My mother was killed a couple of years ago."

"Oh! I'm so sorry."

I shrugged. I didn't really want to talk about it.

"But if you're right, doesn't it seem odd that your mother would keep the boy twin, and my father the girl twin? Or that your mother would agree to it in the first place?"

That was a good question.

"It does. But look, Mom told me that female Travelers were rare; she wasn't sure if they existed at all. Maybe Dad took you because you weren't likely to be a Traveler, and that would make things easier."

A breeze rippled the grass in waves.

Gwen got a funny look on her face.

"Or maybe it's worse than that," she said. "Maybe he married the same woman in two different worlds at the same time. He left your mother, and mine died. We're genetically siblings, and we're the same age, but we aren't twins: we were born in different worlds."

"Ugh," I said. This conversation wasn't leading me to think any better of my old man.

The grass waved.

"March 17th", said Gwen. "My birthday."

"Mine too," I said. "What year?"

"I don't know," she said. "Which one would you like? We moved around a lot, and it was different everywhere we lived. The dates were different in lots of places, too. But my father always said my birthday was March 17th."

"Did he say where you were born?"

"Only once. He got kind of funny about it."

"Well?"

"He said I was born in another world, and that it was a place called Corisande."

I rolled my eyes.

"Corey's End," I said.

"No, I'm sure it was Corisande."

"That might be what he *said*; but I happen to know I was born in the town of Corey's End. Twenty-eight years ago. On March 17th."

"March 17th. Corey's End." She sighed. Then she leaned over and extended her hand. I shook it solemnly.

"Hello, Brother Michael," she said. "I always wondered what it would be like to have a sibling."

"Two siblings, if I'm not mistaken."

"Two? But...oh."

"Tristram," I confirmed. "Mac*Hendry*."

"I thought his last name was Monocle."

"It is, now. Long story."

"Oh. So that's why..."

I glanced over. She was gazing out over the emptiness, remembering. With her old-fashioned blue dress and tousled hair she might have been a pioneer woman a-setting out in front of the cabin. Well, except for the mass-produced folding chair, and the paper cup. And the wall of corrugated sheet-metal behind her.

The black eye was in period, though, I'm pretty sure.

I retrieved my coffee, took a sip. It was cold. Darned concrete, it sucked the heat out of everything.

"Why what?" I said, after a while.

By way of answer, Gwen undid the top buttons of her dress. Reaching inside, she pulled out a locket on a chain. No, two lockets. She pulled the chain over her head, and handed them to me.

They weren't fancy to look at, just two lens-shaped discs of plain brass on a chain. One had a "T" engraved on it; the other had an "M."

"My father gave me these years ago," she said. "He said they belonged to two people from other worlds. If anything happened to him, he said, or if he went away and didn't come back, I should seek them out. But I should be careful, and not reveal myself too soon."

"He said you could find them using these?"

"That was the idea, yes."

"How?"

"Open one. You'll see."

I inspected the one with the "M." "Where's the catch?" I said. "Oh, wait, I see it." Holding it carefully horizontal, I flicked it open. Inside was a curl of something dark and fine.

I looked up. "Baby hair?"

"That's what it looks like to me."

I closed the locket, and handed the chain back to Gwen.

"So you just try to find the person to whom the hair belongs. Of course, he'd have to be a Traveler, or you wouldn't get the right world."

"I figured that out later," she said. "Anyway, it worked a treat.

Well, mostly."

"Mostly?"

"I hadn't intended to end up in the middle of nowhere in a ball gown."

"No?"

"Of course not. Father always told me to do my research, and make sure I knew what was what instead of rushing in like a fool."

I felt a stab of envy, quickly followed by one of greed. What else had that *bastard* told her that Mom hadn't known to pass along to me?

"So I knew what London was like," she continued, "and I knew that I was looking for Tristram. I'd seen you, too; you just sort of popped up at the last minute." She laughed, sort of. "I didn't know who you were, though. Until I saw you take the finder from the man in the stable, I thought you really *were* Tristram's cousin from the Colonies. After that, I didn't know what to think."

"Ah. I'd thought you were too overcome to notice."

She shook her head.

"Overcome, yes, but noticing everything. So I made my plans, and decided on an approach…and after I pushed the button I found myself on the side of the road. You two came around the bend, and, well…I had to make sense of the situation somehow, didn't I?"

"So you invented Gwen the Idiot on the spot?"

"Why, whatever do you mean, sir? Have you been speaking with my wicked aunt?" She smirked. "No, I'd had occasion to use her in London from time to time."

"You took me in completely."

"It wasn't all an act, I'm afraid." She shook her head. "I was a sad trial to Mrs. Illridge, but truly, I had no idea how to sew or mend. It wasn't a skill Father made me learn."

"Skills are good," I said.

"Skills are good."

I pondered that for a while, and drank the rest of my cold

coffee.

"So how did you figure out that I was attached to the other locket?"

"I didn't. I still don't know that for sure, though it seems likely. But you knew about finders, and you looked like Tristram's son, and I knew *he* had to be a singular, which meant that you were. And you were in trouble, *again*, and I really didn't think I should leave you there. You needed looking after."

"Hah! I was thinking the same thing about you."

She looked at me quizzically.

"Idiot, remember?" I said. "Gwen the bird-witted watering-pot. And Stavely had let drop that you'd vanished. But I couldn't figure out how to find you, or how to get back to the inn afterwards without being noticed."

"'Bird-witted watering-pot?'"

"It was a really good act."

"I see that. But why would you want to go back to the inn?"

I shook my head.

"You don't get it, do you. I vanish mysteriously—what's Stavely going to think?"

"Why, that you escaped."

"Uh-huh. From a locked and guarded room on the second floor with windows that haven't been opened since before the Glorious Revolution."

"Well, perhaps you had help—" Her eyes widened. "Oh," she said in a small voice.

"Right. His lordship's going to assume that there's a conspiracy afoot in Grayrigg...and that's not going to end well for my friends there."

"I'm sorry, Michael. So what do we do now?"

"That's a really good question. I think it's time for a council of war."

Chapter 47

"The first thing you should do," said Bernie, "is send a note to Tristram so he knows what's going on."

Gwen looked at Bernie, and her eyebrows did that furrowing thing. You know, that thing you do when you're puzzled.

"No," I said, "that would be the second thing." I spooned the last of the ice cream and hot fudge out of the bowl and into my mouth.

Bernie's eyebrows went up. "How so?"

I swallowed, licked my lips. "The first thing," I said, "is to return to Grayrigg and find out what Stavely's gotten up to while we've been gone, so we can include it in the note."

Gwen looked at me, and her eyebrows furrowed even more. She looked like she wanted to say something, but now Bernie's eyebrows were furrowing too. You know, like you do when you're worried.

"*Not* to Grayrigg," she said. "It's too dangerous. Stockwood, maybe. You want to be on the spot but out of view."

"Well, yeah," I said. "For Grayrigg, read Stockwood."

Bernie's eyebrows unfurrowed. "OK, then. But first I'm heating up the lasagna."

"That would be good," I said, handing her the bowl and spoon. "I'm going to go take a shower."

"Or perhaps Gwen might like to shower first?" said Bernie. We both looked at Gwen.

"You know," I said to Gwen, "you shouldn't frown like that or your face will stick that way."

She really was a picture of perplexity. She looked from me to Bernie and back again, and she was trying to say something but didn't know quite what, and her eyebrows looked like two svelte brown caterpillars having anxiety attacks.

Conversations between couples who have been married for a while can be baffling to outsiders—you've got so much shared context that you can say complicated things in just a few words. And Gwen, for all that she was maybe my twin sister, was more of an outsider than we'd ever had sit at our table. Except for Guy Valens, I guess, though he's not that much of an outsider any more. But still, I didn't think either of us had said anything that was all that hard to follow.

"Is there a problem, Gwen?" Bernie asked.

Gwen struggled to find the right words for a few more moments, then took a breath and said, "Yes, several."

"Such as?"

"You're talking nonsense. I thought you knew something about Traveling, Michael, but it appears that you don't. You simply can't *do* the things you're talking about doing. Finders don't work that way." She got out her fingers.

"First, you can't just send notes to people. You have to Travel in person. Either of us, it seems, should be able to go and find Tristram wherever he is, but we can't just send him a note." She looked at both us, in turn, then raised another finger.

"Second, we can't just go back to Grayrigg, or to Stockton either. You have to have an anchor to do that, and the only anchor we have on that world is Tristram!" She shook her head. "Can't be done." Another finger popped up.

"And third, Stavely might have sent agents to kill Tristram, and I need him alive so that I can find out what happened to my father. The sooner we go find him, the better!"

"Ummmm," I said. "Actually, I think you'll find that we *can* do the things we're talking about doing. At least, we can certainly send Tristram a note."

"How?"

Bernie rose from the table, and came back with a stack of familiar-looking cream paper. "Michael's been writing me notes every day for weeks. How do you think I knew who you were when you popped up in my living room?"

"Why, he's been visiting you, of course." She looked from Bernie to me and back again. "Hasn't he?"

Bernie shook her head. "Only once, until now."

Gwen looked at me. She was still perplexed, but her eyebrows had relaxed a few notches.

"But how?"

I shrugged. "I dunno. I wanted to tell Bernie what was going on, and I couldn't go home—I hadn't realized that Tristram was my brother yet, and I was worried I couldn't get back. So I tried it, and it worked." I shrugged again. "Maybe my finder is special. But if I can send notes to Bernie, I ought to be able to send them to Tristram."

She shook her head in wonder. "I don't think Father knew—knows—that that's possible. OK, so you can do that. But Grayrigg? Stockwood? How do you expect to find *them*?"

"Indirect reference," I said.

She looked blank.

"Not a programmer?"

"A what?"

"Ah. They don't have computers where you grew up?"

Gwen shook her head. "No, pretty clearly not. Mostly I'm understanding what you say without help, I think, but my finder had to translate that word you just used, and I think it gave up. *Computer*? I know what the word means in English, but you seem to have something else in mind."

"Uh-huh. I'll have to show you some time. But look at it this way. Suppose I try to find Louisa Clarenton. What's going to happen?"

"You'll find *some* Louisa Clarenton, out of the infinite number there are."

"Probably so, unless contact with Tristram has made her

effectively singular."

"She might be, I guess, but I wouldn't assume it," she said.

"Neither would I," I said. "So let's take it as read that there are an infinite number of Louisa Clarentons out there. Now, how many of them know *me*?"

Gwen's eyebrows shot up, but they unfurrowed so quickly that I felt my forehead relax in sympathy. I hadn't even realized I was frowning.

"And that works?" she said slowly.

"I did it once. Not with Miss Louisa, you understand. I was trying to get back home to Bernie, before we were married." Bernie smiled at me, and I smiled back. "I don't know if the folks at Stockwood know me well enough for it to work, but I think there's a good chance."

Gwen was oblivious, lost in thought. "That would change everything. I don't think Father knew you could do that, either. Knows, I mean." She looked up, eyes bright with worried tears.

"Have you tried finding your father?" asked Bernie. Trust Bernie. It hadn't even occurred to me to ask.

"Yes, but it hasn't worked," Gwen said. "It's like he's not there to be found." She looked at me. "Haven't you? Tried to find him?"

"You forget," I said. "He left Mom and me when I was very small. I never knew him, and Mom never talked about him. And then, when I got my finder...." I grimaced, waved a hand at myself. "I found out that he was responsible for this. After that, if I'd gone to find him it would have been to punch him in the nose. If I could reach it." I shook my head. "No, I've never tried to find him."

Bernie sat down next to Gwen, and put an arm around her.

"You realize he's probably dead?"

She nodded, looking down. "He might be. He might be. But when he talked about vanishing, about anything happening to him, he didn't talk like he was going to be dead. He just said that I should find Tristram and Michael, and that they might be of help."

My ears pricked up. "Oh, my," I said. "I wonder…."

"What?"

"If he's alive, and you can't find him…don't you see what that means?"

Two pairs of blue eyes stared at me.

"It means that there's a way, there's something, that can block a Traveler from being found."

They gave me the look people give you when they're having a deep emotional moment and you're interrupting with inconsequentials. You know. Then Bernie did the get-on-with-it thing with her free arm—a bit awkwardly, because she'd usually use the arm she had wrapped around Gwen's shoulders.

"Don't you see? If he's alive, that means that there's a way to stop this stream of unwanted guests we've been having to deal with. It means safety." I breathed in, out. I smiled ruefully. "Maybe I want to find that bastard after all."

"OK," said Bernie, "But shower first. Then lasagna."

"Then lasagna. And then Stockwood, and then Tristram. And all that," I said.

"Right," said Gwen.

"Right," I said.

I thought things out a little more while I showered. Showers are a great place to think, and I'd missed them while I was in the Commonwealth. (Yes, I bathed in the Commonwealth. But tubs and basins aren't the same as a good shower.) And it occurred to me that Bernie was right—sending a note to Tristram *was* the first thing to do. I could send him another after we got to Stockwood.

But it also occurred to me that I'd have to write *very* carefully. Tristram was being watched; and I had no idea where he'd be when the note arrived. (*Bernie* was taking a shower when Gwen and I showed up; fortunately our shower curtain is opaque.) I didn't want to get Tristram in trouble if the note fell into the hands of one of Remchester's men.

We talked it out over the lasagna, with Bernie taking notes, and this is what we came up with.

> *Dear Tristram,*
>
> *Melissa's father has come to stay for a few days. He was disappointed with your absence; he had great hopes of finding you here, regarding some paperwork he'd brought from London. Indeed, he is so consumed by it that he's been sharing it with everyone here. He is putting up at B—'s in expectation of your return.*
>
> *We've been much at S—, as you expected, and the ladies greatly wish to see you and expect your return daily. Please don't disappoint them! They wish a quiet reunion before you return home, and have asked me to assure you that A— will make you welcome any time of the day or night.*
>
> *Most of all, G wishes you to waste no more time on her cousin! She is not at all the thing, as I'm sure you have discovered.*
>
> *In great hopes of seeing you soon,*
>
> *Your cousin M.*

I wrote it out long-hand as best I could, and Bernie sealed it up in an envelope addressed to "Mr. T. Monocle, Esq." I considered addressing it to "T. MacHendry" instead, to mislead anyone else who might pick it up; but then, that person might not wish to hand it over to T. Monocle without more discussion than we'd like. And then, any watchers would probably know Tristram's original name in any event, and might wonder why he was choosing to use it.

And then I sent it off, wishing that Tristram knew how to use a finder and could send me a reply.

"So my cousin in Edinburgh is 'not at all the thing'?" said Gwen in her bird-witted voice. "I like that. She's my cousin, of course she's the thing."

"You don't have a cousin in Edinburgh," I said. "Not only isn't she *the* thing, she isn't any kind of thing at all."

"That's true, but if I did then I'm sure she'd be *quite* the thing."

"If she was your cousin she'd be a piece of work, that's for sure."

Gwen was about to wage a response but Bernie stepped in.

"Children! I realize you've got decades of bickering to catch up on, but shouldn't you be off to Stockwood?"

Gwen and I looked at each other.

"Later," I said.

"Later," she said.

339

Chapter 48

When you Travel to a known person or place you've got some leeway in where you land. If I hadn't been so eager to see Bernie, for example, I'd have made it a point to aim for the living room; we keep the center of the floor open so that I don't need to worry about bumping into anything. Well, except for Buster, but he doesn't mind.

We didn't know what was up at Stockwood; Stavely might have taken over the place, or have guards at the door. Alternatively, he might still have most of his forces at the Head with someone watching Stockwood for our return. Either way I wanted to arrive quietly and out of sight, so I aimed for the old stable.

It was silent and dark, just as I'd hoped. I'd loaded my pockets with protein bars before we left, so I downed three of them in a couple of bites each; I'd made two jumps, and even with the sundaes and lasagna as a buffer I needed the refill. Then we moved out. I had only a little while before I'd need to sleep, and we had to either be safe in the house or back home before that happened.

There was no one in sight; and as the stable was screened by trees we had no difficulty moving across the gravel path and in among the overgrown hedges of the garden. There we paused, because there was a rustling noise coming from closer to the house. I motioned to Gwen to stay put; she nodded. Then I crept closer. When you're small for your age, being sneaky is a survival trait.

The sound had a rhythmic quality, a loud rustle-with-a-thwack, like branches springing back in place, followed by a softer rustle, over and over again. *RUSTLE-thwack-rustle, RUSTLE-thwack-rustle.* I couldn't account for it. Certainly I couldn't think of anything a soldier or spy might be doing that would make that noise. Was it yet another of the Commonwealth's Deadly Animals of Death building a home in the neglected garden? It occurred to me that I was completely unarmed, and I suddenly felt naked. I'd have to get armed up as soon as I could.

The sound grew louder as I reached the end of the row, almost creeping on hands and knees. *RUSTLE-thwack-rustle.* I stuck my head around the corner, as close to the ground as I could, to see if I could catch a glimpse of the rustle-thwacker.

Or should that be the thwack-rustler? I never got to settle that, because what I saw was Crosley pruning hedges with a sickle. He'd pull out a handful of greenery (*RUSTLE*) and cut it off with the sickle, leaving the remainder to *thwack* back in place. Then he'd drop the handful into a growing pile at his feet (*rustle*).

Was this the time to be pruning hedges? I ask you. Tristram declared an enemy of the people, Stavely in residence in Grayrigg, Gwen and I on the run, and Crosley responded by pruning hedges.

Mind you, they were well overdue, and there's no time like the present. And he didn't look at all happy about it. But still. It's the principle, etc., etc.

"Pssst! Crosley!" I said as quietly as I could. He didn't show any sign of hearing.

"Pssst!" I said, louder. That stopped him. He released his current bundle, and cast his eyes about, trying to determine where the sound had come from. I stuck out a hand and waved when he glanced my way.

His eyes widened. Placing the sickle neatly on top of the pile of clippings, he hurried towards me.

"Master Henderson!" he said. "Are you all right?"

I made a hushing motion with my hand. "Not so loud."

Crosley winced, and nodded. "Though I don't think there is anyone here but us, Master Henderson. The soldiers were here but they left a quarter of an hour ago, and Miss Clarenton sent me out to prune the hedges. Are you hurt? Is Miss Gwen with you?"

I stood up, and came fully around the corner to meet him.

"I'm fine, Crosley. And yes, she is. Just a minute."

I trotted back down the row to where I could see Gwen, crouched in the shadows under the hedge, and waved at her. She rose and came to join me.

"We're clear," I said. "C'mon."

Crosley had followed me along the path, and he exclaimed loudly when he saw Gwen's black eye and swollen nose.

"Oh, my! Miss Gwen, did those brutes do that to you?"

"Um, well,...." She glanced at me. I shrugged. "No, Crosley, it was an accident," she said. "They never laid a finger on me."

The footman's relief was palpable.

"Bless my soul!" He collected himself. "Miss Clarenton will want to know that you're here. Please, come with me."

Crosley led us through the garden toward the rear of the manor house. As we approached I began to hear something else—a low rumbling, as of many voices, along with a few higher pitched shouts. It wasn't coming from within the house, but from the other side.

Whatever it was, it didn't sound friendly. And it was getting louder.

Time for a look-see...and not from inside the house. I wanted to be able to get clear if I had to.

Gwen was behind me. "Got your little gun?" I said to her, over my shoulder. She nodded.

"Right, then. Follow me."

"Oh, but Master Henderson," began Crosley.

"Not now, Crosley," I said. "Follow along or go inside, it

doesn't matter. But if you come along, be quiet!"

Gwen nodded at him ferociously, and he winced.

A stone path led around the side of the house, hard against the outside wall. I led the way down it, keeping low and trying to walk as quietly as I could. It probably didn't matter...the rumbling of voices was even louder, and I doubted anyone around the front of the house would have any attention to spare for us. But when you're small for age, you've got habits.

I slowed down as we reached the front corner of the manor, the first spot where we might have a glimpse of the drive and the high road, and got down on my hands and knees to take a peek. Gwen and Crosley huddled behind me.

The high road was full of people: two groups of them, facing off.

On one side, almost directly in front of me, were Lord Stavely and his soldiers, along with a number of bowlers. I saw Bowler #1 for sure, but #2 seemed to be missing. As I watched, the soldiers drew up into two ranks facing back toward the town— and the other group.

On the other side, off to my left, were the people of Grayrigg, men and women both, and they did not look happy. I guessed the soldiers had run into them on their way back to the First Lord's Head and made a prudent retreat.

To give Stavely credit he stood in front of his men rather than hiding behind them. He had one arm raised and seemed to be haranguing the crowd, though as he was mostly facing away from me I couldn't make out what he was saying. His soldiers had their guns ready but not leveled.

The good-folk of Grayrigg muttered in response, glaring at Stavely and his soldiers. Their eyes were cold, and filled with judgment. I didn't see any weapons drawn, but I knew they were there.

I shivered. This was setting up to be a massacre.

Bert Wiggins was at the front of the crowd. Him I could hear clearly.

"So where is she, then? Where's Miss Clarenton? You

scoundrel, what have you done with her?'"

Stavely made some response I couldn't hear, and Bert sneered.

"We'll just see about that, shall we?"

At that moment the muttering rose in volume; and then Miss Louisa and Mrs. Illridge appeared in my field of view, hurrying down the drive toward the two groups. They must have been watching from the front of the house. Augustus panted along some distance behind them.

"We're here, Bert, we're all right," said Miss Louisa. The muttering decreased again, and the townsfolk seemed a bit happier. I took a deep breath; maybe there'd be no shooting after all.

Bert nodded at her.

"And what about Mr. Monocle's lad Michael? And Michael's sister? Where are they?" He looked from Miss Louisa to Stavely and back again.

Miss Louisa shook her head, and Mrs. Illridge did the same.

Bert nodded again, and stared at his lordship.

"Can't produce them, can you? What have you done with them?"

Gwen touched my shoulder, and whispered in my ear. "We have to show them we're all right."

I nodded. The last thing I wanted to do was get in the middle of all this, but I know a cue when I hear one. If Bert and company could see that Gwen and I were free and unharmed, we might have a chance of a peaceful resolution. I hated to do it, but I couldn't stand there and watch Tristram's people get gunned down.

I stood up, and took Gwen's hand. She gave it a squeeze back. Then we were running down the path.

"It's all right," I was shouting, "we got free," when Miss Louisa saw us and came running.

"Michael! Gwen! You're all right!" Then she gasped as she looked at Gwen, and an ugly roar went up from the people of Grayrigg.

I'd forgotten about Gwen's black eye.

* * *

It was over in moments.

The roar went up, and the first soldier fell before he could begin to level his gun. His blood was black on his blue coat. The others followed in quick succession.

Bowler #1 had his pistol out and was looking down the sights when he was hit in the stomach. He folded up and collapsed.

Stavely went last. He was looking around at his men, consternation large on his face, when a shot to the shoulder sent him spinning. He was hit several more times before he hit the ground.

And then, for a moment, there was silence. Many bodies lay dead.

Bodies in uniforms. Bodies wearing bowlers. One body in fine clothes, now ruined. None of them had had time to fire a shot.

The crowd of townsfolk began to break up. Wives spoke to their husbands, kissed them, and began the walk back to town. The men came forward and, working in groups, took the bodies off in the direction of the lake. I saw Freddie and his father among them, and also Mr. Mortimer. The snapping trout would have a feast tonight.

Miss Louisa watched them go; then hurried over to where Gwen and I stood frozen. She had a steam pistol in her hand, twice again the size of Gwen's little gun; had she been one of the ones who shot Lord Stavely? I thought she might have been.

"Come inside, children," she said. "It is over now."

Chapter 49

Augustus ushered Freddie into the library as we were finishing our tea—hot and strong, with milk and a touch of spirits. Miss Louisa had insisted, and I was grateful.

He came straight over to the divan where Gwen and I were sitting.

"Master Henderson! You're all right! I was so worried when we didn't find you at the Head."

"I'm fine, Freddie. No harm done." I was beginning to feel a little foggy. "I'm sorry, Freddie. I know I'm supposed to call you 'Bartlett.'"

He beamed back at me. "Call me anything you like, sir, I'm that glad to see you."

And then, more solemnly, "And you as well, Miss Gwen. I hope you are *quite* all right?"

"I'm fine, thank you, Bartlett," she said, dimpling, and he blushed.

Oh. And to think I'd thought Freddie had more sense than to fall for a bird-witted watering-pot like my sister Gwen. He should have known better. And anyway, she was much too old for him.

I stifled that thought. None of my business.

"Please do sit down, Freddie," said Mrs. Illridge. "It makes me tired to look at you looming like that."

"Oh, but Mrs. Illridge—"

"Don't go all manservant with me, Freddie, I've known you

since you were in short pants."

"Yes, ma'am," he said, and settled onto the front edge of an ottoman. At least, I'd call it an ottoman, but it might have been a hassock.

"But how did you get free, Freddie?" I asked. "I thought they'd locked you up in the room next to mine."

He nodded. "They had, sir. But there was some kind of scuffle late last night—was that you, sir?"

"Probably."

"—and then when Stavely and his men set out for Grayrigg, Bert Wiggins came and let me out. Well, Bert and a few others. 'All clear, lad,' he said to me when he opened my door. 'I thought it was time for some autumn cleaning,' he said. But he looked much less cheerful when we found that your room was empty. That's when he gathered up the rest of the town, and we set off after the soldiers."

"Autumn cleaning, Freddie?" asked Miss Louisa.

He shifted on the ottoman—unless it was a hassock—so that he was looking at Miss Louisa.

"They didn't *all* set out for Grayrigg, miss. But we won't have any more trouble with them."

"I see," she said, and there was no mistaking the satisfaction in her voice. Me, I was still in shock. What I'd taken for an angry mob was an execution party—judge, jury, and firing squad all in one. Stavely and his men had been tried and found wanting; and the squirrels of Grayrigg had eliminated the threat to their community. Yes, and cleaned up the mess afterwards.

I sank deeper into the divan—unless it was a chesterfield. The room seemed a long way away.

"But that's not why I'm here," Freddie was saying.

"It isn't?"

"No. It's that I have a message for you."

She looked questioningly at him, and waited for him to speak.

"It's Bert Wiggins, miss."

"Yes, Freddie?"

"He'd—well, we've cleaned up most of the mess, and he wants

to know what else you'd like to have done. You being lady of the manor and all." He looked apologetically at Mrs. Illridge, who arched an eyebrow at him, and then smiled to take the sting away.

"Me? Why—" Miss Louisa paused, and looked flustered. "I suppose I am," she said slowly. She looked at her aunt, who gave her several quick nods. You know, the way you do when someone finally twigs to something that's obvious to everyone else in the room.

"And it is high time you realized it," said Mrs. Illridge. "Young Tristram might own the bulk of the property, but he isn't an Illridge of Stockwood." She glanced at me. *Yet*, her eyes seemed to say. I nodded back. At least, I think I did.

Miss Louisa looked at her teacup for several long moments, and then up at Freddie.

"Very well. First, I would like you to remove all signs of Stavely's presence," she said. "The First Lord will not be pleased with us, so let us not make it easy for him."

"That's already in hand, miss," said Freddie.

"Second, about Tr—about Mr. Monocle's cottage. As soon as the embers are quite cool, I should like the site cleaned up. It might be possible to salvage some of his belongings. I expect that your father is the man to oversee that."

Freddie nodded.

"And third—and third, we shall have to decide what to do about Lord Remchester. Are all of Stavely's men accounted for?"

"No, miss. One is missing."

Bowler #2, I thought.

"Then we must assume that Remchester will hear about Stavely's demise quite soon. I shall have to think." She frowned, then sighed. "And that is all, Freddie. For now."

"I'll tell him, miss." Freddie looked at me. "And will you be staying here, sir?"

I tried to put some words together, but it was too much effort.

"Of course he is, Freddie," said Miss Louisa. She looked at me with concern. "Where else? And I shall have a room prepared for you as well."

"Thank you, miss," he said; and touching his forelock, he was gone.

Miss Louisa looked at Gwen and I.

"Now, I'm afraid you'll have to excuse me. I must think."

"Begging your pardon, Miss Louisa," Gwen said, "but we need to talk first." Her tone was quite unlike her usual blather, neither sullen nor bird-witted, and Miss Louisa, on the verge of rising, did a double-take. "Michael needs to sleep now, but there are some things you should know. And we need to send a note to Cousin Tristram."

Competent Gwen had things in hand. I let go and fell the rest of the way.

I woke up in bed, in the room I'd used on my first night in Grayrigg. My clothes were folded on the bureau, and Gwen was sitting in a chair by the bed.

"Ah, you're awake at last," she said.

"I seem to be." I pursed my lips. "I hope it wasn't you and Miss Louisa who put me to bed?"

"No, it was Freddie and Crosley. He was only gone a few minutes, but you were out cold by the time he came back in."

"That sounds about right." I sat up and stretched. "So, what happened while I was out?"

"I sent a note to Tristram explaining that Stavely was gone and wouldn't be back, and that he should return with all speed. I wasn't sure I'd be able to do it, but I did." She looked pleased with herself.

"And then?"

"And then I had a rather fraught discussion with Miss Louisa."

"Hmmm. And just what did you tell her?"

"It took me a while, but I managed to convey that things were more complicated than they seemed, that you and I are both much older than we look, that Tristram knows your age but not mine, and that we truly are all related on Tristram's father's side of the family. Oh, and that we are truly sorry we deceived her, but we hadn't seen that we had any choice, and we meant no harm."

"And how did she take it?"

"I'd rather avoid a blow-by-blow account, if you don't mind. She was greatly displeased at first, and if she didn't call me a hussy I'm sure she was thinking it. I think she was mostly afraid we'd been taking advantage of Tristram."

"Go figure," I said.

"Why, sir, I'm sure I don't know why she might have thought that," she said in her best Bird-Witted Gwen voice. "But she's calmed down a bit now."

"Did you explain about Traveling?"

"No, not yet. I thought it best to leave that until Tristram is back. But she's going to have to know eventually, I think."

I nodded. "Yeah, that's how I see it. Not sure how that's going to work out, though. They're both pretty stiff-necked."

"But you notice she's beginning to get the grounds back in shape?"

Oh. "No, I hadn't. I mean, yes, I had, but I hadn't put two and two together."

"So there you go. They might need a little helping along, but I think it will be fine."

"What assures you of that?"

"Bernie and I talked books while you were showering. She said that—" and we finished together, "—steampunk regency is still regency."

"You see?" she said. "So it will be fine."

"Oh."

I began to wonder what else they might have discussed, but I let it drop. There are things man was not meant to know.

Miss Louisa gave me a frosty look when Gwen and I came into the breakfast room.

"Good morning, Michael," she said, then turned her attention pointedly back to her black pudding. "I find that you have not been quite truthful with me."

I started to dial my boyish sincerity up a few notches, but realized just in time that that wasn't going to work. So I stood up straight, and took it like a man.

"I'm sorry, Miss Louisa. I'm sure Tristram would have preferred to explain things to you in more detail, but we were pressed for time, and, well, you know, I'm a little hard to explain. And then, you were—" I stopped, a little flustered. "I mean, he was—I mean—" I waved my hands, shrugged, and smiled ruefully. "Well. It made sense at the time."

"Quite," she said. "Well, then, we shall say no more about it." The corner of her mouth made that rueful tilt. "Or perhaps we shall, when circumstances are more favorable. Now, do sit down and have breakfast. I confess, I shall be glad of your counsel."

I filled my plate from the sideboard, and did that thing.

Chapter 50

I was "playing" in front of the manor house when Lord Remchester arrived.

The past week had been kind of like watching a foot race where you couldn't see either of the contestants. Tristram was hurrying south from Edinburgh, or so we hoped; Remchester was hurrying north from London, or so we feared. Who would arrive first?

It all depended. Had Tristram received our notes? Had Stavely sent agents north to arrest him? Was Remchester aware of Stavely's expedition before he left, or only after word reached him of its demise? Had Stavely been working behind Remchester's back, or on his orders? We had to be prepared for any of the above.

And so we made certain preparations; and then I spent a good bit of my day out in plain sight, so that I'd be the first person either would see. Why me? Because Tristram wouldn't dither about whether to speak to me, and if Remchester arrived first it was the safest thing.

Stavely had been a weasel as well as a wastrel: mean and nasty, and vicious in both senses of the word. His enormities had been constrained only by his sense of what he could get away with. No one was safe from him—at least, no one who was in his way. I might be misjudging him, I suppose, not that it matters any more. Between the "squirrels" and the trout, he was history.

But the impression I'd gotten of Remchester from Tristram's book and files was quite different. Remchester was jovial and charming on the surface, but cold and ruthless within. He'd take his time, and see what was what before he acted; and then he'd act with dispatch. But if he was ruthless, he was neither vicious nor mercurial. I might not be safe with him in the long term; but I was confident he'd do me no harm if I was likely to be of the slightest use to him. And of course he knew that I'd journeyed north with Tristram, and he didn't know that I was more than I seemed. I was banking on him wanting to pump me for information, and I have to say I was looking forward to it.

I was sitting in the bower by the drive reading *The Gullslayer* when I heard the rumbling of a motivator in the distance. On a normal day that wouldn't have been unusual, but things were quiet in Grayrigg just now; everyone was waiting for the other shoe to drop. Bert Wiggins was visiting on a daily basis, but he'd been and gone hours since, and we weren't expecting anyone else.

I'd finished *The Last of the Malthusians* early in the week, Freddie having retrieved my things from the First Lord's Head, and though Thompson's books had gone up with the cottage, alas, he'd managed to find me the next of Cowper Madisen's tales among the late squire's books in the library at Stockwood. The Pathfounder was exploring what I thought was probably the Mississippi delta, near what would have been New Orleans if the French had colonized Louisiana in this world. It seemed they hadn't, and given the size of the alligators I couldn't blame them —not to mention the swamp trees that put the "man" in "mangrove." He was seeking the fabled Golden Gulls of Cibola, and not having much luck.

The motivator was approaching from the direction of Grayrigg, which meant that it probably wasn't Tristram. I put down my book and watched as it approached.

It was one of the largest motivators I'd ever seen, not excluding the ones pulling brewery wagons and other heavy freight that we'd passed on our journey north. It was painted red and gold, Remchester's colors, with four postilions in red-and-gold livery, and was pulling an elegant traveling carriage of the same hues. It was similar to but much larger than the elegant carriage that had stopped in front of Tristram's house in London. His Lordship traveled in style.

I'd expected him to be accompanied by a troop of soldiers, but the road behind the carriage was empty. Hah! That was Remchester the merchant all over: he'd have the best motivator-and-carriage there was to be had, and if normal folk made do with two postilions while traveling, why, he'd have *four*, by God! But at the same time he had to maintain his image of being a common man, no better (except in his wits and skill) than anyone else in the Commonwealth. And, of course, the people of the Commonwealth loved him, so there was no need for soldiers!

And in this Remchester was wiser than Stavely; if he decided that Grayrigg needed to be destroyed he'd bring an army and no mistake. Until then, he'd make nice, and avoid looking like a threat.

So no soldiers. It was a show of confidence, and a nicely judged bit of political theater. But I suddenly had no doubt that the postilions were excellent shots, even by the standards of the Commonwealth.

I expected the motivator to turn up the drive, and I was not disappointed. I was in plain sight, the bower having been trimmed back, so I stood up and waited. The motivator stopped when the carriage was opposite me. A window in the carriage door slid down, and his Lordship's majestic and be-mutton-chopped face peered out at me, blinking in the sunlight.

"Ahoy there, lad."

"Good day, your Lordship."

"Just a moment, lad." The window slid up again, and I heard a rapping sound.

There were two footmen riding on the back of the carriage; one of them hopped down and positioned a mounting step by the carriage door. He opened the door and Lord Remchester descended to the gravel of the drive.

He was dressed as he'd been in London. Seeing him again, in light of what I'd learned, I realized that his mercantile appearance was of a piece with the rest of his presentation. It was done for effect. This was no drone, no Stavely; this was a man who knew what he wanted and generally knew how to *work* for it.

He extended his hand to me, and I shook it gravely.

"I am glad to see you looking so well, lad," he said. "You seem quite recovered."

"Thank you, sir, I am. I expect you'll want to go inside?"

He nodded.

"Come with me, then."

He clucked his tongue and waved a finger; and as we turned and began walking up the drive toward the front of the manor one of the footman took up station behind his right shoulder.

His lordship looked down at me as we walked.

"Is your cousin in residence? I must speak with him."

"No, sir, he isn't, but we expect him back any time now." I looked down at the gravel crunching under my feet, then up at his face. Boyish distress and sincerity +10. "Is it true that Cousin Tristram is an enemy of the people, sir?"

Remchester looked grim. "I'll not lie to you, lad, his recent actions don't look good, not good at all." He paused for a moment, and I could see the wheels turning in his head—how to present this to a young boy. Then he continued, "Why, he nearly left poor Miss Stavely waiting at the altar, and that after he'd as good as promised to marry her. That's not gentlemanly behavior, is it, lad?"

I added a hefty dollop of boyish indignation to the mix (though I was careful to keep it both polite and respectful).

"Oh, but that's not true, sir. He never did, I don't care what she says." I frowned pugnaciously. "I've met her, and I wouldn't trust her any farther than I can sling a leviathan. And anyway," I concluded with satisfaction, "he's going to marry Miss Louisa. It's all fixed up."

It wasn't, of course; this was a part of the plan I'd discussed with Gwen, but not with either of the principals. Time enough for that later. I hoped.

Remchester looked surprised.

"Is he really?" he said. "Not to be talking out of school, lad, but I'd understood that she loathed him."

"It was a misunderstanding," I said. "And he couldn't say yes to Miss Stavely until he tried to work things out with Miss Louisa, now could he? Because he's been sweet on her since he was my age."

He looked unconvinced, and a bit puzzled: it clearly didn't seem at all likely to him, but on the other hand why would a small boy lie about such a thing?

Augustus took over at the front door, and led us into the drawing room. Miss Louisa and Gwen rose from the chesterfield (unless it was a davenport) where they'd been sitting side by side. Mrs. Illridge was not present, being down with another sick headache. That was the story; but she'd confided in me earlier in the week that she simply didn't trust her tongue in his lordship's presence.

"He's a jumped-up scoundrel, is His Lordship," she'd said. "I can't see him sitting where my dear husband sat, not without giving him the rough side of my tongue, so I can't."

"Your lordship," said Miss Louisa, and she and Gwen curtsied. Gwen's curtsey was much improved; apparently Miss Louisa had been giving Gwen lessons in deportment while I kept watch.

Lord Remchester clucked his tongue and his footman withdrew, closing the drawing room doors behind him.

"My dear Miss Clarenton," said his lordship. "It's been many, many years, but you're still as lovely as ever."

Miss Louisa looked down, blushing a little. "Thank you, sir. Please, won't you be seated?"

"Why, thank you." He selected an arm chair; I suppose it was the closest he could find to a throne. I went and stood by Miss Louisa.

"As I'm sure you have guessed," said Lord Remchester, "I am trying to locate Tristram Monocle, and also my colleague Lord

Stavely."

"Tr—" she began, and blushed more deeply. "Mr. Monocle is not here sir," she went on, "though we expect him daily."

Lord Remchester noted the blush and glanced at me, and I nodded firmly.

"I understand congratulations are in order," he said.

"Why, thank you, sir," she said. I could tell she was mystified, but she covered it well. "May I have Augustus bring us some tea?"

"Perhaps after our business is concluded," he said. "Now, regarding Lord Stavely. I am assured he came here, Miss Clarenton, yet I find no sign of him." He fixed her with a piercing gaze—the sort of gaze, I felt sure, that he'd have used on the foreman called to his office to explain why the #3 assembly line was underproducing. "I confess to being quite curious."

"Yes, I'm quite sure you are," she said. "But Michael can tell you everything you need to know."

"Michael?" Remchester looked at Miss Louisa, then at me; I gave him a little wave. "Are you toying with me, miss?"

"No, sir, not at all. Michael is much older than he looks, and as he has been traveling with Tr—with Mr. Monocle, I'm sure he can answer your questions better than I can."

He looked at me. "Older than you look? And how old is that?"

"Twenty-eight years, sir," I said, dropping all boyishness. "It's been the curse of my existence."

"Twenty-eight years!" He stared at me, and then looked toward the door, and so toward the front of the house, and the drive. He frowned, and I could see thunderclouds rising. "You were playing me!"

"Yes, sir," I said. "My size is a curse, but it's sometimes useful to be underestimated."

He stared at me. I shrugged. "You know," I said.

After a long moment he chuckled, despite himself, and then burst out into a full-fledged guffaw. (I understand from Cowper Madisen that the guffaws in the Mississippi delta are especially fearsome.) He laughed for a good long time, as the ladies watched in wonder.

"Yes, lad, I do, I certainly do." He pulled out a handkerchief and dried his eyes. "Well, so Tristram's cousin is a prodigy. What else do you have to tell me?"

"I'm not actually Tristram's cousin, sir. I'm his half-brother. But, you know, cousin was easier to explain."

"So that's where old MacHendry went, is it? The Colonies? And here I'd been sure it was France."

"It may have been at first, sir. But I was born in the Colonies." Sort of, I thought.

"Hmmm. So, you've explained why Monocle ignored my wishes and came to Grayrigg. Why did he go further north?"

"Why, I believe that was my fault," said Gwen. I didn't know you could dimple and look sheepish at the same time, but she managed it. Remchester smiled back; and I decided that he was a susceptible old fellow.

"And you would be the young lady that Monocle, ah, acquired, on the road? And how was it your fault?"

"Oh, sir, he might have thought my cousin Eliza lived in Edinburgh."

"Might he? And why would that be?"

"Oh, because I told him so, sir." She nodded. "Well, you see, I had too. He was going to try to send me back to my wicked aunt." She frowned. "But I won't go back, I won't. She beats me."

His lordship regarded her with dismay. "You ran away from home, miss?"

"Why, yes, sir, that's it precisely." She smiled brilliantly. "I ran away from home! And then that carter was so mean to me, and I so shot him in the boot with my little gun."

"In the foot, you mean."

"No, in the boot. And then—"

But Remchester cut her off with a wave of his finger. It was a neat trick; I wondered how he did it.

"And so you sent him to find your cousin Eliza in Edinburgh?"

"Yes, that's right. But he won't find her." She shook her head.

"And why is that?"

"Why, because I don't have a cousin Eliza in Edinburgh. But she'd be quite the thing if I did, I just know it." And Gwen nodded with great satisfaction. She looked like she was going to go on, but Lord Remchester waved his finger again.

"I see. Say no more. That boy always did want to be a knight in shining armor." Then he looked back at me.

"And Lord Stavely? What of him, lad?"

"Are you familiar with squirrels, sir?"

"I beg your pardon?"

"Squirrels, sir. They live in the forest."

"I've heard of them, yes. Harmless, so long as you stay on the road."

I nodded. "Lord Stavely got off the road, sir."

He regarded me for a long moment.

"Well," he said at last, "so what am I to do with you all? What am I to do with Tristram when he returns? He might be a spotless lamb, if what you say is true, and yet he has publicly flouted my authority." He spread his hands in appeal, inviting us to commiserate with him. "He has been declared an Enemy of the People. I can't simply make that go away, it would look bad.

"And then there is the whole affair with Stavely, of which I have received a complete report, I assure you. I can't allow that to pass, you must see that, squirrels or no."

I took a deep breath. Now we got down to it.

"I'm afraid you'll have to, sir."

Chapter 51

"I beg your pardon, lad?"

Remchester's tone was unchanged, friendly and avuncular, but there was an edge to his words even so. A nice sharp one.

"I said that you were going to have to, sir. It's in your best interests."

"Perhaps you might explain that." The tone sharpened, and the subtext was that the explanation had better be persuasive.

"First of all, sir, the people of Grayrigg have done you a great service."

"Have they?" He looked politely surprised.

"Yes, sir. I've seen Tristram's notes."

Remchester didn't flinch—quite. Encouraged, I went on.

"Lord Stavely was becoming more and more erratic year by year, and he was deeply in debt. No doubt you're aware that Stavely was pushing for Tristram to marry his daughter so that he could get his hands on Tristram's money. When Tristram went north, Stavely saw that his game was up, and came north to force the issue." I studied Remchester's face, then nodded. "In fact, I'm guessing that the first you'd heard of Tristram's being drawn and papered was when your agent reported to you on the events here in Grayrigg." Bowler #2, if I wasn't mistaken, though of course Remchester wouldn't know him by that name.

"Truly, sir," I went on. "Stavely acted in a criminal manner, without the support of the Senate, and the people of Grayrigg received him no differently than would have any village in the Commonwealth. Plus he was a fool, sir."

Remchester politely waited for me to go on.

"I've read Tristram's book about the revolution, sir. Even allowing for a bit of whitewashing, it's clear that you only made war on the great estates. You were never fool enough to antagonize the yeomanry…and if you had, you've have brought a great deal more than eight soldiers. Squirrels, you know?"

Remchester didn't nod, exactly, but one eyebrow lowered, and I thought I'd made a point.

"And then, well…you see, your lordship, all Tristram wants at this point is to be left alone. He has no desire to make waves, as we say back home. He didn't make any trouble here in Grayrigg; he wasn't even here. That was all Lord Stavely."

Remchester's eyes flickered over to Gwen, then back to me. Gwen's black eye was mostly gone, but I was sure he'd noticed it.

"And so, I should be grateful?" he said. "But Stavely was one of my oldest supporters, the son of my greatest friend. To do what you're suggesting would require exposing Stavely as a criminal, and that would reflect badly upon me and upon the Commonwealth." He shook his head sadly. "And besides, where's your evidence?"

"Oh, I have the evidence, sir. Gobs of it. You know the kind of organization and detail Tristram's capable of, and it's all noted down in perfect order. If you want to build a case against Stavely, I'm your man."

I waited a long moment.

"And if you want me to build a case against you," I said, "I'm the man for that, too."

"Are you threatening me with blackmail, young man?" His tone remained mild; he seemed almost amused.

"Why, yes, sir." I nodded, smiling. "Got it in one. But it's more like white-mailing, in a way. I've got nothing against you and your Commonwealth, sir. But I've become quite fond of my brother Tristram, and I want him to be happy and safe."

Remchester snorted. "And why should I trust you?"

"You've never done me any harm, sir. So long as it stays that way, why shouldn't you trust me?"

"Hmph. And what's to prevent me from seizing this evidence you speak of? Assuming it even exists; I've seen the remains of Monocle's cottage."

"Oh, it exists, sir. Miss Louisa?"

Miss Louisa rose, and took a manila folder from a side table. The folder looked quite out of place in the Stockwood drawing room, kind of like a toilet at a tea party. She brought the folder to his lordship, and he accepted it gravely; then she sat back down.

"This is a facsimile of one of Tristram's journals." I said. "I've got the original in a safe place, your lordship, along with the rest of his archives. Your agents were never able to locate my father, though I'm sure they tried. You won't be able to find Tristram's archives either. And I can put folders just like that one in the hands of every publisher and journalist in London."

Remchester was leafing through the laser-printed pages in the folder, each one representing a digital scan of one journal page. The blood had pretty well drained from his face by the time he looked up, and the expression on his face was a terrible thing to see.

"But you know," I said, "I really don't want to. I'm sure you have your own sources, and can put together a case against Lord Stavely without my help, or Tristram's. You'll know just how to spin it to best advantage." I regarded him gravely. "Truly, sir, I like your Commonwealth. I don't want to spoil things. Mr. Mortimer down the village is making me a steam velocipede. It's going to be all the crack, sir.

"And you've met Melissa Stavely, sir. Can you blame him? Bit of a battleship, she is. And her father was a menace."

Remchester closed the folder, and looked at me. He was still pale, but I thought I detected a bit of a twinkle in his eye.

"I'd blame him less if he'd simply married the girl." Miss Louisa twitched at that.

"Wouldn't have answered, sir," I said.

"And why not?"

"Stavely wanted Tristram's money. He doesn't have any. Well, not to speak of."

"I beg your pardon?" This time his words were full of good honest surprise.

"He doesn't have any. Well, look at it." I got out my fingers, and counted them off one by one. "He spent his inheritance to buy Stockwood and its environs from Lord Stavely, after Stavely confiscated them from Squire Illridge."

"He did?" said Miss Louisa and Lord Remchester at the same time. They looked at each other, and Remchester continued, "And here I'd thought he'd taken them on his own initiative."

"He did. The details are in that folder. And then," second finger, "his operating funds and confiscations didn't stick to his fingers the way they stuck to Stavely's."

"Really? You interest me strangely."

"And then," third finger, "all of his income went back to Stockwood. Well, until a few years ago. Then he got to keep a little of it." I shook my head. "So, you see, Stavely would still have been rolled up."

Miss Louisa blushed.

Lord Remchester rose to his feet.

"You're a formidable young man, Mr. Henderson," he said. He held up the folder. "Have I your word that this material will never see the light of day?"

"Not in your lifetime, sir," I said. "I can't pledge Tristram any farther than that, not without speaking with him. But that far, yes, you have my word." I walked across the carpet to him, and held out my hand. "You're a businessman, sir. I suspect you won't want a signed contract, not under these circumstances, but I'd be glad to shake on it."

"Hmph. You drive a hard bargain, Mr. Henderson." But he took my hand, and we shook on it. He eyed me solemnly. "Have we any other business, young man?"

"No, sir, I believe that's all. Shall I give your regards to Tristram when he appears?"

"That would be most kind of you," he said.

I opened the doors to the drawing room; Remchester's footman was waiting in the hall. Remchester clucked his tongue, and waved a finger, and the footman fell into place behind him.

Remchester turned to face the room "Ladies. Mr. Henderson. I'll show myself out."

I followed him out, of course. When I sup with the devil I might use a long spoon, but not so long that I can't keep my eye on him. I waited by the bower as Lord Remchester ascended the mounting step and so into the carriage.

The door closed. There were some muffled voices, and some rattling, and I thought I heard the door open and close on the other side of the carriage; and then the window in the carriage door slid open and Remchester leaned his head out.

"I offered him his job back, but he wouldn't take it, lad. I don't suppose you'd be interested? The position is open."

"Uh, no, thank you."

"Then you may have him back with my compliments," he said, and slid the window closed again.

The postilions fired up the motivator, and backed it neatly down the drive and onto the high road; and as it cleared my field of view, there was my brother Tristram standing on the other side of the drive. He looked tired and gray.

Chapter 52

"Hello, Michael," said Tristram. "You appear to have a made a new conquest."

"When you're small for your age," I said, "you have to be extra persuasive. Did you get our notes?"

I waved him over to the bower, and we sat down.

"Yes, and I admit I found them a bit puzzling. Why does it matter that Miss Gwen's cousin 'isn't at all the thing?' I should have said that Miss Gwen herself isn't at all the thing, though I hope you won't repeat that." His mustache gave a ghost of a twitch.

"Oh, that. I was trying to say, elliptically, that you were on a wild goose chase—that Miss Gwen's cousin doesn't exist."

"Leaving Miss Gwen to be the tame goose?"

"You'd be surprised. In fact, you're going to be. But there's time enough for that later." I looked up at him; he looked back, eyebrow raised. "How did Lord Remchester find you?"

"I got your notes, and despite my confusion about the phantom Eliza I was returning south. Stavely's men took me by night at an inn in Carlisle." Rueful tilt. "My phaeton is still there, I suppose. And then Lord Remchester's men, ah, *relieved* them of their duties in Penrith."

I noted the odd emphasis. "Relieved them? How?"

"Decisively, and with dispatch. In the most permanent possible manner." He took out his handkerchief and polished his monocle. "It was all a bit hair-raising."

"You mean that Remchester was on to Stavely the whole time?"

"On to him? Behind him, I should say, driving him every step of the way. And behind me, as well."

"Are you telling me—"

"Oh, yes. He never meant me to marry Melissa Stavely. It was all about forcing her father to reckless action."

I shivered. I'd known Remchester was ruthless; and now I knew why I'd amused him. "Wow. I thought I was playing him, but he was actually playing the rest of us."

"As you say, 'Wow.' Never underestimate him, Michael." His mustache gave a genuine twitch. "Still, I would give a good deal to have been able to watch your performance."

He turned on the bench so that he was facing me.

"I was simply a tool to his hand. A broken tool, that might have been disposed of without regret when it was no longer of use. I find that I am deeply in your debt."

"Not to worry," I said. "What are brothers for?"

"Brothers," he said. He polished his monocle his monocle some more, and I could see that he was deeply moved. "I have never had a brother, before."

"That's what you think," I said.

I saw curtains twitch and faces at the window any number of times while I was filling Tristram in on his new family, but I ignored them—at least until Augustus came and stood pointedly at the front door of the manor.

"How certain are you of this?" Tristram asked as we walked up the drive.

"Fairly. It explains a number of things, including my appearance in Remchester Park. And then, there was a short period of time when everyone in Grayrigg thought that Gwen and I might be your natural children. Purely based on our appearance, you understand."

"Oh, dear. Do we look that much alike?"

I nodded. "Yes, I'm afraid so. Of course, the real question is whether you can activate one of the finders we've been carrying around. If you can do that, I'd regard it as conclusive."

"I can see that."

We walked the last few yards in silence. Augustus met us at he door.

"Welcome to Stockwood, sir," he said, beaming.

"Thank you, old friend," said Tristram.

"Won't you come in? The ladies are in the drawing room."

"By all means."

We let Augustus usher us in, not that either of us needed the help.

Tristram stopped at the door to the drawing room.

"Ladies," he said, but his eyes were only for Miss Louisa.

Miss Louisa, Miss Gwen, and Mrs. Illridge all rose from their places.

"Mr.—Mr. Monocle," said Miss Louisa, leaving me out entirely, but I didn't blame her for it. "Welcome to Stockwood."

"Thank you," he said.

We all sat down, and waited rather stiffly as Augustus brought in the tea things. Tristram didn't know what to say, I could tell, and neither did Miss Louisa, and Gwen and Mrs. Illridge were too amused to be much help.

I waited until Augustus had closed the door and Miss Louisa had poured out, and then I waded right in.

"So," I said. "About the wedding."

Everyone turned to me.

"Wedding?" said Miss Louisa.

"Wedding?" said Tristram. "What wedding?" He looked at Miss Louisa with awful surmise.

"Your wedding, of course," I said to him. "In order to get you off the hook with Lord Remchester, I had to tell him that you couldn't marry Melissa Stavely because you were engaged to Miss Louisa."

"You what?" came two voices in unison, one soprano, one baritone. I glanced over at Mrs. Illridge; she nodded back at me in appreciation.

Tristram stood up. "Michael, I am exceedingly grateful to you, but I will thank you to—"

"Tristram," I said, "sit down, and stop being an idiot."

He stared at me, his angry words hanging in mid-air. He looked over at Miss Louisa for support; she looked away, blushing deeply. He looked back at me, then sat down slowly.

"Tristram," I said, "the only person in Grayrigg who didn't know how you felt about Miss Louisa was Miss Louisa. And the only person in the Commonwealth who didn't know that Miss Louisa would have no one but you was you." I paused. "She was pretty angry at you over the property thing, but she wasn't in possession of all the facts. I think she's over that now."

"Louisa…" said Tristram, slowly. "Is this true?"

And at that I rose to my feet and nodded to Gwen and Mrs. Illridge. "It's lovely outside," I said. "Would you ladies care to join me for a stroll in the garden?"

"Why, yes, Michael," said Mrs. Illridge. "I believe it would be just the thing to prevent one of my sick headaches."

I closed the doors gently behind us.

"You handled that rather well, I thought," said Gwen.

"I'm an engineer," I said. "Problems are to be solved. And if the solution was a bit unusual, well, you know…."

Gwen looked down at me, and made the get-on-with-it motion.

I shrugged. "Regency steampunk is still steampunk."

The wedding took place six weeks later, neither principal being inclined to wait any longer than was necessary to do the thing properly. The banns having been read and re-read, the ceremony was held first thing on a Saturday morning at St. John's, to a capacity crowd; I was the best man, resplendent in a bespoke suit, and Gwen and Bernie were Miss Louisa's maids of honor in matching blue gowns.

Miss Louisa was quite lovely. I had never before seen a wedding veil with goggles, but I have to admit they were practical.

After the ceremony came the wedding breakfast, just for close family, in the dining room at Stockwood; and that was followed by a fête for the townsfolk in the grounds that afternoon.

The fête was much of the reason for the delay; Tristram had been for tying the knot with all speed, once he got over himself, but Miss Louisa insisted on including the townsfolk, and that meant getting the manor and its environs in proper order. And besides, she need to order the material for her dress from London.

Tristram was all for proper order, had always been all for proper order, and so he spent the time keeping Mr. Bartlett and his son Freddie well and truly hopping—them, and a small army of workmen. He also oversaw some modifications to the manor house...after which Gwen and I retrieved his archives from my Unhappy Place, whither I'd dispatched them on Stavely's arrival. Well, I couldn't have sent them home; Buster's a good dog, but he's not to be trusted with bowler hats, dented or otherwise. I'm sorry Tristram, but my dog ate your archives—no, I wasn't going there. We made digital copies of the documents, of course.

I have to say, Gwen was admirably patient throughout; she was itching to go find her father—our father—but I think she was enjoying being part of a family, too. I asked her once if she didn't want to go home for a visit, but she said no.

"I don't really have a home," she said. "Well, except for Father. We moved around a lot while I was growing up, from town to town and sometimes from world to world. I was never able to keep any friends, and I was taught to travel light."

"That sounds like Dear Old Dad," I said. "I guess my mom never got to know anyone in Corey's End until after he left."

"And then, I have no anchor there, Michael," she said. "Between my bandboxes and my bolthole, you've seen everything I own in the world." She shook her head. "With what you've taught me I might be able to go back to the last place we lived... maybe...but everyone I care about is here. Except for Father."

The festivities came to an end at sunset, with Tristram and

Louisa standing at the front of the manor as each of the townsfolk took their leave, shaking hands and laughing.

Bert Wiggins was the last, swaying a little with drink and good cheer.

"I never thought I'd see the day," he said, holding his cap in his hands. "I never did. It's...it's *good* to have you back in Grayrigg, squire." He touched his forelock. "Mrs. Monocle."

"Mrs. MacHendry, Bert," said Louisa.

"Even better," said Bert. "Rubbish name, Monocle." And taking his leave he walked on down the drive, weaving slightly.

"Well, that's that," said Tristram, when he'd quite gone.

"That's just the beginning," said Bernie. "It all starts here."

"Yes," said Tristram. "And I have been waiting my whole life for it." He smiled at Louisa, who squeezed his hand. And in mixed company, too! Shocking, I call it.

And then there was a blue flash, and a surly looking fellow in green overalls appeared between me and Tristram. I tased him in the stomach, Tristram eased him to the ground, and Louisa, who by now had been fully briefed, called for Crosley and Thompson, while Gwen and Bernie relieved him of his finder.

Tristram sighed. "You know, Michael, we really must do something about that."

The End